The Canticle of Whispers

THE AGORA TRILOGY

The Canticle of Whispers

David Whitley

ROARING BROOK PRESS

NEW YORK

Published by Roaring Brook Press
Roaring Brook Press is a division of Holtzbrinck Publishing Holdings Limited Partnership
175 Fifth Avenue, New York, New York 10010
mackids.com

Library of Congress Cataloging-in-Publication Data
Whitley, David, 1984–
  The canticle of whispers / David Whitley.—1st ed.
    p. cm.
  Summary: "In the final volume of the Agora trilogy, Mark and Lily lead the revolution to
unseat the powerful elite and discover the answers to their questions about their origins while
confronting the dark and twisted nature of their destinies"—Provided by publisher.
  ISBN 978-1-59643-615-2 (hardcover)—ISBN 978-1-59643-845-3 (ebook)
[1. Prophecies—Fiction. 2. Fantasy.] I. Title.
  PZ7.W5915Can 2013
  [Fic]—dc23

                                                          2012013789

Roaring Brook Press books are available for special promotions and premiums.
For details contact: Director of Special Markets, Holtzbrinck Publishers.

First edition 2013
Printed in the Unites States of America by RR Donnelley & Sons Company,
Harrisonburg, Virgina

1   3   5   7   9   10   8   6   4   2

For Jamie and Nienke

Contents

Yet pull not down my palace towers, that are
So lightly, beautifully built:
Perchance I may return with others there
When I have purged my guilt.

—ALFRED, LORD TENNYSON

PART ONE

ANSWERS

Chapter One

Echoes

TERTIUS HAD SAID he was going to show her a wonder.

Septima had never been this far from the central caverns before. They had been on the run for days, but up until now they had skirted around their old haunts—swiping food parcels whenever they could, making do with drinking from deep, clear pools of water when they could not. She felt an ache in her belly sometimes, but she was still buzzing with the thrill of it all. She knew that the guardians would catch up soon.

So when, an hour ago, Tertius had told her that he had scouted ahead, and found something marvelous, she was sure that he was lying. Maybe the guardians had threatened him. Maybe he was leading her into a trap.

That didn't stop her from going, of course.

They walked through new and mysterious caves. There was no crystal light here, so they both lit their lanterns. The metal was

3

smooth and warm under her fingers. Everything looked different under lamplight—Tertius's pale face became burnished gold, and his large, dark eyes gleamed with excitement.

Septima stroked back her long, ash-colored hair.

"Is it far?" she asked, daringly. It wasn't her turn to ask a question, but out here they could break all the rules.

"Just a couple more caves away," he said. His voice was high and tense, with none of the music it normally had. She bristled a little. This was *his* wonder; he wasn't supposed to be frightened of it.

Septima was about to speak again, when she heard a strange echo, too far away to make out. Suddenly, she was afraid too, and shrank into her long robe.

"We're near the Cacophony," she whispered. "You never said the wonder was out here. What if it's moved?"

"It won't have," he replied, irritated. "Don't fuss. I don't need to answer you. You haven't shown me anything new for days."

She lapsed into silence, sulking. But it was true. She would have to find something for him soon. She didn't want him to lose interest in her.

She had been near the Cacophony only once before. Back when she had been too young to sing, her tutor had taken her and the others in her section to the outer caves. She would never forget that visit.

She remembered the unfamiliar silence. Their tutor had forbidden them to talk. To speak near the Cacophony invited it to come and find you.

Then there had been the darkness. The tutor had made them douse their lanterns. One girl had refused to go any farther. She had never been out of the crystal light. But the rest of them were braver. They left her, cowering, and walked into the pitch-black caves, stumbling over little cracks in the ground.

As Septima walked now, she felt those same irregularities beneath her feet, so unlike the smooth stone at the Hub. She stared defiantly at the still-burning flame in her lantern. There was no tutor here to make her walk in darkness. For the first time in her life, she was abandoning the rules. She was a rebel.

But now, as she and Tertius moved deeper into the outer caverns, Septima began to hear again what had so terrified her years before: the echoes. They emerged out of the silence—quiet at first, but growing in intensity. Roiling, rushing sounds, like the pounding of a river made up of words and shouts and wails. Septima pressed her hands over her ears, but it didn't make any difference. These echoes seemed to well up from the ground itself.

It wasn't the voices themselves that frightened her, but the passion behind them. Each one roared with joy, or cried in pain. A million voices, all talking at once, each demanding that she listen. She quickened her pace, her heart pounding. It was said to be madness to walk through the Cacophony. The impenetrable barrier that circled their home was an ocean of sound that filled the outer caverns with insane howls and mind-destroying whispers. But that didn't stop people going as near as they dared.

"We don't have to go through the Cacophony, do we?" Septima asked as the echoes faded a little. Tertius didn't respond. He wouldn't talk now. Not unless Septima gave him some new information in exchange.

"I've been here before," she ventured. Still silence. "Six years ago. Just before we first spoke." She bit her lip. Was it enough?

Finally, Tertius turned back, looking satisfied. Septima breathed a sigh of relief. She had balanced their knowledge; they were even.

"No, we don't need to go through. The wonder is just at the entrance to one of the outer caverns." He grinned, his teeth shining in the lamplight. "Not afraid, are you?"

"A little," she admitted. He stepped closer to her. Involuntarily, she pulled back; she could almost feel his breath on her face. That wouldn't do at all.

"Let's get going," she mumbled, her cheeks flushing.

They walked on. She tried to relax, but the rumble of the Cacophony left her on edge. The stone above her seemed to shake with it, as though any moment it might burst out, burying them in the awful sound.

And then, Tertius held up his hand, cutting across her thoughts with the sudden gesture.

"We're here," he breathed.

She squinted into the distance. Just ahead, at the mouth of one of the smaller tunnels, she saw something on the ground. It looked like a pile of cloth. She wrinkled her nose in disappointment.

"Doesn't look like much of a wonder to me," she said, doubtfully. But as they drew near, she could make it out more clearly. No . . . it wasn't cloth . . . it was . . .

"But that's impossible!" She gasped. "Is it one of the Choir? It must be . . ."

"Who?" he asked, triumphantly. "Have you ever seen her face before?"

She looked down. Crumpled at her companion's feet was a girl of maybe fifteen years. Her long, black hair was loose, and fell over her face in swaths. Her skin, too, was dark, and contrasted with her off-white woollen dress, weighed down with dried, flaking mud.

Septima had never seen her before in her life. And that was amazing.

"Is she . . . one of the Orchestra?" She asked, breathless, so excited she forgot that it was not her turn to ask a question.

"Only one way to find out," he said.

6

Slowly, he extended one foot. She felt the breath catch in her throat.

"You can't!"

He looked up, a look of fierce excitement on his face.

"Watch me."

He prodded the form with the toe of his boot. Septima squealed in delighted fear. He was amazing; he could do anything.

The form groaned. They both jumped back. She felt like screaming, but already her squeal from before was echoing around the chamber, and she didn't want to add to it. The guardians might hear them, and take their wonder away.

So she watched, in amazed silence, as the girl raised a hand, and brushed the hair away from her face.

"What . . . I . . . where?"

The girl stared up at the two of them, her eyes wide.

"Where am I?"

Septima's mind raced, trying to come up with the right response. Was this wonder, this girl, really asking a question, without first offering some knowledge?

"Don't you remember?" she asked, cautiously, deciding the only proper response was another question.

The girl seemed thrown by this, and she pushed herself into a sitting position.

"I remember . . . the steps," she began. "So many steps. Going down forever. And the darkness. And then . . . voices . . . calling my name. Getting louder, and louder . . ."

Tertius nearly dropped the lantern.

"You've been through the Cacophony?" he said, abandoning all the rules. "What was it like? Where do you come from?"

Septima turned and stared at him in astonishment. They certainly hadn't earned the right to ask questions like that. Not yet.

"Let's start with something simple," she said, turning to the girl. "Tell us, what shall we call you?"

The girl shook her head for a moment, as if clearing it of smoke.

"I'm . . . Lily. My name is Lily," she said. And then, looking more confident, she rose to her feet. "My name is Lilith d'Annain, from the city of Agora. Now you tell me," she said, looking Septima in the eyes without fear. "Where am I?"

CHAPTER TWO

The Hunt

MARK DREW the filthy blanket up over his face, and tried not to be noticed.

He wouldn't have to wait much longer. Already, he could see that the Inspector was peering less carefully into the face of each debtor. Mark guessed that she had not often taken the time to look at the wretches on the street, and the parade of thin, ill faces was taking its toll. Though, like most receivers, Inspector Poleyn was unmistakably tough; in her the quality was more an unshakable sense of purpose rather than a working knowledge of the streets. It was clear that she would have been far more comfortable guarding the elite in the upriver parts of town, than down here in the tangled alleys of the Sagittarius District.

"Perhaps you could show me only the most likely suspects, Doctor?" she asked, wrinkling her nose in disgust. "I don't have time to interview every debtor that ends up in your . . ." she paused, obviously biting back an insulting term, "establishment."

"I am afraid not, Inspector," replied the doctor, in measured tones. "There have been several fresh outbreaks of fever in recent weeks, and I barely have time to note the patients' names, let alone remember them individually."

Mark risked peeking over the edge of the blanket again. Poleyn was picking at one young woman's wrappings with long, elegant fingers, as though the debtor were something fundamentally unclean. Behind her, Dr. Theophilus ran his own fingers through his thinning brown hair. He was doing a surprisingly good job of appearing helpful, but Mark noticed that he was beginning to sweat. He wondered if the doctor had ever lied to the receivers before.

He caught Theo's eye. The doctor made a frantic signal with the hand behind his back, and Mark sank back beneath the blanket.

"Perhaps, Inspector," Theo said, steering her away from Mark's corner, "you could tell me more about the case? I'm certain I would be able to help."

"I'm sorry, Doctor, but absolute secrecy is vital," the inspector sniffed. "These fugitives have stolen from the Director himself. They must be apprehended, and swiftly."

Under the blanket, Mark suppressed a snarl. Yes, he supposed he had stolen from the Director of Receipts, the ruler of the city. But Mark had stolen nothing which that same man had not first taken from him. Once, Mark had lived in the tallest tower of the city—the Astrologer's Tower, former home of Count Stelli. Mark had been famous, a child prodigy, with a future that seemed endlessly golden, and Snutworth had been his loyal manservant—until Snutworth betrayed him, and sent him to prison. Now, Snutworth was the ruler of Agora, and Mark was hiding among the poorest of the city, trying to avoid the attentions of the law.

"Yes, of course," the doctor said, a little too hastily. "But surely such desperate thugs would much prefer to take shelter at the Wheel, rather than here. They have better supplies, and would likely find an ally in Mr. Crede. I hear that receivers are far from welcome in that part of the city nowadays . . ."

"Investigations are being carried out in *all* likely areas, sir," Poleyn interrupted. Theo had clearly hit a nerve there. "But for reasons I am unable to disclose, it is most likely that the fugitives would hide in this area." She peered closely at Theo. "Are you completely certain that no suspicious figures have recently arrived? Perhaps a boy of fifteen summers, and a young woman with golden hair? She, at least, should not be difficult to recognize—she would be far cleaner and better fed than most of the rabble."

Mark saw a flash of concern cross Theo's face, but he covered it well.

"Inspector, as you have said on numerous occasions, we cater to everyone here at the Temple Almshouse. If we turned someone away merely for being suspicious, our beds would be empty every night. Our doors are never locked."

Scowling, Poleyn turned away, and Theo began to sort some sheets. Mark could see that he was studiously trying not to look at him, or at the cot by the door, where the other fugitive was trying to keep still.

Unfortunately, that was precisely where Poleyn was headed.

"I don't think I've seen this one before," she muttered, pulling aside the blanket. The young woman looked up at her. From this angle, Mark couldn't see if Cherubina was keeping up the pretense. "Perhaps I should examine her more closely."

"Be my guest, Inspector," Theo said, trying to sound unconcerned. "I'm sure that her boils are no longer quite so contagious."

Poleyn snatched her hand back, and despite everything, Mark found himself choking down a gasp of laughter.

This, on reflection, was a bad idea. Poleyn's attention snapped around to his corner.

"You know, of course, that harboring criminals is a serious offense, Doctor," she said, padding over toward Mark. Hastily, Mark drew the blanket over his face again, but he could still hear Poleyn's voice—firm and resolute. "The Director has decided that it is time for a crackdown. Too many people are flouting the rule of law. This ruffian Crede is just the beginning, and we have no intention of letting the rot go any further."

She was leaning over Mark now. Mark could smell her—a clean smell, almost disinfectant, quite a contrast to the rest of the cellar. Mark cringed back under the blanket, his mind racing, trying to come up with something that would force her away. They had been so close . . .

"Inspector, I really wouldn't . . ." Theo began, but Poleyn interrupted.

"I've had quite enough of that, Doctor. Quite enough. It's time to finish these childish games. I'm sure the Director will have many questions to ask . . ."

And then, with a sudden flash of inspiration, Mark flung back the blanket and grasped at Poleyn's lapels, groaning.

"Take me out of here!" he yelled, trying to sound as feverish as possible, scraping his hands, covered in flaking skin, across the sergeant's face. "They're keeping me sick, I tell you!" He rolled his eyes, pushing his lips next to Poleyn's ear, even as she tried to pull away. "You'll help me? Won't you? You'll save me from the medicine? They're all after me, every one!"

Poleyn raised her truncheon, and Mark fell back, whimpering, curling into a ball. Internally, though, he was entirely focused on the sounds of Theo steadying the startled receiver.

"Well, I did try to warn you," Theo replied, with noticeable relief. "That poor young man—mind quite gone, I'm afraid."

Carefully, still acting, Mark peered over the edge of the blanket again. Theo was wetting a rag in a wooden bowl, and offering it to the sergeant. "All part of his condition. A dreadful case. If I were you, I'd wash yourself where he touched you, just in case you develop any symptoms . . ."

With forced dignity, Poleyn took the rag and wiped her face. This time, though, Mark didn't laugh. Despite her distaste for the debtors, Theo had warned him that Poleyn was a highly efficient investigator. If she believed that her quarry was here, she would be back with a whole squad next time. True, the receivers themselves were only doing their job, but they reported to the Director.

And if the Director caught him, Mark wouldn't even have the right to a fair trial, because as far as the law was concerned, he didn't exist.

"Well, I think that is all of the current patients," Theo said, soothingly. "Of course, if you wish to wait until this evening, I'm sure there will be a crowd. It looks like rain, and my assistant Benedicta is planning on an excellent stew. There might even be recognizable meat in it this time, if you'd care to join us . . ."

"That will not be necessary," Poleyn said, brushing down her lapels with a look of disgust. "I am satisfied for the moment that the fugitives are not here, but you shall, of course, be receiving regular visits." Poleyn put down the rag and drew herself upright. Though Theo was almost a foot taller than her, Poleyn seemed to look down on him. "I know what you are doing here, Doctor. How you offer shelter to the debtors and criminals. In happier times, I might have approved. But now . . ." Poleyn looked troubled, and turned away. "The Day of Judgment approaches, and we must all choose our sides . . ."

Despite the tension, Mark saw Theo reach out to her.

"Inspector," the doctor said, gently, "is something distressing you?"

"That is none of your concern," Poleyn muttered, hastily, as though she had said more than she intended. "Now, Doctor, I have other business to attend to . . ."

Looking shaken, Poleyn retreated to the stairs out of the basement. For a tense moment, Mark and Theo listened as she scattered the debtors on the floor above. And then, with an air of finality, she slammed the door.

The doctor sank down onto a stool, head in his hands.

"It's over," he muttered. "Thank the stars."

"No, thank you, Theo," Mark said, sincerely, jumping out of the cot, glad to stretch after hours spent curled up. "Do you still have that cloth?"

Theo handed Mark the damp rag, and Mark began to scrub at his exposed skin, removing the milky film that they had painted on earlier. Before long, the signs of his "illness" were wiped away.

"I never thought hiding right in front of them would work," Mark continued as he soaked the cloth in a bucket of clean water. "If you hadn't come up with this plan, the receivers would have found us, no question."

"I'm still not entirely clear why they are hunting for you," Theo said, miserably. "Or where you've been. Not a word! For over a year! Your father has been moving heaven and earth looking for you . . ."

Mark carried on washing, not quite sure what to say. How could he explain? He barely believed it, and he'd lived through it. He'd traveled through the unknown lands outside the city. He'd seen the vast mountains and dark forests, and the people there who lived in enforced harmony, and punished any deviation with violence. He'd been stalked by the strange, living Nightmare that kept everyone in line, and fought against the mysterious Order of the Lost at the heart of it all, who had captured him, and brought him back to Agora. That had been his life for the last year and a half. It was hard to know where to start.

"Are you going to keep that cloth all day?" said a voice from across the room. Irritably, the young woman with the boils sat up in her cot. Theo had done an amazing job—Mark didn't want to contemplate what he had mixed up to make them look so realistic. Sheepishly, Mark wrung out the rag and handed it over to Cherubina. She dabbed daintily at her face, dissolving the fake boils. She wrinkled her nose. "Now that the inspector has gone, do we have to stay down here in the basement all day?" she asked, unwinding the old shawl they had tied around her head to hide her distinctive blonde ringlets. "It isn't particularly fragrant."

"Patience, Miss Cherubina," Theo replied, cautiously. "I wouldn't move until Laud tells us that it is safe to do so. Inspector Poleyn well deserves her new position, and I am sure that she will send one of her men to watch the Temple for the next few days. I doubt that the Director is quite ready to call off the search."

Cherubina blanched, and Mark winced. He had every reason to hate the Director. Snutworth had betrayed him, kidnapped him, and treated him like little more than a puppet. But Cherubina had been Snutworth's wife. She had lived with him for over a year, half-prisoner, half-prize. Mark could not imagine what that had been like. Certainly she did not want to talk about it, and when Mark had found her imprisoned with him in the Astrologer's Tower, Snutworth's home at the time, she had been all too eager to join in his escape. Of course, as far as the new Director was concerned, she had not run away at all—Mark had stolen Snutworth's property. That was how he thought, and he had the law of Agora on his side.

"Are you sure the debtors won't talk?" Cherubina murmured, clearly shaken. "A lot of them saw our arrival."

Theo raised his head, looking tired.

"There is certainly very little love between the receivers and those who must take shelter in our almshouse," Theo said after a moment's thought. "Still, I wouldn't count on their silence if the receivers start to use rougher methods of interrogation. You won't be able to stay here for long. Perhaps we can find a way to sneak you out." Theo rubbed his temples, looking weary. Mark supposed that the doctor couldn't have been more than thirty, but he seemed to have aged starkly since Mark had last seen him. His hair had receded even more, and his tall, spare frame seemed to sag with the weight of worry. And Mark imagined that his sudden arrival a few hours ago had not helped with that.

"But . . . Mark said that you'd be able to take us in!" Cherubina exclaimed. "You're the only people we can turn to! I don't know anyone in this city, apart from Mommy, and she wouldn't keep me hidden. Not if her business were at risk . . ." Cherubina trailed off, sadly.

"It's all right, Cherubina," Mark said, reassuringly. "I'm sure Theo can find somewhere for us . . ."

"Wait a moment there!" Theo said, firmly. "First of all, before anything else—you have to tell me what's going on." The doctor met Mark's gaze. It was not an unfriendly look, exactly. Mark supposed it would take a lot to truly get on Theo's bad side, but it was a look that demanded answers. "I'm sorry, Mark. I'm glad to see you're safe, really I am. But you can't just . . . *deliver* yourself into our hands like this and expect us to risk everything for you without a little explanation."

In the corner, behind the beds of the most feverish, Mark saw the shattered remains of the packing cases they had used to escape from Snutworth's tower. They had hacked them to pieces, shoving them down in the cellar before the receivers arrived. It had only been an hour ago, but it was all still a blur. He remembered Theo flapping around anxiously, and Laudate, Theo's friend and Mark's former employee, herding the able-bodied debtors out, with menacing instructions to keep what they had seen to themselves. He remembered Benedicta, Laudate's sister, helping Cherubina out of her own case, picking straw and sawdust out of the young woman's curls. He wished Benedicta was still here now, fussing and grinning as she welcomed them back. Mark had met Ben only once before, but that smile had stayed with him—the smile he had so little deserved and which she had given freely. Despite Ben's endless energy, the smile had a kind of calmness that was hugely reassuring. But she had run off, minutes after he had arrived, saying she was going to find someone, and after that, they had all been too busy preparing for the receivers to sit and talk.

"It's rather difficult to explain," Mark admitted. "But I'll try."

"Yes, that is something that we would all appreciate, Mr. Mark." The voice came from the top of the stairs. Mark looked up.

Again, Mark marveled at how much someone could change in over a year. Laudate, known to his friends as Laud, had never been a particularly cheerful young man, but the pressures of running the Temple Almshouse had really taken their toll. His long red hair was unkempt, and there was a scar above one eye from an old wound. Now that Mark had a chance to look at him properly, he could see a wariness in his tread that went beyond his usual cynicism. This was a young man who was used to the world dealing cruel blows, and his attitude at the moment was distinctly hostile.

"I think that you owe it to us, don't you?" Laud said, bitterly. "Call it payment for hiding you from every receiver in the city. Or didn't you know that they're scouring every back street from here to the Aquarian dockyards looking for you?" He cast a cursory glance at Cherubina as he descended the stairs. "They don't name you, of course, but it's pretty clear from the descriptions that you and Mrs. Snutworth are the fugitives."

Cherubina bristled, but Mark laid a hand on her arm. Laud was not the most tactful host.

"Like I said," Mark repeated, "I was being held prisoner, in the old Astrologer's Tower, by Snutworth. And now I find I have to call him the Director . . ."

"I still find that hard to believe," Laud muttered. "Surely everyone would know if the old Director had been replaced?"

"Really, Laud?" Theo asked, reasonably. "We never saw the last one in public at all. I don't suppose it would be too surprising." He frowned, pulling forward another stool for Laud. "You worked with Mr. Snutworth. Would you put such a thing past him?"

Laud conceded that with a shake of the head.

"Perhaps, but I don't see why he had to hold Mark prisoner in his own home." He turned back to Mark, looking a little more ready to listen. "You should still be in jail. When you disappeared last year, we didn't know what to think. Tell us what happened. Right from the beginning."

Mark stood up, trying to gather his thoughts.

"I've been outside the city," he said.

The stunned silence said it all. Even Laud couldn't hide his astonishment.

"That's impossible," Theo said, dully. "There's nothing outside the city. Everyone knows that."

Mark sighed.

"That's what I believed too . . ."

After that, it came pouring out. How he and Lily, his oldest friend, had been forced to leave Agora. About the strange woman who had plucked him from his prison cell, and the care of his long-lost father, to send him out into a strange new world. About the land outside—Giseth—a place of thick forests and lush farms, where all the people lived in harmony, with everyone sharing and no one set above anyone else. How they had taken refuge in the idyllic village of Aecer, and how they had discovered that this supposed "paradise" was maintained by the tyrannical rituals of the Order of the Lost, the red-robed monks, and the absolute power of each village's leader—the Speaker. He told them how he had seen their friends terrorized and attacked for going against the will of the Speaker, and about the mystical Brethren who opposed the monks and had given him and Lily shelter in the forest when Aecer had turned against them. But above all, he told them of the Nightmare—the living dream that haunted the lands. About how it seeped into people's minds when they were asleep, feeding off every suppressed thought and deed, until it drove them insane.

As he spoke, he watched the others' faces. The patients down here were too ill to listen, or at least didn't react if they understood. Cherubina just looked confused; he supposed she was still reeling from their escape. Theo's frown deepened, but he nodded in understanding. Laud's expression, on the other hand, tightened, his lip curling back.

"And I suppose you think we'll fall for this, do you?" he said, suddenly, stopping Mark's story in its tracks.

"I know it's . . . pretty amazing . . ." Mark ventured, but Laud cut him off with a bark of sarcastic laughter.

"It's completely ridiculous!" Laud said, scornfully. "Do you honestly expect us to believe that everything we've ever known about the world is a lie? That there's some kind of living Nightmare waiting outside the city walls?"

"Well of course," Mark replied, his face flushing with anger. "Maybe you should ask the woman next door who bottles people's emotions for a living! What would be the point of me lying to you, Laud?"

"Oh, I don't know, maybe because you don't want us to ask the most important question," he said, darkly. "Tell us, Mark, what happened to Lily?"

Mark froze. Lily had told him so much about the temple, her almshouse, he had nearly forgotten that he barely knew these people. Not anymore. He had worked with Theo and Laud, but at heart they were Lily's friends, and he had come back without her.

"I . . ." his throat went dry. "I don't know. The Director—that is, the old Director—told her that her parents were out there some-where. In Giseth. She was always looking for clues. In the end, the Brethren taught us how to use the Nightmare to find them."

"This same Nightmare that fed off people's dark emotions?" Laud said, caustically. "That sounds like a wonderful plan."

"But it worked!" Mark protested. "The Nightmare doesn't just feed—it links together people's memories . . . or something like that. To be honest, I never really understood completely. But we went into it, together, and we found that Lily's father lived in the Cathe-dral of the Lost, the stronghold of the monks, and we were all set to go there until . . ."

There was a silence. No one seemed willing to fill it.

"Until the monks kidnapped me, and brought me back to Agora," Mark said, quietly. "From what Cherubina told me, it looks like it was one of the first things Snutworth arranged when he be-came the new Director."

"He let me keep all of my dolls," Cherubina added, softly. "Ex-cept the one I made to look like you, Mark. I think you're more of a threat to him than he likes to admit."

More silence. Laud got up to pace back and forth. Theo sat, brooding in thought.

"So . . ." Theo said at last, "she's alive. That's something, at least. All this time, not knowing . . ."

"Not knowing!" Laud interrupted, with a sudden rage. "What do we know now?! That she's somewhere outside the city, looking for her parents? Being tortured by bad dreams, or chased by psy-chotic monks! That's a *great* comfort."

"She can look after herself," Mark said, defensively. "Anyway, it's not as if there's no chance of finding her again. If the monks knew enough to bring me to Agora, that means there must be more who know how to get past the city walls . . ."

"Good luck with that," Laud snarled, bitterly. "With half the receivers on your trail, you won't be able to set foot outdoors. Lily's going to need more help than you . . ."

"I *will* find her!" Mark said, more fiercely than he expected. "I don't care if I can only go out in the middle of the night, and have to crawl through every building in Agora. Even if I have to break into the Directory itself. Someone has to know where she is. She didn't abandon me, and I won't give up on her!"

Mark found his fists clenched. Laud blinked. For the first time, he seemed lost for words.

"Absolutely," he said, quietly. "I'm . . . glad to hear it."

There was silence. Mark was surprised at how vehement his own response had been. But Laud's tone had gotten to him more than anything else. Up until now, he had been preoccupied with trying to escape the receivers. But he had never once stopped wondering what had happened to Lily. Laud had made it sound as if he didn't care.

"We all need to look," Theo said, taking charge. "But first things first—none of us will be much help if we're locked up for harboring fugitives."

"You're definitely sure that the receivers won't come back tonight?" Cherubina asked, anxiously. "I don't think I could stand crossing the city again before I sleep."

Theo thought for a moment.

"You'll be fine for tonight, but we shouldn't keep you here too much longer," he decided. "I'll ask around for anyone who has some rooms to let and doesn't ask too many questions. Perhaps the Sozinhos can help—they are our most loyal patrons, after all. I'll try for two separate places, to see if we can throw the receivers off the scent."

Cherubina's eyes widened in alarm.

"But . . . you can't do that. I . . . I don't . . . that is . . ."

"She's never lived on her own before, Theo," Mark explained.

"She's never even traded for food. It'd be obvious she didn't belong there."

Theo nodded.

"Very well, we'll have to choose a location very carefully then . . ."

Cherubina smiled across at Mark.

"Thank you," she said, softly.

"You can't get rid of me that easily," Mark said, feeling himself relax a little after all his worry. Cherubina looked as if she was about to reply, but at that moment, the door at the top of the stairs creaked open. Everyone turned, anxious.

"Ben! There you are!" Theo said, anxiously, "What were you doing out on the streets? There's a receiver on every corner . . ."

Theo's voice died away. Mark felt his heart jump. Ben was standing there, smiling excitedly, but she wasn't alone.

A heavyset man stood beside her in the doorway. He wasn't old, but every one of his forty summers was carved onto his face. His hair was touched with gray, and his hands shook, but in his eyes was a spark of hope that grew into joy as he saw Mark.

"Dad?" Mark said softly, barely believing it.

The old jailer walked down the stairs. Without really noticing it, the others stepped out of his way. Mark got up.

"I knew you'd come home," said Pete. "But when Miss Benedicta came and found me, I didn't . . . I didn't believe . . ."

Pete's voice cracked. Mark smiled, but when he tried to speak, his throat wouldn't make the sounds.

He was trapped in a city he no longer loved, far from a friend who desperately needed him. He was being hunted by the receivers and didn't know where to turn, or what to do, to prevent his entire world from falling apart. But just for a moment, none of that mattered at all, because his father was hugging him. The father he'd lost, and found, and lost again.

And this time, he wasn't going anywhere.

CHAPTER THREE

Fugitives

"WHERE DO YOU come from?"

"What's it like?"

"Is it under the sun?"

Lily tried to concentrate. The two strangers never stopped bombarding her with questions, their eyes so round and curious that they seemed like little children, even though they appeared to be a few years older than her.

At least she assumed that they were adults—the man's voice was deep enough—but their skin was pale and utterly smooth, without wrinkle or blemish. They dressed like children too; their robes were loose and garishly colored, covered with broad clashing stripes. Their hair was long, tangled, and so blonde it was nearly white, and their dark eyes were startlingly wide as they prattled. But perhaps the most unnerving thing was how alike they were, in their movements and manner. Had she not heard both of them speak, she would have been hard pressed to say which was male, and which female.

"Are you alone?

"Who are you? Really?"

"How did you get down here?"

Lily tried to talk again, but the questions came thick and fast, and she couldn't focus for long enough to answer a single one. She thought about thanking them for finding her, but it didn't seem at all clear that they were going to assist her in any way. Certainly neither had offered to help her up. In fact, as she struggled to her feet, she noticed them pull back, as though she were dangerous.

"There's no need . . . I mean . . . I'm not going to hurt you," Lily said, feeling ridiculous. That was painfully obvious. Her whole body ached. She didn't know how long she had slept on the rough stone floor after she collapsed from exhaustion. Her limbs still shook, though that was only partly from tiredness. But this one sentence was enough to make them stop talking, and stare at her expectantly.

Unfortunately, in the new quiet, she could hear the noise in the background. The distant, echoing voices.

For a few moments, it came back to her. That long, terrible climb down those stone steps, without light, always thinking that her next movement would pitch her down the shaft. And all around her, the voices. Those wailing, cajoling voices that seemed to come from everywhere. In the world above, she had spent night after night running through a living Nightmare that had peeled apart her subconscious thought by thought. And yet somehow that shaft had been worse because of the confusion. All she had been able to make out was her name. *Lily . . . Lily . . . Lily . . .* over and over again until it lost all meaning. It had felt like her whole world was filling with noise.

At some point, she had reached the bottom of the well, and left the stone steps behind. Later, she remembered stumbling through tunnels of rock, her legs jarring on the rough floor, only able to tell where she was from the change of pressure around and above her when the tunnels narrowed, or opened out into caves. And still the echoes had grown, louder and louder, shouting in her ears. As she had tripped and fallen, she had felt as though she were on the verge of comprehension, just a few seconds away from understanding what they were demanding of her. But then the ground came up to meet her, and finally the sounds had been snuffed out.

"Are you listening to anything I'm saying, Wonder?"

Lily snapped out of her thoughts. There wasn't time to dwell on all of that now. These two were strange, no doubt, but they didn't seem dangerous. Besides, they had lanterns. Lily didn't want to be left alone in the dark again.

"Yes, I'm fine . . . I . . ."

"Good. You can still talk then!" the girl said, briskly. "You don't want to listen to the Cacophony. I'll tell you that for nothing."

Lily shivered, but tried to block it out. Start with something simple . . .

"Thank you . . . um . . . I'm sorry, what's your name?" she asked the girl.

"I'm . . . Septima." The girl replied, carefully, with a slightly awkward tone, as though she herself had forgotten it until that moment.

"And you?" Lily asked the young man. He brought the lantern closer to her face. She saw the flame reflect in his large, curious eyes.

"It's not your turn," he said, coldly. "You have to answer our questions first. An answer for an answer." He turned to Septima. "Are all of the Orchestra so dense?"

"Maybe," Septima agreed with a laugh. "Well?" she added, turning to Lily. "Are they? I mean, you'd know."

"Start with an easier one," interrupted the young man. "She looks pretty tuneless to me."

"All right," Septima continued, as if Lily were not standing just a few feet away. She turned back, and again Lily felt the full force of her attention. "Where—are—you—from?" She said, dragging out each word as though talking to a simpleton. Despite everything, Lily bridled a little.

"Agora," she said, truthfully. "Well, that is . . . I came here from Giseth, from the Cathedral of the Lost. But I actually came from up in the mountains, with Mark, and . . ."

Lily trailed off. The two were looking at her very oddly indeed. They appeared confused, which was hardly surprising after her jumbled explanation, but there was something else in their eyes too. A fascination so strong it was almost hungry.

"I'm Tertius," the young man said, simply, his voice full of reverence. "And you have to tell us all about this!"

"Not here," Septima interrupted, she glanced around, and jerked her head over her shoulder. "We've been here too long, Tertius. The guardians won't be far behind."

Tertius nodded, suddenly serious again.

"Shall we take her with us?" he asked. "Or leave her here until we come back?"

Lily looked from one to the other, aghast.

"You're not going to leave me here?" she asked, horrified. "You still haven't told me anything! Where am I? And what are you doing here?"

Septima turned to Lily. "You're in the Outer Caverns of the land of Naru. We're on the run." She tilted her head, as if considering something. "And yes, you can come with us. You're *our* wonder, after all." She snapped her fingers. "Come on, we've a long way to go."

And without a second thought, both of them turned on their heels and began to walk away.

Lily paused for a moment, uneasily. There was something strange about these two. Even their way of walking was odd—crouched but fluid, dancelike, swinging their lanterns around in arcing patterns that threw shifting shadows onto the stone walls and ceiling around them. She knew nothing about them. For all she knew, they might be leading her into a trap. They certainly didn't seem friendly, exactly, and their intense fascination with her appeared to come and go at a moment's notice.

Then again, she didn't want to meet whoever was chasing them through this endless, echoing darkness.

"I'm right behind you," she said.

They walked in silence, which suited Lily. It gave her time to think.

Now that she was no longer terrified, Lily had to admit that she was not entirely clear on what she was doing here in the depths of the earth.

Only yesterday, she had been certain of everything. She had finally reached the Cathedral of the Lost, after many days' travel through forest and swamp. She had escaped an attack from her own guide, driven mad by the Nightmare, and finally stood in the Cathedral cloisters, demanding answers of its scarred gatekeeper. She had come there seeking her father, and she had found him—ill and dying, only able to talk to her through a letter he had written in his stronger days. She had sat at her father's bedside, and held him as he died. After that, she remembered only a mist of grief and rage, and a determination to do something, anything, that would give this journey meaning.

She had been told that she was a Judge—the "Antagonist." That she and Mark were destined to change Agora and Giseth forever. But Mark was missing, kidnapped by the Order of the Lost, and the all-powerful Bishop had proved to be little more than a withered corpse on his throne. All of the prophecies seemed to have fallen apart.

In her apron pocket, she touched the letter her father had given her before the end—a letter that had told her that *The truth lies below, where the darkness echoes.* So when she had broken open the sealed tomb in the deepest crypt of the Cathedral and found steps descending into the earth, she knew which way she needed to go if she were ever to find the answers she craved.

But now that she was here, it didn't feel real. Here, following these two strangers who acted and spoke so oddly, the world above seemed to fade away, like the voices of the Cacophony. Right now, she was hungry, tired, and lost. Right now, all she could think about was finding somewhere she could be comfortable.

"I'm hungry," Septima said, coming to an abrupt halt. "I think we left some food around here."

Lily looked around. She couldn't see anything to distinguish this spot from the rest of the tunnels. The craggy rock made a ceiling not far above her head—now she understood why Septima and Tertius walked the way they did in these cramped spaces. Only the occasional chisel mark on a wall, and the straightness of the tunnels themselves, indicated that they had ever seen a human hand. The air was still and cold, and Lily was glad that she was wearing her thick boots.

Septima fell to her knees and began running her hands over the rocks at the base of one of the tunnel walls. Meanwhile, Tertius held up his lantern to her face.

"If we're going to give you food, you'll have to pay us," he said.

Lily was surprised. Over the past year, she had become so used to Giseth, where everything was offered for free, that she had not expected him to say that. But she supposed that this place, Naru, was different again.

"Of course . . ." she said, swinging her pack off her back, "but I don't have much to trade. I might have some lantern oil left . . ."

She reached into her pack, but Tertius shook his head.

"Don't you know anything?" he said, scornfully. "Or doesn't the Orchestra trade knowledge?"

Lily wasn't sure what to make of this question. What Orchestra did he mean? And then she remembered how they had acted when they first found her, how eager he had been as she began to explain herself . . .

"You want knowledge? About me?" she ventured. Tertius snorted.

"So you *do* understand," he said, wearily. "I guess you must just be slow then. Yes—answers, information, secrets. Anything hidden." He stretched, and yawned. "Think of something good. I'll wait."

Lily resisted the urge to give a sarcastic reply. Her stomach was beginning to ache, and if all he wanted in payment was a little information, that wouldn't be difficult. For a moment, she considered telling him about her quest—about everything she'd learned at the Cathedral of the Lost. But she decided against it. She could satisfy his desire for facts without having to give away her most precious secrets.

"I come from a city called Agora . . ." she began.

"What's a city?" Tertius interrupted, immediately. Lily raised her eyebrows. But, then again, why would he know? She didn't suppose that there were many cities down here.

"It's a place where a lot of people live, all together . . ."

"Like the Hub, then?" Tertius replied.

"I don't know," Lily said, truthfully. "Is that where you come from?"

"You get your questions later!" he snapped. Lily pulled back, as if stung, and Tertius lowered the lantern. "Continue," he said, in a quieter tone.

"Well . . . Agora's made up of buildings and streets, and it has a river, and squares, and . . ." Lily frowned. It was impossible to know what they would understand. How would they react if she told them Agora's true nature—a city where anything could be bought and sold, where children were bartered by their parents, and memories, thoughts, and emotions were traded on the open market. To an Agoran, it would have been simple, to a Gisethi, horrific. But what would it mean to the people of . . . what did they call this place? Naru?

No. Best to stick to the simple facts.

"It's divided into twelve districts . . ." she tried again.

"Sagittarius, Libra, Gemini, Aquarius . . ." Septima began to rattle them off from her position on the floor.

"All named after the signs of the Zodiac," Tertius added. "Yes, yes, we know that."

Lily looked from one to the other, astonished.

"But . . . if you know about Agora, then why didn't you know what a city is?"

Tertius shrugged.

"I'd never heard it described like that before. We know all sorts of facts—but we've never actually been there. It's hard to join the details together, sometimes. How many people?"

"What?" Lily asked, her head still spinning. How could they know about the districts, without knowing Agora?

"How many people in this city?"

"Um . . ." Lily frowned, "I don't know . . . it's huge . . ."

"More than 576?" Tertius asked.

Lily blinked, incredulous.

"Yes, quite a lot more. More like a hundred thousand, at least."

Tertius gasped. On the floor, Septima stopped in her search to turn and stare.

"That's impossible!" she said. "There wouldn't be enough food! We have shortages all the time, and there's only a few of us . . ."

"Five hundred and seventy-six?" Lily guessed.

Tertius nodded.

"Well," he added, "574, now that we've escaped."

Lily frowned.

"Escaped?" she asked.

"We're on the run," Septima chimed in, returning to her search. "They've been chasing us for three weeks now. We shouldn't wait here too long, or they'll catch up."

Lily grimaced. Just her luck to team up with criminals. She had hoped to be accepted into this new society.

"Who'll catch up?" she asked, trying to sound casual.

"The guardians . . . aha!" Septima's tone changed to one of triumph. With a flourish, she pushed aside a pile of loose rocks and pulled out a thick, padded, cloth bundle, tied up with string. "I knew I'd left a food parcel around here somewhere." She looked critically at Lily. "I think Lily's given us enough knowledge to pay for a bit of food, don't you think?"

Tertius nodded, grudgingly, and Septima undid the string.

"It's your turn to ask a question," she prompted, as she spread out the cloth. "After telling us about the hundreds of thousands . . ." she shook her head, dreamily. "That's a real wonder. That's special. You can ask anything you like."

Lily frowned. Septima unwrapped a loaf of bread and large piece of cheese. They didn't look particularly old, but Lily doubted that they could have been made down here. It didn't look like the place for cows and grain.

"You're on the run, you said?" Lily asked, breaking off a piece of cheese.

Septima nodded, airily.

"Have been for weeks," she said, almost proudly. "We've led them on a chase, of course, but they're closing in. We'll need to find our way to the rails again soon. Maybe sneak back into the dining caverns near the Hub for more supplies."

Lily reached forward to tear off a piece of bread; the cheese had really sharpened her hunger. As she did, Tertius pulled his own hand back sharply. Lily had noticed both of them do this before. Even though they sat near to each other, they never came close to touching.

"The Hub?" Lily asked, trying to piece together the fragments of information.

"The center of the Inner Caverns." Septima cupped her hands into a dome shape. "It's miles away. We won't want to go back there for long. If we're caught . . ." she hunched over. "They say they throw you into a tiny cave, with any other prisoners. You can feel their *breath* on your face!" She shuddered. "It's obscene."

Tertius stretched out a hand toward her, and waved it. It looked like some kind of comforting gesture, again, without touching. Respectfully, Lily shuffled a little farther away from them.

"But, why are you running?" Lily asked, "What did you do?"

Tertius crossed his arms, defensively.

"That's for us to know. Have you told us *your* biggest secret?"

"We wanted to know something that was forbidden," Septima confessed. "We didn't just want to trade secrets, we wanted an artifact from the world above. Something we could show off, something solid. We wanted to find a wonder!" She smiled. "And we did. You."

"But why?" Lily persisted. "What's it for?"

"For?" Septima replied, blankly. "It's everything."

"I mean," Lily swallowed the last lump of bread, "why are you collecting all these secrets? Is someone hiding them from you?"

Septima twirled a strand of her white hair, and stuck it in her mouth. She seemed lost for words.

Tertius leaned back against the side of the tunnel.

"Why do you breathe?" he asked. "Why do you eat? Knowledge rules our lives. We ask questions, we tell each other facts, and secrets. The more you know, the better you are." He broke off. "That's what it's like for all the choristers. That's how it's been forever."

"Tertius . . ." Septima said, warningly. The two exchanged glances, and lapsed back into silence. Lily got the strong impression that he had just said too much. Which, if knowledge really was all they cared about, wasn't that surprising. Lily supposed that she hadn't paid enough for that information yet.

For a few moments, they ate in silence. Septima brushed crumbs from her lips.

"What are you doing here, Lily?" she asked suddenly, in a much more serious tone.

Lily knotted her fingers, wondering how much she should admit. Of course, she could swear them to secrecy, but if they traded knowledge here like possessions in Agora, she couldn't be sure that someone else wouldn't find the right price, and then Tertius and Septima would hardly be likely to keep her safe. They still seemed to look on her as a thing rather than a person.

"I'm looking for . . ." Lily trailed off. What exactly was she looking for? There were so many things that had been hidden from her: Her real purpose, as the "Antagonist"—one of the fabled Judges; the secrets that were hidden in the Midnight Charter, this document that seemed to rule her life. But these would have taken too long to explain. And anyway, she wasn't sure if she trusted these strangers enough to tell them this yet. And then, unbidden, the right answer came into her head. The answer that made her feel profoundly guilty, because it wasn't the first thing she had thought of.

"I'm looking for my friend, Mark," she said. "He was kidnapped, and I need to find him."

Septima stroked her hair, absently. Lily had expected some kind of reaction, but she seemed less interested by this than when Lily had been describing Agora.

"That doesn't sound like something that just anyone would know," she said, thoughtfully.

"The Conductor might," Tertius muttered, darkly. Septima shivered.

"Lily wouldn't want to ask him anything," she replied, quickly.

"Why not?" Lily asked. "Is he someone important?"

"He's evil," Septima said, with a surprisingly matter-of-fact tone.

"Brutal," Tertius agreed.

"A fiend of a man. He's enslaved all of our friends," Septima remarked, growing increasingly heated.

"He's the reason we're on the run," Tertius added. "The reason we left everyone we know to trudge through these outer caverns."

"Lucky for you," Septima said. "We'd never have found you if it wasn't for him."

"True," Tertius said.

They sat in silence.

Lily shifted, uneasily. For a few moments, when talking about the Conductor, they had suddenly animated, sounding genuinely fearful. Now they were listless again, as though nothing had happened. It was almost as if their emotions switched on and off at will. The more time she spent with this pair, the less comfortable she became. But right at the moment, they were all she had.

She was about to speak again when she heard something far off. A distant echo. For a moment, fear gripped her—had they wandered back toward the Cacophony? But Tertius and Septima's reaction made it clear that the danger was of a far more immediate kind.

"The guardians!" Septima hissed. "I knew they were following us. We shouldn't have waited here for so long!" She glared at Lily, as though it were her fault. "Find somewhere to hide," she hissed.

In a second, Septima snatched up the cloth, and she and Tertius doused the flames of their lanterns. Blinded in the sudden darkness, Lily felt her way behind some thickly clustered stalagmites.

She heard them before she saw them—the soft, steady tread of thick-soled boots. Then she saw an approaching light, and their shadows, dancing on the wall. She just had time to see Tertius and Septima, cowering in little alcoves on the far side of the tunnel, before she ducked back down behind the rocks.

She peered out. The pursuers didn't look too terrible. They were a small group, walking closely. Like Tertius and Septima, they were slim, pale, and androgynous, though they looked stronger than her new friends. The only difference she could see was that each one wore thick gloves that reached up to their elbows, and strips of cloth tied across the lower half of their faces. Lily narrowed her eyes. Those gloves looked scuffed, well used. Considering Tertius and Septima's reactions to physical proximity, she imagined that if these "guardians" were allowed to touch their targets, they must be feared indeed. As for her—she could probably escape from one or two, but there were ten in this group, and she kept her head down, until they had disappeared into the distance.

Tertius and Septima remained pressed against the tunnel wall until long after the guardians had gone. Then, in a sudden movement, Tertius heaved a great sigh of relief.

"That was close," he said, breathing dramatically.

"You all right?" Septima asked, with genuine concern. Lily noticed her hand, hovering a foot from Tertius's shoulder.

"Fine," he replied shakily. "Come on, Lily. This way . . ."

"Mm . . ." Lily said, distracted. Fortunately, Tertius and Septima didn't seem to notice as they set off that Lily chose to walk a good distance behind them.

For people who prized knowledge so highly, they didn't seem to be all that observant. Lily had been well hidden, but Tertius and Septima had barely had time to conceal themselves at all.

In fact, she was pretty sure that the pursuers had seen Tertius and Septima quite clearly. And they had stared right through them, as if they were invisible.

CHAPTER FOUR

The Wheel

"YEAH?"

The big man filled the door so completely that Mark was amazed he had fit through it in the first place. He stared down at Mark without hostility, but with an implacable knowledge that no one was coming through his door without permission. A smell of stale beer and smoke assaulted Mark's nose, but he couldn't see a single thing behind the man's bulk. Whatever was happening here, it was the last place Mark would have expected to find Cherubina.

For nearly two weeks, Mark and Cherubina had been living in a small, musty building in the Aries District. It was an ideal hiding place—drab, empty, and practically indistinguishable from the other gray houses around it. Even if they were spotted in the area, the receivers would have no idea where to start. The residents of Aries kept their own counsel—they weren't the sort to snoop.

Even so, they barely ever left their few cramped rooms. Receiver patrols were getting more and more common, and Mark still jumped when he heard their shrill whistles. They had the occasional visitor—usually Pete, Mark's father, bringing food for them. Neither Mark nor Cherubina could trade for food themselves; their signet rings would have been recognized instantly when the receivers checked the merchants' records. Those visits from his father had been one of the few things making these last days bearable. The others had warned the old jailer to be careful, but nothing would keep him away. Mark and Pete hadn't spent more than a day in each other's company for over three years, and they were determined to make up for it.

But those visits were brief, and usually it was just Mark and Cherubina, alone. Cherubina never spoke of her time in Snutworth's tower, and honestly, Mark didn't want to ask—so it had been down to him to keep them both entertained. And he had tried so hard to keep up their spirits, to assure Cherubina that the Directory had too much to worry about to chase them for long. But as the days passed, he ran out of stories, and patience. He wanted to be out there, trying to find Lily. And instead, he would look at Cherubina and see that every day she was a little less thankful for her rescue, and a little more sullen. He couldn't blame her—she had exchanged one prison for another. Before long, whole days could pass in silence—Mark pacing up and down, suffocating from inaction, and Cherubina sitting silently, stitching away at a series of increasingly mournful rag dolls.

In the end, Mark couldn't stand it any longer. He began to go for walks, just short ones, to clear his head. He was careful—he kept away from receiver patrols, and he was always back by the time his father paid a visit. Pete was worried enough as it was.

So when Cherubina had followed his lead and started to take walks herself, Mark hadn't been too concerned. Mark made her wear a headscarf to cover her distinctive curls, and he was glad to see her starting to feel less trapped.

But then she had begun to go out more and more frequently. She wouldn't tell him where she was going.

And then, just an hour ago, he had found the note.

Cherubina was out again, and as he looked to see where she had put the last of the bread, he knocked over her sewing basket—the one possession she had insisted was hers alone. The little piece of paper had fluttered to the ground among the spools of thread. It had a single sentence scrawled on it, and Mark had read it without thinking:

"Meeting at the Wheel—Taurus 8th, third hour after noon."

Taurus 8th—today's date. He wanted to stuff the note back into the sewing basket and forget he had ever found it. This was none of his business, and he had plenty to worry about. If it had been anyone else, he would have left well enough alone.

But this was Cherubina. Until two weeks ago, she had never been outdoors without an army of servants.

He put on his jacket.

It didn't take him long to find the Wheel—a famous taproom in the depths of the Taurus District. But he had to admit that he hadn't expected the guard at the door.

"I'm . . ." Mark floundered, his confidence deserting him. "I'm here for the meeting."

The huge man nodded.

"You're late," he grunted. "Mr. Crede's already started."

He stepped to one side, revealing a dark and smoky interior. Somewhere in the back of Mark's head, a warning note sounded. He was sure that he had heard the name "Crede" before, if only he could remember.

He looked up at the thug. For a moment, he considered asking what kind of meeting this was. Fortunately, a second later his common sense reminded him that he was supposed to know already.

"So, Mr. . . . I'm sorry, I didn't catch your name," Mark said, trying to sound polite. The man gave an unpleasant grin.

"Nick, and don't you forget it. Don't think you'll be getting any favors from the 'Mr.,' though, boy. There's no pecking order here; everyone's equal under Crede."

Mark noted the tension in Nick's huge arm as he held the door. Maybe not any social order, but Mark bet that if any disagreements came up, they'd be solved very swiftly, and directly.

"So . . . Nick, has my friend arrived yet? I promised to meet her here. You'd know her if you saw her, she's got these blonde ringlets . . ." Mark trailed off. Nick was shaking his head, and grinning that disturbingly predatory smile.

"Not for me to say. You going in, or not?" he said. "Everyone's welcome, but everyone goes without a name. Protection against spies. But of course, you know that. Whoever told you where to come must have filled you in, yes?"

Mark swallowed, he'd given himself away there. Nick might have been here as muscle, but he certainly wasn't dumb.

"Of course," Mark agreed, hurriedly. "No problem."

Shakily, he walked past the man, but as he did so, he felt a rough hand on his shoulder.

"Don't worry, boy," Nick said, a little more kindly. "Doesn't matter why you came. Everyone here gets a fresh start."

For some reason that was difficult to fathom, Nick's reassurance made Mark more uncomfortable than his threats. There was something in the way he said it that suggested this fresh start wasn't optional. Once you went through that door—you were one of them.

"Thanks," Mark said, and stepped in.

To Mark's relief, the taproom beyond was much less sinister, although it was dimly lit and thickly crowded. Through the tobacco smoke, Mark groped his way toward the bar, with a thin and sour-looking barman serving pint pots of muddy beer. He sat on one of the barstools, and as his ears adjusted to the hubbub, he heard a voice from the far side of the room.

". . . they hunt us down, force us to hide—like rats. But should we be cowed by this? Hah!" There was a sound, as if someone had banged a metal tankard on a table. "I say this. When, in a thousand years, Agora is naught but dust, and our last fine building has crumbled away, the rats will still be here. Multiplying until their hour has come. Don't be offended by being called a rat, my friends. They need nothing but each other, and they cannot be destroyed."

Mark looked sharply into the corner, where he could just make out the silhouette of the speaker.

"The time is near, my friends," the voice continued. "So near, we can taste it! And then, the receivers will regret the lengths they've pushed us to! Remember, if you shake up a rat's nest, you'll be bitten for your trouble!"

The whole room roared its approval, and as it did, a breeze stirred through the smoke, someone raised a lantern high, and Mark could see Crede.

He was tall and ragged, with stringy blond hair and an imperfectly shaved face. Physically, he was not terribly inspiring—he looked like a man who had spent too many nights passed out on the floor. But his stance and eyes told a different story. Every movement, every second, spoke of a man brimming with passion. As Mark watched, the story that Laud had told came back to him. The story of the Wheel, Crede's rival almshouse—of the things he was prepared to do to ensure a better life for those who sought his aid: theft, intimidation, even attacks on receivers. Laud had received a beating at the hands of Crede's thugs, one of whom, Mark was sure,

41

had been the one who had greeted him at the door. As Crede moved, the whole crowd shifted with him, riveted by his every gesture. And they listened as if their lives depended on it.

"The receivers are already learning their lesson, my friends! They cower in their parts of the city, patrolling outside the houses of the elite, so that the wealthiest will think that they are still safe." He laughed, a short, cruel burst. "Soon they will not dare interfere again, and we can take to the streets, and ensure a fair deal for everyone. Because as long as the Directory remains in power, how can the ordinary man or woman get a fair deal for themselves? What value do they place on the lives of ordinary people? We believe that humanity is worth more than the market price!"

The room erupted into applause. On his stool, Mark shuddered. He remembered those words. But last time he had heard them, they had been spoken by Lily. In an odd way, Crede reminded him of Lily—she had always been determined that the world should be more fair. But Lily had planned to do it with compassion, not by starting a war.

Mark tore his gaze away to look around the room. The way Laud had described Crede's operation made it sound like an army in the making, especially considering the way they antagonized the receivers. And it was certainly true that there was a sprinkling of people who, like Nick, looked as though they weren't here for the speeches. But at the same time, most of the listeners were much more inconspicuous: men, women, even children, mostly poor from the looks of their clothes, and all captivated.

"Hey, you," the barman grumbled. "You going to order a drink or what? Crede can set up shop here, but I need to make my living as well."

Hastily, Mark shrank away, trying to mingle with the crowd. As he did, he caught a glimpse of a small, dark-haired woman, watching silently from a doorway. For a second, he was sure that he had seen the woman before.

"Miss Devine?" Mark said to himself under his breath. "This isn't your kind of place at all . . ."

Mark remembered Miss Devine, though he had met her only once. She was the neighbor of the Temple Almshouse, and officially a glassmaker by trade. But her real business was rather more strange—extracting and selling the emotions of others. When Mark had been a rising star of the Agoran elite, it had been fashionable to pass around a few tiny bottles of emotion at parties, and Miss Devine had been the best supplier. But what was she doing here? As far as Mark remembered, she was doing well, and hardly interested in the rights of the downtrodden . . .

"And now, my friends, there is someone I want you to meet," Crede pronounced at full volume. "Comrades, don't think that our only support comes from lowly folk like us. Why, even some of the highest in the land have joined our cause, so moved are they by our plight! I present to you, Miss Serapha, the daughter of the elite!"

"Serapha?" Mark said, turning his head. "That sounds . . . familiar . . ."

He stopped, mouth agape. There, with the crowd opening out around her, was Cherubina.

"Is this not a symbol of our cause?" Crede said, bowing gallantly in Cherubina's direction. "Started by the purity of a young maiden—Miss Lilith—and after her mysterious disappearance, continued by such shining examples of charity as Miss Serapha, who willingly gave up an elite family to live among us. Whatever the Directory may say, as long as such people flock to our cause, we know it is just and true!"

There was a cheer from the crowd around. Cherubina remained still, her eyes cast demurely down—standing in a borrowed dress, under a false name, and being praised as a heroine of truth.

Mark thought that it seemed to sum up Crede's movement pretty well.

He waited until Crede moved to another part of the taproom, still talking, and the crowd followed him, away from Cherubina. Then, he crept toward her, and grabbed her shoulder.

"Ma—?" Cherubina gasped as Mark pulled her into the quietest corner of the room. Mark glared at her furiously, and she hastily swallowed the name. She had promised not to say it in public. "What are you doing here?" she whispered.

"What am *I* doing here?" Mark replied. "In what way is becoming a symbol of a revolution keeping a low profile?"

"I'm finding us some allies," Cherubina replied, proudly. "Aren't these people just like your friends at the other almshouse? Except, of course, Crede actually takes action. They say that the receivers don't dare come into the Taurus district anymore . . ."

"Fine, fine," Mark said, glancing around to check that no one was listening to them. Fortunately, Crede was still very much the center of attention. "But how did you know about this place at all?"

Cherubina smiled in a way that she clearly thought was mysterious.

"Mr. Crede sent me a note—one of his men slipped it under our door. He said I might be able to help them. At first, I went because I was curious, and because they promised to protect me, but now . . ."

"How did they know about you?" Mark interrupted, and then shook his head. That much was obvious; he recognized several ragged figures here that had been at the Temple Almshouse. News obviously traveled fast in the underworld. "I wish you'd told me," Mark said, uneasily. "Didn't you think that one or two of these people might let the receivers know where you are?"

"What would be wrong with *Miss Serapha* coming to the meetings?" Cherubina replied, with all the subtlety of a brat of four summers.

Mark sighed, and raised his hand to touch Cherubina's ringlets. "There are more things than names that can draw attention to us," he muttered. "Did you know Miss Devine is here as well?"

"Who?" Cherubina replied, deeply uninterested.

"Miss . . ." Mark looked around, but the emotion peddler had vanished in the crowd. He dismissed her with a wave of the hand. "It doesn't matter. Someone we don't want following us. The point is, anyone could be here, even an undercover receiver."

"Nick on the door knows every undercover receiver that dares to work at this end of the city," Cherubina replied, with a touch of pride, "Mr. Crede's not stupid, you know."

"Baiting the receivers when they're already on edge. Promising fairness to everyone in Agora . . ." Mark sighed. "He doesn't look or sound like someone who's very closely in touch with reality."

"He's trying to make a difference," Cherubina said, quietly. "And so am I. All my life I've been a prize, used by other people. Not anymore."

"No," Mark muttered, sarcastically. "And your 'purer than a lily' act there certainly wasn't Crede showing off his new possession."

"He's the Director's enemy, so that makes him our friend," Cherubina said, loftily. "Crede said I'm too valuable to let anything happen to me. He already knows where we live. I've seen some of his men watching me as I come home. He's keeping me safe."

"It doesn't work like that," Mark insisted. "He isn't really out to help people. He's after as much power as he can grab. You think he really cares about you?" Mark took her hand. "By all the stars, Cherubina, this isn't a game! I thought you did some growing up over the past year . . ."

Cherubina snatched her hand away, furious.

"Don't you *dare* talk about that dreadful time again. Don't you *dare* treat it like a joke!"

45

"Then you shouldn't treat our hiding like it doesn't mean anything!" Mark snapped back, barely trying to keep his voice down anymore. "We're hiding from *him*, Cherubina, from Snutworth! Even if he doesn't really care, he'd take you back out of spite—you know he would."

"That's why I need proper protection," she said, scornfully. "You think just because Crede's got vision he's stupid? He understands everything. He was just telling me before you arrived, now that Snutworth's the Director, we have to plan carefully . . ."

Cherubina trailed away as she saw Mark's expression.

"You told *Crede* about Snutworth?" Mark whispered. "You told him who you are?"

Cherubina crossed her arms, defiantly.

"It's my secret," she said. "I can tell who I want."

Mark stared at her, marveling.

"Do you have any idea what he could do with that kind of knowledge?" Mark said, quietly.

"Of course I do," Cherubina said, intensely. "He told me himself. Right now, the people are scared of the Director—they think he's a myth, all powerful." Mark detected a hint of Crede in her tone, as though she were repeating something he had said. "But as soon as they know that he's just an ordinary man . . ."

"An ordinary man?" Mark interrupted, putting his head in his hands. "A few years ago, he was my servant, and now he's the ruler of the city! There's nothing ordinary about him, and you know it. And anyway, that hardly robs him of his power—or have you forgotten about the receivers? Dad says that they've stepped up their training. Some of them are even practicing with swords, not truncheons. You really believe that Crede's army of thugs is going to be able to fight them?"

"So you think we should just do nothing?" Mark was amazed to see that Cherubina's eyes were wet. She seemed to be almost crying, but her voice was still dangerous. Mark gingerly laid a hand on her shoulder.

"I'm saying you shouldn't be getting involved in this. I hate Snutworth as much as you do, but you can't keep obsessing over him. You've escaped—you need to live your own life . . ."

Cherubina met his gaze.

"And how can I do that?" she asked, softly. "By doing everything you say?"

Mark pulled his hand back, stung, but Cherubina was unrepentant. She turned her back, stiffly.

"I need to get back," she said, pointing to the crowd, still ignoring them, enraptured by Crede. "He wants to introduce me to some of the new recruits."

"You're just a tool to him," Mark protested, feebly. Cherubina didn't turn around.

"Maybe," she admitted, "but at least he's doing some good. He's not sitting at home, waiting for Daddy to visit. He can keep me safe." She glanced over her shoulder. Her anger seemed to have gone; now she looked sad, almost disappointed. "Why don't you go? Crede is handing out bread, and we don't have much to trade. I'd ask you along, but he only gives handouts to men of action."

And then, before Mark could reply, she walked away, mingling in the crowd.

Mark couldn't think of a single thing to say. Not as he left the smoky bar, the sound of Crede's speeches ringing in his ears. Not as he crept through the streets, and returned to their lonely house.

Not even that night, when the receivers walked past, ringing the new curfew bell. All he had was a jumble of thoughts about Cherubina's safety, and his own inability to decide what to do. But by then, it didn't really matter.

Because, by then, it was clear that Cherubina wasn't coming back.

CHAPTER FIVE

Harmonies

LILY DIDN'T KNOW where she was anymore.

Every time she woke and lit her lantern, the rocky passageways disappeared into darkness on either side. She began to wonder if they went on forever.

It was hard to tell how long she and her new friends had been traveling; they hadn't seen their pursuers once since that first encounter. They had slept fifteen times, that was certain, but whether this had any bearing on day or night it was impossible to say. She was tired most of the time, but considering the constant walking and stone surfaces where she was forced to sleep, that was hardly a surprise.

On the second "day," they had found a cache of lantern oil, and Lily had been given her own lantern. She had taken to keeping the flame low after she woke up, and then raising and dimming it through the day, making her own sun. She found it strangely comforting.

It wasn't that the tunnels were dull. Often they opened into caverns of breathtaking beauty, with rock that rippled across the walls like water. Or they would find a cave full of quartz shards that burst through the floor to make scintillating forests of crystal. Even when they had to crawl through spaces barely wide enough to breathe, the rock under their hands and knees was mottled with a hundred different tones, textures, and colors. Under normal circumstances, Lily would have been fascinated.

But she found herself longing for the real forests of Giseth, or even the crowds of Agora. There was no chance of meeting anyone new down here. If they heard the sound of approaching footsteps, they had to hide. Lily had tried to get Septima and Tertius to explain again why they were on the run, but all she got for her troubles were veiled comments about the evils of the Conductor, and increasingly suspicious looks.

That was the other problem. She could cope with sleeping on rock floors, with nothing but her pack for a pillow—she had suffered worse. She could cope with being lost, and the lack of light and stale air. But her companions were another matter. She was beginning to suspect that accompanying Tertius and Septima anywhere was not a good idea.

If anything, their behavior became even stranger as time went on. Unless Lily mentioned it, they seemed to have forgotten that they were being chased. In fact, they couldn't seem to latch on to one thought for more than a few minutes. They chattered continuously, but never about anything of importance. Occasionally, they claimed to be fleeing to a secret rebel encampment, but they seemed to have little idea of where to go. If anything, their journeys were simply from one concealed food parcel to the next, and even that was strangely convenient. At first, they claimed that they had left the food there, in cases of emergency. But it soon became clear that it never even occurred to them to take any of the food with them. In fact, they carried no supplies at all, apart from their lanterns. They slept, sprawled on the floor, without any need for comfort, brushing the dust from themselves in the morning, and washing in the pools of water that formed in the damper caverns.

Above all, they didn't seem to have any plan. On the seventh day, Tertius led them on a breakneck chase through a maze of tunnels, only to show them a smooth, egg-shaped nugget of crystal growing out of a wall. Septima stared at the amber stone in delight, watching the light of her lantern play off its surface.

Lily leaned against the wall of the tunnel, thinking of all the similar crystals they had seen, growing from the walls, in their journeys through the tunnels. She remembered her own tiny crystal, the one that had led her here, still buried in the depths of her pack. It was one of the crystals that Verity, her father's sister, had brought to Agora. She had thought it so strange when she had first found it; she could never have imagined that she would find a whole land of them.

But in Naru, they were everywhere. Some glittered beneath her feet, barely larger than a fingernail, others covered whole caverns with splendor. No two were the same; they were of every color and shape, but all shared a kind of shifting translucence. Stepping into a whole cavern lined with them was an unsettling experience, as though the solid rock around her was dissolving into smoke.

But that wasn't the oddest thing about the crystals. She hadn't discovered that until she had tried to sleep.

The crystals whispered.

They were very quiet, too faint to understand, like the distant babble of the Cacophony. But in the silence, she could hear them, the sound rising and falling like a million echoes a long way away.

"Can't we get moving again?" she asked, testily, trying to conceal her unease. Septima didn't bother to look at her.

"Not until we've examined this one," she said, still gazing intensely at the egg-shaped crystal, which pulsed faintly in the light of her lamp.

Lily shifted. She was sure that she could hear more whispering coming from this amber gem, but her ears could just be playing tricks.

"What's so special about these crystals anyway?" she asked, trying to cover her unease.

Septima turned around, her expression smug.

"Shall we tell her?" she asked Tertius. He shrugged, sourly.

"I'll show her. This one is good to look at, but it's too garbled to be useful."

Septima giggled in delight. She was clearly enjoying knowing more than Lily. Lily refused to rise to her bait.

"You wanted to know how we know so many facts about the world above, when we've never seen it?" Septima asked. "Come here, and put your ear to this crystal."

Lily approached, tentatively. The smooth gemstone seemed to be glowing with its own light. Tertius noticed her hesitation, and smirked.

"It isn't hot. We shine our lanterns on these crystals, and they take in the light, but not the fire."

Tentatively, Lily bent her head, and pressed her ear up against the crystal's smooth surface.

"What am I supposed to . . . ?" she began, but Septima shushed her.

Tertius began to sing.

When speaking, his voice had been harsh. But now, it emerged in a sweet, high series of notes—no real words, just an oddly haunting melody. Lily was so surprised that she didn't move, keeping

51

her ear against the crystal. For a moment or two, all she could hear was Tertius's voice, resonating inside the crystal, gaining overtones that hummed and sparkled.

Then, suddenly, she began to hear words. But these weren't coming from Tertius. This was a different voice altogether, swimming up from the depths of the crystal.

She recognized this new voice. It was her own.

What's so special about that crystal?

She pulled her head back in surprise. Tertius stopped singing and laughed, but Septima cleared her throat in an exaggerated way.

"These crystals rule our lives," she said, as if reciting a lesson. "Something about them allows them to resonate for years, maybe even centuries. We think that every word spoken, every sound made in the world above is captured by seams of crystal in the stone beneath your lands." She traced a path across the rock wall, revealing a line of glittering stone leading up to the crystal. "And the resonance builds, passing from crystal to crystal, until it reaches the caves of Naru. After that, it's only a question of sifting through the noise to find the secrets. Every crystal unlocks new treasures for us."

As if to demonstrate, Septima sung a sudden top note, bright and clear, and the crystal rang in response, its light growing. At first, Lily heard only a burst of unintelligible echoes—like a crowd far away. Septima changed notes, singing up and down a scale. As she did, some of the voices faded away, and others rose to the surface.

Don't be offended by being called a rat, my friends, . . .

A man, making a speech.

You going to order a drink or what?

Another man, sour and ratty.

All my life I've been a prize, used by other people. Not anymore.

A woman. Lily craned forward; she was sure she recognized that voice. If she could just listen for a few seconds more . . .

52

Septima stopped singing. Almost instantly, the voice faded into nothingness, and the light within the crystal guttered and failed.

"Of course, sometimes all you get is nonsense," Septima said, airily, apparently not noticing Lily's disappointment. "But find the right crystals, and you might hear anything ever spoken in the lands above."

Lily marveled. Back in Agora, the Director would have longed for a tool as powerful as this. To be able to listen in on any conversation ever held, any word ever uttered. It was extraordinary, amazing.

No, she realized. It was terrifying.

"*Anything?*" she said, aghast. Tertius scratched his chin, nonchalantly.

"Well, in a lot of the crystals, most of the echoes are too faint to hear, of course," he said. "The best ones are back at the Hub. Out here you usually only get little pieces of worthwhile knowledge."

"Speaking of worthwhile knowledge," Septima said, turning her back on the crystal. "That was a lot of answers we just gave you, and I don't remember you answering many questions for a while. You'd better tell us something new soon, Wonder." She frowned. "Anyway, there's nothing worth listening to here anymore. Let's go."

And completely ignoring the crystal that had so fascinated her moments ago, Septima strode from the cave, leaving Lily even more confused.

After that, Tertius and Septima were unusually hostile for the rest of the day. Lily tried talking to them, but they had soon wrung her dry of trivial facts about Agora, and the more time she spent with them, the less keen she was to share anything more personal. And as soon as she stopped talking, their interest began to wane.

For three days after that, they were sullen and moody. But it wasn't until they awoke on the eleventh day that either of them would say what was wrong.

"I don't think much of this wonder anymore, Tertius," Septima announced, suddenly, as they were eating. "She hasn't told us anything new for a while. Why do you want to keep feeding her?"

Lily swallowed in alarm, not sure whether to be frightened or insulted. Tertius smiled, enigmatically.

"You need patience. She'll reveal more if we give her time. She's one of the Orchestra, remember? They're not like us."

"You've mentioned the Orchestra before," Lily said, anxious to change the subject. "Who are they?"

Septima glared.

"Questions, questions, all the time, and never any knowledge to pay for it," she said, darkly, and then rolled her eyes. "The Orchestra! You know . . . up there." She waved her hand toward the stone ceilings. "The world above. The Orchestra provides the music, while the Choir," she gestured to herself and Tertius, "sings the song. You can have that for nothing, that's common knowledge." She sniggered. "You're right, you know; she's pretty tuneless."

Tertius began to giggle. After that, Lily couldn't get any sense out of them for an age. Every time they looked at her, they dissolved into laughter.

On the twelfth day, she decided to put her foot down.

"Where are we going?" she asked, suddenly. Tertius looked back, an expectant look on his face. Lily sighed. "All right, you want some knowledge first?" She took a breath. "The village of Aecer is the nearest Gisethi village to Agora, and its leader, the Speaker Bethan, used to be the village's tale-spinner. Now can I ask a question?"

Tertius pulled a face.

"What's a tale-spinner?"

Lily felt her fists clenching in frustration.

"A tale-spinner is something between a teacher and a

storyteller. And that's all you're getting until you tell me where we're going!"

Tertius exchanged glances with Septima, brushing his long white hair out of his eyes.

"We're running away," he said, as if she were simple. "Away. Not toward anything. We'd hoped to find a wonder, but since that didn't turn out right," he looked down his nose at her, "we'll just have to keep going until we find another one."

"And what will you do if you find one?" Lily asked, used to ignoring the insults by now.

Septima looked at her nails, thoughtfully, pointedly refusing to answer. Lily leaned back against the wall. How could she make this work?

"Tell me, have you two ever heard of the Midnight Charter?"

Septima's head snapped up.

"What do you know about that?" she said suspiciously.

Lily smiled.

"Quite a lot, considering I'm mentioned in it. And I'm willing to share."

Tertius frowned, and leaned closer to Septima. He whispered, but because he had to whisper loud enough for Septima to hear without getting too close, Lily also heard every word.

"That's top quality information. Only the Oracle knows about the Charter."

"She could be lying," Septima replied with a glare. "You can't trust the Orchestra—everyone knows that." Tertius pulled on his hair in frustration.

"She needs us. Think! If we found out something the Oracle didn't know . . ."

"Who's the Oracle?" Lily asked.

There was a stunned silence. Septima looked as though her eyes were going to pop out of her head.

"The Oracle is . . . the Oracle," she said, stupefied. "She knows everything. They say, if you can tell her something she doesn't know, she'll reveal every secret in the world."

Lily smiled. Finally, a plan had presented itself.

"All right, this is the deal," she said, stepping closer to them to make them uneasy. "You take me to the Oracle, and before I tell her my secrets, I'll tell you. Then we share the truth. Deal?"

Tertius and Septima exchanged glances again.

"You could be lying," Tertius stated, flatly.

"What have I got to lose?" Lily replied, keeping her voice level. She couldn't back down now. This Oracle sounded like a much better place to start finding answers than these two.

Septima breathed out.

"It had better be worth it," she said. "We'll take the Rails. The Conductor won't expect us to come that way."

Tertius nodded, wrapping up the last of the food.

"It's a few days' walk away. Come on, Wonder."

Decisively, he set off.

"Can I ask just one more question?" Lily said as she followed. Septima glared.

"What?" she said, peevishly.

"What are the Rails?"

Septima's lips curled into a smug grin.

"Something you'll never forget," she said.

Three days later, they reached the Rails.

At first, they didn't look too impressive—nothing more than two parallel metal tracks, running down the center of a flat tunnel.

"Is this it?" Lily asked, trying to keep the disappointment out of her voice. Septima nodded distractedly.

"The rails run all through the tunnels out here," she explained.

"They even go as far as the edge of the Cacophony, near where we found you."

"Well, I have to say," Lily mumbled as they continued down the tunnel, "I wouldn't call these unforgettable . . ."

As they progressed, Lily noticed that the tunnels were growing wider and more regular. The air in the tunnel began to stir, blowing strands of her dark hair across her face. Then, she heard the noise. A whirring, clanking sound, quite unlike the eerie echoes of the Cacophony. Ahead, Lily began to make out a cold glow of light.

"Hush," Tertius said, suddenly, looking down. His dark eyes were hard, and serious. "We're about to get to the Rail Nexus," he said. "Follow us. Don't speak; don't draw any attention. Do exactly what we do. And remember, you owe us for this."

Lily nodded, keeping her mouth shut.

Then, with alarming swiftness, Tertius and Septima bounded forward, into the light. Surprised, Lily raced forward, toward the mouth of the cavern—and stopped dead.

The cavern was huge, stretching so far up that it almost looked like a sky. Up in the roof, Lily could see huge lumps of crystal, glowing with their own inner light, casting a strange, bluish radiance over the entire cavern. All around the edges, Lily could see people, dressed in the same garish colors as Tertius and Septima. But the most striking thing about the cavern, the thing that took her breath away, was that it was filled from top to bottom with a vast array of spinning, whirring, and interlocking clockwork gears.

Ahead, behind a large cluster of machinery, Lily could see Septima beckoning to her. She darted a look around, but the other figures seemed to be distracted, tending to their enormous contraption. As she hurried across to her companions, Lily couldn't suppress a shudder. She had seen a mass of clockwork like this only once before, in the cellar of a secret house back in Agora. And there, her life had been threatened by a madman.

"What—?" Lily began, but Septima shushed her, and pointed deeper into the machinery. Lily squinted. In the depths of the clockwork, she could make out a series of shapes, like oddly shaped carts. Inside one of them, she spotted a flash of white. Tertius's hair, she was sure of it.

"After you," Septima said, gesturing toward a ladder, propped up against the side of the machine. Grimly, Lily took hold, and began to climb.

Unsteadily, she reached the cart. It was larger than it had looked from the ground, and even contained a few seats. Tertius shrank away from her as she stepped in, and Septima gracefully hopped in behind her, one hand on a large lever at the back. Lily glanced up at the clockwork spinning around them, and then peered over the side. Sure enough, the cart's wheels were slotted into a pair of thick, metallic rails.

"You might want to sit down," Septima said. Lily turned back to look at her, opening her mouth. But before she had a chance to ask, or even move, Septima shrugged. "Suit yourself," she said, and pulled the lever.

The bottom dropped out of the world.

A few seconds later, Lily realized that she had been thrown to the floor of the cart, her head spinning as it lurched forward. She dragged herself up, and instantly wished that she hadn't—the cart was racing through a narrow, winding tunnel, coming loose from the tracks on every turn. She tried to shout, but the wind whipped her words away, as Tertius and Septima stood up, and snatched at the stalactites that hung just above the track, even though actually touching one would have struck their hands off in a second.

Lily wanted to yell, to scream at them to slow down. But then she saw the expression on Septima's face. It was thrilled, desperate, determined to touch these rocks, even if she was thrown from the cart to her death. And it was terrifying, because she just didn't care.

Lily crouched down, and tried not to look.

The cart hurtled along the tracks, its wheels screaming against the metal. Lily was no longer looking out. She huddled in the bottom of the cart, while above her, Tertius and Septima laughed with delight and whooped as the cart lurched and dipped. In the background, Lily could just hear the crunch and whir of the gears as they powered the cart along.

And then, just as suddenly, it stopped.

Lily groaned, her head spinning. She looked up. Septima and Tertius were standing over her, lit from behind.

"We're here," Septima said. "Welcome to the Hub, Lily."

Cautiously, Lily pulled herself to her feet, and looked out over the edge of the cart, shielding her eyes against the sudden brightness.

The Hub was dazzling—an immense, monolithic pillar of crystal glowing and radiating a brilliant cascade of light. It stood at the center of a cavern so huge it dwarfed the Rail Nexus. As Lily watched, the colors in the Hub shifted and merged, like smoke. Lily remembered, buried in the depths of her pack, her own little crystal that had led her here. That too absorbed light, glimmering with a tiny flame. But this was like an inferno to that flame. It would have been hard to look at it under normal circumstances, but after spending the last few days squinting in the darkness, the sudden brilliance nearly knocked her backward. Even Septima and Tertius, she noticed, averted their eyes, as though the light was painful to them as well.

"You . . . live here?" Lily asked, blinking furiously. Septima laughed.

"No one could live under the Hub itself—the flame of truth burns too brightly. Except for the Oracle . . ."

Tertius silenced Septima with a look and stepped out of the cart, standing between Lily and the worst of the light. He was unsmiling.

"But we've brought you here," he said, seriously, "because no lies can survive beneath its light." He leaned closer—closer than he had ever come to Lily before. "Tell us quickly, is it true?"

Lily's eyes began to adjust. Behind Tertius, she began to make out the silhouettes of people, clustered around the Hub, dressed just as brightly as her companions. As she watched, one small figure detached itself from the group, and began to walk toward them.

"Is what true?" Lily said, suddenly confused and fearful.

"Are you mentioned in the Midnight Charter?" Tertius said, more forcefully.

"Tertius . . ." Septima said, suddenly scared. "He's coming."

"Tell us now!" Tertius nearly shouted. "We need something to bargain for our safety!"

"Why? Who's coming, who . . ." Lily's confusion mounted, and then her words stuck in her throat. "The Conductor—you brought me to him, didn't you?"

"Tell me!" Tertius snarled, all pretense of friendship gone. "You stupid, tuneless piece of . . ."

"Now, now, this won't do at all . . ." said an unfamiliar voice.

Tertius and Septima stiffened, and turned together. Lily poised herself to run, to try and get away, and stopped.

The Conductor stood before them. He was middle-aged, plump, and wore a pair of thick, heavy spectacles. He was a little shorter than Lily, and clad in a black, dusty gown, quite a contrast to everyone else, though he was still pale and white-haired. He was also, Lily noticed, with growing surprise, completely without any kind of guard or escort. He held no weapons—nothing more threatening than a slim, white baton, which he tapped against his forehead absentmindedly.

Tertius and Septima stepped backward. Lily was amazed to see they were trembling.

"Perhaps," he suggested, in a warm, slightly uncertain voice, "you might want to introduce me to your guest?"

Without warning, Septima flung herself on the ground before the man's feet.

"Spare me, Conductor! I've brought back the foul brute!"

Tertius gasped as Septima crawled forward.

"Tertius found an outsider, sir, a member of the Orchestra! He was holding her captive."

Tertius glared at her.

"You stole my idea!" he accused her. "When did you decide to turn traitor?"

"Two days ago," Septima said, with pride. Tertius laughed, triumphantly.

"Then you're too late. I decided I was going to turn you in three days ago. Just as soon as I had the Wonder's best secret."

Septima sprang up from the ground, indignantly.

"How do I know that? You might have made that up now. Anyway, that just makes you a rotten traitor."

"But you just said . . ."

"Why don't you just rot away and die, Traitor?"

"You disharmonious load of old . . ."

The slanging match grew louder, and more vehement, incorporating some fairly graphic hand gestures. Throughout it all, the two squared up, a yard apart, their faces flushing with the effort.

In the midst of all this, the Conductor came closer to the cart, and, tucking his baton behind his ear, gave Lily a weary smile.

"Would you like some refreshment, young one? I fear this argument will continue for quite some time."

Dazed, weary, and utterly confused, Lily nodded dumbly, and got out of the cart. Then, watched silently by the people clustered near the shining Hub, she followed the Conductor, the wailing shrieks of her former friends ringing in her ears.

Ten minutes, and a strong cup of tea later, Lily felt a little better.

"You mean . . . they weren't on the run at all? Really?" she asked, still not quite believing it. The Conductor shrugged. He had taken her to his comfortably furnished cave, a few minutes' walk from the Hub. The bare stone was disguised with throws and rugs, and the Conductor had insisted that she sit on a large canvas bag filled with feathers. He stood in the corner, busying himself over a little stove, heating up the water for his own cup of tea. Its little flame cast a pleasant glow over his features, a contrast to the cold light from the faintly glowing cluster of crystals in the ceiling.

"In a sense, they were," he replied, thoughtfully stirring the infusion. "A few weeks ago they disappeared. Some of the others in their sections said that they had been struck with wanderlust. So naturally, I ordered the Guardians to watch over them. We left a few food parcels in their way, just enough to keep them safe. I must admit, as soon as the Guardians told me about you, I was looking forward to your arrival. Orchestra members are not unknown or unwelcome here, but it has been years since we have had any visitors. I was tempted to invite your companions back to the Hub a couple of days ago, when it looked as though they were about to abandon you, but in the event, I'm glad that we did not. It is vital to let wanderers return of their own free will."

"But, they told me that you had been cruel to them, hurt their friends . . ."

The Conductor frowned, and scratched his chin. "Well, I think I might have commented on the tenors' tuning a few weeks ago. Really, when the wanderlust is upon them, they're looking for any excuse." The Conductor leaned back, crossing his hands across his stomach. "I remember, when I left the Hub for the first time, I had been given three fewer grapes than my friend. I managed to work that into an entire conspiracy against the baritones—it took me nearly two months before I came back." He chuckled, and came over to sit on a chair of his own, bearing a rough wooden plate. He offered it to her. "Would you like some cake? I baked it myself, quite a novelty."

It had been hours since Lily had last eaten. Cautiously, she took a slice of cake. It was dry but serviceable. As she chewed, she tried to get her thoughts in order. It wasn't easy. Whenever she began to get close to understanding this place, it was as though someone changed all of the rules. Agora and Giseth had their secrets, but at least they had some consistency. But everything she had learned about Naru seemed to alter at a moment's notice. Who could tell whether the Conductor was telling her the truth now? Tea and cake was no indication of trustworthiness.

"What do you think?" the Conductor said eagerly, taking a piece of cake himself. "Our food arrives in parcels from the land of Giseth, winched down in boxes. The Gisethi believe that they are appeasing certain ancient spirits of the earth, which does ensure that we get good rations, if a little bland. Very little grows down here. I'm so glad they sent a few sacks of grain this time, though I fear that few of the choristers would have the patience to bake anything."

Lily nodded distractedly.

"I have so many questions," she mumbled, "but I'm not sure if I can ask them. I'd rather keep my secrets to myself . . ."

"Oh, don't concern yourself on that account, Miss Lily," the Conductor said, pleasantly. "You are a very unusual case. I am quite happy to waive our usual conventions of knowledge trading simply for the pleasure of conversing with someone new. Outsiders in Naru are rare indeed, and if you find your way here, I believe you should be treated as an honored guest. I lay my little offerings before you. Food, comfort . . . and a few choice morsels of truth."

Lily shrank a little, embarrassed at her suspicions.

"You're very generous," she said, meaning it. The Conductor shook his head.

"You are paying me back a thousand times, in a way your traveling companions never really appreciated. To see a real member of the Orchestra, to converse and understand the lands above . . ." For a moment, he looked at Lily more intensely, a sparkle in his dark eyes. "It is a rare and precious thing, more valuable to me than you can imagine. I never thought it would happen in my time as Conductor. You are truly a wonder, my dear, truly a wonder."

Lily knew that he meant it kindly, but she shivered at hearing that word.

"Tertius and Septima called me that," she muttered. "It made me feel like some kind of possession."

"Tertius? Septima? Who . . ." the Conductor began, and then his faced creased with a look of recognition. "Ah, were those the names that your companions chose? Yes, yes, that would be likely. They often take names based on their numbers . . ."

"Those weren't even their real names?" Lily muttered, dully, barely able to be surprised by anything anymore. The Conductor finished his cake, thoughtfully.

"They were real, for a brief time, but they were hardly permanent. To be honest, Miss Lily, I am surprised that they did not change them partway through your acquaintance. The choristers take on new identities more often than they change their clothes. It allows them to view their knowledge from every angle, every mindset, without becoming dangerously attached to any one belief or idea. And, of course, it is entertaining. Soprano Seven and Tenor Three—sorry, Septima and Tertius—have kept their names for an unusually long time, but the wanderlust can cause that. When the world becomes more exciting, self-interest dwindles."

Lily put down her cup, trying to take this all in, and found that she couldn't. It was all too much, too alien. She found herself focusing on the room around her, the strange mixture of odd and familiar. The stove, the food chest, the chairs, and table. All were normal, if a little oddly designed to fit in the cave. But the whole space was lit by a glowing crystal, whose light flowed and pulsed as though a swarm of glowing motes were trapped within.

"This happens a lot, then," Lily said, trying to sound sympathetic. The Conductor nodded.

"All but the very youngest sing in the Choir, after they have left their tutors. It is a sheltered life, so most of the choristers go through wanderlust at some stage. I remember my mentor telling me that a Conductor must always be prepared to begin each performance and find he has lost half of his best singers, though it has rarely been that bad." The Conductor sipped his tea. "Honestly, I find it hard to blame them. Any of them. Life here is a little disappointing. We spend our waking hours soaking up information, listening in to the echoes of distant lives. We know more facts about the lands above than most of you who live there. But the actual experience needed to join those facts together, and form a clear picture of the world . . . that is quite a different matter." He rubbed the back of his hand, wistfully. "Most of us could tell you exactly how the days grow longer and shorter throughout the year, but we have never seen the sun. We live by hours and weeks that mean nothing in these caverns. And the most important things to us are things that can never be touched."

Despite herself, Lily reached out to touch the Conductor's shoulder. Reflexively, he shuffled back.

"Forgive me, I mean no offense. I know that in your culture that would be a gesture of sympathy, but—"

"No, I'm sorry," Lily said, embarrassed, remembering the way that her former friends had reacted to the possibility of physical contact, as though it was something obscene.

"The touch taboo is an old part of our culture," the Conductor explained, "taught to us from the cradle. I suspect it began to ensure that we all remained here, in Naru." He looked sadly down at his own hands. "Without this fear, we may have all succumbed to wanderlust and joined the Orchestra long ago. But our purpose is to gather knowledge, not experience true life. The thought of how you live in the lands above, crushed together, feeling each others' breath upon your faces." He shuddered. "Ours is a purer existence, free from so much complexity. But perhaps the wanderers, just for a moment, understand what we have lost."

Lily put down her empty teacup, her head spinning.

"This place is nothing like what I expected."

"Really?" The Conductor smiled, "and what did you expect?"

"I expected . . ." Lily frowned, trying to think of how to phrase this. The truth took her quite by surprise. "Answers. I actually expected that all I had to do was to come down the steps, and there would be someone waiting who knew everything. Who could explain why there have been people interfering with my life for as long as I can remember. Why my father sent me to be brought up an orphan, why conspiracy follows me around . . . It was going to be so very simple." Lily couldn't help but smile at the absurdity of it.

The Conductor put down his cup.

"You were looking for harmony. That is not terribly surprising. We all are, to an extent—all so overloaded with facts and thoughts and half-formed ideas, and looking for a pattern where they fit. Well, Naru can certainly provide answers, if you are willing to find them." He smiled. "We must talk more. It would be fascinating to see if I am right about some of the mysteries of Agora. And then, of course, there is the Oracle. She will want to see you."

Lily wanted to ask about the Oracle, she really did. But right now, there was too much to take in, too many confused thoughts filling her brain. She felt a shiver go through her. Up until today, she had thought of the Conductor as someone to fear—the tyranni-cal ruler of this dark, claustrophobic underworld. She had clung to this, the one solid fact in this strange new land. And now she had met him, and he was the closest thing she had down here to a friend.

Not for the first time, she wondered what Mark would do.

"I have so many questions . . ." Lily said, doubtfully. "But I think they can wait."

The Conductor looked as if he were about to speak again. Then, in the distance, Lily heard something: a human voice, singing a note. Soft and pure, it seemed to resonate through the caverns. The Conductor rose from his seat.

"The Oracle will answer your questions properly, after you have slept. But now, it is time for the rest-tide concert." He plucked his baton from behind his ear and, shyly, bowed to Lily. "It would be an honor if you would come to listen. No Orchestra member has ever heard the Choir since I became Conductor."

Lily looked up into his face. So unfamiliar, with his huge, mel-ancholy eyes, but so welcome right now. And she laughed.

"Why not?" she said, quietly. And then, in case she had hurt his feelings. "I mean, I'd love to."

The Conductor smiled, uncertainly, and then drew aside the curtain at the front of his cave. Lily hauled herself to her feet to follow him. Beyond, Lily could see the other Naruvians beginning to drift toward the central cavern. Lily noticed that the light from the Hub had dimmed. Now she could make it out more clearly, a towering but natural crystal spire, shooting up from a deep cre-vasse. All around it, on semicircular platforms carved into the cavern walls, the Naruvians were gathering, separating into men and women. Lily could make out Tertius and Septima, finding their places on opposite sides of the Hub.

"I must take my position," the Conductor said, apologetically. "Please, find somewhere that you are comfortable."

As he walked away from her, Lily settled herself down, sitting cross-legged on the ground, wondering what was going to happen. She watched as the Conductor climbed up onto a podium of rock, tapping his baton to silence the rumble of chatter.

In the sudden quiet, Lily could once again hear a distant echo of voices. A little like the Cacophony, but more orderly—more controlled. Almost like a heartbeat, or the rise and swell of the tide.

And then, Lily saw Septima begin to sing. Softly at first, and then with growing power, a glorious solo line that rang higher and higher. Then, one by one, the other women joined her, and the men followed in a cascade of sound.

And Lily nearly laughed. Because in all her time hearing Tertius and Septima talk about "the Choir," she hadn't realized that it was the literal truth.

There were words somewhere in the texture, singing about almost anything. Lily caught snatches of lovers' confessions, of parents' sorrow, of laughter and fear and torment. The light from the Hub began to increase; a million different colors striving for dominance in its smoky depths. And then the Conductor flourished his baton, and the voices blended into one soaring tune, that rose and harmonized and echoed from the crystal walls of the cavern until the whole space thrummed with its vibrations, and the Hub glowed with a dazzling blue that made Lily feel as though she were standing under the summer sky.

And just for a moment, despite her tiredness, and confusion, and apprehension, Lily felt elated. Questions could wait for tomorrow. For now, she was happy just to sit there, and marvel that such a mad, impossible place could produce anything so beautiful.

CHAPTER SIX

The Warning

"ARE YOU SURE about this?"

Mark adjusted the wide tricorn hat, making sure that it obscured his face, and turned.

"I have to try, Ben. I can't let Cherubina stay with Crede."

Benedicta nodded. She had come over to visit that morning, apologizing for his father, who couldn't come until the afternoon. She had barely been there ten minutes before Mark had outlined his plan to her in one long, restless gabble.

"I know Crede's dangerous," Ben said, frowning, "but surely Laud could go and talk to him? Or maybe Theo? What if you get seen by the receivers?"

"The receivers are far too busy with Crede's mobs to worry about me," Mark said, only a little more certainly than he felt. "Besides, you think I'll be safe once Cherubina really opens up to Crede? He'll probably sell my location to the receivers in exchange for leaving him alone." He looked at Ben, attempting a smile. "You'll keep Dad distracted?"

Ben nodded, though not happily.

"I'll go straight to the prison and keep him talking. As long as you're back by the fourth hour, it won't be a problem—I'm supposed to be visiting the Sozinhos. But you really should tell Pete you're doing this. None of us want you to put yourself in danger . . ."

"He's been a jailer for too long," Mark muttered. "He'd lock me in if he could."

"He might not be wrong," Ben insisted. "The receivers are getting really jumpy."

"Don't you want to rescue her?" Mark asked. Ben raised an eyebrow.

"Do you think she wants to be rescued?"

Mark didn't reply, angrily pulling a scarf up to his chin.

"You don't need . . ." Ben began, but Mark interrupted her, sharply.

"Maybe not, but I have to try!" he said, hotly. "I have to do *something*! Cherubina was right; I don't know what I'm doing! I don't have the first idea where to start looking for Lily. I can't even help out at the Temple. And Dad means well, I know, but if I'm supposed to be so important, then I can't keep hiding. I have to do something, and if it means rescuing one of the few friends I have left from the stupidest decision she's ever made, then I'm going to do it!"

Ben stared at him, as he stood, breathless. Then, very carefully, she raised a finger, and tapped the scarf.

"I was going to say that you don't need the scarf. It'll just draw attention to you—it's nearly summer."

Sheepishly. Mark breathed out and unknotted the scarf.

"Thanks, Ben." He tossed the scarf to one side, awkwardly. "I know it's a lot to ask. I mean, we barely know each other really . . ."

Ben shushed him.

"You're Lily's friend, and the Directory's enemy. That's good enough for me." Her smile faded. "You think I'm helping you out as a favor? Crede had my brother beaten by thugs, the Directory made our parents vanish, and the former Lord Chief Justice himself organized the murder of my sister." Benedicta looked away. "I don't trust any of them, and if I thought that I could help you today—if I thought Crede would listen to me—I'd be going with you, and nothing in the world could stop me. You and Cherubina are part of the Temple now. Part of *us*." Ben turned back, a wistful look in her eyes. "Believe me, Laud and I need all the family we can get."

Mark stood there, taking in what she had said. He wasn't quite sure how to react, though he felt sure that he would never be able to say how grateful he was. So instead, they stood, awkwardly, and for a moment, Mark thought of asking Ben to come with him after all. He wasn't looking forward to confronting Crede.

But she was already opening the door.

"Remember, I can't keep Pete busy for long," she said, hurriedly. "Go to Crede, and get straight back here. If you're not back by the fourth hour, I'll get Laud and Theo, and we'll storm the Wheel together."

And despite everything, Mark laughed.

"Now that's something I'd like to see," he said.

Mark was nearly at the Wheel when it happened.

It started simply. A squad of receivers passed by and Mark, anxious not to be seen, slipped into a side alley. As he did so, he was jostled by a large man.

"Mr. Crede's expecting you," he said, softly.

Mark started, and looked up into the big man's face, recognizing Nick, the doorman from the Wheel. He put a finger to his lips.

"No time to chat, boy," he said with a grunt. "Business."

"What . . . ?" Mark began, but Nick had already shoved his

way out of the alleyway, and toward the receiver squad. In his hand, he held a large cobblestone.

Mark realized what was about to happen a few seconds before it did, just long enough for him to turn and run.

Behind him, he heard the crash of people falling to the ground, shouts and calls. Soon enough, the receiver whistles stung his ears, and the street behind him dissolved into a brawl. Fortunately Mark was far enough away to avoid getting caught up, as he slipped through the gathering crowd, unable to get the sight of that cobblestone out of his mind. He hoped that Nick was planning to put it through a window.

By the time he reached the Wheel, he was not surprised to see the door ajar. There wasn't the slightest chance of gaining the element of surprise. *Still*, he thought, as he pushed the door open and stepped into the darkness beyond, *if he meant me harm, then I'd know about it by now.*

The interior of the Wheel seemed less oppressive without the crowd jammed to the rafters, but it was still dark and smoky. The shutters were closed, and the room was lit by thick tallow candles. For a moment, Mark thought that he was alone. Then his eyes began to adjust, and he saw Crede—sitting with his feet up on a table, entirely at ease, staring directly at Mark.

"Crede," Mark said, trying to sound more confident than he felt, "I want a word with you."

Crede beckoned to him, casually.

"Of course, of course," he said, "always a pleasure to talk to someone so . . . infamous." He added the last word lightly, as though it were a joke. In a way, he was more unnerving now than when he was filled with the fire of his speeches. "Would you like a drink?"

Mark shook his head, tightly. He wasn't going to accept any hospitality from this man.

"Or perhaps something a little more special?" Crede suggested, languidly reaching into his jacket pocket, and pulling out a leather drawstring bag. "Can I tempt you to my own, personal poison?"

He tipped a few milk-colored spheres from the bag into the palm of his hand. Mark recognized them at once, though he hadn't seen them since he had walked among Agoran high society. Back then, they had been in vogue.

"Still taking other people's memories, Crede?" Mark asked, coolly. "They told me you used to be an addict."

Crede shrugged, careless of the insult, and popped one of the memory pearls into his mouth. He swallowed, and closed his eyes, savoring.

"I prefer to think of myself as a connoisseur. Ah . . ." he gasped, as the memory spread through him. "The remembrance of a first kiss. So tender."

Mark felt sick. He wondered how desperate someone would have to be to sell such a precious memory—to have it lost to them forever, so this man could have a few moments of enjoyment.

"You are oddly quiet, Mr. Mark." Crede said, opening his eyes and putting away the drawstring bag. "Are you waiting for anyone else to arrive? Have you brought any of your friends? Or your father, maybe? I hear he likes to keep an eye on his little boy."

Mark clenched his jaw at Crede's barbed comment. He found himself consciously deepening his voice as he replied.

"My father knows nothing about this. And in any case, I don't need his permission to do anything."

Crede smirked.

"Miss Cherubina tells quite a different story."

And there it was, out in the open. In a strange way, it was a relief. Now Mark didn't have to bring up the subject.

"Where is she?" he asked. Crede waved his hand, airily.

"Somewhere near, I think. I didn't want to take up all her time; that wouldn't be the act of a gentleman."

Mark refused to rise to Crede's mocking bait.

"I want to see her," Mark said, controlling himself. "Now."

"It seems such a shame to disturb her," Crede said, taking his feet off the table. "She's probably resting. She was up half the night, telling me all sorts of astonishing things. I thought that after she told me about the new Director, nothing she could say would surprise me again, but . . ." he shook his head, a genuine look of amazement on his face. "The things you have seen over the past year, Mr. Mark . . . just astonishing."

"She had no right to tell you that!" Mark said, rather louder than he intended. To his irritation, he heard his voice squeak. It had broken back in Giseth, but he'd thought that it had settled by now. "Those stories were . . . personal," he added, gruffly.

"Come now, Mr. Mark," Crede said, smiling. "After facing the dangers of the Nightmare, and fighting through hordes of fire-crazed villagers, you still worry about secrets?" He laughed. "The truth will set us all free."

Mark's jaw was so tightly clenched it hurt. Crede was treating his time in Giseth like some great joke. Cherubina hadn't thought twice about telling him everything about that dreadful place. Lily was probably still out there, and this little slum dictator was laughing about it. For one second, Mark pictured himself picking up one of the tankards and staving in that greasy head.

Instead, very slowly, he asked the question again.

"Where is she, Crede? I think I need to have a word with her."

Crede's smile disappeared.

"She chose to come to me, boy. She's a big girl; she can take care of herself."

Mark shook his head.

"No, she's not," he said, realizing the truth of the words as he said them. "She's never had to make her own decisions. She doesn't know how. Even when she lived with . . ." Mark bit his tongue, not wanting to mention Snutworth's name, ". . . with *him*, she was protected, in a way. Maybe she'll learn, like I've had to. But until she can really choose, I won't let you use her like this."

Crede nodded, seeming almost reasonable.

"I understand, Mark. I'm sure your friends have told you terrible things about me. I imagine Laud has shown you the scars that my men gave him, and Theo told you how I threatened him at the Temple." Crede leaned back, spreading his arms wide. "And I'll tell you something else—everything they've told you is true. Every. Single. Thing." He fixed Mark with a look. His ease was gone, banished by a sudden intensity. "I'd do it all again. Everything I have done has been necessary."

Mark couldn't look away from Crede's eyes. Whatever this man had done, Mark realized that he believed every word he said. That did not help at all. If anything, it made him more eager to make a rush for the door.

"Necessary?" Mark replied, warily. "Don't tell me—there's a war coming, and you need your army."

Crede laughed.

"Coming?" he said, scornfully. "It's already here. The revolution has begun, and the Director and all his hordes can't do a thing to stop it."

"I've seen how this ends, Crede," Mark said, with feeling. "Cherubina told you about my time outside Agora. Did she say what happened in the village of Aecer, about the revolution they had?" Mark tried to block out his memories of that night—of the fire, and the screams of rage and fear. "They tore their leader to pieces; they had their 'victory.' And in the morning, nothing had really changed."

"We will do better," Crede said, springing up. "We have no choice." His voice changed, growing louder, as though he were giving a speech. "Tell me, Mark, when you were coming here today, didn't you see riots break out in the streets? Aren't the receivers just weeks away from a full-scale attack on our own people?"

"I saw one of your men start that riot," Mark interrupted, hotly. "The receivers were only doing their duty."

"Their duty!" Crede shook his head, a look of disgust crossing his face. "And is it their duty to attack the weak and defenseless? You've seen the victims here, the debtors with nothing to trade—no hope, no future. Do you think they only go to the Temple? My alms-houses are full of them. When Inspector Poleyn's lackeys want to pick a fight, they go after the weak, and no one cares. At least when Nick gets involved, everyone sees the receivers pull out their weapons." He leaned closer. "Can't you see I'm not your enemy, Mark? Maybe I'm not perfect, not as pure as . . ." he paused, "as pure as a Lily. But I could help you. The Director will never find you here."

"Why are you interested in me?" Mark muttered. "You've got my stories, for all the good they'll do you. No one will believe a word. And you've got Cherubina; she makes a far better figurehead."

Crede shrugged.

"Possibly. She's pretty, no doubt, which doesn't hurt." He gave a smile that made Mark distinctly uncomfortable. "But she wasn't Lily's friend. Not like you." Crede leaned forward. "Don't you see? Lily is the key. She's the ideal—the symbol of what I'm fighting for, no matter what those cowards running the Temple think." Crede straightened up. "She would have seen the need for revolution, and my followers know that. I'm just her spokesman. Look at me, Mark—no one would follow this face." Crede touched his own cheek. "Everyone knows that I used to be a crook. When the Directory's doors are broken down, it'll be in Lily's name, not mine."

Mark stared at this man, who said he was marching to war in Lily's name, and he felt his anger cool into contempt.

"And until then, you'll keep sending out Nick, with a cobblestone in his hand?" Mark said bitterly.

Crede's smile vanished.

"I don't have the time for your stubbornness, boy," he said, coldly. "The revolution will not wait for those who can't make up their minds."

"You don't get it, do you?" Mark replied, hotly. "I don't care about revolution. I just want my friends back."

"What friends?" Crede said, sharply. "In the end, the only people who'll stand by us are those who share our dreams." He fixed him with a stare. "I have many who share mine, Mark. And soon, we will awaken." He leaned back and closed his eyes. "You'll want to leave now."

For the first time, Mark agreed.

By the time Mark returned to his safe house, he was deep in thought. It had been a long walk—the scuffle with the receivers was still going on, and had spread across several streets. Mark had needed to make a detour to avoid being swept up in it. But truthfully, he barely noticed where he was going. Crede's words had rattled him more than he cared to admit. He was still pondering them as he opened his door, glad to have a moment to himself.

"Hello, Mark," said a voice.

Mark stopped in the doorway. His father was sitting on the other side of the room. He had found Cherubina's old chair, and was sitting facing the wall.

"Hi, Dad," Mark said, finding his voice. "Did Benedicta . . ."

"She did everything you asked," Pete said, without turning around. His voice trembled a little. "She didn't admit that she was supposed to keep me talking. I worked that out myself."

Mark nodded. He wasn't going to apologize. He'd meant to spare his father the worry, but he'd been doing what needed to be done.

"I've been to see Crede," he began to explain, "I know you said I should stay hidden, but . . ."

"You weren't here." Pete got up, and turned around. His eyes were red rimmed. "Can you imagine what I felt when I opened the door, and you weren't here? That you'd vanished, again? Do you know what it's felt like, these last years?" His voice grew louder, more desperate. "Don't you understand that the Director himself is after you! Why couldn't you tell me where you were going?"

"You can't protect me just by trying to hide me away," Mark said, gently putting a hand on his father's shoulder. "I understand, I really do. But I'm part of this now. I'm the 'Protagonist,' whatever that means. I'm a foretold Judge, and you know that Snutworth's going to keep looking until he finds me."

Pete met his gaze, fiercely.

"I lost you twice, son," he said. "The first time, it was my own fault—I know that. I traded you away like an old coat, like you meant nothing to me. And when I saw you rise in the world, I . . ." he faltered, his eyes dropping. "I was prepared to let you go, then. But you came back to me. We found each other. For twelve hours, we were a family again. And then you were gone, and I . . . I . . ."

Pete's voice faded away. Mark took his father's hands.

"All the time I was in Giseth, Dad, I tried to come back," he said, looking his father in the eyes. "Every day, I wanted to. If we get through this, we can spend the rest of our lives making up for these few years. But right now, my friends need my help. Lily, Cherubina, . . ." He moved a little closer. "I haven't been a little boy for a long time. But even a man needs his father."

Pete nodded, relief flooding across his face.

"Then let me help," he said, at last. "On your terms, this time."

Mark took his father's rough hand and shook it firmly. It made him feel older than he ever had before.

Pete smiled.

"Now," he said, more cheerily. "We've got plans to hatch."

Mark frowned, his good mood dampening.

"I wish I knew what to suggest, but visiting Crede was a mistake. Cherubina's gone for now, and I still have no idea where Lily could be . . ."

Pete crossed his arms and sat down again, thoughtfully.

"The Director would know."

Mark laughed, bitterly.

"And I'm sure he'd just love to tell us."

Pete smiled.

"But what if we had someone on the inside? Someone in his office?"

Mark looked at his father. He hadn't seen that expression on his father's face for so long. It almost looked like excitement.

"You know someone in the Directory?" Mark said, amazed. "How? Who is he?"

Pete smiled.

"*She* is the person who sent me a letter when you disappeared, to tell me that you were alive. I suppose I should have been grateful for that, but at the time, all I could see was that this woman must know where you were. So I chased her down. It took me a long time, but I found her in the end." He sat down, with a new confidence. "Her name is Miss Verity, and she's the Director's secretary."

Mark gasped. He had met Verity; she had been the woman who had unlocked his cell door and led him out of Agora. But more than that, Verity was Lily's aunt, the one who had brought her to Agora in the first place.

"If you can contact her—" Mark began, but Pete frowned.

"I promised I'd leave her alone, once you were back in Agora," he said, doubtfully. Mark folded his arms.

"I didn't promise her anything," Mark said, with steely determination. "I'll tell you what to write. She's got a lot of explaining to do . . ."

CHAPTER SEVEN

Resonances

IT HAD BEEN such a relief to sleep in a bed again.

It was hardly a typical bed—a niche carved out of the stone wall and stuffed with cushions. But after days of sleeping on a rock floor, it was heavenly. And Lily was so tired that she did sleep, despite the aches and pains, and despite the fact that it was never quite dark in the Conductor's rooms.

As she awoke, slowly and heavily, this was the main thing that occupied her sluggish thoughts—the people of Naru lived in constant half-light. Glowing lumps of crystal, like smaller versions of the Hub, were set in every wall, the light dancing in their smoky depths and rippling over their faces like watery reflections.

She had wanted to keep on sleeping. She had been dreaming that she was back in Agora, with her friends. And Mark had been embracing his father, and Ben and Theo were dancing, and Laud had smiled and taken her by the hand. She would never have thought that she would long for Agora's crowded streets and corrupt, grasping people. But at least there, she understood how people behaved—what drove them, and made their lives complete.

Down here, it was like staying in a madhouse.

But the Choir had begun to sing again, a harsher melody this time, with loops and whirls, and sudden piercing top notes. She couldn't sleep through that. So instead, she had risen, and put on her freshly washed dress and apron. She was glad that she had talked the Conductor out of giving her Naruvian robes to wear, although she was beginning to see why they might dress in this way—in a world of stone and dim light, only the brightest colors stood out at all.

Thoughtfully, she looked over to where she had dumped her pack, and then knelt down to open it. It was nearly empty—her food had been eaten long ago, and the hunting knife that she had taken from Wulfric, her Gisethi guide, was still sheathed and untouched. But among the few strips of cloth that would have served as bandages, she found what she was looking for—the letter from her father, rolled and tightly bound with ribbon, a tiny pair of brass scales, and a small, irregular crystal made of the same smoky material as the resonant crystals that dotted the walls. She stared at this last object for a moment.

"Maybe . . ." she murmured to herself. As an experiment, she held it close to her mouth and began to quietly attempt a tune. She hadn't sung anything since her days as a tiny girl in the orphanage, and her voice was still croaky from lack of sleep, but after a moment or two, she managed a passable few notes. But no hidden voices emerged—this crystal was definitely Naruvian, but it held no resonance.

"Well, that would have been far too easy," she said to herself, slipping the crystal and letter into her apron pocket as she got up. She paused before putting the scales away, feeling the shapes of the two symbols carved onto the pans of the scales. One, a lily flower growing out of an open book, was a symbol she knew very well. It was also carved onto the brass ring that she wore on her finger—her signet ring, her personal sign. The one thing about her that still marked her out as an Agoran. The other, a starfish, was Mark's symbol.

Mark . . .

Lily felt a stab of sadness. She hadn't seen Mark for nearly a month now, ever since the Order of the Lost had spirited him away. She'd traveled a long way to get him back, but she was no closer now than she had been before.

With a resolute sniff, Lily dropped the scales into her apron pocket and pushed aside the heavy velvet curtain at the mouth of the cave that acted as the Conductor's home. There was no more time for dithering. She still had no idea where Mark could be, but if this Oracle really did know as much as Septima and Tertius seemed to think, then she must be the best person to start asking.

Although she couldn't help but wonder what someone who impressed the inhabitants of a realm like Naru would be like.

The last notes of the Choir's song were fading away as Lily emerged. Already the choristers were wandering down from their platforms, chatting in groups of two or three. As they all kept their distance from each other, this hubbub was loud, each conversation trying to drown out the next, without any thought for privacy.

More surprising, though, was their reaction to her. These Naruvians were supposed to be obsessed with knowledge, with new things, and she must have been the most extraordinary person to walk among them for years. Yet they seemed determined to ignore her, scattering if she attempted to get their attention. Their shimmering clothes—simple robes and tunics, glimmered in the undulating light from the Hub. As Lily walked among them, fragments of their conversations emerged out of the noise.

"It can't be true, can it? No, not possible . . ."

"You'd better believe it. This is top-quality knowledge! So what will you give me for it?"

". . . So she thought no one else would turn up, just wasn't her lucky day!"

"Everything I know about the village is worthless! I've nothing but old news . . . this is the worst day of my life! Why did they have to go and get a new Speaker?"

"Well, he had been dead for several days . . ."

". . . that's no excuse!"

Every time she caught a hint of something familiar, it dissolved into a sea of nonsense. The Choir began to move faster around her, rushing over to greet new people and spurn others. It was like no crowd she had ever been in, so loud and yet so separate, as though each person wanted to be everywhere and nowhere at once. Lily began to feel quite disoriented, stumbling from one group to another, trying to pick out the Conductor. She was so absorbed in this that she hardly noticed Tertius and Septima until they were almost face-to-face.

The pair stopped in front of her. For a second, they glanced at each other, and back at Lily, in a slightly puzzled way, as though she had been someone they had met once, a few years ago. And then, Septima turned back to Tertius, and resumed their conversation.

"You'll never believe it," she continued, her eyes wide and excited, her hands fluttering. "She's going to stay with Crede! What do you think he'll do now?"

"Who cares?" Tertius grunted, stepping around Lily as though she were invisible. "Why are you always listening to the Agoran echoes anyway? I heard something really good from Giseth last night. One of the monks is missing. His Speaker is frantic."

"Really? That's amazing!" Septima gasped in delight as she trailed after him. "Um . . . what's a monk, again?"

And then Septima and Tertius were gone, vanished into the chatter. Lily stared after them, mouth agape. Had it really been only yesterday they had been screaming at each other as they betrayed her to their "enemy"? And had they really been talking about Agora? For a moment, she thought about running after them, to ask what they had heard—did they have any news of her far-off home? But then, all they would be able to offer her were meaningless fragments, bald facts without understanding or experience. They'd probably been listening to voices from Giseth for years, and yet Septima still had no clear idea of what a monk was. Just like she had known a hundred details about Agora, but could not picture a city.

Then again, Lily thought, as she continued on her way, was it that surprising? No one in Giseth needed to explain the monks to each other because they saw them every day. Lily shook her head, trying to imagine what it would have been like to be brought up a Naruvian, to know so much, and understand so little. It seemed like only the Conductor talked sense around here.

At least, he had yesterday. With a shiver, Lily wondered if the Conductor would remember her when she found him. He had seemed more sensible, but age was no indication of stability here. A pair of old men had already passed her, squabbling like schoolboys over whether sheep or goats would make the best pets. Lily wondered if they had ever seen either.

To her relief, when she did see the Conductor, lingering near his podium, he returned her gaze, and even raised one chubby hand to give a little wave. It wasn't a particularly friendly greeting; he looked more nervous than anything else as she approached. But here, that was more than enough.

"You're early," he observed, nervously twirling his baton. "I hope you were not unsettled as you approached—I have told the Choir not to bother you with questions, but I fear they were not terribly subtle."

Lily nodded, thoughtfully, as the choristers filed out of the Hub chamber, until only the two of them were left beneath the eerie glow of the crystal spire.

There was an uncomfortable pause. Lily wondered what passed for small talk down here.

"Um . . ." she glanced around. "The Hub is very bright today," she ventured. The Conductor nodded, distractedly.

"A lot of knowledge was brought to it, and has yet to be taken by the Oracle," he mused. "Many have called knowledge a light in the darkness—in Naru, this is the literal truth." He paused. "But I am not the one to explain such things to you. Do you want to see the Oracle now? We can wait; she is very patient . . ."

"I'd like to see her now, if that's all right." Lily said, eagerly. After traveling for so long, she didn't want to delay a second longer. The Conductor nodded, still oddly reluctant.

"It's not far."

The Conductor shuffled toward the Hub, and Lily followed. As they drew nearer, Lily began to hear something. It felt like a low buzzing in her ears, but the closer she got to the Hub, the more pronounced it became, vibrating through her whole body. Not painful exactly, though uncomfortable. But the strangest thing about it was that it was oddly familiar; it seemed to peak and flow just like the song the Choir had been singing as she awoke.

She turned to ask the Conductor about this, but he was already disappearing down a set of stone steps, hidden behind one of the choir platforms. Lily hurried after him.

The light of the Hub was soon replaced by a blue-tinted gleam, cast by smaller crystals set into the walls of a descending tunnel.

"Watch your step," the Conductor warned her, turning back,

his dark eyes like mirrors in the strange light. "I can guide you part of the way, but you must approach the Oracle alone."

"You won't be coming with me?" Lily asked, surprised. The Conductor shook his head.

"It is not right to visit the Oracle without being summoned." He tucked the baton behind his ear. "And I do not care to visit the Resonant Throne. It is not a comfortable place."

"But, if the Oracle is your leader, why does she stay there?"

The Conductor sighed.

"She does not sit there out of choice. It is the only place that she can hear all of the echoes—beneath the Hub, where every secret it absorbs is released."

They walked on a little, in silence. Something was nagging at the back of Lily's mind.

"So, the Oracle hears everything said in the world above?" she repeated, slowly. "Millions of voices, all at once? Wouldn't that make it just a meaningless babble?"

"For most, yes," the Conductor said. "I am sure you have seen that for the choristers, the sense of the whole truth is less important than the fragments they can call their own. But the Oracle is the most gifted of us all—she truly listens. She remembers. She can bring our secrets together into sense. That is why she rules. And of course, the Oracle does not just hear simple echoes." The Conductor grew somber again. "There are more secrets in the world than those that are spoken aloud."

The stone steps came to an end, to be replaced by a rough-hewn corridor. The glowing crystals were becoming more sparse, and the Conductor walked ahead into the gloom. Lily wanted to reply, but she found all her attention was required to feel her way, and not trip.

"That is why we sing," the Conductor continued, half to himself now, so Lily had to strain to hear him. "We spend our days in search of trivia, disjointed pieces of information, and we bargain with them among ourselves. But in the end, their true purpose is to make the Song. We take the secrets we have discovered and weave them into a harmony, as an offering to our ruler. The Hub then focuses everything down to the Resonant Throne, where the Oracle directs its flow. She banishes worthless babble to the Cacophony in the Outer Caverns, and absorbs our songs, rich in true knowledge and wisdom. Nothing is hidden from her. Nothing."

Lily was silent. The more she heard about the Oracle, the less she liked the thought of meeting her. How many times had she shouted in frustration through her short life? How many words of bitterness and rage, how few words of love and friendship? She hoped that the scales balanced in her favor, but to meet someone who would know every word she had ever uttered was an unsettling prospect.

"But, if she knows everything, why does she need you?" Lily asked, hoping she didn't sound too tactless. The Conductor frowned.

"I and the Choir have our purpose, set down by ancient laws. We preserve her harmony, keep the song flowing, and protect her physical form. In return, we are fed, we are comfortable, and we have endless truths to find. We know our duties; there is no unrest in our land. We have little need of strong feelings, they are . . . dangerous." The Conductor turned away a little, his voice softer— more contemplative. "And it will remain this way, until the Day of Judgment."

Lily was about to ask him what he meant, when he came to a sudden halt, and gestured down the tunnel.

"No more questions," he said. "We have arrived."

Up ahead, Lily saw a stone archway, set into the wall. A thick curtain of dark velvet stretched across it, and at one side hung a tasseled rope. The curtain pulsed and waved, as though there was a strong wind beyond it, though on this side, as ever, the air was still and dead.

"Go and meet the Oracle, my young wonder," the Conductor said, as he reached the arch. "But be aware, she will know everything about you."

Lily faced the curtain, fighting the urge to put it off, to run back to the Hub, and the madness that she almost understood. A strange shiver passed through her, and she felt herself tense.

"She doesn't know my thoughts," Lily said, with more bravado than she felt. "I'll have something to surprise her."

The Conductor met her gaze. Not for the first time, she was struck by something deeply sad behind those nervous eyes.

"No, Lily. Even your thoughts are not your own. She will know those too. She has always known them."

Lily took a step back, involuntarily.

"How?" she breathed. "That's impossible. Has she ridden the Nightmare? Has she been spying on me?"

The Conductor shook his head.

"No, child, she listens to the Canticle."

Lily felt her fists clench. Every time she thought that she understood what was going on, the Conductor pulled out another story. She gritted her teeth.

"And what's 'the Canticle'?" she asked, pointedly. "Capital *c*, presumably? Are you ever going to tell me what's really going on here?"

The Conductor pulled back, in alarm. Lily looked down at her own hands, her knuckles white with tension, no less shocked. Where had that outburst come from? She must have been more on edge than she thought.

"I . . . I'm sorry," she mumbled. "You've told me so much, and all for free. It's just . . . it's a lot to take in . . ."

The Conductor nodded, mollified.

"I understand. Even I find it hard to believe in the Canticle of Whispers, and I have heard it myself. It is the quietest song, but the most potent. It can be found only in the deepest caverns, its music composed of hidden thoughts, desires, and dreams. Even thoughts, it seems, leave an echo." He paused, rubbing the side of his nose. "We all take our turn to listen. It is not a pleasant experience. Even the most curious return eagerly to the Hub after a few hours. There is something in it that unsettles our souls. Only the Oracle has the strength to spend every day in intimate communion with the souls of millions, to have her whole being filled with the music of humanity." The Conductor wiped his brow with the back of his hand. "It takes its toll even on her. Even she cannot listen to every mind at once. Remember that." He reached for the rope to pull back the curtain. "Oh, and one other thing. If you approach her throne, then do so on your knees."

Lily frowned, her anger not quite cooled.

"Why does she demand that? She's not my ruler."

"It's nothing to do with what she wants," he said, quietly. And then, to Lily's surprise, she saw him smile, rather wistfully. "She wants for nothing. Except perhaps for one thing. And I doubt that you'll be the one to give it to her."

He pulled on the rope. Beyond, Lily could see a stone corridor, smoother than most, and filled with an odd, milky light.

For a moment, Lily turned to the Conductor, not knowing whether to thank him for his guidance, or blame him for sending her in so unprepared. But the Conductor had turned away, averting his eyes from the corridor. Whatever was beyond, he didn't want to see.

"Thank you," she said. He nodded, once.

Lily stepped into the corridor.

Lily felt a sudden, unexpected breeze. Maybe it was just a vibration, but the air in this corridor was moving, going in and out like the breathing of a great beast. The light, too, was odd, coming from some source up ahead, but seeming to fill the air all around her.

Lily's only company was the sound of her boots on the stone. She tried to plan what she would do, how she would approach the Oracle, but every time she tried, the Oracle's omniscience rose up like a barrier. She couldn't introduce herself; the Oracle would know. She couldn't say she was looking for Mark; the Oracle would know that too. It felt as though everything she could do had been decided for her already. For Lily, who prided herself on her independence, it was a crushing feeling.

But still, she walked on. Up ahead, she could see the passage reach its end, and beyond it, something shone. She stepped forward, trying to see what it was, shielding her eyes as the light grew in power and intensity.

And then, with a lurch, she was at the mouth of the tunnel, and all her senses deserted her.

The cavern was larger even than the Hub chamber, and filled with weird light that flowed over the walls, dazzlingly bright. She could barely make out the stone walkway at her feet, but she could see enough to know that it was narrow, and that it stretched out over a vast chasm, a sheer drop onto wickedly sharp spars of rock. Above, the measureless height of the chamber took her breath away. She tried taking a step forward, but as she did, that dreadful buzzing from the Hub returned to her ears, hitting her like a wall. It was louder now—no longer musical, but pulsing like a heartbeat. Lily gasped, feeling a splitting pain through her head as the light grew more intense.

"Speak."

One word. One single sound, but it cut through the noise like a knife—cold and sharp. Lily felt her mouth fly open, almost beyond her control.

Ahead, the light faded, the buzzing vanished. And Lily saw the Oracle.

She saw only glimpses, at first: the edge of her granite throne, on a high spar of rock, directly beneath the point of an immense, inverted spire of glowing crystal that plunged down from the roof of the cavern, and was clearly the base of the Hub; the tip of a headdress, sparkling like a star; the shifting jewels on her cape picked out like the night sky. Then, gradually, these points resolved themselves into a woman.

At least she assumed it was a woman. The voice that she had heard had been female, and not especially old or young. But that was the only clue. Every inch of her body was swathed in a jeweled robe, headdress, and mask. No, not jewels—resonant crystals, each one dancing with light.

The Oracle sat so still, in all her finery, that for a moment, Lily thought that she must be a statue. Then, the figure moved its head, and that same voice resonated through the cavern.

"Speak, Lilith."

This time it was louder, but no less cold. There was not a spark of interest there, no warmth, but no dislike either. She had never heard a voice that seemed so commanding, and at the same time so indifferent.

Lily found her thoughts had quite deserted her. Instead of speaking, she walked a little closer, slowly growing accustomed to the odd, distorting light. She was nearly halfway to the throne now, halfway across the narrow stone walkway that stretched over the chasm. Her footfalls rang unnaturally, the echoes whirling over her head, until her own approach felt like an army drumming in her ears. Her head spun. Involuntarily, she reached out her arms to keep her balance. The rock bridge beneath her seemed thin and precarious, and she felt herself beginning to topple toward the edge. In a flash, she remembered the Conductor's warning, and sank to her knees. Here, with the stone beneath her hands, she felt a little better, and crawled forward, until she was nearly at the throne.

"Why . . . why am I feeling like this?" her speech came out thick and slurred, not really expecting a response.

"The resonance in this chamber is dangerous," came the reply, clipped and polished. "You are growing used to it. Lie down. It will pass."

Unsteadily, Lily did as she was told, resting her cheek against the cool stone. Gradually, the vibrations stopped, and Lily risked a look up. From down here, the light from the Hub above refracted through the crystals on the Oracle's crown, creating a shifting halo of light.

Lily raised her head.

"I'm here," she said, to the Oracle.

There was a pause; Lily struggled up onto her knees, but didn't try to move any farther. She didn't want to fall down again; if she slipped from the stone bridge, it was a long way down.

"I can see," the Oracle said, without a trace of sarcasm or irritation. "You wish answers. Ask your questions."

Lily looked up, amazed.

"Just like that?" she said. "No objections? No speech telling me I am not ready to know?"

"My being is truth," the Oracle replied. "Ask."

Lily staggered to her feet.

"Who am I?" she asked, softly. "Why did my father send me away? Where is Mark? Is he all right? Is he hurt?" Her voice grew louder, her questions coming fast. "Why does everyone say we're important? What is in the Midnight Charter that makes us so special? What are these secrets that everyone is keeping from us? Why . . . ?" Lily faltered, growing quiet again. "What is our role, Oracle? Our place? Can you tell me?"

There was a long silence. Lily heard her own words disappear into the shifting sounds of the Resonant Throne, joining the buzz of a million other words that hovered around the Oracle like a miasma. And then, the Oracle spoke.

"All this I can say."

Lily felt an overwhelming wash of relief. She felt like laughing, like jumping for joy. Already, she pictured herself reuniting with Mark, with her other friends, of the Midnight Charter's prophecy torn up and trampled in the streets. For one, blissful moment, everything was wonderful.

Then, the Oracle raised one gloved hand.

"But first, the price," she said. "Truth begets truth; no knowledge is free. That is the way of Naru."

Lily nodded, hastily.

"Yes, yes, of course. What would you like to know? I've traveled all over the worlds above. There must be so much that I can tell you." She racked her brains. "You've heard about Giseth, I'm sure, but do you know what it feels like to see a spring dawn? Crisp and clear, and bright . . ."

"I know," came the reply, hard and final.

Lily was startled. She tried again.

"Do you know about the Nightmare? About all the things I saw in my dreams when it had me in its grasp? You know, my friend Laud turned up all the time, he had eyes that shone and . . ."

"I know."

"Oh . . ." Lily faltered. The Canticle could even see into dreams? That hardly seemed fair. She thought back, far back, trying to think of something that wouldn't be remembered, something totally unimportant. Unless, of course, you were trying to please some-one who thought they knew everything. "When I was a little girl," Lily began, "back at the orphanage, there was this corner. We were all crowded into these tiny rooms, but none of us would sit in that corner. I never knew why, never thought about it until now, it was as though we were frightened of it . . ."

"I know." The voice was not annoyed, or weary, it was simply stating a fact. "I know everything spoken in the lands above, and everything thought, and felt, and dreamed. The Choir sings that which is revealed to the world, and the Canticle whispers all that is hidden."

Lily stopped, feeling the force of the Oracle's eyes from behind her silvery mask. She dropped her head, her confidence draining away.

"Then, what can I give you?" she asked, quietly.

"One thing," the Oracle said, her tone as icy and impersonal as ever. "One fact. One secret, something tiny, but something that has been hidden from me. Taken from my mind. The Canticle refuses to show me, unless I am told directly, and I must know." The Ora-cle moved her head, and though Lily could not see her face through the glittering mask, she felt the power of the Oracle's stare.

"Of course!" Lily said, spreading her arms. "What is it? What don't you know?"

The Oracle didn't reply. Lily's words echoed around the cham-ber, coming back to her distorted and mocking. *Don't you know? Don't . . . know . . . you . . . don't . . . know. . . .*

There was something wrong here. The Oracle was silent again, implacable, more still than any human being had a right to be. Lily remembered the corpse of the Bishop of the Lost, forever sitting on his throne. If she hadn't heard her speak, Lily would have won-dered if there was anything at all behind that crystal mask.

And then, it struck her.

"You don't know, do you?" she said, amazed. "You don't know what this secret is. And you expect me to find it anyway?"

"Tell me." The Oracle leaned forward, and for a brief moment, Lily heard a quaver in that hard, clinical voice. A tremor of emotion, though which emotion was impossible to say. "Truth begets truth. Tell me! Tell me!"

The Oracle's voice rose higher, an imperious command. The walls of the chamber echoed it back, the Hub flared with light, sparking off the Oracle's headdress. Lily felt another wave of nausea pass through her, as the vibrations from the Oracle's voice shook the stone walkway. She collapsed onto her hands and knees.

"My lady, I don't know where to start! Please, can't you tell me anything?"

"One truth," the Oracle said, no less firmly, but perhaps with more resignation. "One truth, one fact is the key. Most important . . ." she paused, and then, in a softer voice, almost human, she continued. "Most important to who I was."

"But what *is* it?" Lily tried again, desperately. "What is the secret?!"

Lily's voice echoed through the chamber, reverberating, coming back to her loud and shrill, hurting her ears. And the Oracle's mask stared. As the echoes mixed and bounced and faded, she stared.

"I can't remember," she said.

After that, the Oracle spoke no more. By the time Lily left her, she had not moved again.

Later, as she returned to the Hub, with the Conductor leading the way, she told him all that had happened. Strangely, he seemed almost relieved.

"Perhaps it is a blessing, child," he reassured her. "It is dangerous to go to the Oracle without some idea of what you are looking for. Truth is a powerful thing. This way, as you search for her answer, you may find your own."

"Yes, I suppose," Lily replied, distantly.

"And I might be able to assist you," the Conductor fussed. "I can show you the best resonance stones . . . or I could take you to the Canticle itself. Even the Oracle will not have been able to listen to it all. There is still hope, child, and I for one would be sorry to have you go just yet, when there is so much we can learn from each other . . ."

Lily was nodding, but she wasn't really listening anymore.

After everything she had been through. After the horrors and the weariness, and the years of not knowing, she was so close. This secret, whatever it was, was the key to everything. The Oracle knew the truth; Lily knew that as deeply and fundamentally as she knew her own name. Once she knew what was happening to her, really knew, everything would be clear. She could find Mark. She could return to Agora. She would defy them, turn the tables on these shadow men and women who took titles instead of names and thought in prophecies and visions. She would win, and could have a life of her own again.

This secret would solve everything.

And she was going to find it.

CHAPTER EIGHT

The Page

VERITY SHOULD HAVE been terrified.

As she sat at her desk, she could hear the sounds of the visitor, shouting and raging in the next room. He had done little else since he arrived. The New Director had told her that he was normally a quiet man, that he had taken a vow of silence, but she wasn't surprised. She had met men like him before, so repressed by tradition and beliefs that when they finally broke free, there was a lot to say.

But that meant nothing.

The New Director was also not in the best of moods today, although it was not obvious. He smiled as easily as ever, and never spoke without calm and consideration. But there were little signs that, as his secretary, she had already started to notice. He hadn't called her in yet to offer the visitor wine. He always did that. He liked to present a mood of conviviality, to be the perfect host. He was keen on perfection, generally.

But that meant nothing.

She nodded to Chief Inspector Greaves as he waited with her in her office, sitting very still and upright. The Chief Inspector was never loud, and the hardest to understand of all. He wore the golden braid of his rank uncomfortably. She was sure that he would rather be out, chasing down criminals—making Agora a safer place.

But that meant nothing.

She glanced at the fireplace and remembered the letter that she had burned there that morning. Only the stars knew how Pete had managed to smuggle it to her. Maybe none of the clerks wanted to check through the fifty-page report on the well-being of prisoners that had arrived on her desk yesterday afternoon. It wasn't a long letter, and at first, she had been so relieved to hear that Mark had returned to Agora without her assistance. She was sure that Pete was just writing to thank her. But as she had scanned the rest, her mood darkened. He still wanted her help, to find Lily this time. How could she know where Lily was? Hadn't she watched over her for years? Hadn't the Director forced her to let Lily go, even though it broke her heart? Pete had his son back; he had no right to worry about Lily as well. She wasn't part of his family.

No, Lily belonged to her. Lily was Verity's brother's daughter.

Verity's brother was dead.

And that—that meant *everything*.

Verity hadn't been planning to reply. If the visitor hadn't come, she would have been the Director's secretary still, in mind and deed—quietly doing her duty. Then, that morning, everything had changed.

It had all begun a few hours ago. The Director had sent her down to the tunnels, to welcome a guest from the world outside. Verity had tried not to think of Lily as she walked those ancient corridors. Tried not to remember leading Lily to the door—the only way out of the city by foot. She had hoped that the old Director would let Lily travel by boat, and leave by the secret locks used by the riverboat captains. But the old Director was firm—Lily was to have no companions except for the boy, no help at all.

All that time, that long walk, Verity had not spoken to her niece once. Lily must have thought her so cold, when all the time she knew that if she spoke at all, she would have broken down and told her everything.

So when she went to the door this morning, heard the sound of knocking, she had broken into a run. Maybe it would be Lily, maybe fate was being kind to her at last. She had turned the key with a trembling hand.

She flung the door open. It wasn't Lily. It was a scowling man in russet-red robes.

"Finally," Father Wolfram said, pushing past her. "Take me to the Director."

It had been a long walk back to the Directory, and an even longer wait as the red-robed monk had his private conference with the Director. Greaves had been summoned, the Director had canceled all other appointments, and still the door to his chamber had remained closed. In the end, Verity had gathered an armful of papers and quietly eased the door open. The old Director had never minded her doing this, and her curiosity was overwhelming. She hadn't seen a member of the Order of the Lost since she was barely more than a girl. She imagined that she and Wolfram were the only people from Giseth in the entire city.

The sight that met her eyes was almost comical. Wolfram was pacing around the Director's desk, his limping gait doing little to disguise his anger. In contrast, the Director sat at his ease, his green eyes gleaming in the candlelight.

"Father Wolfram, calm yourself," said the Director, his tone always reasonable. "I assure you, all of our efforts are going into finding the boy. But this is not Giseth. The people of Agora are strong-willed, and there are many places he could be hiding."

"You told me you ruled this city, Director," Wolfram replied, bitterly. "That in serving your interests, I could prevent disaster falling upon my own land. If I had known that you have so little power . . ."

"Power is a curious thing, Father," the Director replied, with deadly calm. "Sometimes quiet observation is just as potent. I would have thought that a man such as yourself, who normally holds to a vow of silence, would realize that."

Verity suppressed a smile as Wolfram grunted in response. She was about to make her presence known, when the Director caught her eye. She had seen that look when he had been one of the former Director's servants. When he had been no more than Mr. Snutworth, a useful spy. It was a look that was very calm, entirely reasonable, and made it clear that you were *not* to interrupt.

Very slightly, she nodded her head.

Wolfram did not seem to notice this exchange, and continued his complaints.

"I have tried patience, Director," he growled, "and the only result has been to waste time. I brought you the boy, and in return, all you sent to me was a letter saying that the girl must be found as well. I have spent weeks tramping across Giseth, searching every village. I know that Sister Elespeth of the forest Brethren knows more than she is telling, but she refuses to talk to me, and she is a difficult woman to find." Wolfram struck the Director's mahogany desk with his fist, scattering papers. "I have sacrificed much for this search. My own village of Aecer is in chaos without my guidance; half of my fellow monks believe that the Nightmare has addled my wits; my vow of silence is in tatters . . ."

"All for the greatest possible cause," the Director said, mildly. "But surely, if Miss Lily's goal was the Cathedral of the Lost, that would have been the best place to search?"

Wolfram grunted.

"I tried, after my initial searches came to nothing. I even commandeered a riverboat from its task of bringing food to Agora to speed my journey through the marshes. But the porter turned me away, claimed he had seen no such girl, and none of the Order were willing to talk."

Snutworth raised an eyebrow.

"Could you not prevail upon the girl's father? I understand, from our records, that he is a member of your Order, residing in the Cathedral?"

Wolfram waved a hand dismissively.

"Brother Thomas was dead by the time I arrived. I do not think that we can rely upon my fellow monks to retrieve her . . ."

Verity hadn't heard any more. It had taken all of her self-control not to drop the papers she was holding. She had left the room without a sound, not caring if the Director saw her go.

Her brother was dead. Her magnificent, perfect brother was dead, and they had treated his death like a footnote. She felt the last ties of loyalty snap. The old Director—the *real* Director, not this treacherous usurper—was gone. She had no reason to stay anymore. No reason to remain trapped in this rotting old building, serving a man who looked at her as though she were nothing more than a tool.

Now she was about to commit a crime. She was about to commit the most dreadful betrayal, to break every rule that she had ever followed, everything her brother had beseeched her to do when he sent her to Agora nearly fifteen years ago.

But she would do it without a shred of regret, because her brother was dead. And now Lily was her only family.

"Miss Verity?"

Verity emerged from her thoughts with a start. The Chief Inspector had stood up, and was pointing to the clock on the wall.

"It is now the second hour. Should I interrupt? I have no wish to keep the Director waiting."

She looked at Greaves, his craggy face full of concern, and made herself smile.

"Do go in, Chief Inspector," she said, brightly. "I'm sure the Director would appreciate the interruption."

He returned her smile, a little hesitantly, as the sound of Wolfram's shouting rattled the door.

"I can certainly believe that," he said. "But wouldn't you prefer to announce me?"

Verity picked up the papers on her desk.

"No," she said, trying to keep her voice flat and efficient. "I'm afraid I have other work to attend to."

And before her face could betray her, before her shell could crack, she turned on her heel, and walked out of her office for the last time.

Every step she took felt more final. She knew, at the moment, she could still turn around, still return to her office, where she was safe. She had hidden in this building for nearly fifteen years. She had been the Director's personal secretary for ten. For half her life the Directory of Receipts, a building that inspired fear in every Agoran, had been home to her.

It would have been so simple to turn back, to give up. What was her brother to her, anymore? She hadn't heard from him in years.

But he had been the only family she had.

No, that wasn't true. She had family. She had a niece. A wonderful niece, an extraordinary young woman. Her brother's daughter. And right now, the Director and his men were looking for her.

She had neglected Lily for too long. The least she could do was to make sure Lily's friends found her first. And there was only one way to do that.

Verity made her way through the endless corridors with practiced ease, and in little time, she came across the right door. The room beyond was like so many in the Directory, miles of shelving stuffed with ledgers and books, a record of every trade made in Agora since its foundation. Row after row of facts and rules. No one ever opened these books, just knowing that they were *there* was powerful enough. The air was thick with dust and secrets.

She knew what she was looking for, but was not quite certain where she would find it. She walked between the stacked shelves. No, not here. These books were all printed. Too new. She took a left turn, passing a few huddled clerks with quiet authority.

There, that was more like it. She was deep into the bookshelves now, where the older records were kept—the ones that were handwritten with spidery ink. Deeper and deeper she went. Here the lamps were only sporadically lit, and were set high up on the walls, for fear that one would set the precious books alight.

For one strange moment, Verity fantasized about taking one of those candles down, and holding it to the nearest ledger. She pictured herself waiting as it caught fire, and then the next, and the next, the whole Directory going up in flames, giving everyone in the city a fresh start. Debtors and elite alike, free from the tyranny of their past.

But it was only a fantasy, and she had just seen the book that she was looking for.

With fumbling fingers, she prized it out of the shelves. It was a thick, old volume, loosely bound in brown leather, and she leafed through it, hurriedly. She found what she needed, and with a single tug, ripped the page from the book, tucking it among the other papers she was carrying. She wished, not for the first time, that she had pockets in her skirt or blouse, but this would have to do. She returned the book to the shelves with a furtive shove. The bookshelf wobbled for a moment, but aside from a shower of fresh dust, there was nothing to show that she had ever been there.

Her heart pounded as she traced her steps back through the stacks, trying to remember her route. Was it left here? Or right? It had been so easy when she had come in. But of course, she hadn't been carrying anything out of the ordinary. She hadn't been so close to freedom.

She turned the corner, and stopped.

Just ahead, in a row she hadn't passed before, a tall, stately woman in a businesslike dress was taking down a book from a top shelf. Verity stepped back, out of sight. She recognized that woman— Lady Astrea, the Lord Chief Justice, the most powerful woman in the city. She was second only to the Director in rank, and yet here she was, struggling to take down books without assistance, in an obscure corner of the Directory.

Verity almost laughed. So many secrets, everywhere. That was what living in the Directory had done to her. She had seen too much, known too much, until in the end, nothing mattered at all.

"I wonder what she's looking for," whispered someone behind her. "I do hope it is something important. The Lord Chief Justice shouldn't be wasting her time on filing."

Verity felt her blood turn to ice. She knew that voice all too well. Slowly, she turned.

"Director," she said. One word. She knew that there was no point in trying to explain herself. Lying to him was a waste of breath.

"Miss Rita," he said, using the short, familiar version of her name and smiling, pleasantly. "I hope I am not intruding on your work, but I wished to consult you."

Verity paused for a moment too long. She tried to respond instantly, to pretend nothing was amiss. But she could tell that the

Director had noticed that pause. His eyes were not as friendly as his smile.

"Of course, Director, I . . ." she tried to think of something to say. "I thought that this was a good time to do some paperwork, as you were in a meeting . . ."

"Indeed, most enterprising," the Director replied, walking away from Lady Astrea and motioning for Verity to follow, so they could talk without being overheard. Wretchedly, Verity obeyed. "Father Wolfram and Chief Inspector Greaves are enjoying each other's company even now," the Director continued, "but I had no wish to hear the good Father's story a second time."

He laughed, lightly, as though making a joke. Verity decided against forcing herself to smile. Far better to be bland, to slip under his notice. That was how she had lasted this long. Even the former Director was a man best avoided.

The Director looked at her quizzically, and sighed.

"Dear me, I hope that I shall find your sense of humor eventually, Miss Rita," he said. "I know that I could not face my duties without it. Now, about this paperwork, I think I should check it through, just in case there is anything that I have not dealt with."

He plucked the papers from her arms before she could react. Her eyes widened. She felt her pulse begin to race.

"There is no need, sir—it is entirely trivial," she said, hurriedly. The Director barely looked up as he flicked through.

"No detail is entirely trivial, Miss Rita. Surely you must know that."

"But sir, I . . ." her throat dried as he continued. And then, he pulled out the torn page.

He stared at it. The paper was old, and smaller than the other documents, clearly not part of the pile. Verity couldn't speak, couldn't think. All she could hope for was that he wouldn't realize what he was looking at.

The Director smiled, and put the page back among the papers.

"Most delectable, I'm sure," he said, mildly. "Yes, it seems that everything is as it should be."

He handed the papers back, and walked away, leaving Verity standing in the storeroom.

In a few moments, she would walk out of that room, down to the tunnels, and leave the Directory. She wouldn't make a fuss. She would be as calm and authoritative as ever, and no one would challenge her.

But through all of this, she would barely notice anything around her. Because all she could think of was the Director's smile. Not a false smile, something far worse.

It had been a smile of contentment, and triumph.

"Did you find what you were looking for?" Wolfram asked, sourly, as the Director reentered the office. The Director walked to his desk, without speaking.

"In a sense," he replied, at last. "I found what I was expecting to find, though perhaps a little sooner than planned. But this is all to the good."

"Director," Greaves got up, breaking his silence. "I feel I must protest. Is it really necessary to spend our resources hunting for Mark and Lily? My receivers are overstretched as it is dealing with the Crede situation, and it would seem that Lily is not even within the bounds of the city."

"You know nothing," Wolfram muttered with contempt.

"No, no, Father Wolfram, the Chief Inspector has a fair point," the Director said, silencing Wolfram with a look. "Greaves, you will concentrate on Crede. Perhaps some kind of meeting would be appropriate; we have ignored him for too long. As for you, Wolfram," the Director's tone became more confidential, "I think that we will soon have the answer to all of your concerns."

"How can you be certain?" Wolfram asked, clearly ruffled by the Director's calm. The Director sat back behind his desk.

"Because of a page from a very old book, Wolfram," he said, quietly. "If I am right, it will do a great deal of our work for us."

Greaves looked from the monk to the Director. He wasn't quite sure what was going on, and that worried him. But then again, he had nothing but worries nowadays.

"I must say, Director," he said, "I would be grateful for such a page. If I may ask, what did it say?"

The Director looked at him then, but if there was a secret in those inscrutable eyes, Greaves could not see it.

"Nothing at all, Chief Inspector," he replied. "At least, nothing that would appear significant. And that is the beauty of it. If used at the right moment, *nothing* can be the most powerful thing in the world."

Greaves looked at the Director, the man who had been a servant just a few years ago, and now sat behind the mahogany desk, ruler of Agora. If anyone knew about power, it was him.

It was not a comforting thought.

CHAPTER NINE

The Legend

MISS VERITY was just as Mark remembered her.

She had arrived at the Temple without warning, in the midst of a fierce downpour, clutching Pete's note, and asking to be hidden from the receivers. By the time Ben had fetched Mark, she was already sitting quietly in the cellar room with Laud and Theo, dry but still shaking, as though her world had fallen apart.

Mark stared. She looked so like Lily that he was amazed he hadn't noticed the resemblance the first time they had met. She was a little more disheveled than he remembered, and definitely more apprehensive, but she was still the woman who had freed him from his cell, and banished him from his home. The same woman he had seen in Lily's dreams, the aunt who had brought her to Agora. The woman who had, in her own way, started it all.

To her credit, she didn't waste time. As soon as Mark had closed the door, she began to talk.

She spoke softly, but clearly—without trying to justify her own actions, or excuse them. She told them about her role as the Director's secretary, and how the Directory had changed ever since Snutworth had taken over. She talked of the receivers training for battle, and the increasing number of secret meetings. But most importantly, she talked about Lily. About how she had made it to the Cathedral of the Lost, and how she had vanished from the face of the earth.

"Vanished?" Laud asked, sharply. "You don't mean . . ."

"Father Wolfram said that she had gone somewhere called 'the Land Below,' and the rest of the Order would not let him follow her. Wherever she is, I think she is safe, for now."

"Wolfram is here?" Mark said, his heart sinking. Verity nodded.

"Yes, though he no longer abides by his vow of silence. To be honest, I'm not sure if the Order would recognize him as one of their own any longer."

That gave Mark little comfort. All this time, he had been picturing Snutworth alone as his enemy. But Mark remembered Wolfram. He remembered that hard, unfeeling stare that seemed to drag out your inner thoughts, that absolute belief that only he knew what was truly right. Snutworth was disturbing because Mark had never been able to fathom his true motivations, but Wolfram was the opposite. His beliefs were his whole life, and right now, it seemed, he believed in Snutworth's cause.

"Never mind about that!" Laud said, testily. "One man makes little difference. Tell us about this 'Land Below.' "

Verity nodded, but it was Mark she turned to.

"I was the old Director's private secretary for years," she began, confidentially. "In all that time, he mentioned this land only once, after I had fetched him a certain book from the oldest library." She reached down and pulled up the hem of her floor-length skirt to reveal a large patch sewn onto the inside, making a pocket. Carefully, she pulled out a single page, torn from a book, and held it out to Mark. "I think this might help."

Mark took the page. It was old and worn, covered in faint ink. He squinted at it.

"Sugar . . . barley . . ." he blinked, trying to make out the words. "Is this a recipe? What does it mean?"

Miss Verity smiled.

"Some things need a little illumination, before they give up their meaning," she said. "Hold it up near the lantern."

Cautiously, Mark did as instructed. As soon as the light shone through the old parchment, a few dark shapes that had looked like water stains resolved themselves into clarity.

The Sozinhos possess both the door and the key to the Land Below, although they recognize only one.

It seemed ridiculous. The Sozinhos weren't involved in any ancient conspiracies—they were just musicians. This message made no sense at all.

But it was a clue. At last, they had somewhere to start. And that was all they needed.

The rain was fierce as Mark, Laud, and Ben trudged through the sodden streets of the Leo District an hour later, cloaks and coats pulled up around their faces, their boots soaked through. Mark glanced at his companions, a little way ahead of him. It had been all they could do to keep Laud from setting out instantly, without coat or hat, despite the terrible weather. Even now, his walk was full of tension, and though Ben was calmer, she was no less determined to follow this up. Theo had wanted to join them, and nearly had until Ben had pointed out that someone needed to mind the

Temple. As they left, the doctor had been asking Verity to repeat her story, just in case there was anything they had missed.

Then again, their sudden energy was hardly surprising. Mark was already frantic with worry, and for him, it had been barely two months since he had last seen Lily. But for those at the Temple, their friend and leader had been lost for nearly a year and half.

Mark adjusted his hat, trying to prevent a trickle of water finding its way down the back of his neck. It was not particularly cold—this was late spring rain—but it was pervasive. To Mark's surprise, he thought of it as "growing rain." In Giseth he had welcomed storms like this, knowing that the following day he wouldn't have to water the crops. It was a strangely happy memory, one of the few times in his recent life when everything had been very simple.

No, now that he thought about it, his life had never been simple. Not since he had first met Lily, when they had both been nothing more than servants, back in the tower of Count Stelli. Even then, it had looked like his life was mapped out, as the apprentice of Dr. Theophilus—until the day they had exchanged lives. It had been such a simple decision at the time; Lily and he had swapped masters because he was scared to venture out into the city, and Lily longed to escape the Astrologer's Tower. That had been the first time they had parted since they had known each other, the first time their lives divided onto two paths that had never quite become one again, even after all the time they spent together in Giseth. What would have happened if they hadn't swapped places? Would Lily have had his life, and been the prodigy who fell from grace, giving Snutworth the keys to his power? Could Mark have started the Almshouse, and inspired Crede's revolution? Somehow he doubted it; most likely they would have both been unrecognizable by now. Perhaps the Directory would never have noticed them, and they would be leading dull, predictable lives, with no more knowledge of prophecies, charters, and other lands than most of Agora. Perhaps some other children would have taken their place, or perhaps nothing would have happened, and Agora would have continued on the same as it always had, waiting for the Judges who never came.

The trouble was, Mark wasn't entirely sure which life he would have preferred.

The Sozinhos' large, comfortable house loomed through the driving rain. Mark banished his musings to the back of his mind, and hurried to catch up with his friends, just as Benedicta pulled the bell cord.

The door was answered by an old servant, and once they had introduced themselves, he quickly ushered them in.

"The master and mistress will be pleased to see you, Miss Benedicta," the old man said as he took their coats. "I hear they have been missing your visits."

"This is rather more than a social call," Laud muttered.

"In which case, sir," the servant said, with unflappable calm, "perhaps I should show you in right away. I am under instructions not to disturb their rehearsals, but I suspect that they will make an exception on this occasion."

They followed the old man through the corridors of the grand house. As they progressed, Mark began to hear the sound of singing, one deep baritone, the other a pure, high soprano. Something about it comforted him and even seemed to soothe Laud's nervous energy. By the time the servant pushed open the doors to the practice room, Mark felt more ready to be sociable.

Signor and Signora Sozinho were sitting side by side at the harpsichord, both singing, their voices swooping and caressing each other. As they sang, their hands darted in and out on the keys. Even the rain drumming on the windows was reduced to a gentle patter that seemed to provide an accompaniment all its own. Mark knew that he should speak, that there was no time to lose. But just for a moment, he was lost in the music, and wouldn't have broken it for anything.

The old servant coughed. The music stopped; Signora Sozinho turned her head, and her eyes widened in surprise.

"*Carissimo,* look!"

Her husband blinked, and then a great smile came across his face.

"Miss Benedicta, Mr. Laudate, and . . ." he stopped, and stared. "By all the stars . . . Mr. Mark! I thought you had vanished from the city forever!" He jumped up, smoothing back his graying hair with a flourish. "You should have given word that you were coming! We must have tea fetched. I shall ring for the maid . . ."

"Thank you, Signor, but—" Mark was overwhelmed. He had liked the Sonzinhos well enough when he had known them, but that had been long ago, in a different life. He had expected Ben to do all the talking.

"We never believed in your disgrace," the Signor interrupted. "No doubt you have been in hiding. Very wise. After this little trouble with Crede is over, the city will be ready for a bright future."

"I think it is terrible that so many of the elite believe that the Temple and the Wheel are no different," the Signora added, turning to Ben. "As if we would be patrons of Crede's army! Of course, we understand now why you haven't been visiting, Crede must be causing you so much trouble . . ."

"Signor, Signora," Ben said, trying to stop them. "We appreciate this, but we need to ask you about—"

"Yes, yes, of course," the Signor said, "we want to hear all of your news, but we must sing the rest of this song for you first. We have written it especially for the latest gala, but we'd much rather have the opinion of people who are not trading for our services—we get a much more honest reaction . . ."

Laud closed his eyes, his hands curling into fists at his sides.

Hastily, Mark reached into the inner pocket of his coat, and pulled out Verity's crumpled page.

"Signor Sozinho, we've got to ask you something. It's about this page, we think—"

"Not that we object to the employment," Signor Sozinho continued, blithely. "The elite are holding more and more parties nowadays. I believe they are attempting to ignore the Crede situation, but it is only a matter of time before . . ."

The Signor didn't get any further. In one movement, Laud yanked the page out of Mark's hands, grabbed a lantern from a wall bracket, and pushed both into the Signor's face.

"Read it," he said. "Please."

Puzzled, and temporarily silenced, Signor Sozinho took the paper and looked at the hidden writing, as Laud held the lantern. Slowly, all of the good cheer left his face.

"Leave us," he said to the servant, who swiftly withdrew. He beckoned to his wife, who also read it over his shoulder, her confused frown growing deeper.

Laud looked at them both, putting down the lantern.

"We need to know how to reach the Land Below, Signor, Signora," he said, levelly. "We think Lily is down there."

Mark watched the Signor's face. He was obviously trying to keep all emotion out of it, but he looked deeply troubled.

"Lily is in Naru?" the Signor said, dully, sitting back at the piano stool. The Signora fumbled with the edge of her sleeves.

"I had thought that it was only an old family legend," she said. The Signor smiled, sadly.

"Ah, *carissima*, it is. A bedtime story. The land of Naru, a world of secrets deep beneath our feet. A wonderful fantasy." He looked up at Laud, regaining his composure. "I'm sorry, but whoever has given you this is playing a trick on you. It doesn't exist."

Laud's expression darkened.

"I have the greatest respect for your musical talents, Signor," Laud said, "but you are a terrible liar."

A flash of anger crossed the Signor's face.

"You think I would lie to you? After all I owe to Lily? This tale is a fantasy. Everyone knows that there are no lands outside the city."

"Everyone is obviously mistaken," Laud replied, sharply. "*Everyone* should be prepared to accept that there are stranger things going on in this city than *everyone* thinks."

"Laud, perhaps we should . . ." Mark tried to interrupt, but the young man waved him aside. The Signor's lip curled in response.

"If you are going to be childish, Mr. Laudate, perhaps we should wait for another occasion so we can discuss this like adults."

"Because, of course, claiming that Lily is trapped in a fairytale land is entirely plausible . . ."

As Laud and the Signor grew more heated, Mark noticed Benedicta out of the corner of his eye. She seemed to be making signs with her hands, while staring significantly at the Signora.

"I don't know what to make of all this," the Signor muttered. "You come here unannounced, burst into our parlor, drip water on the harpsichord, . . ."

The Signora nodded, making an answering sign, and both she and Benedicta quietly got up to leave the room.

"Lily's life could be in danger, and you're thinking about water stains?" Laud shouted.

Mark, shaking his head, followed the women out of the room, closing the door behind him.

He found the pair relaxing in a pair of armchairs in the anteroom, being served tea by the old servant. The servant barely looked up when Mark approached, but silently filled a third cup. Benedicta smiled.

"Glad you joined us, Mark. It was getting a little tiring in there."

Mark winced, apologetically.

"I'm sorry, Signora," he said. "I don't think Laud was in the mood for conversation."

The Signora smiled, sadly.

"My husband will let no one talk to him at the moment. He worries too much about the current situation," she shook her head. "A dreadful time is coming. There is already conflict in the streets. Such times are not good for musicians who rely on the elite. I cannot see us composing revolutionary anthems. So my *carissimo* was ready for an argument. As for your brother, Ben," she looked toward the door, where Laud's shouts were growing louder by the second. "I think he needs to let some of his anger flow; it is how he expresses his concern."

"He's very worried about Lily," Mark said. "We all are."

The Signora nodded, a curious smile on her face.

"Perhaps, but not in the same way, I think . . ." she said, thoughtfully. "A lot of memories are coming back today." She looked at Benedicta. "The language of signs . . . I remember that. Not a happy memory."

"We always knew how to talk without speaking," Ben said, simply, and then leaned over to touch the Signora's hand. "Signora, we really do need your help. Lily helped you, when you thought you had no future. Can't you do the same thing?"

Mark watched the Signora's face. She seemed to be fighting some inner restraint. And then, quietly, she spoke.

"It is such a strange tale," she said. "My husband told me when we were first married, but I never truly believed it."

Mark reached to pick up his teacup.

"Believe me," he said, adding sugar, "you get used to that feeling quickly when we're around."

The Signora laughed.

"That is true." She looked up and around at the room. "You would think that this fine house would be enough for the Sozinhos,

116

no? Perhaps it is, for we do not live in the other two houses that we own. One of them, I did live in, for many years." She frowned, drawing her shawl a little tighter as though a cold wind had started to blow. "That was where you first met me, dear Benedicta, where I spent those unhappy years, away from my *carissimo*. But the third is the oddest of all." She frowned. "It is an old house, ancient as my husband's family, full of endless corridors and secret doors. But family tradition says that its greatest secret is a way to leave the city itself, and travel down to Naru." She shook her head. "I have never been to that house myself. Neither has my husband, except to check that the locks are secure. But perhaps . . ." She brightened. "Verso, one of our servants, worked in the University libraries for many years. He tells me that he spent some time researching our family history. Maybe he would know if there is any truth in the tale."

Mark felt his heart sink.

"And where do we need to go to find him?" Mark said, wearily predicting another slog through the rain, another obstacle before they could start to do some good.

"Not terribly far away, sir," said the old servant.

Slowly, Mark turned his head. He hadn't really looked at the servant before. He was an elderly man; he must have seen more than eighty summers, and was clearly not in the best of health. But there was a lively intelligence in those rheumy eyes.

"Can you help them, Verso?" the Signora asked, quietly. "I wouldn't be surprised if it was nothing but a story."

Verso bowed, slowly.

"No story, ma'am," he replied.

Signora Sozinho looked at her servant and sighed, as if a weight had been lifted from her shoulders.

"I am glad to hear it," she said. "Take whatever time you need."

Verso bowed again.

"May I see the page, ma'am?" he asked. Signora Sozinho got up, passed it over, and then withdrew into the next room, as though glad to be rid of the responsibility. Verso read over the page once, and then held it up to the light for a moment. He frowned, pursing his lips. "Yes, yes, of course," he said, slipping the page into his pocket. Then he looked from Mark to Ben, appraisingly, rubbing his chin with one gloved hand.

"You wish to go to the Land Below?" He said, his voice a little less deferential than before. "Legends say that it is a dangerous journey, but the rewards are high. They say that every secret in the world is hidden there—quite a treasure trove, such power . . ."

Ben interrupted him.

"We don't care about that," she said, bluntly. "We're going there because Lily's there, and she'd do the same for us."

Verso stared down at them, a curiously searching look for an old steward. Most servants were worn down by a lifetime of submission.

"You would risk such a journey for one person? Risk descending into a world that might not even exist, on the word of a single sentence and a servant who, for all you know, may be senile?" He frowned. "You would do that for her?"

Mark wanted to explain. He wanted to talk about how she had crossed a country to rescue him, when he had been taken. He wanted to explain how they had grown closer during their time in Giseth, and how he had no focus without her. He wanted to say how much she had done for Agora, how much the city needed her back.

He didn't. He said the first thing that came into his head. Which also happened to be the truest of all.

"Of course. She's our friend."

The old man nodded, pleased.

"Then might I suggest you pack some belongings for an expedition? I fear it is not likely to be an easy journey . . ."

CHAPTER TEN

Thoughts

THE CAVE WAS SMALL, claustrophobic, and deep beneath the Oracle's throne room. It was also surprisingly cluttered with statues, ornaments, and wooden chests. The Conductor put down his lantern on the floor, casting his shadow across the room.

"What is this place?" Lily asked, uneasily.

"A memorial," the Conductor replied, "a place of remembrance."

Lily shivered. The crushing disappointment of her audience with the Oracle two days before was still fresh in her mind; she was burning to start her search for the unknown secret, and the Conductor had brought her to a place that appeared to be a tomb.

"At least, I believe it is," the Conductor said, almost casually. "No one has been buried here for years, and truth be told, no one but the Oracle herself knows anything about those who rest here, but that is not important. At the moment, this chamber is the best place in all Naru, outside of the Resonant Throne, to hear the

Canticle. The Canticle drifts around the lower caverns, but it often rests here." The Conductor gave a half-smile. "Perhaps it finds the atmosphere appropriate. Listen."

Lily waited, but she could hear nothing but the thudding of her own heart. Idly, she began to look around the cave. Now she could make out the brass plaques, set at intervals around the walls. The first few were heavily tarnished, the later ones gleamed, but all but the last bore the same inscription. A name, and two dates. The span of their lives. Lily wandered closer to look. The newer plaques bore only one name and a sign, just like the engraving on a signet ring. But the oldest had two names, like her father, and like her, of course, though she had only discovered that a month ago. Before her father had signed his name on his last letter, she had never heard of anyone having more than one name. It seemed that it had been more common, long ago.

The last plaque was blank, and looked relatively new. Lily breathed on it, and traced her own name in the cloud. "Lilith d'Annain, 129– . . ." A morbid thing to do, but that felt appropriate here, among the dead.

And at that moment, she heard it.

It was like a sigh at the very edge of hearing. Normally, she would have been amazed, perhaps even thrilled at the prospect of the Canticle of Whispers, of hearing others' thoughts. Among these grave markers, though, that was not a sound that she particularly wished to hear.

"You can listen for as long as you want," the Conductor was continuing, oblivious to her mood. "You won't be disturbed. No one has been down here for years."

Lily looked around the room. Many of the chests were open, and much of the contents were spread out beneath the glow of the crystals set into the walls.

"No one?" she said, arching an eyebrow. The Conductor

wandered over to a large shape in the center of the room, covered with an embroidered cloth.

"No one but me," he admitted. "I was curious. We see so few objects from the world above, and this chamber has some spectacular wonders—I was sure that their former owners wouldn't mind a little investigation." He turned back, his round, sad face illuminated by the light. "I do not think that they would have wanted to be forgotten."

Lily knelt down beside one of the chests. This one was small, and inlaid with rosewood. She saw that, among the jewels, there was a small, wooden rocking horse. She couldn't guess how old it was, but the paint was barely chipped. It had never been played with.

"I suppose not," she said, frowning. "You really don't know who they were?"

The Conductor began to pull away the cloth from the object in the center of the room.

"I did ask the Oracle, once, when I was first made Conductor. But she refused to tell me. She said that it would be revealed only when the time was right. Now, talking of wonders," with a final heave, he pulled the last of the cover away, "what do you think of this?"

Lily stared. In the light of the lamp, it looked like a large, strangely shaped harpsichord. But as she came closer, she noticed that there was no keyboard, and that something in the main body of the instrument was shining in the lamplight. It looked like a series of glass bowls, lying on their side, each slotted inside each other.

"Well?" the Conductor asked, proudly. "What do you think of the glass armonium?"

"Well . . ." Lily replied, not certain what to say. "It's very . . . impressive, but what does this have to do with the Canticle?"

The Conductor smiled, seating himself on a stool in front of the instrument and pumping a pedal, setting the glass bowls spinning.

"Listen," he said.

With careful precision, the Conductor licked his finger, and touched the edge of one of the bowls.

A single, pure note rang out. Lily knew that sound. She had heard it often, when she had been cleaning glasses, and amused herself by running one wet finger around its edge. It hummed and sparkled, all at once. The Conductor spread his fingers to touch more of the spinning bowls, and the tones joined together in a chord.

Then, he began to play.

Lily scarcely noticed what he played. Anything would have sounded haunting on that strange instrument, with its ghostly tones. But as the music rang through the cavern, something else happened. The whispers began to grow clearer.

It was almost as though they were attracted by the armonium, or maybe its tones were sharpening her hearing, focusing her on the right sounds. Whatever it was, the voices grew clearer, skittering through her head in sudden, furtive bursts.

Can't do that, no, that's dangerous . . . What if he finds out? No, he's too busy with his guests . . . She seems pleasant, but who knows what she must have suffered . . . I'll find her, I have to find her . . .

Lily clutched her head. Other people's thoughts were singing in her mind. She felt her heart leap and her skin prickle. She smiled. This is what she'd been searching for, all this time. This was what had propelled her out of Agora, and through Giseth. There was so much truth here. So many answers . . . if only she could grasp them . . .

What's the point, why should I go on? . . . I love him, I know it's wrong, but I love everything about him . . . stupid man! He'll get himself killed, and I'll be the one to do it . . .

The Conductor stopped playing. The whispers faded back into

an incomprehensible hiss. Lily rubbed her aching temples, the new thoughts already slipping from her mind.

"I have no idea how it works," he said, getting down from the glass armonium. "I think that it was left here as part of the grave goods. But something about this instrument's sound seems to resonate with the Canticle, and make it easier to hear."

Lily didn't reply, unable to get away from the exhilarating experience of the Canticle surging through her. It felt like having pure information running through her brain, crisp and undiluted, but tantalizingly incomplete, like a burned parchment.

A burned parchment . . .

An image of the fragment of the Midnight Charter that Lily had found back in Agora swam into her mind. That piece of parchment had started everything. Nothing had been the same for her since that night—since she had found a few incomplete sentences that seemed to rule her life. In all this time, had she just been looking to fill those blanks?

So be it. She knew what she needed to search the Canticle for. It wasn't likely that the Oracle's one unknown secret would be anything trivial.

"Thank you, Conductor," she said, and meant it. "I think I can carry on from here."

He did not argue. She had a look in her eyes that could not be resisted, but as he shuffled to the exit, he did look back.

"Remember," he said, softly, "we Naruvians spend our entire lives looking for secrets, and even we do not care to spend too long with the Canticle. Some thoughts can tell you too much."

But Lily was already sitting down at the armonium, and she barely heard him.

The days passed.

I'll hide him, that's what I'll do . . . should I have fish or fruit? . . .

Everyone's marching to a new beat, a new rhythm . . . I can't cope with this . . . Fish, fruit, what's the difference? . . . What should I pack? Where did I put it? . . .

At first, she left to eat in the communal canteen, and sleep in her own, private cave. But as time went on, she spent more and more time down in the tombs. Sometimes she looked up from the instrument and saw some bread and dried meat waiting for her on a tray, perched on one of the chests. She never saw who brought it for her. If she was hungry she ate, carving hunks of food with the hunting knife she had fetched from her pack. Occasionally she remembered to sleep. But most of the time, she pressed the pedal, spread her fingers across the armonium, and let the Canticle sing to her.

Is now the moment? Not yet . . . Is he looking for me? Maybe he is, but I'm safe here; the doctor will look after me . . . Can I trust her? . . . . Can I trust him? . . . I know I've seen this fabric somewhere before . . . that face! I recognize that face . . .

The more she searched, the more she wanted to know. Mostly, she remembered that she was supposed to be looking for the one truth that eluded the Oracle. But sometimes, she couldn't resist the sheer beauty of it. She would sit back and let a million disjointed thoughts flow through her mind, her whole body shivering with the music of it all.

Have to keep the trades up, maybe I can eat this week . . . The last steps are in preparation, and yet this man delays, what is he thinking? . . . Water under the bridge, my friend, we'll never meet again . . . Did he just goose me? The nerve . . . pain never stops, why won't it stop? . . .

It didn't seem to matter what she played, which was just as well as she could barely pick out a tune. Instead, she learned to focus her mind, to guide the endless stream of whispers. Two images were always at the front of her mind. The Midnight Charter itself, whole and complete, giving up all its secrets, and her friends: Laud, Ben, Theo, Mark.

Won't tell, can't tell the secret, not just yet . . . WHY WON'T IT STOP . . . why won't she stop playing that violin? She's no good . . . Where are they? Where are they? There should have been a message . . . what happened out there? . . . What—what do we do now? . . .

Sometimes she searched through the whispers for other things, for old and forgotten secrets. The oldest thoughts still echoed through the chambers after their owners were long dead. She could tell they were ancient—the voices were faint and scratchy, although she couldn't tell if they were men or women. But the fragments she picked up fascinated her.

These crystals; they have the most extraordinary properties . . . it's a ridiculous notion! Preposterous . . . but imagine if it worked . . . our Society, our lives' work, proved right . . . remember, lay those stones just right . . . it'll never work, someone's bound to tell . . . someone did tell, they've been removed. Disappeared . . . The others are keeping the faith, the whole city believes in our cause . . .

Sometimes she searched for her friends, trying to hear those familiar voices in the maelstrom of thought. But whenever she was sure she could hear Mark, or Laud, or Ben, or Theo, she caught only tiny, incomprehensible fragments.

She makes herself useful, I thought after a life in an office she'd never take to this work. Shows what I know! . . . Will she want to come back? Maybe she found her father after all. What if she doesn't need me—no, need us, anymore . . . There's still preparations to make, why wouldn't Mr. Verso say anything more specific? . . . She's still with Crede? Why? I'm doing something now; why doesn't she see?

But mostly, Lily plunged through, listening to everything, as though the whole world were filling her head. Thoughts from the lands above rushed through her, each one fading as she heard it, until she was left with only a feeling—a spark of truth. Dark thoughts, funny thoughts. Thoughts she herself would never have had in a thousand years. Thoughts that shamed her, or made her laugh, or cry, or shudder.

I'll wait for them, they won't suspect a thing . . . green is so elegant, so intelligent . . . It'll be a night he'll never forget . . . look at her, shacked up with the rebel. She wasn't worthy, none of them are worthy . . . Mathilde asked about him again, twenty-five summers and she's acting like a babe in arms. But still, I feel it. Oh stars, I feel it . . . Round and round and round and round we go. Wheee! . . . Won't suspect a thing . . . not a thing . . .

And then, all of a sudden, she would hear one of her own thoughts, echoing back at her, and the Canticle would be full of whispers about her. Of people calling her name. Everyone waiting for her opinion, her beliefs—for Lily to swoop in and save the day.

I have to keep on searching . . . searching for answers. She always looked for answers . . . Lily would know the answers . . . Lily IS the answer, that's what he said; I wish I had known her . . . Lily will soon know . . . Lily will never know . . . Lily and Mark, Lily and Mark, so perfect and so wrong . . .

And that would go on and on, spiraling into a chorus. Until they filled her brain and bones and soul, and the entire world was whispering her name.

Lily is the key . . . Lily, where are you? . . . Lily, forgive me . . . Lily is our inspiration . . . Lily is at the heart of everything . . . Lily . . . Lily . . . Lily . . .

"Lily!"

Lily's fingers slipped, and the sudden flash of pain as she pulled her finger from the spinning glass jolted her back to her senses. To her surprise, she realized that the last of the voices was still calling her name.

"Lily, can you hear me?"

She swiveled on the stool. A young man stood by the lantern, mostly in shadow.

"Who . . . ?" Lily asked, still disoriented, finding it hard to match what she was seeing to the echoes that were still bouncing around in her head. A moment before, she had been all knowing, in tune with the thoughts of millions. Coming down to earth was harder every time.

"It's Tertius," he replied, and stepped a little closer. Lily could see that he was holding a silver tray, probably taken from the grave goods. "I brought you some food."

Lily's vision cleared, and she was able to focus on the face.

"Is that for me?" Lily asked, stretching, feeling an ache in her back. How long had she been sitting there? It was impossible to keep track of time in this sunless land. She glanced at the lantern—it was nearly out. That was why there were so many shadows.

"Let me do that," Tertius said, hastily putting down the tray, and pulling out an oilskin, to refill the lantern. Lily waited in the dark, bemused.

"You're very helpful, suddenly," she said, wondering if it would last.

Tertius laughed, high and nervous.

"Just trying to make a change," he said, fumbling with the lamp. "The Conductor said that you were down here, and I thought you might want some company." Lily heard him striking a spark with a tinderbox, and lamplight filled the room. Now that she could see clearly, Lily noticed that Tertius was no longer dressed in bright, clashing colors. He was wearing a brown tuniclike garment, and seemed to have tied his flowing hair into a ponytail, in the Agoran way. As he looked around, he noticed a plate of uneaten food on the floor, and frowned at her.

"You know, you really should eat," he reproached her. Lily

looked at the food. She supposed that she was hungry, in a way. But she didn't want to get up from the armonium. There was still so much more to find. Idly, she slipped her foot back onto the pedal, until the bowls were spinning, and touched the largest. A single note keened into life, along with a tiny rush of whispers. Tertius spun around, excited.

"Is that it?" he said, awestruck. "Is that the Canticle?"

Lily took her finger away, and the note faded.

"I thought so," she said with a weary smirk. "You're not interested in me; you just want to hear the Canticle."

Tertius looked crestfallen, his whole body slumping in shame.

"Can't I want both?" he said, in a voice so small and childlike that Lily couldn't stop herself from softening. She swiveled around on the stool.

"You and Septima had me all to yourself for days," she said, leaning forward, curiously. "As I remember, I was a disappointment."

Tertius straightened up, and attempted a haughty flick of the head.

"Don't talk to me about Septima. We aren't speaking anymore. She never appreciated you." He smiled, shyly. "I never understood before. The Conductor told me what you're doing down here, trying to find out something even the Oracle doesn't know. He meant it as a warning, but I think it's amazing. Just *amazing*." His eyes grew round and wide, and despite her tiredness, Lily smiled.

"You find lumps of rock amazing," she said, deadpan, getting down from the seat. "I just need answers, that's all. If the Canticle can find the truth for me, I'll use that. Otherwise, I'll try something else."

Tertius's mouth gaped, as though Lily had just given the most brilliant speech he had ever heard. He came closer, and Lily tried not to laugh.

"But that's just it," he said, with growing intensity. "You're looking for *answers*. I've searched for facts and secrets my whole life, but I've never come across an answer. Not a real, final answer."

Lily frowned.

"I'm not trying to find out the meaning of life," she said, thoughtfully. "Just the answers that matter to me. What's happened to my friends, why everyone seems to think I'm so important . . ."

"You don't know?" Tertius interrupted.

Lily looked at him. Before, his stare had been strangely endearing. But now, there was something too intense about the way he looked at her. He looked almost hungry.

"No," Lily replied, surreptitiously looking to see if he was between her and the exit. "I'm just a girl. I don't follow anyone's prophecies. I'm not important."

"But you are!" Tertius said, a little too loudly for comfort. "You have such drive, such . . ." his eyes filled with realization, ". . . focus. You know what you want, and you go out and get it. Little more than a month in Naru, and you're on the verge of finding everything you want!" He advanced toward her, a rapturous smile on his face. "You're perfect."

Lily shrank back, and felt the armonium behind her, blocking her way.

"Now look, Tertius," she said, hurriedly, "this is really flattering, but you could be just the same as me, you know. All you have to do is have a goal, something that really matters to you." She pointed to the cave mouth. "Go on! Go out there, and get what you want."

"I know what I want," Tertius said, quietly. "Nothing's ever mattered to me as much as understanding *you*."

Lily tried to escape, but Tertius was already right in front of her, his eyes huge and strange, as if they would drink her in.

"Tell me how you do it!" he said, more forcefully. "I have to know!"

Suddenly, without thinking, Lily pushed him away.

Tertius screamed. He collapsed backward, as though Lily had stabbed him in the chest. Lily stared at her hand.

"I barely touched you," she said, amazed. He looked up at her, aghast.

"But you *did* . . . you touched me!" He sounded ill, his breathing quick and fast, his already pale face was deadly white. "With your bare hands! That's . . . that's . . . urgh . . ." He crawled away across the floor. "You filthy *thing*!"

Lily looked down at Tertius, crawling away from her. Her first instinct was to bend down, to help. But as she moved closer, he shrieked again, scrabbling away from her across the stone floor, knocking over the tray of food in his desperation.

And then, to her surprise, Lily felt herself getting angry. Maybe it was relief, maybe a reaction against the fear, but she felt her lip curl, and her heart pound faster.

"What? You think I'm going to give you some kind of horrible disease?" Lily asked, scornfully. "I thought I was 'perfect.'"

Tertius looked as if he was trying to reply, but he was overcome with dry retching. He lay shuddering on the floor. And Lily stood over him, her fury growing. She felt that strange shudder pass over her again, the one she felt every time the Canticle was near, and this time she didn't try to push it away. Instead, she laughed— a hard laugh, fueled by exhaustion.

"You want to know how to focus?" she asked, scornfully. "Maybe you need to stop seeing knowledge as the end of everything! The Oracle knows every secret in the world, and what good does it do her? She's stuck in her chamber, all alone."

Tertius raised his head, and finally managed to speak, through quivering lips.

"You couldn't understand," he said, dragging himself to his feet. "She is pure, unfettered by the world. I thought you were like her." He shook with revulsion. "But you're just an animal, a deviant, a—a . . . creature of the flesh!"

He spat the last words as though they were a curse, but Lily only laughed again, more harshly than she intended.

"It's just your body!" she shouted. "How can you be so disgusted with something that's part of you? No wonder you can't focus. You hold everything at arm's length." She stepped forward, and Tertius recoiled. "Real truth isn't just facts," she continued, passionately. "It's something I've been looking for my whole life. Something I longed for when I sat crying in my corner at the bookbinders because there was nowhere in the world where I fit. I was an orphan—a girl with stupid ideas above her station. A danger to society."

She was snarling, but she just didn't care. All the anger she'd been keeping under wraps was pouring out of her. She'd spent days with nothing but Truth, and she couldn't have stopped herself now even if she wanted to. She seized Tertius's wrists, not caring as he squirmed in fear and disgust at her touch. Behind her, the Canticle chattered and whispered, growing in volume, buzzing inside her head.

"And I never gave up looking for the truth," Lily continued, pulling him closer so her breath was in his face. "Never stopped looking for my parents. Never stopped tearing down all the lies in Agora and Giseth, trying to find something real. I know more about *meaning* than you Naruvians ever will, until you finally decide to let a single lasting emotion, a single real feeling in to those empty shells you call your souls." Tertius struggled, his face growing paler than ever as she squeezed his wrists, digging her nails into his skin. "Because real truth is something that matters, that you feel deep down in your guts and your heart. It's something that makes you understand who you are!"

Lily's words echoed around the cave, multiplied by the Canticle a thousand times.

Who you are . . . who you are . . . who . . . are . . . you . . . who . . . are . . . you . . . .

And suddenly, in a moment of perfect clarity, she knew what the Oracle's question was.

She loosened her grip, and Tertius tore himself free, his whole body shaking. But she had already forgotten about him, as he ran for the exit. Already forgotten about the food, slopped all over the floor. In the back of her mind, a part of her wanted to go after Tertius and check that he was all right. A part of her knew that it wasn't like her to be so cruel to him, that something was wrong, terribly wrong. But she drowned that nagging voice in a million others, whispering all around her. She saw everything clearly now—as clear and bright as glass. He was just another distraction.

She sat down at the armonium, once again.

"She doesn't know who she is," Lily said, exultantly, to the empty air. "She knows everything in the world, but not where she fits in."

She spread her fingers over the armonium, her body shivering all over, and reached out for the Canticle.

"I'll find you, Oracle," she said, with all her heart. "I'll find your name."

And the whispers echoed through her mind.

CHAPTER ELEVEN

The Descent

"ARE YOU SURE we're in the right place?" Mark asked
Laud, who stood beside him, poring over Verso's instructions.

"It looks like it," he replied. "Though I admit, it is not what I
expected."

It was a modest house of red sandstone, toward the center of
the Virgo District. Entirely respectable, almost dull. Mark walked
up to the oak door and tried the handle. It swung open, without
even an ominous creek. For some reason, he found that unsettling.

"After you," he said, gesturing to his friends. Ben and Laud
shouldered the backpacks that Theo had provided, stuffed with
food and heavy bottles of water. They were fully prepared; it had
been two weeks since their visit to the Sozinhos. But Verso had been
most particular. He would guide them, but only when he had made
his own arrangements. When his letter arrived this morning,

Theo had read it out with visible relief. Waiting had not been pleasant for any of them.

For a brief moment, Mark wished that the doctor had been able to join them—but it would be suspicious if the temple were abandoned, and Lily wouldn't have wanted that. And Lily was the point of this whole journey—Lily was the reason the three of them were stepping through this door without a clue where it would lead.

The house inside was dimly lit, but Mark could still recognize a kind of shabby grandeur. The walls were paneled in dark oak, and the furniture had a respectable solidity. At the far end of the entrance hall, one of the doors stood open, the glow of a candle visible.

"Ah, how punctual," said an old, scratchy voice.

Verso appeared in the candlelight. The steward still managed to walk with graceful deference, despite his bent posture, and Mark noticed that although he was dressed in tough, outdoor clothes, he was still wearing his spotless white gloves.

"Well, Mr. Verso?" Laud said, stiffly. "We're here. We're ready. How far is it to this secret entrance?"

Verso smiled, rubbing his rheumy eyes.

"Not far, sir. Under the dining room, in fact."

Mark tried to suppress a laugh. Verso turned to him, peering into his face with a trace of amusement.

"I wasn't aware that the dining room was a particularly humorous place," he said. Mark shook his head.

"It's not that; it's just . . . really?" Mark said, grinning sheepishly. "A secret entrance to another land beneath the dining room? Isn't that a bit ordinary? I was expecting a cobweb-hung mausoleum." He sighed. "Stupid, I suppose."

Verso turned away. Just for a second, there had been something oddly wistful about the old man's eyes.

"Not entirely, sir," he said. "This way, if you please."

Verso led them through the corridors, up and down a bewildering number of steps. The house was larger than it had seemed, and it obviously hadn't been lived in for a very long time.

"Mark does have a point," Benedicta said, as they made their way through the dining room—the table set for six, but covered in a thick layer of dust. "Why is there a path to Naru in an ordinary house like this?"

"The question, Miss Benedicta, might more accurately be put this way," he said, picking up a sturdy oil lamp from a dresser. "Why would anyone build an ordinary house over the path to Naru?" He lit the flame in his lamp. "Down these stairs, if you please."

The stairs descended for quite a distance, turning from fine wood to stone. The corridors down here were servants' quarters, and the wooden doors were old and warped.

"All right," Mark said, somewhat frustrated by this cryptic old man. "Why would they?"

Verso smiled.

"As you astutely said, sir, because it was such an unlikely place." Verso pulled a key from his belt to unlock one of the older-looking doors. "The man who used to live here was known as the Last. Some called him a madman, but that is a label we often give to those who see with disturbing clarity. In the end, his family insisted on him "retiring" to this house." With a satisfying click, the key turned, and Verso pushed the door open. "Which was, of course, exactly what he wanted. This house, he felt, needed to be guarded. The fact that he was essentially a prisoner here did not concern him. I think perhaps he was indeed a little unbalanced, at the end."

"You seem to know a lot about him," Laud said, suspiciously, following Verso through the door, to another wood-paneled corridor. Verso looked back.

"Naturally, sir," he said. "I was a servant of his, in my youth, though only for a short time. Before he went the way of all things,

135

he entrusted me with some very important secrets." Verso turned suddenly, and reached out to one of the wooden panels on the wall. He pushed a knothole, and the panel slid to one side. "This one, for example."

The room beyond was dark, and Verso shined his lamp in.

"Lady and gentlemen," he said, with a bow, "welcome to the Last's Descent."

Beside him, Mark heard Ben and Laud gasp. The room was probably large, but it was hard to tell, as it was mostly filled with a vast array of gears, interlocking over the ceiling and walls. In the center of the room was a circular metal platform, ringed with rails and suspended from thick iron chains that disappeared up into the mass of cogs. Beneath the platform was a deep stone well that plunged far beyond the range of the light. Verso entered the room and began to adjust some levers on a contraption near to the door. Mark followed, but Ben and Laud remained in the doorway.

"Aren't you coming?" Mark asked.

"I don't trust this," Laud said, his face grim. "It reminds me of the Clockwork House."

"Well, as I understand it, Mr. Laudate, Naru is a considerable distance *that* way," said Verso, pointing down. "I suppose we could always move the platform and find a rope . . ."

Laud silenced him with a glare.

"The last time I stepped into a room decorated this way, I was on the trail of my sister Gloria's murderer, and was nearly burned alive. I would appreciate it if you would take me seriously." Distractedly, he touched his left arm. Mark knew there was a long, livid scar there, given to Laud by that same murderer.

Lily had told Mark the story of that terrible night during their travels. She, Laud, and Ben had been cornered by the murderer, a disturbed receiver called Sergeant Pauldron, in the strange Clockwork House, deep in the Agoran slums. Laud had tried to grab the killer, and in return Pauldron had opened Laud's arm nearly to the bone with his knife. But still, Laud had held on, distracting him, letting Ben escape, and keeping Lily safe until help arrived. That had been almost two years ago now, but one look at Laud and Ben showed that the memories were still raw.

Verso dropped his head in a slight bow.

"My apologies, sir. I was attempting to lighten the mood." He looked over at the platform. "I do not relish this descent myself."

"You're coming with us?" Mark asked, surprised. Verso rubbed one wrist, thoughtfully.

"Indeed, sir. Much as it would be agreeable to say that I am showing you the Descent out of nothing but the goodness of my heart, I have my own reasons for visiting Naru." He pulled another of the levers, and with a shuddering wrench, the largest of the gears above began to turn. "And that, sirs, miss, is all I am willing to say on the subject. Now, if you would join me."

Verso walked purposefully onto the platform, his step only a little unsteady, leaning heavily on the rails as he lowered himself into a sitting position on the metal floor.

"The descent will begin in a few minutes," he said, breathing heavily, from the exertion of sitting. "I advise you to join me."

Mark looked back to Laud and Benedicta, hovering in the doorway.

"Are you coming?" he said, jumping onto the platform, making it rock a little. "For Lily."

Silently, hand-in-hand, Laud and Ben joined him. As they settled themselves down, the last of the cogs above began to turn. And then, with a lurch, the chains began to let out, and the platform began slowly to descend.

"She'd better be down there," Laud muttered, as they sank into the darkness.

* * *

Mark woke just before they reached the bottom of the well.

He pushed himself into a sitting position, surprised to find that he had fallen asleep at all. The descent had hardly been a smooth ride. The platform jarred on the rock walls of the well, and even when the going was easy, the chains continued to rumble overhead. The light from above had long since vanished, and they had extinguished their lanterns after the first few minutes, when it was clear that the journey was going to be long, and they didn't want to waste oil. He supposed he had been more tired than he thought.

He looked around at the others. Laud and Ben were curled up, though he couldn't see their faces from here. But Verso was still sitting, upright and propped against the platform rails. He almost looked as if he were enjoying himself. Every now and then, he produced a leather bag from his pocket and slipped a small boiled candy into his mouth, savoring the flavor.

"Aren't you going to share, Mr. Verso?" Mark asked. Verso turned to face him. For a second, he looked startled, almost guilty.

"Forgive me, sir, but no," he said. "You must forgive an old man his treats. I have been saving these for a long time."

Mark watched hungrily as Verso pulled another candy out of the bag. This one was particularly tempting—deep blue and shiny, glinting in the dim light.

Slowly, an odd thought crept over him. He checked, the lanterns were all extinguished. The top of the well was far away, and doubtless the candle up there had burned out anyway. So how could he see anything at all?

Mark held up one hand. There were no shadows; it was as if the light—faint and bluish—was coming from all directions.

"Ah yes, the light," Verso said, amiably. "Might I draw your attention to the walls, sir?"

Mark looked. At first, all he saw was stone—rough, uneven stone, certainly, but nothing out of the ordinary. And then he noticed the tiny veins of crystal, extending through the rock, and glowing. Faintly, yes, but just enough to bathe them all in deep twilight.

Mark turned back to Verso. He couldn't understand why he was so unsettled. The light was hardly a threat. Then again, perhaps that was the problem. He had been expecting surprises, and dangers. But this light was alien, like nothing he had known before, except perhaps in the dreaming depths of the Nightmare.

Mark was about to speak when, without warning, the platform struck something, and pitched violently to one side. All four were jostled into a struggling heap.

"Looks like we've reached the bottom," Ben said, pulling herself up, and then glancing back in alarm. "Mr. Verso, are you all right?"

She helped the old man to his feet. He was unsteady, and coughed a couple of times, a contrast to the calm figure of a moment before. But he quickly regained his composure and patted her hand.

"Thank you, my dear. Quite well enough." He looked up. "Ah, it seems our journey is not yet concluded."

Mark followed Verso's gaze. In one side of the well, there was a carved archway in the stone. Beneath it sat a wooden cart, half-covered with more clockwork gears. It rested on a pair of metal rails that disappeared through the archway, and down a rocky corridor, sporadically illuminated by lumps of faintly glowing crystal.

"At least we won't need to waste the lamp oil," Laud muttered, staring down the tunnel, before facing the old man. "Now that we're down here, Verso, do you have anything you want to say? A couple of words of warning, maybe? Any clues on what we have to do?"

Verso leaned heavily against the stone wall, and mustered a smile.

"This cart appears to have been left to provide the only way onward. Perhaps I might be allowed to inspect it? Unless you would prefer to walk?"

Verso met Laud's gaze, and again, Mark thought he saw a flash of steel behind those amiably polite eyes. Laud closed his eyes and clenched his jaw.

"Fine," he said, through gritted teeth. "You'd better get to work."

A few hours later, the four of them stepped from the cart on unsteady legs. It hadn't been a bad journey—the corridor was straight, and the cart rode surprisingly smoothly—but the speed had taken them by surprise. They had never moved so fast in their lives. Mark was sure they must have been halfway out under Giseth by now.

But although the rails had come to an end, the stone tunnel had not, and there was no option but to continue on foot.

They made slow progress—partly out of caution, and partly because Verso could not walk very easily. In fact, the farther Verso went, the shakier his steps became. Perhaps it was the strange crystal light, but the wrinkles on his face looked deeper than before. Despite this, Laud continued to press on, striding forward with burning purpose, often barely waiting for the others to catch up. And it was quiet, so quiet that all Mark could hear was the pounding of his own heart in his ears.

Without warning, Benedicta stopped.

"What is it?" Laud asked. Ben looked around at them all. In the faint light, she looked puzzled, but not frightened.

"It's probably nothing, but—our footsteps aren't making any sound," she said.

Mark stared at her. Of course, now that she said it, it was obvious. He looked at the stone that lined this tunnel. It was black and dense, of a kind he had never seen before.

"This rock feels normal," Ben said, touching the walls, "but— look." She knocked the edge of her lantern against the black rock. Or rather, they saw her do it, but the metal lantern made no noise at all.

"Right," Laud muttered. "Glowing crystals, sound-absorbent rocks. Do you think it's time for the monsters to arrive?"

As if on cue, there was a sudden rasp. Laud spun around, brandishing his lantern like a weapon, but Ben was faster, and stopped his hand.

"It's just Verso," she whispered, as the old man broke into a fit of hacking coughs. Ben hurried over to Verso, and gently patted him on the back.

Mark eyed Laud's lantern.

"You think that would help in a fight?" Mark asked. Laud shrugged.

"Not perfectly," he admitted. "Burning lamp oil can't be pleasant, but it rather makes me wish I'd brought something a bit more threatening." He looked farther up the tunnel. "I thought I heard something up there, a moment ago. Shall we scout it out?"

Mark looked back at where Benedicta had sat Verso down, his back propped up against the wall.

"I don't think Ben should stay with Verso," Mark murmured. Laud raised an eyebrow.

"I don't imagine that the old man would be particularly dangerous. And Ben's dealt with much bigger threats than eighty-year-olds who can barely stand."

Mark shook his head.

"It's not that. I want to ask him a few questions. I think he was about to tell me something during the descent." Purposefully, Mark raised his voice, loud enough for Ben to hear. "So that's settled, you and Ben go on ahead. I'll stay with Verso until he's rested."

Laud looked at the old man curiously, but didn't object.

"Come on Ben," he said, "it can't be much farther."

"You realize that now you've said that, we'll be walking for hours," Ben replied, deadpan, as she joined her brother.

"Sarcasm doesn't become you, dear sister . . ."

141

"Well, I suppose it runs in the family . . ."

Their voices quickly faded away down the tunnel. Faster than usual, in fact, probably due to the black rock.

Mark sat down beside the old servant. Verso's wheezing was still very bad, and he continued to rub his wrists through his gloves. The old man turned, but didn't quite meet Mark's eye.

"Did you want something, Sir?" he asked.

"Answers would be nice," Mark admitted. "Look, I appreciate you bringing us down here, I really do, but I can't trust you. In fact I think you've gone out of your way to make us distrust you."

Verso frowned.

"I'm not sure I entirely follow you, Sir . . ."

"You've been acting mysteriously since the moment we met," Mark interrupted, firmly. "You obviously know more than you're telling. All those secrets you hint at, all those little pauses. You told the Sozinhos you only know about this place because you'd researched their family history, and then you turn around and tell us that you used to work as a servant to the Last. You don't add up, Verso, and sometimes I think you're doing it on purpose."

Verso continued to rub his wrists, thoughtfully, giving nothing away.

"So, do you trust me, Mr. Mark?" he asked, at last.

Mark thought for a moment.

"I don't know. I probably shouldn't, but if you'd wanted to betray us, you could just have lied about the way down."

Verso turned away. His eyes were unfocused, as though he were remembering.

"Lying would be easy," he said. "It always is. But truth, now that is a difficult thing indeed. I have known so many truths. From tiny facts to huge secrets, and every one is a burden. But this is a place where truths must be faced."

Mark looked into Verso's eyes. For a few long moments, he examined the old man, trying to get into his head. There was something he was missing here, something obvious.

"You know a lot for someone who's been a servant all his life," he said.

Verso chuckled, which turned into another attack of coughing.

"Servants have a great deal of time to think, sir," he said, once he got his breath back. "We have little else to do, without the freedom to make our own decisions. I know many secrets, yes, but I can do nothing with them. Every action I have taken, every choice I have made, has been determined by greater forces."

Mark put his hands behind his head.

"That sounds like an excuse to me."

Verso turned to him, sharply.

"What do you mean?"

Mark shrugged.

"A lot of people use that excuse—'I was just doing what I had to.' Those are usually the people who are too scared to try something new." He studied Verso's face, carefully watching the old man for a sign of weakening. "There's always a choice."

Verso twitched.

"You understand nothing, boy. The years still stretch before you, full of possibility. You haven't even seen sixteen summers yet. What do you know of duty, of sacrifice, that fills a whole lifetime?"

"Not much," Mark interrupted, with a slight smile. "But I know I was right about one thing. That wasn't the speech of a lifelong servant."

Verso looked straight at Mark then, and Mark felt the force of his stare. But it was an oddly approving look.

"I would like to tell you all, Mark. I would. And you will know the truth, soon enough. But I am here for my own reasons, and you are not my confessor. First, I must—"

"Mark! Verso! Where are you?"

Ben's shouts drowned the old man's words. She was running down the tunnel, breathless and excited. She was closer than she seemed, another effect of the strange black rock—Mark had not heard her approach.

"Ben, what are you—?" he managed to stammer out before she reached him, grabbed his sleeve, and pulled him to his feet.

"We've met them! And they know where she is! Come on! We've found her!" Ben pulled at him, babbling. Mark yanked back his arm.

"Slow down, Ben. Who are you talking about?"

Mark stopped speaking, realization stealing over him. There was only one person she could be talking about.

"Lily?" he said. Ben laughed.

"Yes, Lily! Who did you think?" she said, mockingly, hitting the side of his head in a playful tap. "Laud's with the people who live down here now . . . They're a queer bunch . . ."

But Mark was no longer listening. He and Ben raced back along the corridor, leaving Verso struggling to catch up.

The other end of the tunnel opened out into a large cave, filled with tables, cooking pots, and a crowd of people. Mark registered a confused, chattering mass of white hair and bright, garish clothes. But one—a portly, round-faced man—was deep in conversation with Laud, who looked happier than Mark had ever seen him before.

"Is she . . . ?" Mark asked, trying to get his breath back. Laud nodded, furiously.

"Down in the lower caves. The Conductor, here, has been explaining it to me. He's been very obliging, but don't offer to shake his hand. I thought he was going to faint." Laud pressed his hands to his temples, as if trying to shake his thoughts into some kind of order. "Apparently, they have to offer assistance to anyone who comes out of the silent tunnel, so they're going to take us to her right away . . ." And for the first time ever, Mark saw Laud's face split with a genuine grin of delight. "No tricks, no traps, they're going to help us because of some ancient rule. At last these old secrets are working for us!"

Behind them, Verso finally caught up, wheezing but excited.

"Well, my boy, are you going to wait here all day?"

Mark snapped into action, turning to the portly man, the one Laud had called the Conductor.

"Can we go right away?" Mark asked, eagerly. The Conductor swallowed, nervously twisting a baton behind his ear with his free hand.

"Yes, but . . . she has asked not to be disturbed . . ."

"I really think she'll make an exception for us," Mark said, laughing.

The Conductor bowed his head, obviously giving up on his attempt to understand what was going on.

"Follow me," he said.

Mark barely registered the wonder of Naru as he followed the Conductor. He, Laud, Ben, and Verso were led through caves of extraordinary splendor, past towering pillars of crystal and fathomless depths. He didn't even stop to look at the people, with their huge, dark eyes and curious chatter. He caught Benedicta's eye, and saw in her the same thing that he was feeling—relief. Wondrous, blissful relief. In the end, it had been strangely easy to track Lily down. It hadn't taken months of perilous travel; they hadn't had to fight their way through the Order of the Lost. And now, at last, he could admit all the things he had been fearing. She wasn't dead. She wasn't alone, or mad, or captured by enemies. She wasn't suffering because she had gone chasing after him. It wasn't his fault.

The Conductor led them to a small, dark tunnel, sporadically illuminated with crystals. Mark could make out steeply descending stone steps.

"She is down here," the Conductor said, anxiously. "But, she is listening to the Canticle. Perhaps you would rather wait . . ."

Mark didn't hear the end of that sentence. As one, all four of them were already clattering down the steps.

Ben and Laud hurried forward, determination in their eyes. Behind him, Mark heard Verso struggling down the steps, leaning against the wall for support. Despite his eagerness, Mark turned back to ask if the old man needed any help.

"No, no," he gasped. "You go on. I'll catch up."

Mark nodded and, free of his charge, he flew down the steps, passing Laud and Ben. Up ahead, Mark could hear a strange sound. A haunting, floating kind of music. And all around them, there was another sound, just out of hearing—like a thousand whispers, speaking all at once. But still, they pressed on, deeper and deeper, with the sounds growing ever louder, until their ears rang.

And then they were at the mouth of another cave, and they saw her.

She was sitting with her back to them, at a strange harpsichord, made of polished, black wood. Her hands were frantically moving across a series of spinning glass bowls, producing wild music. Her head was thrown back, every inch of her body was tense, moving this way and that with the flow of the whispers that raced around the room. She was so totally absorbed she seemed almost part of the sound itself.

"Lily?" Ben said, astonished, but Lily didn't hear her.

"Lily!" Laud shouted at the top of his voice, but there was no reaction.

Scarcely knowing what he was doing, Mark ran forward, knocking over a discarded plate of food, and dashing a lantern to the ground. He reached the instrument.

He caught a glimpse of Lily's eyes, and faltered. They were fixed, ecstatic. She was mouthing along to something he couldn't

146

hear, filled with passion he couldn't guess at. She looked extraordinary. But she looked nothing like his friend. She was barely human.

He slammed his hands down on the spinning bowls.

There was a shrieking discord. And the whispers fled.

Lily convulsed as though struck by lightning. Mark reached forward, but Laud was already there to catch her as she fell back, and Ben took her hand as she flung it out.

She shook, babbling something about truth, and secrets, and being so close.

And then, to his relief, her eyes began to focus.

"Get off me . . . I need to go back . . . I need to . . . what . . . I . . . ?" She peered at him, as if through a haze. And then her mouth fell open. "Mark? Mark!" She flung herself forward, grabbing his face. "It . . . I . . . what?"

"Glad to hear you've been practicing your oratory," Laud said, in a tone that mixed humor and tenderness so perfectly that Mark barely recognized it. Lily twisted her head around, and laughed in delight.

"Laud!" she cried, clasping him in a hug.

"Do I have to insult you to get a mention?" Benedicta asked, warmly. Lily turned her head, her smile broadening.

"Ben! I can't believe it . . . how did you find me? I thought I knew everything here, but . . . how?"

"Well, we had a little help," Mark replied, spotting Verso appearing in the cave entrance. But before he could point out the old man, Lily reached out an arm, and grabbed Mark in a tearful embrace.

"I thought . . . this would be it . . . the rest of my life with nothing but the dark, and the whispers and . . . oh . . ." Lily hugged all three of them so tightly Mark thought his back would break.

"It's a miracle; it's . . ."

147

She stopped. Mark looked up, smiling. But Lily's cheer had vanished. She was staring at the entrance to the cavern, with a look of wary hostility.

"What's *he* doing here?" she asked.

All eyes turned to Verso, standing quietly at the base of the stairs.

"He led us here," Ben said, clearly puzzled. "Without him, we'd never have found our way . . ." Ben trailed off, clearly alarmed by Lily's expression. "What is it, Lily? Do you know him?"

Slowly, Lily nodded.

"Mark, Laud, Ben," she said, quietly. "I'd like to introduce you to the ruler of Agora."

Quietly, as though shedding an old skin, Verso seemed to change. He straightened, his limbs ceased to tremble, his whole attitude altered. Authority settled on him like a cloak. When he spoke again, his voice was clear, and utterly calm.

"How pleasant to meet you again, Miss Lilith," said the Director of Receipts.

CHAPTER TWELVE

Revelations

LILY STARED at the Director. He had changed since she had last seen him, sitting behind the mahogany desk at the center of the Directory. His skin was a little paler, his wrinkles more entrenched. But even in the scuffed boots and patched jacket of a servant, there was no mistaking that face.

"Though, I fear you are a little out of date," the Director continued, walking into the cave with an easy tread. "I have been deposed in your absence. Mr. Snutworth now holds my office, and much good may it do him. But yes, when we last met, I was the Director. I must admit, I had not expected that our next encounter would be in the mausoleum, although it is somewhat appropriate."

Beside her, Mark and Ben stood silent, their faces plastered with almost comical looks of disbelief. Laud, on the other hand, did not take long to recover. He tensed in Lily's arms, and pulled himself free.

"We trusted you . . ." he said, his voice low and dangerous.

"I don't believe, Mr. Laudate, that I ever betrayed that trust," the Director said, with infuriating calm. "You asked me to lead you to Naru, and to find Miss Lily. I achieved this objective with a minimum of fuss."

"Don't give me that!" Laud shouted. The cavern rang with his voice, and Lily heard another whirl of whispers, fluttering like frightened bats. "Do you expect us to believe for one second that you led us down here just to be helpful?"

The Director shook his head.

"Not at all. That was my primary reason for not revealing my identity. I suspected that if I had, none of you would be disposed to accept my aid. And I did not want to make this journey alone." He rubbed his wrists, thoughtfully. "It is, perhaps, a journey that I have waited too long to undertake."

Lily put a hand on Laud's shoulder, to stop whatever cutting remark he was planning.

"He did bring us back together, Laud," Lily said, quietly. To her surprise, Laud relented, and relaxed a little, though he still gave the Director a filthy look.

"But . . ." Mark spluttered, finding his voice again, "Cherubina said you were dead! And what about the page that Verity took from the Directory? The one that led us to the Sozinhos? Did they know all this too? What . . . what . . . ?"

"Such eloquence," the Director said, with a slight smile. "I'm disappointed, Mr. Mark, particularly after you came so close to the truth as we journeyed here. You certainly knew that I was no old servant, but you lacked the imagination to wonder who else might know such secrets."

Mark scowled.

"I suppose I expected the Director to be a bit more impressive," he replied, sourly.

Something in this seemed to wound the old man.

"Perhaps you are right, boy." He wandered over to the brass plaque near the entrance, the only one that had no name engraved upon it. "But then, I held that position for twenty years, and despite some legends to the contrary, I am entirely human. All greatness must end. And where better than here, in the mausoleum?"

Lily stared at him. His power seemed to be ebbing from him with every moment. Almost unconsciously, she remembered the plaque next to the blank one. Carved with a single name, and dates. *Procuria, AY 56–124.* But it was the second date that was fixed in her mind—Agoran Year 124. Twenty years ago.

"Who was Procuria, Director?"

The Director smiled, sadly.

"My predecessor. Director before me, and a musician. In fact, I believe that you are sitting at her armonium. It must have taken a great deal of effort to bring that down here, but she always was a very stubborn woman. I suppose she never wanted it to leave her side."

Lily nodded, understanding. But Mark was still fuming.

"So what was this journey really about?" he muttered. "Why did you need us to bring you here?"

"Mark," Lily said, quietly. "I think this is where all the past directors are buried."

The Director nodded.

"Quite correct, Miss Lilith. This journey, Mr. Mark, is my very last."

Mark seemed chastened by the Director's words, but still looked at him with distrust. It was only then, in the silence, that something the Director had said really penetrated Lily's brain.

"Snutworth is the Director?" Lily said, amazed. "Your old servant, Mark?"

Mark nodded.

"It's a long story, and it looks like we didn't know the half of it."

He cast a significant glance at the former Director. The old man smiled, faintly.

"Yes, indeed, I should have been interred here months ago," he said, lightly touching the brass plaque. "Snutworth's plan was not only cunning, it was very nearly successful. He left me in a most dreadful state." The Director held up his hand, and smoothly pulled off one of his gloves. In the pale light, Lily gasped. The scarring across his wrists was thick and painful, she could still see the edges of crude stitches. The Director winced. "But I have lived a long time, and I was not to be defeated. I lasted long enough for Miss Verity to find me." He pulled the glove on again, smiling fondly. "Dear Rita. It was fortunate indeed that she had not gone to her chambers, but was preparing to meet Mr. Mark's father, and needed to creep past my office to use the secret tunnels." He rested his hand against the plaque. "She found me just in time, I believe, and sensibly did not raise the alarm. Doubtless Snutworth would have ensured that only guards loyal to him were stationed in the Directory that day . . ." he frowned. "You will understand that I know little of what happened next. I was very weak. But I was able to direct her to my instructions. I had . . . prepared for an event such as this."

"You thought Snutworth was going to attack you?" Mark asked. The Director shook his head.

"Not him, specifically, although looking back I should have realized that he would be the only one with the intelligence to manage it. But I knew that powerful men rarely die of natural causes. I knew that one day, I might have to fake my own demise, to disappear so perfectly that even the Directory, with all its resources, could not find me. To do that, I would not merely have to hide. I would need to become a different person."

Slowly, he reached into his pocket and pulled out a small,

drawstring bag. From it, he tipped out what looked like a few small, colorful, boiled candies.

"Miss Verity followed my written instructions to the letter. She took me to a doctor, without saying who I was, to heal my wounds. She provided me with a false name and signet ring. And then, she took me to the memory extractor, and left me there, so she would never be able to say where I had gone. I knew that if Snutworth found me, he could extract the last of my secrets this way, and I chose to lose myself on my own terms." He sighed. "My whole self was stripped away by the extractor, each pearl of memory disguised in a truly harmless form."

"The candies . . ." Mark breathed. The Director nodded.

"I would have taken them all before our journey, but there were some memories I did not dare recall until we were safely out of Agora. Even now, there are a few last details that I have kept from myself." He tipped the candies back into the bag. "My memory extraction technician was truly an expert. He even labeled the candies in a cipher, and told me the code when I awoke, so I would know which to take first." The Director rolled the candies around in the palm of his hand, looking a little wistful. "I must admit, it was a relief to be Verso for a time. To lead a simple life. Having my years as Director settle back upon me was an . . . unpleasant experience. There were many days I would prefer to forget." He shook his head. "After the process was complete, the technician promised to even remove his own memory of my presence, and crush it beneath his heel. I was left believing myself to be an old servant, confused by advancing years. Not a single soul in Agora knew Verso to be anyone special. My only clues were this sealed bag of 'candies,' and a note, in my own handwriting, warning me that I had a greater purpose, and that this bag was not to be opened until I received the sign to become myself again." He paused for a moment. "Fortunately, I had also been kind enough to write myself a good reference for the Sozinhos. After all, I needed a place to work."

"Why them?" Ben asked, finding her voice. The Director smiled.

"They guarded the Last's Descent. The few memories I had allowed myself to recall included all my knowledge of the Sozinhos. I knew that, one day, I would have to take the Descent myself." He frowned. "As Verso, of course, I did not fully understand the significance of these memories, but the note I had left myself was clear—I had to enter their service. It was risky, of course—they had no real reason to take me on. At first, I tried flattery, pretending to be an old librarian, fascinated by their family history. This brought me little success. But when I explained that I was pursued by a cruel former master and needed to stay away from the public eye . . ." The Director met Lily's gaze. "Fortunately for me, they are charitable people. I think I have you to thank for that. They even agreed to pretend to the world that I had been their servant for years."

"But," Mark looked even more baffled, "what about the page from the old book? The one Verity went to such trouble to get?"

The Director rubbed his chin, thoughtfully.

"Ah yes, the page. My lifeline." He pulled the page from his pocket, smoothing it out. "I had told Verity that it would show the way to me, should the need arise. I must admit, she used it rather sooner than I was expecting, but perhaps that was all for the best." He held it up to Mark. "What do you see here?"

Mark glared at it.

"It's just a recipe," he said. "You need to hold it up to the light."

The Director smiled again. "Really, Mr. Mark? Would you expect me to hide my true meaning so simply? That message led to my hiding place, but it did not alert Verso that it was time to turn back into me. I needed a message that only I would understand."

Mark looked down at the page again, and the light of understanding dawned in his face.

"It's a recipe for boiled candies," he said, softly. The Director nodded, returning the page to his pocket.

"For all his short life, Verso knew those candies were important. So when this ancient page appeared, borne by strangers . . ." He sighed. "He knew . . . that is, I knew . . . that my last reprieve was over." His sigh grew more pronounced, and he leaned against the wall for support. "But I have little time left. My health is far from ideal, and I must save my breath for my confession. Is the Oracle prepared to see me?"

His last words were addressed to the Conductor, who had appeared at the entrance to the chamber.

"She will already know that you are here," the Conductor said, solemnly. "Will your friends be joining you?"

"No," the Director replied, "this confession is for the Oracle alone." Absently, he wiped his gloved hand across the blank plaque. "The Directory and the Cathedral of the Lost are built on the same black stone we encountered in the tunnel. It silences all echoes—even the Canticle. I believe that the ruling founders did not want their thoughts overheard. But we pay a price for this privacy—all secrets must be given up eventually. Every Director ends his days before the Resonant Throne, making his final confession."

He turned to go.

"You're staying right here."

The Director turned back. Lily realized that she had spoken—the words had come out of her mouth before she could stop them. But after everything she had been through, after all the hours she had spent with the Canticle, searching for anything that could help her, she wasn't going to let the most knowledgeable man she had ever met walk away.

"And why, might I ask?" replied the Director. "I am quite certain that you could stop me leaving, if you wished. But I fail to see what that would accomplish . . ."

155

"Stop!" Lily shouted. "Stop treating everything like a game!" She approached the old man. A shiver passed through her, and behind her she heard the Canticle begin to buzz. "I trusted you," she said, her fury building. "Mark and I went out into Giseth because I believed you when you told me we were Judges, that we were important. Since then, I've been at death's door, had a village full of friends turn into murderous maniacs, fought off a creature that fed on all my worst nightmares, watched my father die in front of me, and been forced to live in this maddening hole. And do you know why? Because I wanted some answers! I wanted the end of the story you could have told me in the first place! So you owe me something, Director. You owe me the truth."

Lily found that her breath was coming out in gasps. The old man looked at her, with an odd kind of respect.

"Really, Miss Lilith, I am not as useful as you think," he said, utterly calm. "The Oracle will tell you everything you need to know." He smiled. "Once you have given her back her name, of course."

For one long moment, Lily seriously considered punching him in the face.

"I don't *know* her name," she snarled.

The Director smiled. Then he held up something, between the tips of his fingers. A tiny memory pearl, the last of its sugary coating falling away.

"No, Lily. But I did."

The Director had been in the Oracle's throne room for nearly an hour now, but Lily had barely noticed the time go by. As soon as he had left them at the entrance, drawing the velvet curtain behind him, all of her joy at seeing her friends again had flooded back, replacing the sudden and surprising rage. Since that moment, they hadn't stopped talking.

Some of the stories she found hard to believe—picturing Cherubina as a revolutionary figurehead took some effort. Some were all too easy. Sadly, she did not find it difficult to see Snutworth becoming the Director. She had met him only a couple of times, but that had been enough. He was everything about Agora that she had hated. It was all too likely that he would achieve anything he desired.

It was overwhelming to hear Ben's excitable tones again, to argue with Mark over where he had embellished his stories of their time together, and to hear Laud's remarks, so sharp but tender. She barely paid attention to what they said, just listening to their voices was enough to enchant her.

They had made her tell them her own stories, of course. But she found that she was barely able to get them straight. She had heard so many secrets in the Canticle, lived so many lives, that her own story seemed small in comparison. When she came to the death of her father, though, she found that the memory was so real and sudden, so unlike the whispers, that fresh tears sprang to her eyes. The three of them hugged her again, and she felt safe in their embrace, as though she was waking up at last from a very bad night.

"How long . . . how long has it been?" she asked, at length. "It's hard to keep track of days, down here."

"A couple of months since we last saw each other, I think . . ." Mark said, shaking his head, "but . . ."

"Longer for us," Laud said, intensely. "So much longer."

Lily looked at Laud. She realized that he had been staring at her ever since they had first arrived. Even during her argument with the Director, his eyes had barely strayed. She dropped her head self-consciously.

"No need to stare, Laud. I'm not going anywhere."

Laud hastily turned his gaze away.

"I'm sorry, it's just . . ." he broke off. "That is . . . I—we—I always knew that you'd be back, Lily. I want you to know that. You said you would. I knew you'd come back . . ."

Lily took his hand, confused. Laud seemed to be struggling with something, but as he opened his mouth to try again, a voice cut across them all.

"It is done."

The voice sounded tired, and old, and relieved. It came from behind the curtain, and as they turned to face it, Lily saw a withered hand draw the curtain aside. The figure that emerged was almost unrecognizable. He was a little like the Director, but the Director with all of his pride and strength drained away. He hunched and wheezed, and looked at them through watery eyes.

"Well, that was certainly a powerful experience," he said, laughing weakly. "When the Oracle takes your confession, you leave nothing out. I had not expected the resonance in the chamber to be so overwhelming."

Benedicta rushed forward to offer the old man her arm. He pushed her away, lightly but firmly.

"I neither deserve, nor want your help, Miss Benedicta. Reserve that noble soul for those who are more worthy." He looked up at Laud, who looked surprisingly angry at the Director's return. "And there is no need to curse me, Mr. Laudate. I am no one, now. Save your energies; there will be plenty of time to use them." He turned to Mark. "Guide her well, Protagonist. There is no true Director now, and the Day of Judgment is nearly upon you." He laughed, feebly. "Of course, that might all be nonsense. You know, I'm really not sure anymore. The approach of the end will do that to all our certainties."

"What are you going to do now?" Mark asked, with a cautious tone. The Director sighed.

"I shall find the Conductor. He will know the proper arrangements. The funeral of a Director is a quiet affair. I shall not expect any of you to attend." He pulled himself up straight, regaining his dignity. "Now, there is one last promise to fulfill."

The Director came close to Lily, steadying himself on her shoulder. Then, with careful deliberation, he slipped the last memory pearl into his mouth. He hesitated for a moment.

"Miss Lily," he said, "it is not far from here to a path back to Agora. You could take it; return home without asking any more questions. You already know so much, and I can promise you this— the truth will not make you happy."

Lily took hold of his hand. Deep inside her, the whispers rose up again.

"I have to know," she said, meaning it with every fiber of her being.

The Director sighed.

"Then I am sorry, Miss Lilith. I hope you will forgive me."

He leaned close and whispered something into her ear.

The world stopped.

The Director pulled back his head, and looked her in the eyes. Lily stared back at him, speechless.

"It is the truth," he said. "Go, and tell her."

Lily walked forward, in a daze. Behind her, she heard the old man shuffling away, back down to the mausoleum. She felt Laud take one arm, and Mark, the other. She saw Ben in front of her, asking her what the Director had said, with mounting concern. But it was as if all of them were miles away. It was like she was back inside the Canticle—all she could hear was the truth, resounding inside her own head. She broke free from their grasp, pushed aside the curtain, and walked into the Oracle's chamber as though she were the only person in the world.

Every part of her seemed to have shut down—her mind, her voice, her senses. Mark, Laud, and Ben buzzed around her, exclaiming about the Oracle's cavern. She dimly felt their awe as they edged out onto the stone walkway over the spines of rock, and gazed up at the vast crystal suspended over the Resonant Throne. She watched her friends collapse to their knees from the vibrations, but somehow the resonance couldn't touch her now.

And then, she stood before the throne. And the Oracle looked down at her from behind her crystal mask, as impassive as ever.

"I have brought you Truth, Oracle," Lily said, her voice thick and heavy. "I have brought your name."

Lily's words echoed far louder than they should have done. Her friends struggled to their feet, hands clasped over their ears, as the words grew into a sound like the blast of trumpets.

The Oracle leaned forward, her face only a few feet from Lily's own. Her gloved hands gripped the arms of the throne.

"Tell me," the Oracle said, her voice bearing an unmistakable note of tension.

Lily stared at that masked face, and finally let herself form the words that the Director had whispered.

"Your name is Helen d'Annain," Lily said. "And you are my mother."

There was dead silence. Behind her, Lily heard Mark and Ben saying something to each other, amazed. Laud took her arm. And she wanted to look at him; she was sure that his face would have been full of sympathy. But she could not move. She could do nothing but stare at the woman on the throne, looking for any reaction at all.

Around her, Lily felt a vibration in the air, a faint rumble from the cavern, as though a shower of distant whispers had been set all a flurry. But the Oracle's body did not show this; the crystal mask did not move. When her voice emerged again, it was steady, and devoid of emotion.

"Yes, that is true," she said.

Lily's eyes grew hot. She wanted to cling to the Oracle, or to strike her—to beg for love or to curse her for not even remembering that she had a daughter. But when she opened her mouth, her voice was still and cold.

"My father said you were dead," she said, dully. "Why did he lie?"

The Oracle's reply came readily enough.

"He did not lie, Lily. Listen."

From around the cavern, the voices of the Canticle began to increase. Then, out of it all, another voice emerged, clearer than the others, but still distant—an echo from far away. Lily recognized that voice. It was her own—reading aloud the letter her father had left for her as he lay dying:

Your mother would probably have approved. But I buried her long ago.

Lily almost laughed, but the sound caught in her throat, strangled.

"So, that's what he meant," she said. "He really meant 'buried.' He put you in the earth."

"Helen d'Annain became the Oracle soon after your birth," the Oracle intoned, speaking her own name as if it were a distant relation. "Her husband objected, but she wished to go. It was a great honor. But her memories were taken from her. All Oracles must live without a self. For self brings only emotion and disharmony, and destroys the balance of the Resonant Throne."

Lily turned away from the Oracle, sickened.

"Lily . . ." Laud said, softly, but Lily wasn't in the mood to listen. She looked back at the Oracle. Outwardly, she gave nothing away. But inside, she felt the whispers of the Canticle growing louder.

"You remember nothing about me?" Lily asked, feeling a pain in her chest.

The Oracle hesitated. Again, the room seemed to shake slightly, the light in the crystal spire above pulsed and strained, as though agitated. This chamber really was attuned to the Oracle's mind. The echoes responded to the slightest disturbance.

"I remember all things," the Oracle replied. "Facts from a hundred thousand lives. I know every one of them."

"But you don't feel them, do you?" Lily retorted, almost willing there to be another disturbance, another wave of vibrations in the air. Anything to show that this woman who claimed to be her mother was feeling something.

"I cannot. All truth is equal in my sight," the Oracle said, a tiny tremor in her voice. Lily felt the pain spread through her—a terrible, gnawing ache.

"What's the use of a million lives if you can't live even one?" she asked, louder. This time, the vibrations hit her in the stomach, and she and her friends fell to the floor, the whole room shaking. One of the stalactites in the roof cracked, and fell into the chasm yards away from the walkway, splintering with a thunderous crash as it hit the floor far below.

Mark crawled over to Lily, winded from his fall.

"Lily," he said, gently. "I understand. I really do. This must be terrible for you, but . . . if the Oracle really can answer our questions, shouldn't we ask them first? You've found her now, and she's alive, and well. You can make her remember, in time . . ."

Lily sighed, looking up into Mark's trusting gray eyes. The pain within her subsided a little.

"You're right," she said. "I came here for a reason."

Mark helped her up. Laud smiled reassuringly. Only Benedicta still looked troubled as she got to her feet.

"Lily, are you sure?" she asked. "It's been a big shock for you. The Oracle isn't going anywhere . . ."

"She's been looking for answers for so long, Ben," Mark reproached. "We all have. I wouldn't mind asking a couple of questions myself."

"But don't you think you've just found an answer, a big one?" Ben said, awkwardly. "Maybe if we get used to this first . . ."

"It's all right, Ben," Lily said, quietly. "I want to know. I *have* to know."

Ben frowned, still looking unconvinced. Lily turned back to the Oracle.

"Ask," the Oracle said, with the patience of the ages.

Lily cleared her mind, looking for the right question to ask. In the midst of all her confusion and pain, a spark of excitement stirred. This was it. It didn't matter that this *thing* had once been her mother. She was going to get the truth. The truth was what really mattered. That was what had always mattered.

She smiled at her friends, but they didn't look entirely reassured. Perhaps her smile was a little too wide. She realized she was breathing in quick bursts. But she couldn't let herself think about that now. All of the secrets of the world were laid out before her. What should she ask?

And then, in an instant, she knew.

"What is in the Midnight Charter?"

The Oracle cleared her throat.

"The Midnight Charter," she began, as though reciting from the document itself. "Text begins: It is hereby agreed that the knowledge contained herein will be the sole property of the Libran Society, and that until the time when the Antagonist shall arise, and begin the conclusion of the experiment, all those involved will refuse to acknowledge these secrets, and work only to ensure the survival of Agora and Giseth, and to preserve the structure. Be it also laid down, that those charged with watching over the Antagonist and the Protagonist must, with full support of the Society, keep all knowledge from them until the Day of Judgment.

Any major breach in these measures will render the project null and void, and will lead to dissolution of both, as stated below.

"Furthermore, it must be made clear to all inhabitants of the first phase that every dweller in Giseth, and every citizen of Agora, has the duty to keep the existence of the outside world, and their own arrival, secret from their children. This will ensure the sanctity of the project until the Last shall fall, and then the full purpose of the Libran Society's greatest experiment will be able to progress, confident that the truth will be secure until the Day of Judgment . . ."

"Project?" Mark interrupted. "Experiment? What are you talking about? And why are we part of this? What are the Protagonist and the Antagonist supposed to *do*?"

Lily felt her desperate smile begin to freeze on her lips. Something about this was wrong, very wrong. She remembered Pauldron, the receiver who had read the Midnight Charter. She remembered his ravings, how he had believed that the whole city, the world, was unreal—nothing but a glorious dream. She remembered how her father had called them all the children of the lost, abandoned by the outside world. What was happening here? No . . . what had *happened* here?

"This experiment," Lily said. "When did it begin?"

When the Oracle replied, she seemed almost satisfied.

"Nearly 144 years ago. Twelve grand cycles of twelve years . . ."

As she spoke, her voice seemed to be joined by another. A ghostly echo of a man's voice, distorted but jovial—a voice of triumph.

Twelve times twelve, my Libran brothers and sisters! Our most perfect of numbers. Enough time to build the city, to populate our new lands with our most loyal followers, and to ensure that every member of the original generation lives out their days, so that the new generations will grow knowing only our created world. Our Agora, our Giseth, the testing grounds for our greatest balance of all!

The voice faded. Suddenly, Lily was afraid. Her excitement was gone. She didn't want to know what the voice had meant. She wished that she'd listened to Ben. She wanted to leave, wanted to go home.

But somehow, she kept asking, kept pushing for more.

"This Libran Society, were they the same people as in Agora?"

The Oracle replied, her bland tone never wavering.

"No, the first Libran Society was a group in the world outside our lands. A gathering of thinkers and philosophers who saw balance in all things as the key to a perfect world. And they were rich, wealthier than even the greatest merchant in Agora. They believed that under their guidance, the world could find a perfect way of life." For a brief second, Lily thought she heard a flicker of emotion, like an ironic sigh. "One day, they were challenged to prove it. To create that perfect world."

Lily heard Mark gasp.

"Agora? It was Agora, wasn't it?" he said.

The Oracle seemed irritated by the interruption.

"Not quite, Protagonist. The true Libran Society knew that balance was everything—that even their own vision of perfection might be corrupted, and would need a counterbalance. So they founded Agora and Giseth—opposite, interdependent, in perfect balance. They populated it from the outside world, with others who believed in their vision to the point of madness, who willingly swore never to tell their children about their past, on pain of death for them, and all to whom they revealed the truth."

"The Last . . ." Mark said, slowly. "He guarded the Descent down here . . . He was the last to know, wasn't he? The last to have seen the world outside, before the experiment began."

"Yes," the Oracle replied, "the Last had seen six summers when first brought to Agora. Not quite the youngest, but the last to die. A curiosity."

Lily felt a flash of anger. To hear a man's whole life dismissed in a footnote was inhuman. She wanted to shout, and demand that the Oracle apologize. She shut her eyes, her skin prickling. She couldn't let it get to her. Deep inside her head, the whispers of the Canticle sounded like they were mocking her. The more she discovered, the more she wanted to understand. There would be time for dealing with emotions later. There had to be.

"But this place, Naru," she said, "this wasn't part of the plan, was it?"

The Oracle turned her blank, masked face to her.

"Naru is not a true land. It was created to watch the experiment for the Librans. They planned that their successors would visit every few years, to review the latest results. We still gather information, though all but I have forgotten the reason. Now, it is just our way."

Again, a voice emerged from the chorus of whispers. The same excitable man—a long-dead Libran.

The natural crystals in the empty lands we have chosen have extraordinary properties! Their resonant abilities should allow us to record all manner of facts without venturing into the lands themselves and disturbing the projects. My colleagues have even speculated that they could be made to resonate on the frequencies of thoughts, or memories . . . even pure emotions, allowing them to be drawn out of a body and kept in solution! . . . I feel that calling my ideas preposterous is not entirely fair, Sir . . .

The voice faded again. Mark was shaking his head in disbelief. Ben and Laud exchanged glances, bewildered. Outwardly, Lily knew that she looked calm. But that was only because her hands were clenched so tight her nails were pressing into her palms. The arrogance of those ancient Librans! To turn a whole country of people into the Naruvians—to warp their lives so far that they never touched, never felt—never knew anything more than broken, fragmented facts. Just to keep their precious experiment pure.

No, she couldn't think like that. She couldn't think about how everything she had known, every person, and sight, and experience in her life had been planned as part of a grand social experiment. So many lives, bent and warped to fit their scheme. To create their "perfect" world.

"So what went wrong?" Lily said. Her tone was mocking now. It barely sounded like her own voice at all.

This time, the sound of the echoes flared up once again, as though the Oracle's mind were in torment. But when she answered, it was in the same, flat, reasonable tone as ever.

"The messages stopped coming. The Society said that something had happened in the outside world, but that the project should continue. That they would contact us again when they could. Then nothing, until one ship arrived at the cliffs beneath the Cathedral in Giseth. A ship with red sails, loaded with gold and silver coins. But the crew were nowhere to be seen. Only one man remained alive onboard, and before he died, he babbled that a disaster had befallen the outside world. Maybe he was right. Or perhaps the Librans simply abandoned us. Whatever the truth, from that day to this, we have heard nothing. The monks took the coins, which they had no use for, and bound them into the walls of the great Libran Cathedral of Truth. And it was renamed the Cathedral of the Lost, for that is what we are, now. Lost forever."

Lily wondered whether she should have felt sad, or even horrified. But instead, a great flood of relief washed over her. A crumb of comfort, at last.

"So, the experiment is over," she said.

"No, Antagonist, the experiment continues. You have seen to that."

Lily stared. She couldn't even speak anymore.

"What do you mean?" Laud asked, angrily, in her place.

"They knew that at the end, after 144 years, they would need some means of judging the success of their experiment," the Oracle replied. "They knew that the people within their experimental societies would have formed different opinions. All they needed were two—one of whom bore the Agoran mindset, and one the Gisethi. One who thrived in their perfect city, where every trade was balanced and fair, and one who fought against it, and exposed any flaws. The Protagonist and Antagonist—to be chosen toward the end of days—would sweep through Agora and Giseth, and purge them of their imperfections. Each would play their role. Together they would travel the lands. Together they would see everything. And together, they would cause chaos and conflict, as impurities were removed. And then they would judge the project's success, and find the perfect balance."

At the base of Lily's spine, the strange shiver started up again. All her plans, and thoughts, and beliefs . . . it was all part of the grand plan.

Mark swayed beside her, his face drained of color.

"You're saying that our lives . . . our parents' lives . . . everything was for this? Everything was to *prove* a *point*?!" He shouted the last words, furious. The chamber rang, and a billion shouts returned from the walls, making them all stagger. Lily wanted to shout too, to blaze with fury. But she felt cold. The shudder spread through her. Her knees buckled.

"No . . ." she muttered, disbelieving. "It's not true. I wasn't at home in Giseth, not really . . ."

"But you were," the Oracle continued, with passionless determination. "You saw faults, and you burned them away. For that is what you will always do, Antagonist. Already, revolution is brewing. Agora is splitting into factions. Giseth is ravaged by doubt, and rage, and violence. Already the experiment is coming to its conclusion. Your chaos is a refining fire. And none escape its flame."

Lily couldn't move. She could barely breathe. In her head, the whispers were back, stronger than ever, the Canticle within her echoing the one in the chamber. And every voice was saying the same thing—that the Oracle was right. Everywhere she'd gone, she had brought chaos. Her Almshouse movement was breeding revolution and violence in Agora every day. She'd gone to the peaceful village of Aecer, and thanks to her the villagers had torn their leader limb from limb. Even the Nightmare, that dreamscape of hidden feelings, had turned hellish every time she had ventured there. Never once, in her struggling, fighting, messy excuse for a life had she done anything that hadn't left its scars all around her. And still she'd forged on, her way lit with self-righteous anger. Telling herself that she was doing good.

"Lily . . . are you all right?"

Laud was talking to her, but she couldn't focus. She was sweating now, her unwanted thoughts coming thick and fast. All her life, she had been a rebel. That had been her identity. That had been more important to her than the family she didn't have, than the friends she kept losing. She'd been ready to die for her cause. Ready to do anything. But she hadn't died. Others had bled and died for her. She wasn't a leader. She wasn't a savior. And now, according to the Oracle, she wasn't even original. She was nothing at all.

"No, I won't accept this!" Mark was shouting at the Oracle. "I've been my own man, I tell you."

That . . . that was it.

Lily laughed, suddenly. High and pained. All the whispers stopped, as though holding their breath. It was a lie. All of it. It had to be. There was nothing wrong. Nothing at all. It was all . . . so clear . . .

"Mark . . ." that was Laud's voice, warning. "I think something's wrong with Lily. Lily? Can you hear me? Lily?"

But Lily pushed Laud away. She couldn't look at him now. What face could she show him?

"It's all right," she said, quietly. "It's all a trick, isn't it? The Oracle's lying. The Director lied. It's all lies . . ."

She kept repeating it, over and over, walking closer to the Oracle, staring at that blank crystal face. This wasn't her mother. That wasn't the truth she had searched so long to find. She couldn't be the daughter of a soulless machine. She couldn't have spread chaos and pain to fulfill the plans of long-dead overlords. That was what she was telling the whispers—the pain-fueled echoes in her head. They had no power over her anymore.

Because she understood them now. In her sudden clarity, she saw the truth of the Canticle. She could feel the brooding, desperate weight of the Nightmare, hiding inside it. She laughed again, a choking sound that hurt her throat. She knew the Nightmare's ways from her time in Giseth—knew how it lived in the spaces between thoughts, feeding on dark emotions. But down here, in a land where no one truly cared about anything, it had been starving. All it had needed was one head to hide within. One heart that felt true emotions. It had been crafty, luring her into the Canticle with promises of knowledge. It had nearly taken her. But now she was free.

"Lily?" Ben said, grabbing her wrist. "What are you doing?"

Lily shook off her friend. There was no time for distractions now. Her mind was clear, and clean, and focused. She had beaten the Nightmare. She would drive it, and all its lies, out of her head, out of the Canticle. And she would be left with the Truth. That shining, wonderful Truth that would give sense to her life. The Truth would never harm her. Never leave her alone, with only her fears and emptiness.

"Lily?" Laud asked. "Lily, what are you doing?"

"I'm ending the lies," she said.

In one frantic movement, Lily reached up, pulled the mask from the Oracle's face, and flung it to the ground. It broke, scattering the crystals onto the rocky floor, bouncing to oblivion. Lily stared.

The Oracle's face wasn't so like hers as Verity's had been—though the skin was dark, Lily had obviously inherited her looks from her father's side of the family. But there was something in it—the set of the chin, the shape of the nose—that made it unmistakable. Only the eyes were different. Not a different color; they were that same dark mirror that Lily's were. But while Lily's pierced, the Oracle's were depthless pools. Drawing in, but giving nothing out at all. There was no feeling in those eyes. Nothing at all but cold, terrible knowledge.

"Every word is true, my daughter," she said.

In the distance, Lily heard someone shouting and screaming at the top of their lungs. It sounded a little like her. No, it *was* her.

The Canticle's whispers filled her mind. Her mother was a monster. A monster just like her. Hide, children, because the Antagonist will come, with her fiery eyes, and burn down your world.

She was running now, wasn't she? Maybe. Had she fallen over? Had someone caught hold of her arms?

Every moment of her life predicted. All that suffering and pain around her, calculated and worked into a theory. And she'd played her part. She'd given those around her false hope, even as she led them to their deaths.

She shook herself free. Someone crashed to the floor.

They had been abandoned. The Librans had left them here. A mad experiment, without a watcher.

She was still shouting and screaming, without words. There was a terrible grinding, cracking sound.

They were nothing; she was nothing. There was no meaning to any of it. Just suffering, and pain, and fear, and . . .

She was running. She tasted something hot and metallic in her mouth. Someone else was screaming now.

They were nothing, and . . .

Still running. Still shouting.

Nothing at all, and . . .

Her mind was fuzzy, so quiet.

Nothing, and, and . . .

Just keep running. Keep running.

And then . . .

And then . . .

CHAPTER THIRTEEN

Cracks

LAUD OPENED his eyes.

He was lying on the ground. He raised his head and shook it, trying to clear the fuzz. He must have blacked out for a moment. There was a ringing, rumbling sound in his ears.

"Don't be an idiot, Mark! Wait for the shaking to stop!"

"But I have to go after her . . ."

Laud's vision came into focus. The stone walkway beneath him was rolling like water.

He staggered to his feet. The two voices he had heard resolved themselves into Mark and Ben. His sister had a firm grip on Mark's arm, but just as Laud tried to speak, there was another tremor, another burst of echoing noise, and the two of them fell to the ground once again. Behind them, Laud saw the Oracle, sitting back on her throne, her eyes and mouth tight shut, a roar of sound all around her.

Where was Lily?

In a flash, Laud's brain cleared. He remembered Lily's scream, still echoing. He remembered how she had run from the throne room, fighting off all who would stop her with manic strength.

And he remembered her eyes. He really wished that he didn't. What the Oracle had told them was dreadful, horrific. He had barely taken it in himself. But it had affected Lily a hundred times worse. She hadn't looked like the girl he had known. Her eyes had been as dead as those of the Oracle.

He glanced at Ben. The tremors seemed to be dying down, and Mark was with her. She was safe, for now. Without another thought, he ran, following Lily.

The tremors didn't stop as he pushed past the curtain and out into the tunnels. Alarming cracks ran up the walls, and some of the glowing crystals lay on the floor. As he vaulted up the stone steps, he saw something glinting on the ground. It was the tiny brass set of scales that had been in Lily's apron pocket. She had shown them to him less than an hour ago. She had definitely come this way.

At the top of the steps, the Conductor was waiting, nervous sweat pouring down his face.

"Sir? What happened?" he stammered. "I was coming to pay my respects, and the earth shifted with pain. And then Miss Lily appeared and—"

"Where is she?" Laud demanded, grasping the Conductor's sleeve. "Where did she go?"

The Conductor blanched, pulling back from Laud's touch as though it burned him.

"The Rail Nexus," he gasped. "But don't follow, sir. When the rock shakes like this, the Oracle is in distress—the smaller tunnels aren't safe . . ."

But Laud was already running.

A few minutes later, a cart holding three people flew along the rails, sparking with every turn. At the front, two Naruvians stood, operating the cart, their long white hair blowing behind them. The man had given his name as Tertius, and seemed nervous. But the young woman, Septima, was laughing as though the whole thing was a wonderful game. Behind them, Laud crouched, his pack of supplies thumping against his back with each jarring turn.

For the fiftieth time, Laud cursed that he hadn't been a little faster. He had actually seen Lily's cart disappearing down the rails, away from the Hub chamber. But by the time Laud had managed to get any of the Naruvians to help, Lily had long since vanished into the echoing depths. He hoped that Mark and Ben were following behind, but he couldn't worry about that. At the speed these carts traveled, Lily could be miles away by now.

"We're nearly at the Rail Nexus!" Tertius shouted back. The cart swerved, Septima whooped, and the tunnel opened wide. They screeched into a vast cavern, filled with a mass of clicking, whirring machinery. Laud leaped from the cart before it had stopped moving, stumbling across the rocky floor, and grabbed a terrified Naruvian engineer by the front of his robe.

"Have you seen a girl come through here?" he asked. "Dark, scared, possibly screaming?" The engineer nodded, recoiling from Laud's grasp, and pointed to one of the side tunnels, where another set of rails disappeared into darkness.

"She . . . she took a cart . . . please . . . let me go . . ."

Laud dropped the terrified engineer. As he did so, Tertius scurried past him, to prepare another cart for their onward journey.

"What *fun*!" Septima said, adjusting a couple of dials on the central machine. "We're off hunting!" Laud scowled at her, but she was already finished, and climbing into the cart behind Tertius. As Laud hurried to join her, the ground gave another lurch, dropping him to his knees. In the distance, he heard a deep, grinding rumble. And something else—something that sounded like an echo of the Oracle's voice.

You will not leave me . . . you will not leave, my daughter . . .

"Lily . . ." Laud said, scrabbling back to his feet. He had to keep moving. These tunnels weren't safe. If he could just bring her back to the Hub, he'd be able to calm her down. She'd listen to him, to her friends. She just needed to stop running.

He piled into the cart, and Tertius threw the brake handle. They powered forward, the clockwork monstrosity setting them flying down the rails toward the new tunnel.

The Oracle's voice was louder now; there was an edge of pain to it.

Stay . . . stay . . . stay forever . . .

With each word, the tremors increased, and the grinding noise overhead grew worse. Laud looked up. Cracks were running all through the cavern roof. The rock bulged.

"Faster!" he yelled. Septima reached forward and pulled another lever.

The cart streaked forward.

The tunnel swallowed them up.

And the world fell down around them.

Laud pulled himself from the wreckage of the cart and stood on shaking legs. He was bruised all over, but nothing seemed to be broken. He coughed, wiping dust from his eyes. In the dim crystal light, he could see that the tunnel had collapsed both ahead and behind them, sealing them in. Tertius had been thrown free, and was already clawing at the mass of rubble that blocked their way back to the Rail Nexus. He looked shaken, and his robes were torn, but he was unharmed. Septima hadn't been so lucky. She sat against the wreckage of the cart, a long, deep cut down her leg, glistening with blood. But she was still smiling, though her eyes were damp.

"You . . . you certainly know how to take us for a ride!" she said, brightly, through the pain.

Hastily, Laud bent to examine her leg, but she drew it back.

"It's all right," Laud said, quickly. "I've worked with a doctor." Septima stared back at him.

"No touching," she said, fiercely. "What are you, a monster?"

Laud sighed with frustration. Was everyone down here insane?

He untucked his shirt. It wasn't exactly clean, but it was better than his other clothes, covered in dust from the cave-in. It was an old shirt, and already a little ragged. He tore off a strip from the tail, and dangled it in front of her.

"At least keep it covered," he said. Septima looked at the rag suspiciously, and then grabbed its trailing end.

As she dabbed at the wound, Laud stared down at the cart. Its mechanism had been crushed. If any of them had been standing a few feet farther back . . . His morbid thoughts were interrupted by the sound of another ominous rumble. He spun around. Tertius was pulling small stones out of the rubble. As Laud watched, a larger rock began to tremble and slide out, just above the young Naruvian's head.

"Get away from that!" Laud shouted. "You'll bring the whole thing down."

Tertius pulled back, just as the rock crashed to the ground. For a second, the whole tunnel shook again, and Laud flung himself to the ground . . .

Then, nothing. The ceiling stayed up. Laud straightened, his heart pounding. There was now a little gap in the rubble, where the rock had moved. Light was shining through it. Moving carefully, ready to throw himself under the remains of the cart in an instant, Laud crept up to the gap, and peered through it, back into the Rail Nexus.

He wished he hadn't. The cavern was a mass of mangled clockwork. Part of the ceiling had collapsed onto the central mechanism, and gears, chains, and rails lay buckled and broken everywhere. Every tunnel was blocked, every exit sealed. Here and there, Laud could see a few shapes lying amid the wreckage. Shapes he didn't want to inspect too closely. Near them were tatters of multicolored cloth.

He rested his forehead against the stone, his head swimming. These tunnels had looked so solid. But when Lily had argued with the Oracle, something had happened. It was as though the tremors in the air had drawn strength from their distress. He remembered those echoes, which sounded like the Oracle, crying out for her daughter. But that couldn't be it. The Oracle wouldn't have let her own people die, just to stop Lily escaping. Would she?

He looked again into the Nexus, his thoughts seeming to whisper back at him from the echoing rocks. What if Mark and Ben had been following him? What if they'd been caught in the cave-in? What if Lily hadn't gotten far enough ahead? What if he, and these two, were the only ones left . . . ?

He straightened up with a grunt, the whispers fading. There was no point in thinking like that. Not now. Ben and Mark were resourceful—if they were alive, they'd find a way out of this.

He turned his attention to the other end of the corridor. It was pointless trying to get back into the Nexus; it could take days to clear the path back to the Hub. But the rubble at this end didn't look too bad. The cavern roof appeared stable, and if he just moved a few of the rocks, maybe he could make a gap large enough to squeeze through.

"Can you help me move this?" he asked, looking over at Tertius.

But the young man didn't seem to hear him. He was sitting on the ground, his whole body curled up, and his head resting against the wall. His long hair covered his face, and he seemed to be moaning.

"I know this is difficult," Laud said, gruffly. "But if we work at this, we'll be out of here in no time. Then we can get help." He gestured to Septima. "Your friend is hurt. Doesn't that mean anything to you?"

Tertius didn't move. Laud frowned, but didn't waste any more breath on the man. He took off his jacket and began to tease the rocks out of position, his fingers scraping on the rough stone.

"You're still trying to follow her?" Septima said, suddenly.

Laud kept working.

"I'm trying to get us out of here," he said, grunting with the effort. "We need someone to bind your wounds properly. You must have someone you'll allow near it."

"We have the Guardians for that," Septima said, her voice breaking with pain. "They deal with . . . touching . . . urgh . . ." she make a revolted noise. "Maybe this isn't so bad . . . I've never been in pain before. It's . . . kind of . . . exciting . . ."

Laud glanced over his shoulder. She was prodding at the cut, shuddering with each touch.

"Don't do that," he muttered. "Just . . . keep it clean. I'll bring back help, when I get out of here."

"There's no help that way," Septima said, softly. "There's just *her*. Lily. Our wonder." She yawned, seemingly forgetting about the pain in her leg. "Everyone's wonder, especially yours. We nearly died and you're still chasing after her."

Laud clenched his teeth, but continued to work at clearing the rubble.

"She's my friend," he said, defensively. "I'd go anywhere to get her back."

179

Septima laughed.

"Why? She's interesting, I suppose, but you already know everything about her. She'll just get boring, like everyone else."

Laud bit back a sarcastic response. There was no point; he doubted whether she would understand. He turned to face Septima.

"It isn't about what I already know. It's about *her*. Her mind, her spirit . . ."

"Oh *that*," Septima laughed. "That's easy. I'll be Lily for you. I'll sound just like her." She folded her arms, frowning. "I must discover the truth," she said, dramatically. "Nothing will stop me! I'll save the world . . ."

"Stop that!" Laud shouted.

His voice echoed around the tunnel. Laud realized that his fist was raised, and tightly clenched. He had nearly struck her. Septima looked surprised, but not half as shocked as Laud was himself.

"She's shattered," Septima said, suddenly serious, her laughter vanishing as quickly as it had come. "Broken. She heard too much of the truth. She won't want to be found, now. Knowing too much will do that to you." She met Laud's gaze, and held it. "Why do you think we don't take anything seriously?"

Laud turned back to his work, deeply shaken. He hadn't expected to react like that, but to hear that girl imitating Lily, mocking everything that made her special . . .

"She'll come back," he said, shifting the rubble once more, the slow work calming his nerves. "She has to. Not just for me, or Mark, or any of her friends. For Agora. We need her. The city is collapsing, rallying to the cry of a maniac who uses her words. We tried to keep her vision alive, but it's been corrupted by a hundred thousand desperate souls. There's going to be blood, and we can't stop it without her. Her heart, her strength, her purpose." Laud dropped his head. "She can't break. Not Lily."

There was a long pause.

"You're quite a friend," Septima said.

Laud refused to reply. For minutes, they were silent, with nothing but the scrape of the rocks as Laud worked them loose, making himself a gap large enough to wriggle through.

Eventually, he was done. He stuck his head through the hole. The tunnel beyond looked stable enough, and a few crystals in the walls were still glowing, enough for him to see the metal tracks continue off into the distance. This was the path Lily's cart had taken.

Laud looked back. Septima was even paler than before now, the brightness in her eyes more clearly pained. He clenched his jaw in frustration. Lily was probably still ahead, tantalizingly close if her cart had stopped working. But he couldn't leave this young woman here, with only her useless friend for company. Someone had to fetch help.

"Can I get back to the Hub this way?" Laud asked Tertius, who was still curled up, leaning against the tunnel wall. No answer. He strode over to him, shouting in his ear. "By all the stars, is there a brain under all that hair?"

"Help is already coming," Tertius replied, suddenly. "Listen."

He brushed his hair from his eyes, and stood up. Set into the wall, where he had been leaning, Laud saw a small, round gem, light dancing in its heart.

"Isn't that one of those resonant crystals?" Laud asked, surprised. "Like the one over the Oracle's head?"

"Listen . . ." Tertius said, gesturing down. Laud crouched, putting his ear against the crystal. As he did—Tertius began to hum, the same sound he'd been making before, but this time, Laud could pick out the tune.

The crystal began to buzz, sounds emerging from its depths.

. . . I don't care. If Laud and Lily are somewhere down there, behind the rock fall, we're not leaving without them . . .

That was Benedicta's voice. Laud felt his eyes prickle with tears. His little sister was alive!

The echoes are growing . . . That was the Conductor, sounding panicked. *Something is happening in the world above. In your home. The Judges must return to Agora. That is the Oracle's wish.*

We're not doing anything that madwoman says! That was Mark, shouting so loud that even the echo rattled the crystal. *I'm the only Judge here, and I say Agora can look after itself. We came all this way for Lily, and she wouldn't abandon us . . .*

But it may take days to clear the rubble, or weeks! The Oracle is calm now, and she has heard their voices. She knows that Mr. Laudate and Miss Lily are alive. But Miss Lily is still running. You will never be able to reach her . . .

Laud bit his lip. He was so much closer. But even if her cart had failed, she was getting farther away every second.

"Ben . . . Mark . . ." he said, into the crystal. "Can you hear me? I'll go after her . . . don't worry . . . I'll find her . . ."

Tertius stopped humming, and the echoes began to fade.

"They won't hear you," Tertius said, softly. "Only the Oracle will hear. But the other echoes are growing stronger. You'll be lost in the noise."

Laud glared at him.

"What other echoes? What are you talking about?"

But even as he said it, the crystal began to resonate again. New sounds were emerging from it. Shouts, screams. The roar of a crowd. They were chanting something.

The Stone . . . The Stone . . .

"I don't . . . understand . . ." Laud said, trying to hide his unease. "What *is* that?"

"The echoes from above," Tertius said, his voice shaking. "From Agora. Every voice, raised in terror, and violence. Something

has happened in the world above. In your home. Something . . .
terrible . . ."

The echoes from the crystal grew clearer.

Blood for blood . . . Death for death . . . The Wheel turns at last . . .
The Wheel . . . The Wheel . . .

Laud pulled away, aghast, but the shouts from the crystal were
loud enough to hear, even as he backed away. There were no words
anymore. Just screams, and sobs of rage and pain.

"Can't you stop it?" he shouted at Tertius. But the young man
was now cowering against the far wall.

"The world is out of joint," he whimpered.

"The Day of Judgment is coming," Septima added, her eyes
fixed, as though she was repeating something she'd heard, long
ago. "And Agora will be the first to burn. The Judges are needed.
Find her."

Laud stared at them, backing away. He wanted to go; he wanted
to find Lily, more than anything. But he couldn't. Not like this.

"I . . . no . . . I can't . . . I can't leave my friends . . . I can't go
after her on my own . . ."

"Find her!" Tertius said, suddenly, his voice joined by a hundred others, filling the air. Every crystal in the tunnel flared
with light. And above it all, he heard the sound of the Oracle
herself.

Find her! The Oracle's voice called out. *Find my daughter and*
bring her home!

Laud pressed his back up against the rubble. Tertius and Septima seemed almost entranced, their eyes glazed. They were no
longer speaking. They were wailing, their voices matching the
shouts and screams that still rang from every crystal.

Laud turned, fear and determination pushing him onward,
scrabbling through the gap he had made.

"I'm sorry Ben, Mark . . ." he whispered, as he landed on the other side. "I . . . I can't wait for you.'

And he ran into the darkness.

Hours later, Laud staggered down the tunnels.

Nowhere, nothing, nobody . . .

He was getting used to the voices by now. He remembered Lily telling him about the Cacophony, of the maddening echoes that haunted the outer caves. Back then, in that precious hour he had spent talking to her before the Director had returned from his audience with the Oracle, and everything had gone wrong, it had seemed harmless. But she had never warned him how loud it was.

We must try, Director. We cannot ignore them any longer. The people will not stand for it.

He held his lantern low. The flame was dim, but just enough to see the iron tracks, and to make sure that he didn't fall into any sudden drops. Lily had to have gone this way, along the rails. It was his only lead.

I'm not theirs! I'm not . . . I'm not . . .

The voices ebbed and flowed. Lily had said that the Cacophany was made up of sounds from the worlds above, fragments that forever echoed through the tunnels. Some voices were old and serious, some light and carefree. But all sounded lost among this sea of sound.

He was right. I should never have come. Never known, never known . . .

Sometimes, he thought he heard a voice he recognized. It was tantalizingly familiar. A distinguished voice—an older man with many cares on his shoulders.

You must consider, Director, that they are not the only ones to blame. We cannot let war break out in our streets.

Sometimes he walked; sometimes he tried to sleep. But the voices wouldn't let him rest for long. They were building, rising into a storm, reverberating off the endless stone around him until his head shook with it. Above it all, the old man's voice came again, loud and fearful.

Please listen, dear friends. We are not enemies. We are not—

There was a gasp. A shout. Cries and screams. But Laud struggled on. The air of the tunnels howled with the noise.

The stone! The stone! The stone!

Laud wanted to stop, to clasp his hands over his ears. But he couldn't, because there, ahead in the darkness, was the sound of Lily's voice. Tiny and alone, but still somehow audible in the maelstrom.

They'll never find me. They'll never come . . .

"I will, Lily," Laud whispered, so softly that he could barely hear it. "I will."

And he carried on, his own words blowing back at him, as he walked deeper into the storm.

I will . . . I will.

I fear, sir, that the mission has failed.

I will . . . I . . .

May the stars watch over us all.

PART TWO

TRUTH

CHAPTER FOURTEEN

The Stone

"MARK, did we do the right thing?"

Mark looked over at Benedicta. This was the first time she had spoken for hours. They had both been quiet over the last few days once it had become clear that no matter how much they shouted, and raged, and pleaded, they weren't going to be able to follow Lily and Laud.

They had started the weary trek back to Agora three days ago. With the Rail Nexus destroyed, the carts no longer worked, and the journey that had taken mere hours on the way there had been a long slog through the silent darkness. Once their frustration had faded, there hadn't been much to talk about. Or rather, there had been, but by mutual consent, they had chosen not to. There was no point in wasting their energy worrying, when there were more miles of tunnel ahead. Even when that "morning" they had finally reached the Descent, Ben had only flashed him a tired smile as they had climbed aboard, activated the controls, and the machine had rattled into life, to hoist them back up to Agora.

Mark sat up, rubbing his back. He had been lying on the metal platform, trying to sleep. Ben was already standing, holding on to the rails around the platform, watching the sides of the rocky well as they slipped past.

"I don't know," he admitted. "Did we really have a choice?"

They hadn't. That was what Mark kept telling himself. The tunnels had been impassable. They had stuck it out for two days, helping to clear the rubble. But although they had finally made it into the Rail Nexus, the tunnel where Tertius and Septima had been trapped was still too weak, too likely to collapse. They had been forced to slip food through the tiny hole in the rubble just to keep the young Naruvians alive. Mark had raged at the Conductor, insisting that there had to be another way; that they couldn't leave Laud and Lily in the outer caverns, all alone. And through it all, the Conductor had been begging them to return to Agora, saying that the Oracle could hear shouts and screams coming from the world above.

"You know that we'd have gone after them if we could have, no matter what the Conductor said," Mark said, trying to sound reassuring. "But we weren't doing any good down there, not anymore. And Laud *will* find her."

"I don't mean that," Ben replied. She turned to face him. In the strange, soft light, her face looked washed out, paler than she really was. She bit her lip. "I trust Laud. Once he's set his mind to something, he'll finish it. No, I mean, should we have let Lily visit the Oracle?"

Mark wanted to answer immediately, to say that of course they should. That Lily would never have delayed for a second.

Except . . .

"You think we could have made her wait?" he asked.

Benedicta sighed, leaning back against the rail at the edge of the platform.

"Maybe we should have tried," she said. "Maybe if we'd had time to talk to her, to prepare her, she wouldn't have run off, the Oracle wouldn't have gotten upset . . . those workers wouldn't have died, Mark."

Mark frowned, remembering the Conductor berating them as they surveyed the wreckage of the Rail Nexus, shouting that Lily had poisoned the Canticle, and disrupted the Oracle's control. Without the Oracle to provide order and harmony, he said, the Canticle's echoes had spiraled out of control, until their wild resonance had shaken the caverns to their core—with fatal results.

At first, Mark hadn't believed the Conductor. Surely, he thought, Lily's confrontation with the Oracle couldn't have been responsible for all this death? But as they had picked their way across the devastation, Mark had heard a sound he had hoped to never hear again. Behind the ominous rumbling that continued in the rock overhead, he could just make out a familiar mocking, eerie whisper.

He should have recognized the Nightmare in the Oracle's throne room, where its dark suggestions had hung in the air. He should have felt it lurking in the Mausoleum as Lily greeted them. But he had been too swept up by all the other revelations, too happy seeing Lily again after so long, he hadn't understood the danger they were in.

Then again, apparently neither had Lily. The Conductor had explained that the Nightmare could hide within the Canticle, feeding on unguarded minds. Suddenly, the strange behavior of the Naruvians made sense—always flitting from one thought to another, never letting themselves feel true emotion, lest it overpower them. An unhappy way to live, but it had kept them safe. Until Lily had come.

After that, it had been hard to argue with the Conductor. And no matter how hard Mark and Ben had worked to clear the rubble, the Conductor had never wavered in his opinion. The Oracle wanted them to return to Agora, and the best thing they could possibly do now was to follow her wishes, before she lost control again.

"It isn't what I'd hoped for," Mark admitted. "Slinking home and hoping for the best. That isn't what Lily would do. We've beaten the Nightmare before. Together, we could do it again . . ."

"But we aren't all together, are we?" Ben said softly, looking out at the rocky walls as they slipped slowly by. "I don't think we ever were, this time. We were all so desperate to rescue Lily, to bring the truth to light, we didn't really pay attention to her . . ."

Mark fiddled with his cuffs, noticing for the first time how badly frayed they were.

"We didn't have a choice, Ben," he began. "Lily wasn't going to leave without finding out the truth, and we needed to bring her home as quickly as possible." He sunk his head into his chest, trying to mask a growing feeling of guilt. "It's not just for our sake, you know that," he said, hastily. "Agora needs her. It needs someone other than Crede to lead the ordinary people—to stop the fighting in the streets, to stand up to Snutworth. The Oracle was right about one thing: Lily knows how to light a fire, and make everyone see the world a different way." Mark set his jaw, feeling so very tired. "We need her."

"You sound like Crede," Ben said, quietly.

Mark stared at her, too shocked to reply. Ben's eyes glinted in the dim, bluish light radiating from the stone walls.

"We told each other we were going down there to rescue a friend," she said, softly. "But if we'd really wanted that, we'd have calmed her down. We'd have looked after her better. Crede's spent all this time treating her like a symbol, and now we're doing the same."

"But . . . we need her," Mark said, alarmed at how much Ben's words rang true.

"Yes, we do." Ben knelt down in front of Mark, looking him in the eyes. "As a friend, not a savior. Lily started up the Temple Almshouse, but we've spread its message. Without all of us, it would never have become as important as it is. We kept it alive." She put her hands on Mark's shoulders. "This isn't just her fight anymore. It's our city, our world." She smiled. "When Laud finds her, and he *will* find her, shouldn't we be able to show her that we've made a difference, our way? Wasn't that what she always wanted? For everyone to be free, and make their own future?"

Mark smiled, tentatively. He wished he had Benedicta's confidence.

"I'll . . . try," he promised, meaning it.

For a long moment, the two of them didn't speak. They sat together on the floor of the platform, listening to the rumble of the long chain above, raising them ever higher, taking them home.

"But . . ." Mark said, at last. "I'm not sure I can match Lily's resolve."

Ben's smile grew sad.

"That might not be such a bad thing," she said. "Maybe what we need is a little more flexibility. I mean, if there's one thing those ancient Librans had, it was resolve." She sighed, turning away. "I still find it hard to believe that no one let the truth slip. Not once. All those years lying to their children, pretending that Agora was an ancient city . . . even a threat of death wouldn't have stopped me from talking."

"I don't think it was about that," Mark said, cautiously. "Don't you remember what the Oracle said? Those first settlers took that oath willingly. Maybe they were mad, but I think they really believed they had to keep the secret, to make their perfect world. They probably thought they were doing the best for their children, by giving them a better place to live and not burdening them with the truth." His mood darkened. "It was like that in Giseth. It wasn't just the Nightmare that kept people in line—it was so much easier not to think. Not to wonder. Just to accept that you should live your life the way everyone else did." He shook his head. "I suppose, when you're struggling to survive, who has time for history?"

Ben nodded, thoughtfully.

"Maybe we should keep it that way," she said, stretching. "The last thing we want is something else to make people angry. Those street mobs are bad enough already . . ." she paused, putting her head on one side.

"What is it?" Mark asked, seeing a look of concern pass over her face.

"Mark," she said, quietly, "can you hear something?"

Mark listened. He wished that he hadn't.

"Isn't that shouting, coming from above?"

Ben nodded, nervously.

"Sounds like a lot of people," she said.

"Mmm," Mark said, uncomfortably. "More than usual. A lot more."

"But I'm sure the rocks are just echoing it, making it sound louder," Ben said, hastily. "Just like back in Naru."

"Yes, of course," Mark replied, a little too quickly. "I'm sure that's it."

Neither of them wanted to remember what the Oracle had said about shouts of terror on the streets of Agora. Certainly not now that light was beginning to filter down from above, and their journey to the surface was nearly over.

By the time they reached the Last's house, the noise had died away. But it wasn't a peaceful kind of quiet—there was a tension in the air.

That feeling only increased as they slipped down the corridors and out into the Virgo District. Mark was surprised to find that it was mid-morning—they had lost all sense of time in Naru. It was a beautiful day, bright and fresh, but the streets around the Last's house were deserted.

"So . . ." Mark said, keeping his voice low. "Which way back to the temple?"

Ben frowned.

"This way," she said. "At least, I think so. I don't remember that stall being there . . ."

Mark looked more closely. The stall was very much out of place—a rickety, wooden construction perched on the corner of this elegant street. It looked like it had been thrown together in a few minutes.

"I'm sure I'd have remembered that," he agreed. "Maybe we turned the wrong way?"

He approached the stall, trying to get a better look. There didn't seem to be any wares on display, apart from a large, brass hand bell. The proprietor, a surprisingly elegant woman with a pale, tired face, was staring glumly the other way. She looked tense, but harmless enough.

"Should we ask?" Mark whispered to Ben. Ben considered.

"I'll ask," she said. "The receivers are still after you, remember?"

Mark agreed, slipping out of sight behind one of the nearby houses. He watched Benedicta approach.

"Excuse me," she said, "I wonder, could you tell me how to get to . . . ?"

The woman jumped.

"Oh, forgive me," she said, stumbling over her words. "My nerves are all shot to pieces, but that's hardly a surprise. We must be vigilant against the . . ." she trailed off, looking Ben up and down. A note of suspicion crept into her voice. "I don't remember seeing you in this area before. Who is your mistress, girl? You're obviously a servant."

"Actually," Ben said, patiently, "I'm not. I'm just trying to get back to the Temple Almshouse in—"

Ben got no further. With a shriek, the woman grabbed for the hand bell on the counter beside her, and swung it wildly, its shrill peals shattering the peaceful morning.

"Receiver! Receiver needed here quickly! Oh, by all the stars come now!" she shouted.

Alarmed, Ben jumped back.

"What's going on? What . . . ?"

In the distance, Mark heard the answering shriek of whistles.

"Run!" he shouted, and broke cover.

The two of them sprinted down the cobbled streets. The whistles were joined by cries of fear and alarm. All around, upstairs windows opened, and masters and servants alike joined in, shouting for the receivers. In the distance, they could see an approaching line of midnight-blue coats. Mark dodged down an alleyway, and Ben nearly barreled into him.

"The receivers . . . are they . . . ?" Mark managed to gasp, too afraid and confused to make any more sense.

"I don't think they've seen us," Ben panted. "We're nearly at the Central Plaza—that's the fastest way back home. At least . . ." she reconsidered, all of her confidence draining away, "it was when we left."

Mark took Ben's hand and gave it a comforting squeeze.

"Run now, questions later?" he asked. Ben nodded.

"Definitely," she said.

They dodged through the streets, the whistles fading into the distance. Every now and then, they passed another of the rickety stalls. It was obvious now that these stalls were watch posts—civilian volunteers ready to summon the receivers. But Virgo had always been a sedate district. Six days ago, when they had left Agora, there had barely been any receivers here at all. Now, it was all they could do to keep away from their patrols—every few minutes they spotted another blue coat, and were forced to duck into alleys or wait, breathless, behind abandoned carts. Every receiver that hurried past them bore the same haunted look, and no one seemed to have slept for days. But it was only when they approached the Central Plaza, only when they heard the sound of shouting carried on the breeze, that they realized that whatever had happened, it was far bigger than they had thought.

Mark and Ben crouched in the shadows of the Virgo District archway, and stared. The plaza looked like a battlefield. The stalls that normally covered it had been pushed together to form a crude barricade, curving in an irregular line across the plaza, stretching from the Taurus District archway to the Sagittarius Bridge on the other side of the wide marketplace. No, Mark realized with a jolt, the barricade wasn't limited to the plaza—it stretched out into the city as far as Mark could see. Agora had been slashed in two, and the Sagittarius District, their home, was on the other side.

On this side of the barricade, a detachment of receivers was patrolling up and down, tension written all over their frames. Mark couldn't see the other side, but from the noise, it sounded like there was a large and very angry mob, screaming a litany of curses, and crashing against the barricade.

"Blood for blood, a fair trade!" they were shouting. "The stone will strike anew!"

For a brief moment, Mark wondered what they meant, but then he shoved it to the back of his mind, along with all the rest of his worries. It was strangely easy to do, because none of this felt real. This city was his home; it couldn't just change like this, not when they had only been gone less than a week . . .

"Mark!" Ben whispered, jolting him out of his thoughts. "Look! I think I can see a way past the barricade!"

Mark followed her gaze, and nodded. Some of the broken stalls that made up the barricade had been piled up across and under the marble bridge that led to the Sagittarius District. It looked like it had been a rush job, and there were definite gaps in the barrier under the bridge. Large enough for them to slip through.

Just at that moment, there was a sudden cry from the other side of the plaza. A few ragged figures had struggled over the top of the barricade, and begun to rain down pieces of wood and stone on the startled receivers. For a minute or two, the receivers were thrown into confusion, before rallying to arrest the rioters. It didn't take long, but it was long enough for them to miss Mark and Ben, running across the other side of the plaza, and scrambling down the bank beside the Sagittarius Bridge.

Ben went first, and Mark followed quickly behind—squeezing past the debris, scraping his arms and legs on the unfinished marble under the bridge. The piles of wood groaned ominously, and more than once threatened to give way and plunge him into the river, but he made it to the far bank, and hauled himself up to where Ben was standing, staring into the distance.

"Come on," he said, picking at her sleeve. "What are you looking at?"

And then, he saw the other side of the plaza.

Bonfires belched smoke into the sky, and around them, crowds of people shouted their defiance at the receivers. But what most caught his attention was the central fire. It was larger than the others. On it lay a life-sized effigy, dressed in a blue and gold Chief Receiver's uniform, burning to ash.

And behind it, clearly visible despite the smoke, were two people he recognized. One, he had expected to see: Crede's right-hand man, Nick, his massive frame looking all the more intimidating as he roared out curse after curse. But it was the other figure that shocked him.

Her hair was disheveled, her clothes plain, and he had never

seen her with such a look of fury. But there was no mistaking
Cherubina.

Ben grabbed his hand.

"You're right," she said, "it's time to go."

"But—" Mark stammered. Ben squeezed his hand tighter.

"You want them to see us here? It's time to *go*."

And even more confused than before, Mark turned and ran
from the plaza.

Mark and Ben hurried to the temple in silence. Near the plaza, the
streets were swarming with people—angry people, fearful people.
One or two had the same look of hard fury that Mark had seen in
the rioters, and the majority of them looked scared. But the most
disturbing thing by far was that no one appeared to be trading. As
they ran on, the crowds thinned, and by the time they reached the
familiar streets around the temple, they were alone again. All of
the shops were shut, the hawkers absent. Even Miss Devine's shop,
which usually had a few hollow-eyed emotion addicts loitering
around, was closed and silent.

As the temple came into view, they saw that the guiding light
was extinguished, and the familiar queue of debtors was nowhere
to be seen. Mark ran up to the large, wooden door and tried the
handle. It was locked.

"But . . . we *never* lock it," Ben said, joining him. "Not during
the day. The temple's doors are always open."

Mark knocked on the door, but there was no response. Then he
began to hammer on it, rattling the hinges, but still there was no
response.

"Maybe the receivers attacked," Ben suggested, frowning. "No,
that makes no sense; they're all on the other side of the barricade,
and you couldn't slip a whole squad past the rioters the way we
came . . ."

"This isn't the receivers," Mark said, darkly. "This is Crede's doing."

"Quite right, Mr. Mark, in a way," said an all-too-familiar voice.

Mark spun around. Beside him, Ben bristled.

Miss Devine stood in the doorway of her establishment, a trace of amusement on her face.

"Miss Devine," Ben said, guardedly, "what do you want?"

Mark had never heard Ben sound so cold, but that was hardly surprising. Ben's sister, Gloria, had been one of the emotion seller's most loyal customers. That addiction had ruled her life, and ultimately led her to her death. But if Miss Devine was at all uncomfortable in Ben's presence, she did not show it.

"Very little," Miss Devine replied, "although I must admit that your rather violent knocking did make me curious. I wonder where you two could have been. I haven't seen you for days . . ."

Mark opened his mouth, already concocting a cover story, but Ben cut him off.

"Ignore her, Mark. She's probably in league with Crede."

Ben turned her back on the woman, her shoulders tense, but Miss Devine's reaction was the last thing Mark was expecting. She laughed. A hard, bitter sound.

"I'm afraid not, Miss Benedicta," she said. "Mr. Crede is dead."

There was a long pause. Suddenly, all of the things that they had seen on their way here seemed to make sense—the feeling of boiling anger, the outright war between receivers and rioters. Crede had been dangerous, but he was also a leader, a way to focus all the anger he stirred up. But with Crede gone . . .

"How did it happen?" Mark asked, barely taking it in. Miss Devine crossed her arms, and for a moment, she seemed lost in thought.

"It began five days ago," she said, keeping her voice low, but without drama. "It was extraordinary news—everyone was talking about it. Chief Inspector Greaves had announced that he wanted to meet with Crede, to negotiate an end to the riots. Some thought it was a trick, while others, your friends in the Temple Almshouse included, believed he really was willing to offer a deal to stop the violence in the streets." Miss Devine shrugged. "Few thought it would succeed, but Crede did agree to a public meeting, an hour before sunset that same day."

"Was it a trap?" Mark asked. Miss Devine's look was inscrutable.

"That is what Crede's supporters say, but I doubt that Greaves is capable of such ruthlessness. I went to see the meeting; of course, there would be no customers at such an exciting time, and I am interested in public events."

"Yes, I thought you might be," Mark muttered, remembering Miss Devine's presence in Crede's meetings. If the emotion seller heard him, she gave no indication.

"By the time I arrived," she continued, "the plaza was full. I had to watch from the Sagittarius Bridge. Even so far away, I could see that the debate was already . . ." she chose her word carefully, "intense. They had set up two of the Agora Day podiums, so they could talk without getting too close, and to stop their supporters from coming to blows. They were supposed to be alone on their platforms, but both had a few friends with them. Mr. Nick wasn't with Crede, but Miss Cherubina was," Miss Devine's lip curled for a fraction of a second. "She looked quite a firebrand. Greaves had Poleyn with him, of course, to keep the receivers on his side of the plaza under control. Not a tactic that was likely to be successful."

"I doubt you did anything to help," Benedicta said sourly. Miss Devine ignored the comment.

"At first, the event was predictable. Greaves offered empty words of understanding, and Crede made his usual speeches, denouncing everything the Directory stood for. The crowd was on his side. But I must admit, as time went on, Greaves became more convincing. He talked about honor, and trust. About going forward as equals. That seemed to strike a chord with Crede. But the crowd was not so easily swayed. They began to argue among themselves." Miss Devine began to talk a little faster, getting into her story with unpleasant relish. "Fights broke out, scuffles between debtors and the elite servants became larger, and more violent. Then things started to fly through the air. Little objects—bottles, cloth bags, even vegetables. Some of the traders were making a good living fueling that argument.

"And then, someone threw a cobblestone.

"It wasn't large, but it soared straight toward Crede's platform. I don't know if it flew wide, or if it struck its target. But I know this—Crede fell in an instant."

Mark felt the blood drain from his face.

"Did he . . . ?" he began to ask, but Miss Devine cut him short.

"Crede died in Miss Cherubina's arms," she reported, dispassionately. "The crowd's fury was something to behold. Greaves barely escaped with his life, and several receivers didn't make it. The first riot went on all night—it seems like both sides had made plans in case this happened. The fighting simmered down a couple of hours after dawn, but by then there was a barrier stretching all the way across the city." Miss Devine gestured out at the empty street. "And we, Mr. Mark, are in the part of the city that is full of rebels demanding blood for their leader's murder."

The three of them stood in silence. All Mark could picture in his mind's eye was a single image—Cherubina cradling Crede, a dreadful wound on the side of his head, the crowd raging all about them. And in the background, the looming shadow of Nick, Crede's right-hand man, just as Mark had seen him last—a big cobblestone clenched in his fist.

To one side, they heard the sound of wrenching metal. Mark

realized that it was coming from the door of the temple—the sound of a key turning in a rusty lock.

"Well," Miss Devine observed, "it seems that your knocking attracted the attention of your friends after all—perhaps they feel it is safe enough to open their doors again." Miss Devine turned away, a cold smile on her face. "I'm not certain that it is wise."

She went back into her shop, shutting the door behind her.

Dumbly, Mark and Ben stared at each other. This was too much to take in; they needed a moment to adjust, a moment to prepare themselves for facing their friends.

They didn't get one. The door to the temple inched open.

"Who's there? We're not open, we . . ." the voice emerging from the temple stopped with a gasp, and the door was flung wide open.

"Theo!" Verity called, delighted. "It's Mr. Mark and Miss Benedicta! They're safe!"

Through the door Mark could see Theo, making his way toward them with a look of joy and hope. And behind him, there was a whole crowd of frightened people, waiting for some good news. He attempted a smile.

Verity looked past them, still beaming.

"And Lily? Is she with you?" she asked.

Mark's smile vanished as quickly as it had come. It looked like it was now his turn to tell a story.

"Well," he began, "She might be a little longer . . ."

CHAPTER FIFTEEN

Believing

IT WAS NATURAL LIGHT, Laud was sure of it.

He urged his aching legs to keep climbing. This winding stone staircase had seemed endless at first, but now he could see something that was almost like daylight, filtering down from above.

His throat was parched, and his stomach ached. He had finished the last of the food some time ago, though how long ago he couldn't say. He had slept a couple of times since then, but he had taken to sleeping whenever the chatter of the Cacophony lulled for a few moments, rather than keeping to any sort of schedule. He must have been wandering the tunnels for days, but sometimes, it felt like years. Or hours.

He realized that he was muttering to himself, counting the stone steps as he climbed them. That had started fairly quickly once the lantern oil ran out. He preferred hearing his own voice to the endless echoes in the pitch-black caverns.

What will come? Why? Which? Where? Whom? Wherefore?

"One thousand, five hundred and fifty-eight . . ." Laud muttered to himself. He had lost count of the steps a while back, but anything was preferable to listening to the voices. At the moment they were asking questions, which wasn't too bad. But sometimes they whispered secrets that made him blush, or screamed abuse and threats. At one point, when he had been negotiating his way through a tunnel lined with fiercely sharp spears of rock, they had done nothing but prattle inane greetings, so that he felt as though an army of idiots was following him, just out of reach, and impossible to shut up.

But all of that he could take. He knew that the voices, however loud, were nothing but sound. The trouble was, sometimes the sound was familiar.

He had expected that hearing Lily's voice would be the worst. And it was true that he could always pick it out of all the others, however distorted. But in a way, that gave him hope. Even if she was crying or raging, she was still alive. It kept his weary, blistered feet moving on.

No, the worst parts were the old echoes. The sounds he hadn't heard since he was tiny.

Sometimes they were so simple. The call of the nut seller who had lived across the street. The sound of his friends, playing. Yes, he remembered. There was a time when he'd played and he'd had friends. Before his parents had been taken from him and he'd had to go and work. Before he'd seen what the city was really like.

Still, it could have been worse. He could have heard Gloria, his dead sister. The Cacophany could have summoned her voice—just a little too bright, as she tried to take over from their mother. It could have found her last words to him, promising to give up taking the bottled emotions she needed to get through the day.

He heard those words often enough in his dreams.

So many people had left him. And now he'd left. Benedicta, the last of his family, was far away. In the tunnels, surrounded by empty echoing words, there was no companion but himself. And he didn't know himself well enough to be comfortable with that.

He'd expected some great revelation, some profound truth. But all he found was that his need to keep going grew even stronger. He couldn't explain it, couldn't rationalize it away or turn it into a pithy one-liner. He simply couldn't let Lily slip through his fingers again.

He looked up. Yes, that was definitely light up there—a jagged opening, just around the next twist of the steps, growing wider by the second. He put out a hand to steady himself against the wall, and noticed for the first time that his fingers were raw and scratched, reminders of the number of times he had fallen in the dark tunnels. He risked a look down. His breeches were torn, his boots nearly worn out. He pushed a few strands of lank red hair out of his eyes. By the time he finally reached Lily, he wouldn't be a particularly comforting sight.

Still, he thought as he reached the top of the steps, that might be an advantage. If any trouble came his way, one look at his wild face would convince anyone that he meant business.

He grasped the edge of the opening, hauling himself out from the shattered remains of something that looked like a tomb. He blinked in the sudden light, streaming down from an opening in the roof to this stone chamber, far above. It almost looked like some kind of crypt . . .

He felt the tip of a blade press into his back.

"What business have you here, dweller in darkness?" a raspy voice said, close to his ear.

Without stopping to think, Laud spun around, catching the unseen man off guard. The knife clattered from his assailant's hand, and Laud put his foot on it. Then he focused on the man. He wore a russet red habit, the hood up, cowling his face.

"Is this how you greet all your guests?" Laud asked, his

sarcasm covering his nerves. He didn't know if this man was alone, and he darted a look around the circular chamber. The man stood back, warily.

"You are not welcome at the Cathedral," he said. "We have sealed the path to the lands below. Only the Judges may pass."

Laud studied the man. He didn't look much of a threat, especially considering how easily Laud had disarmed him. But he couldn't afford to be delayed.

"It's a good thing that I'm one of the Judges, then," he said, keeping his voice entirely matter-of-fact. "My name's Mark; I'm the Protagonist."

The red-robed man's attitude changed instantly, and he threw back his hood to get a closer look. Despite himself, Laud flinched. The man's face was covered with so many thick, livid scars that he barely looked human. He reached out to Laud with equally ravaged hands.

"Thank the stars," he exclaimed. "I've been waiting for you. Wolfram said that you had been captured, but I knew that the Protagonist would never be imprisoned, and after Miss Lily emerged from the tomb, I was certain . . ." He stopped, and his ruined face shifted into something like a frown. "I thought that Wolfram said you were blond?"

"Has Lily come this way?" Laud interrupted, hastily. The man immediately nodded.

"Yes, but you should know—"

"Where is she?" Laud interrupted.

The man raised his hands.

"I tried to stop her," he said. "I could see she was in distress, poor child. She can't have eaten for days . . ."

Laud grabbed the front of the man's robes.

"Where. Is. She?" he asked, with menace.

The man calmed down.

"In the marshes," he said. "But you mustn't go after her. You should rest, prepare yourself . . ."

"Do I have time to rest?" Laud asked, not letting go. "Do I really have that choice? Will Lily be safe if I delay?"

Even beneath the scars, it wasn't hard to see the guilt.

"No, but I can't let you both go out there. One of you should be ready . . ." he stopped. Laud wasn't quite sure what the expression on his face was, but if it conveyed even a fraction of his thoughts, he wasn't surprised that the man had stopped protesting. He felt within seconds of snapping.

"I'll show you to the door," the man said, quietly.

Outside, the fog formed a thick, choking blanket, though the cold air was still welcome after weeks in the tunnels.

The man, who called himself Honorius, the porter of the Cathedral, had warned him to take care on the path down to the marshes, but Laud found himself running along, jogging stones off the pathway.

Honorius had warned him that he should rest. That if he needed to come back, not to return to the shining Cathedral, but to find his way to the sanatorium, on the other side of the headland. There were soft beds waiting there for him and Lily. But Laud only ran faster as he reached the bottom of the cliff.

And, above all he had warned him to be careful. Not to venture into the heart of the treacherous swamps, where something called the Nightmare reigned.

Laud wasn't good at following advice.

The instant he stepped into the marshes, he felt it. A sense of being watched, like a pressure in his head. He had experienced something like it, back in the throne room of the Oracle—but there it had been hidden, at the edge of his thoughts. Here, its presence pressed in on all sides.

He began to slow, the mud sucking at his boots. Something was muttering in his mind, telling him to turn back. That Lily didn't want to be found. That she would laugh at him for following her. That he was useless, worthless . . . not worthy of her attention . . .

A cloud of insects billowed up from the ground. Laud jumped back, swatting at them, and his thoughts cleared.

"Don't bother," he snarled at the fog. "I've been through worse than you, Nightmare. I'm not going to be put off so easily."

He planted his feet and focused on one thing. Lily. Her face, her voice, her uncrushable spirit. The way he remembered her.

"Lily!" he called.

His voice was swallowed up by the fog.

He trudged on. The fog suffocated him. He could see nothing, except for its long white tendrils. The mud beneath him grew soft and slushy, but he forced himself forward.

"Lily!" he called, over and over. "Lily!"

And then, suddenly, he heard her.

"You didn't bring flowers."

The voice was almost a whisper, right next to his ear. Laud jumped, pitching forward into the mud.

"Have to bring flowers when you're visiting a lady. That's manners."

Laud struggled to his feet, and turned back.

Lily stood lightly on the surface of the mud. Her skirt was streaked with the filth, and hung heavily from her thin frame. Her body swayed, as though in a stiff breeze. She laughed, but did it without smiling. And her eyes roved and turned in her head, never settling for an instant.

Laud looked at her, aghast. Something was wrong, so very wrong. The girl who looked like Lily leaned forward, peering at him.

"Flowers? Lilies? Lilies for the dead, and the near dead, and the always dead." Her voice was strange and tight, but it flowed as though she didn't have a care in the world. "Flowers for the never alive, though? What would those be? Roses maybe. I wanted roses from you. Why did you never bring them?"

She unfolded her arms and reached out to touch his face. Laud noticed that her nails were bleeding.

"Lily?" he said, taking her hand, "I'm so glad I found you . . ."

"Found me? Did you?" Lily smiled. "Good. I've been looking for me all day." She slapped his hand away. "Look, don't touch. I break easily."

She spun around with surprising ease, and the fog closed around her.

"Lily?" Laud said, in alarm. "Lily, where are you?"

"Everywhere, stamped into this land, she is," Lily's voice replied, growing fainter. "Can't get away from her. You'd think she was the only person in the world . . ."

Laud reached out for her, but all he could hear was her voice—light, high, and unnatural.

"Wait!" Laud said, running after her.

"Keep your thoughts nice and lush . . ." Lily sang. "It likes them that way. Full of fear, and regret . . ."

Lily reappeared in front of him, spinning on one foot.

"Lily . . ." Laud shouted. "Please, just stop and listen to me."

"No thanks," she said, lightly. "Listened too much already. Always looking for people to tell me things. Shouldn't have done that. Too much, you see. All full up. No more. No more."

She stopped, suddenly tense, looking at the fog around her.

"It's coming again," she said, quietly. "Don't stay. You won't like it."

"What?" Laud said, shaking his head. "What do you . . . ?"

Lily began to scream.

Laud grasped her, begging her to stop, but she kept on—louder and louder, until Laud had to let go and clamp his hands over his ears. But he couldn't block out that sound. So desperate, so pained—the fog around them seemed to shimmer with it, whirling around Lily as though it was dancing for joy.

And then, in an instant, Lily was quiet again. She smiled, in a vague way.

"That was less than usual," she said, her voice rasping from the strain. "It must be getting bored with me."

"Who?" Laud ventured, uncovering his ears. Lily blinked.

"The Nightmare, of course . . . aren't you . . . ?" Her eyes widened in fear. "No, that can't be you . . . you're not here!"

She seized his hand, pulling it close to her eyes to inspect it.

"It looks real, smells real . . ." she licked his finger, still crusted with mud, and spat. "Tastes real too, I think. But it doesn't sound right. Laud would have talked more by now. He was never quiet. Always sharp, always bittersweet . . . not like salt and mud . . ."

Laud felt his mind cloud over again. He almost wanted to reply in kind, to let his mind roam like hers. To forget all the stress and danger, and chase her through the marshes, lost in her world.

But he couldn't. He needed her back.

"Lily, it's me," he said, grasping her hand. "The real me."

"Who is the real you, Laud?" she asked, her eyes focusing. "Do you know everything about yourself? Are you sure you haven't been someone else for as long as you can remember? Have you betrayed yourself, Laud?"

She let his hand drop.

"The betrayal of our fathers," she said, solemnly. "They left us alone. Forsaken. All on our own, dancing to a music they stopped playing long ago. We could have been wonderful, with their guidance. But they left us. Left us to go wrong, to wallow in suffering, to never, never be able to put it right . . ."

Laud could see that he was losing her again. Her eyes were beginning to glaze.

"Lily, don't go," he said. "You're not alone. I've followed you all this way."

"No," Lily said, shaking her head, whipping her matted hair back and forth. "Not really there, not real. Just a trick. Too sincere, too gentle. Not the Laud I know."

Despite himself, Laud's eyebrow raised.

"You'd rather I made a comment about the mud? It looks like you've been wallowing in it . . ." Laud began, and then stopped. Lily had pulled something out of her apron that glittered in the dim light. A short, sharp, hunting knife.

"Have to fight the nightmares," she said, quietly. "You usually crumble with a single touch. And if you're too solid, I'll just have to try a little harder." Laud stepped back. "You know, I wish you were real." Lily said, sadly. "I so wanted to see Laud again, more than anyone else. But you knew that. You always knew."

She lunged forward. Laud dived to one side, but the mud slowed him down, and Lily's knife cut open the sleeve of his shirt. He grabbed for Lily's hand, trying to wrestle away the knife, but she fought back with terrible strength, flinging him to the ground. He lay, sinking into the marsh as she loomed over him.

Laud panicked. He tried to think of a way of proving that he was real, but all of his wits were deserting him. He couldn't look away from Lily's eyes—usually so calm and reassuring, but now desperate, on the verge of collapse. He couldn't think, couldn't reason. All he could think about was that look. He brought up his left arm to shield himself.

Lily raised the knife again. And stopped.

Her gaze was fixed on his arm. Or rather, on the old scar that was now exposed. A scar he had gotten protecting her from another madman, who had also thought that the world was nothing but an illusion.

The knife fell from her hands, and sank into the mud.

She looked down at Laud. Her eyes were full of tears.

"Laud? That's really you, isn't it?"

It was her voice—her real voice, tired and frightened, but nothing like the strange singing tone from before. Laud grabbed a thick clump of marsh weed, and hauled himself into a sitting position.

"Took you long enough to work that out," he said, his voice shaking. As he spoke, the fog around them began to grow thicker, stroking them like living tendrils.

"You shouldn't stay here. I won't be myself for long," Lily said, rapidly, gulping her tears away. "I get . . . flashes of truth. Real vision. I'm sorry Laud, you've come all this way and I'm not worth finding."

"I'm not going to dignify that with a response," Laud replied, struggling to his feet. "Come on, you need to get out of this marsh— away from the Nightmare. There's a sanatorium nearby; the scarred man said he could help."

Lily shook her head.

"I'm not going."

Laud frowned.

"I'll carry you if I need to."

He reached for her, but Lily stepped back.

"You don't understand," she said, her voice trembling. "The Nightmare won't let me go. It followed me from Naru. Whispering in the Canticle, laughing on the wind. Reminding me of what I did . . . of what I am . . ." Lily's eyes lost their focus, her breathing coming in short gasps. "All those people—in the village of Aecer, in the tunnels . . . All that death . . ."

Laud put his hands on the sides of her head, forcing her to look at him.

"What are you talking about?" he said. "Is it that earthquake, back in Naru? That was the Oracle's fault; she was trying to stop you and she lost control . . ." He cradled her head. "You can't listen to this Nightmare . . . it's just trying to confuse you . . . it was an accident . . ."

"And the revolution in Agora?" Lily shouted, pushing his hands away. "Was that just an accident? The Nightmare set the echoes ringing in my head, every time I tried to sleep. Didn't you hear it, Laud? In the tunnel? Didn't you hear the battle cries, the panic? Just like Giseth . . . just like Naru . . . everywhere I go, I bring nothing but death!"

The fog was swirling around them now. There were shapes in that fog, shapes that Laud didn't want to look at too closely. Things with claws and teeth. Laud tried to focus on Lily, but his own fears were getting harder to ignore. *Ben will be back in Agora, by now,* said new whispers in the back of his head, *and Mark, and Theo. And you left them behind to follow this poor, mad girl. Will you ever have a home to go back to?*

"All this time, I thought I was helping," Lily continued, her voice more sad than scared. "Showing people a new way to think. That they didn't have to keep living the same mistakes, over and over again, fighting over scraps or suffocating each other with traditions. The future was ours, Laud. A proper future, where everyone would be whole . . . not empty, not searching for some purpose they'd never had . . ."

Lily began to shake, violently. For the first time, Laud noticed how thin she was, like a dream herself.

"Lily, just listen for a moment . . ." Laud said, desperately, but she didn't seem to hear him anymore.

"But this isn't my future. It's theirs," she muttered, her voice growing frenzied as the Nightmare closed in. "The ancient Libran experiment, right on schedule. Who cares how many have to die? Who cares that they left us all alone? They won—and we're all paying the price."

"Lily—"

"But what does it matter?" she asked, her voice fading in and out. Laud could feel the Nightmare now, slithering through the mud and air, settling on Lily like a haze. "We're not real. Not proper people. Who cares if we have mothers who are soulless machines and dead fathers who abandon us to fate, as long as the great project survives?" She laughed, harshly. "Such little lives, Laud. Walking our little paths until we drive ourselves into the dust, making patterns that no one is left to see . . ."

"Lily!"

"I wanted happiness, Laud," she said, her voice resuming its high, mad whisper. "For me, for everyone. I thought my ideas could bring it. I didn't care who I sacrificed to bring about my world, because I was so *sure*. Just like them, those Librans. But it's all twisted. Every bit. A whole life of longing and I'm worse than the Nightmare, worse than Snutworth. At least they never thought they were doing good. But no one told me that the music stopped playing, the world's moved on, and I'm just twirling and sinking and dying and . . ."

"By all the stars, listen to yourself!" Laud grabbed her shoulders. "Do you really think it's all down to you?" Laud shouted. "You think the rest of us were just sitting around, waiting for the great Lilith to turn our world upside down?" He met her gaze, utterly serious. "You think everyone followed, and struggled, and died, just to please you? The Lily I remember wouldn't think that. The Lily I remember didn't care about prophecies, or anyone's ancient plans. She just rolled up her sleeves and got ready to help the next debtor who came through the door. Because that's what she did—help. All day, every day. Trying so hard she nearly forgot that she was only one person. One person with an amazing, inspiring idea."

Lily stared back. There was a spark of her old self in those rolling eyes—frightened and unsure.

"But, everything I did . . . all that death in my name . . ."

"Which name?" Laud said, fiercely. "Lily the Antagonist? Lily the Revolutionary? Those aren't you. Good or bad, this is bigger than you now." He put his face closer to hers, touching her forehead with his own. "This is you. It doesn't matter how many names you have, or who your parents were, or anything like that. It doesn't matter to me, or to Mark, or Ben, or Theo. You're Lily. You're good, and compassionate, and stubborn, and angry, and wonderful." He brushed a strand of hair from her pinched, frightened face. "You're not perfect, and why would you want to be?" He looked her in the eyes. "But you're close enough for me."

Lily held his gaze. For a few seconds, they said nothing. Laud felt the beating of her heart.

And then, she opened her mouth, and wailed.

It was a long, pained wail, like a baby's cry. And Laud drew her close, and held her. Held her until his ears rang and his heart shuddered. And all around them, the fog bucked and roiled and shivered with the sound.

Laud didn't let go. Not as her cry faded into a rasp, and then a sob.

"I . . . I . . ." Lily began, her voice weak.

"Aren't you ever going to let anyone else get a word in?" Laud asked her, fondly. Lily pulled back a little, her eyes clear, but immensely tired.

"It's just . . . look . . ." she said, raising a shaky finger, to point behind him.

Laud turned and looked. In the distance, far across the marshes, he could see the setting sun.

"The fog . . . it's gone . . ." Lily mumbled, swaying.

Laud caught her as she fell.

CHAPTER SIXTEEN

The Punishment

"YOU MUST ADMIT, Chief Inspector, that it was not quite the outcome you had anticipated."

Greaves stared at the floor. It wasn't out of shame. He knew that his negotiations had been working, at first. Perhaps if he and Crede had talked longer, they might have brought peace back to the city they both loved. He had nothing to be ashamed of.

No, he looked down, because he was afraid that if he looked the Director in the eye, he would forget himself, and let his contempt show.

He had already faced Lady Astrea's anger on several occasions over the past weeks. He could forgive her that—she was his superior, and her home, the former Astrologer's Tower, lay far too close to the barricade for her to live there anymore. She had fled the tower in the middle of the night, and arrived at the Directory with her composure ruffled and looking for someone to blame. She hadn't come to this meeting. As far as he could tell, she was spending most of her time in the Directory libraries, looking up prison records. He had not asked her why.

No, Astrea's fury was justified—she didn't want the city to be torn in half any more than he did. But now, as the Director sat behind his mahogany desk in the huge, candlelit office, Greaves was sure he detected a note of triumph in his voice.

"Indeed, sir," Greaves said, at last, "it is not what I would have hoped." The Director nodded, thoughtfully.

"I am glad to see that you are so calm, Chief Inspector. We will need to maintain our clarity of purpose in the coming weeks."

"Absolutely sir," Greaves said. "With your permission, I would like to recruit some Directory clerks to send over the barricades to begin talks again. I fear that the sight of a receiver uniform would not be welcome at the moment, but we need an official representative in the rebel side of the city . . ."

"There will be no talks, Chief Inspector," the Director said, softly.

"Sir, it has been nearly three weeks," Greaves continued. "Naturally we had to give them time to mourn Crede's death, but surely now that the flames of revolution are cooling, this would be the perfect time to seek peace."

"There will be no talks," the Director said, busying himself with paperwork. "No negotiation, no compromises. The revolutionaries have chosen to defy the Directory, defy Agora. They have traded our guidance for their own rule, and so they shall live in a city without protection, or order. Or food." The Director looked up, leaning back in his chair. "The stocks in the downriver warehouses will soon run out, and the Directory controls the supply of food from Giseth."

Greaves could not prevent himself from flinching at that. Before his promotion to Chief Inspector, he had believed, like everyone else outside the Director's private circle, that there was nothing beyond the city walls. To hear the land that lay out there discussed so casually unsettled him. The Agorans who were still loyal to the Directory saw him as the representative of law, and of justice. Yet here he was, planning the future with people who lied as easily as breathed.

"Of course, we will have to ration food in the Upper City as well," the Director continued, ignoring Greaves's discomfort. "But our stocks will last until the Gisethi harvest, and the next delivery." He reached for a decanter, and poured himself a glass of wine. "The revolutionaries will not be so fortunate. They shall starve, until they can resist no more. A suitable punishment, I feel, while we deal with more important matters."

"With respect, sir," Greaves muttered, "what could be more important than the lives of our people?"

The Director met Greaves's eyes with an implacable gaze.

"Do you think that I am not interested in the lives of our people? Believe me, Greaves, I have the interest of everyone in our city at heart. I simply have a more long-term solution in mind. You gave them the opportunity to redeem themselves, and they have responded with violence. So now, they have forfeited any right to decide their own destiny."

Greaves felt his jaw tighten.

"I serve Agora and her people, sir. I swore an oath."

"No, you swore an oath to the Directory. You traded your loyalty, Chief Inspector, for your title, and your authority." The Director sat back, never looking away. "Nevertheless, I appreciate the difficulty of leading this campaign. The receivers will need to be ever vigilant, and it is not safe for you to be on the streets. Therefore, I am appointing Inspector Poleyn as the street commander. You will be confined to the Directory, for the present time. And now," the Director gestured into the corner of the candlelit hall, "I have a meeting with Father Wolfram, if you would excuse us."

Greaves turned, trying not to show his surprise as Father Wolfram materialized out of the shadows. For a man who wore such distinctive red robes, he was very good at being inconspicuous.

The monk hadn't said much since those first few days at the Directory. At first, Greaves had wondered if he would be an ally, a man to challenge the Director on his own terms. But whatever they talked about in their private meetings had rapidly won him over, and now everyone knew that he was the Director's right-hand man.

Despite this, even Greaves, with all his long service, couldn't work out exactly what Wolfram did. Officially, he was an adviser. He had many hushed conversations with the Director, about a "process" they were working on, and the question of the "vessel." It sounded ominous, but no worse than the many whispered conversations that the Directory of Receipts had seen over the last years.

But there was more. Greaves had seen Wolfram send letters to Giseth, and send out agents to scour the city and the lands around. Greaves had made his own investigations. He knew that Wolfram was still searching for Lily.

Even that made no sense. The Director knew exactly where Mark was—he had shown Greaves a letter from an old friend telling him that the boy was back at the temple, and yet he sent no one to interrogate him and find out where Lily was. The barricades would be no barrier to the Director if he had really set his mind on something. Greaves had asked him about this once, but had received only one of those uncomfortably tiny smiles, and the assurance that Lily would return more easily if led by her friends, not captured by her enemies.

Yet still, the Director's agents searched—as if finding Lily were the most important task in the world. Yes, she had been an agitator in her day, but the city had more than enough of those now. This was a time for action, not for messing around with ancient prophecies.

"Chief Inspector?" The Director's voice broke into his thoughts. "You are still here, I see. Is there anything else I can do for you?"

Greaves could think of several responses to that, most of them unspeakable in this hallowed office. But he bit all of them back. He did not understand this man, but he was still his Director, his ruler. And he would protect the rule of law, because at the moment, that was all his poor, wounded city had left.

"If I am to remain in the Directory, what am I to do?" he asked, at last. He had to ask it, but he didn't like the way it made him sound. He was Chief Receiver, not an office boy. The Director pondered for a moment.

"Set up a guard around my office," he said, "your best men and women, naturally. And arm them with swords, Greaves," the Director added. "Truncheons are all very well, but our private offices must be especially secure."

"It sounds like you are expecting trouble, sir," Greaves observed. The Director adjusted some papers on his desk, and caught the eye of the silent Wolfram.

"We must be prepared for every possibility, Chief Inspector," the Director said at last. "I suspect that when the crisis comes, it will be swift indeed. But I doubt this will happen just yet." The Director picked up his pen. "No, I believe that, for the moment, everything will be very quiet."

Greaves did not find this particularly reassuring.

CHAPTER SEVENTEEN

The Noose

MARK ADJUSTED the cloth mask over his nose and mouth and looked down at the woman who lay coughing on one of the pews, her face as pale as the grave. She was just like all the others that morning. This was a simple infection and, in normal times, she would have fought it off easily. But these were not normal times. With so many people crowded together in the slums, the usual illnesses had been spreading faster than ever before.

He looked over his shoulder, to where Verity was crushing some herbs with a mortar and pestle, perched on the temple's altar.

"Is Ben back with those supplies yet?" he asked. The barricade had moved again yesterday, and a little more of the Gemini District was now on their side. Most people had taken the opportunity to scavenge for food, but Ben had realized that one of the museums was now accessible, and she had thought that there might be some old medical equipment.

Verity shook her head, not looking up.

"Not yet," she said, wearily. "I still say that she shouldn't have gone alone. The streets aren't safe—Nick's thugs might keep order, but you can't trust them." She brushed away a stray strand of hair from her face. Mark couldn't help but notice that gesture. It was so like Lily.

He had told Verity and Theo everything about what had happened in Naru, of course. In a way, he wished he hadn't. It hadn't even occurred to him as he'd been telling it that Verity would have known the Oracle. But the Oracle had been her brother's wife. As it was, though, this had been the part of his story that Verity had found the most believable.

"That sounds like Helen," she had said. "She was always more interested in facts than people. I never knew why Thomas wanted to marry her. Monks of the Order don't usually marry. I suppose it had something to do with the Midnight Charter, or the Bishop." She had looked down at her hands. "Everything did, for him."

She hadn't talked about it since, hadn't once asked about Lily. But every time the door opened, she looked up with such hope in her eyes that Mark knew she hadn't given up.

Then again, he was sure that he did the same. It had been eighty days since he had last seen Lily and Laud in the throne room of the Oracle. The summer was at its height, and there had been no word from either of them. Mark couldn't even return to Naru and ask if there was any news, not while the Last's Descent was far behind enemy lines. There was nothing any of them could do but wait, and hope.

They needed Lily now more than ever. The city was at war. The barricade had split the city in two—Upriver Agora, where the elite cowered behind their receiver guards, and the downriver districts, with twice the population and half the supplies. The revolutionaries were roaming the streets, to ensure that everyone on the downriver side supported their vision of the future, with arguments and threats. The receivers were doubtless doing the same on the other side.

Some of the corner preachers had built up Lily's image into something divine. Inspired by Crede, the martyr for the cause, they were claiming that all it would take to win this fight would be someone like Lily to lead them to victory. To them, she was a saint, and a savior.

Mark wished he still had that kind of faith.

"Mark?"

Mark snapped out of his thoughts. Dr. Theophilus had come over and was looking at him quizzically, the deep, dark circles under his eyes more noticeable than ever.

"Sorry," he said, "I was thinking about, um . . . that is . . ." Mark rapidly changed the subject, "Ben's been gone a long time."

Theo nodded.

"I'm sure she is being cautious, but she has chosen a dangerous part of the city to investigate. I've heard it looks like a hundred years have passed. Half of the buildings are in ruins—there's a line of overturned carts stretching from the University to the Astrologer's Tower. Practically every receiver in the city is in Gemini, or on the Central Plaza." Theo attempted a smile, gesturing around to the vast crowd of people that filled the temple, sitting or lying on the stone floor. "At least we've no shortage of rags—I think we're going to need more bandages."

Mark chucked at the black humor of it all.

"I don't see what you're laughing about," Verity muttered, her voice tight. "We've taken on another twenty patients today. How are we going to feed them?"

"We'll manage," Theo said, with calm assurance. Neither of them bothered to keep their voices low. Conversations like this had become all too familiar to worry the debtors.

"How, Theo?" Verity replied, stepping around the altar and coming toward him. The strain of it had been creeping over the formerly dignified secretary for weeks, and now she seemed close to snapping. "The Aquarius warehouses are nearly empty, and no one in the downriver districts ever saved much food. You know what will happen when we run out."

Mark and Theo exchanged glances. Yes, everyone knew. For the first week, it had seemed like Crede's dream of a city without exploitation would come true. Mark remembered seeing Nick, Crede's burly henchman, handing out free bags of grain and fruit at the warehouses. But as supplies had dwindled, and the barricade remained, Downriver Agora had returned to its old ways. Most people still used their signet rings to seal contracts and trade for what little food was left, but without the receivers to make the contracts official, they were little more than pieces of paper. No one was there to make people honor their agreements, and Nick and his street thugs were taking the law into their own hands. No wonder so many more were coming to the temple for refuge.

"We have to keep going, Rita," Theo said, firmly.

"No, we don't," Verity replied. "Maybe we can still treat their illness, but we can't feed them. We don't have enough for ourselves. We didn't want this revolution; it didn't happen in our name, or Lily's. It wasn't anything to do with the temple. Why should we . . . ?" she trailed away, all her energy deserting her. "Why do we have to keep fighting?"

Mark stared at her. He wanted to give an answer, but he was too tired, and too confused himself, to think of one.

The doctor took Verity's hands.

"Because they look to us," Theo said, with absolute conviction. "Because this temple, this almshouse, has become their only guiding light. And leaders, no matter how unwilling, have to try to lead, or every single person who falls is our fault."

Verity nodded, quietly, and Mark breathed a huge sigh of relief. He thanked the stars that Theo was here. For the first time in several weeks, he felt almost peaceful.

The door slammed open, shattering the moment. Mark turned his head.

Ben stood in the doorway. She was flushed and panting hard, as though she had been running.

"Ben! What are you . . . ?" Theo began, but Benedicta shook her head.

"No time. They're probably already there." She wheezed, trying to catch her breath. "It's Nick, and his revolutionaries. I tried to get back as fast as I could, but . . ."

"Slow down, slow down," Theo said, clearing a pile of blankets off one of the pews. "Are they coming here? Surely not; we've treated so many of their men."

"You don't understand," Ben gasped. "They're launching another attack. I heard it from one of their people, but it's already going ahead. We might be too late . . ."

"What are you saying?" Mark said, alarmed. "You think we should try and stop it? The receivers can look after themselves. You're talking about a hundred people at most . . ."

He trailed away. Ben knew all this; she wasn't stupid. So why had she come back to warn him? She stared him straight in the eye.

"It's the prison, Mark. They're attacking the prison. They want to free all the inmates. That means the jailers are standing in their way."

Mark froze.

"Dad . . ." he said. Then he grabbed his jacket.

"Mark, think about this," Verity said, trying to stop him. "You don't know if your father is there; you can't face down an angry mob on your own . . ."

"Let him go, Rita," Theo said, softly. He touched Mark's arm.

"Hurry. I'll stay and watch over our charges. Someone has to care for those who get left behind."

Mark nodded, grateful, then turned to Ben.

"Let's go."

They smelled the fires before they saw them. The smoke spiraled into the hot, dry air. Mark, already sweating from the run, felt their heat as they neared the prison.

"The prison's right next to the receiver barracks; it's mad," Mark shouted as they ran.

"The receivers are all over the city—the barracks are practically deserted!" Ben replied, swerving around a corner. "That's why they're striking now."

Mark groaned. He hadn't seen his father since he had returned—they were on opposite sides of the barricades, but a few letters had been smuggled through. Mark had comforted himself with the thought that it was safer for his father on the upriver side of the city. It didn't look particularly safe now. The barricade here was smashed down, and the streets beyond were almost deserted, but they showed signs of many footsteps passing, breaking up the dry mud. Here and there, a frightened face peered out from a side street, but until they came to the prison itself, they saw no trace of the mob.

But they heard it, growing clearer every second—the roaring chant of anger, magnified a hundred times. Mark had heard that sound before, back in a Gisethi village, when the rage of years had erupted. It wasn't a sound he had ever wanted to hear again.

By the time he and Ben could see the crowd, louder than they could have imagined, their eyes stung from the smoke. It looked like the rioters had burned their way through the doors. The few receivers who were still conscious huddled together, guarded by a gang of thugs.

But Mark barely gave them a second glance. His eyes were drawn to the scaffold.

A rope noose swung in the breeze. Nick stood beside it on a newly erected wooden platform, holding the other end of the rope. And there, next to him, was Pete.

Mark launched himself forward, crashing into a wall of backs. He clawed at the crowd, but they were packed so tightly they shrugged him off with ease. He sprawled back, and felt Benedicta grab him and haul him to his feet.

"Let go!" he shouted, barely audible above the roar of the crowd. "That's my dad up there!"

"Shhh . . ." said Benedicta, the relief clear in her face. "It's not what we thought. Look again."

Mark stared up.

She was right. It wasn't quite as bad as it had looked. His father was there, certainly, along with one or two other jailers. But they weren't there to be executed. They were escorting one of the prisoners—thin and dirty, his head covered with a sack. As they watched, Nick secured the noose around his neck, and stood him on a barrel. Mark saw his father close his eyes. He heard the crowd's shouts build to fever pitch.

The barrel was knocked away. The prisoner kicked at the air a few times. Then nothing.

Mark turned away, sickened, as the mob roared their pleasure.

"Feed the beast," a voice whispered, nearby.

Mark turned, looking down.

It took him a moment to recognize the old man who crouched beside him. He was gaunt and ragged—wearing the tattered coat of a once-rich prisoner. But his loose old skin had once been full of flesh. And he recognized the smell—rotting flowers. Even in prison, he had still used that oil.

"Ghast?" he said, amazed. His old prison mate, the one-time

lawyer with dark ambitions, had not taken well to prison. When Mark had left his cell, nearly two years ago, Ghast had already lost his senses. In the time since, he appeared to have grown worse. He crouched on the ground, peering up at Mark with sunken eyes.

"They came to set us free," he said, grinning. His teeth were still good, after all this time. They made quite a contrast. "Free! How could I be free? The shadow has me at every turn. He has them, too, all of them. The shadow's always one step ahead."

Mark shivered. "The shadow" was the name that Ghast gave to Snutworth. Everyone knew that he was the Director, by now, but no one had any idea what he was planning to do about the revolutionaries—and the receivers were hardly likely to tell. Whatever it was, though, Mark couldn't believe that letting them storm the prison would be on his list.

Ghast poked him in the ribs with one bony finger.

"You should rejoice, little star," he muttered. "The beast has eaten your enemy. That bluecoat guard with the poisoned mind. What's his name?" Ghast shook his head. "He cast a pall over everything—said the world was a lie, said everything was a madman's dream . . ."

"Pauldron?" Ben interrupted. "Is that who you mean?"

Ghast turned his eyes to her.

"That's him, red angel. He called Agora a beautiful dream. Well, maybe he's woken up now. Or maybe he sleeps forever." He pointed at the scaffold, where Nick was cutting down the swinging corpse. "An enemy of the new order, as much as the old," he said, more calmly than before.

Mark looked back at Ben. There was a small, disturbing part of his mind that was pleased. He could see that same guilty look in Ben's eyes, and he could hardly blame her. That mad receiver had murdered her sister, and scarred her brother. And yet . . .

"He kept saying that Agora wasn't real," Ben said, reflectively, watching as Pauldron's body fell to the ground. "And in a way, it isn't. At least, that's what the Oracle said." She frowned. "I suppose we never really knew what was going through his mind."

"Too late now . . ." Ghast laughed, clapping his hands in delight. "But that was just the starter. The beast won't be satisfied with just one. Aha! Here comes the main course."

The buzz of the crowd grew more heated. Mark craned his neck, trying to see who was being led onto the scaffold now.

It was a haughty old man, his iron gray hair loose and unkempt, his once-good clothes arranged in as dignified a way as possible. But despite the change, Mark realized that he had seen this man before, though rarely out of his wig and chain of office.

"Lord Ruthven," he breathed.

"He had your cell, little star," Ghast said, rubbing his hands in glee. "So proud, so sure of his destiny. Well, here it is. Enemy of the people, enemy of all." Ghast grew louder. "Death to him! Death to the traitor!"

The crowd around began to pick up the chant. And above it all, Nick pointed to the former Lord Chief Justice, and began to recite a list of his crimes. The big man's voice was deep, and slow, but Mark could hear every word.

"This man was a leader of the old regime," Nick said, above the growing shouts of the crowd. "He must be punished for opposing the people, for leading the receivers, for upholding laws that led to starvation, and for threatening Lily, great symbol of our revolution."

There was a cheer. It was a sound that yearned for blood.

"No," Mark said, quietly.

"What?" Ben asked, turning sharply.

"No, this isn't right," Mark said. He felt his chest tighten. Everything about this felt wrong. He looked into the crowd. There were little children, sitting on their parents shoulders, cheering. There were old men and women waving and shouting with rage and joy.

And up above his father, his movements slow and sad, was readying the noose.

"Mark?" Ben asked, alarmed. "What are you thinking? You aren't going to . . . ?"

But Mark moved before she could stop him, before he could let himself realize what madness this was. Everyone was mad today, so why should he be any different?

This time, the crowd was huddling around Pauldron's body, leaving the path to the scaffold a little clearer, and Mark found it wasn't too difficult to fight his way through. He pushed past waving arms and thickly packed bodies until, unseen, he was at the base of the scaffold.

Benedicta emerged from the crowd behind him, panting.

"Don't do it," she said. "It's madness, suicide, it's . . ." She met his gaze. He hoped that some of his determination showed in his face. She sighed. "Why do I bother?" she said, and knelt down. "I'll give you a boost."

Mark managed a tight smile as he stepped onto her interlaced hands. She was surprisingly strong.

The crowd were so focused, that for a moment or two, they didn't notice the newcomer on the rickety platform. Only Pete turned, and his eyes widened as his son approached.

"Mark! What are you doing?" he whispered.

"I'm here to stop this," Mark said, simply. He felt strangely calm. He was already in as much danger as he could possibly be; there wasn't anything else to do but get on with it. Without explaining any further, he reached up to take down the rope.

A huge hand closed over his.

"What do you think you're doing, boy?"

Nick's face was inches from his own. Mark looked up. Crede's former assistant really was a giant of a man. The crowd had gone utterly silent.

Mark stared up at Nick, unblinking. He was tired of being scared.

"I'm taking down this noose," he said, loud and clear. "It's not needed anymore."

It worked. Nick was so surprised that his grip faltered. Mark freed his hand and continued. The knot began to loosen in his hands.

Nick took hold of his jacket.

"I don't know what you're planning, boy, but—"

"Mark," Mark replied, calmly. "My name is Mark. One of Lily's friends." He raised his voice loud enough for the whole crowd to hear. "You're really going to threaten me, the last person in Agora to see Lily?"

This time, it was enough to send a buzz through the crowd. Nick frowned, but didn't let go.

"You use her as your symbol, Nick," Mark continued. "Do you think that she'd want this? Did you ever actually meet her? Because I remember *his* trial." Mark jabbed a finger down at Pauldron's crumpled form. "I remember that she was offered his life. And she turned it down. She wanted to heal, not destroy." With every sensible part of his mind screaming at him, Mark turned back to the noose, ignoring Nick, but making sure his voice carried across the whole square. "She'd have done what I'm doing now."

He finished untying the knot. The noose unraveled, becoming a single length of rope. The crowd gasped, a hundred conversations breaking out—curious, confused, tense. All this time, Mark didn't move. On the surface, he probably looked calm. But inside, he was panicking. Inside, he was remembering Nick, a cobblestone clenched in his hand, and much later, Crede, felled by a similar stone.

"But you didn't know Crede, Mark," said a voice from the crowd.

It was a cold voice, and hard—it sounded nothing like it once had. But Mark recognized it. And now, he looked.

Cherubina had kept the ringlets. Everything else had changed—the frills and gowns had been exchanged for a simple working dress, the look of exaggerated sweetness for a dark stare. But the ringlets were still there, still golden.

"We want our due," Cherubina said, her voice cracking with emotion. "They killed Crede when he was trying to make peace. They hate us. All they want is to see us back under their control." She clenched her fists—so like a little girl having a tantrum, had it not been for those hooded, furious eyes. "I say it's time for justice. It's time for them to feel the will of the people, the will of us *all*."

Mark felt his blood freeze. He had heard those words before, too. He had seen the result—the ruin, the graves, the savagery of the mob. He opened his mouth to protest, to try and calm them down.

He heard someone beside him laughing. Slow, and mocking—without a trace of humor.

Lord Ruthven stepped forward.

"Justice?" he said, addressing the crowd with contempt. "You have no concept of justice. Crying and whining because your lives aren't fair, when every person in Agora starts the same way—with nothing but their skill and ambition. I was a wigmaker's son, and I rose to be Lord Chief Justice. But because I did my job, because I upheld the laws and traditions that keep this city great, you see me as your enemy?" He stood straight and haughty, his voice never wavering. "Well, I am. I was the enemy of your conman prophet. I was the enemy of Lily, and all her disruptive ideas. I am the enemy of your weakness, and your desire to ruin everything that could have made you worthy. So string me up if you will, and call it justice. You'll still be nothing more than children, breaking their toys because they lost the game."

A roar of fury emerged from the crowd. Nick shoved Mark away from the rope, and began to retie it. Mark staggered, the wind knocked out of him.

"Crede was no conman," Nick growled. "He was everything to us. *Everything.*"

It was genuine, Mark was sure. He could hear the shake of grief beneath that anger. For a split second, he inwardly apologized to Nick for ever thinking him guilty of Crede's murder—whatever he was, he was loyal. But that same loyalty was about to lead him into a terrible mistake.

"Don't listen to Ruthven!" Mark shouted, to Nick and the crowd. "Don't let him tell you what you are; you're more than that!"

"So we should listen to you instead?" The voice of Cherubina, loud and clear. "Why are you trying to save him? He tried to have you killed! Why do you care about that *thing*?"

"I don't!" Mark shouted. This was so unexpected that the crowd was silenced. Cherubina looked like she was about to speak again, but Ben had worked her way through the crowd, and grabbed her hand, distracting her. It was long enough for Mark to gather his thoughts.

"I don't care about him," he repeated. "I wish I could say that I did, but you're right. I think the city would probably be better off without him." He gestured out at the crowd. "But I do care about *you*. You've been scared your whole lives, I know. So have I. Because this city demands it—it makes you force yourself to the top, or lie in the gutter in fear. Now the city's falling apart! People are starving in the streets, worse than ever before. And you're cheering because you think you have a victory. But really, what's happening here?" He pointed to Lord Ruthven. "When you take away all the revenge, all the politics . . . One pathetic madman is already dead, and one more helpless old man is going to be killed in front of you." He bit his lip. In a moment, all his resolve would desert him, and he'd have to run. But just for now, he had them. "Just think for a moment," he pleaded. "Would Crede want this? He dreamed of change, but striking at those who can't fight back sounds like business as usual to me." He lowered his voice. "Would Lily want this? You say you fight for her vision. As I remember, human life was what she fought for above everything else."

"Lily's dead," said Cherubina.

She wasn't raising her voice anymore. Despite the huge crowd, despite Nick's threatening presence, it felt more and more like a private conversation. For a second, Mark remembered the old times, when they had taken tea together, and never mentioned anything more serious than cake. And now, Cherubina was standing at the head of a lynch mob, looking at him with something between fury and desperation.

"We all know Lily's nothing but a symbol," she said. "Her ideas—we all dream of them. I wish I'd known half of what I do now, the one time I met her. But this isn't her city. She's gone. It's our city now."

"No," Mark replied. "She's alive. But you're right; it's our city. Our future. And it's up to us to find our own way." He looked around at the crowd, trying to reach all of them. "I didn't like Crede, but when he died, he gave you all a chance to fight. And you want to begin it by lynching a harmless old man?" He glanced at Ruthven, standing stiff and proud, and glared. "He isn't worth our attention."

Lord Ruthven moved faster than Mark would ever have thought possible from a man of his age. The blow wasn't strong, but it was so unexpected that Mark reeled back.

"How . . . how *dare* you!" Ruthven spat at Mark, his face contorting in fury. "I was the Lord Chief Justice! I am the most important prisoner here! I ruled the Libran Society . . . I was . . . I was . . ."

Mark did nothing. Just looked at him. Desperate, Ruthven turned to the crowd.

"I know such secrets . . . such power, the likes of which you cannot conceive! I was nearly Director! I matter! I'm important . . . you can't . . . you can't ignore me . . ."

But already, the crowd was beginning to talk among themselves, to turn away.

Nick flung the rope to the ground.

"We have achieved much today," he shouted. "The strongest fighters should secure the barricade again, before more receivers arrive. The rest of you, come, there is food back at the Wheel."

He passed Mark as he left the scaffold, giving him only a single look. Strangely, it seemed to contain a hint of respect. Mark, for his part, waited until he was sure most of the mob was looking away, before staggering, all of the tension that had been keeping him going leaving his body. His father appeared behind him, to help him steady himself.

"Dad," he said, quietly, "never let me do that again."

"I thought you didn't want me to tell you what to do?" Pete said, relief and pride flooding his voice.

"Yes, and look where that gets me," Mark replied, realizing that his legs were shaking. Pete laughed a little.

"I don't think it's quite over yet," he said, pointing.

Mark followed the line of his father's finger. Past the former Lord Ruthven, kneeling slumped beneath where the rope had once hung, crushed and silent. Out into the thinning crowd.

He saw Benedicta, smiling and waving. And beside her, Cherubina, looking straight at him, with an expression of fury.

Later, much later, Mark and Cherubina got a chance to talk.

If Mark had thought that the crowd would just dissipate peacefully, he was wrong. The revolution had been looking for someone to focus on ever since Crede's death, and suddenly Mark had stepped into the spotlight.

It was as if half the city had suddenly remembered that the

Temple Almshouse had started everything. They were besieged with offers of help, not to mention offers of violent assistance in breaking through the barricades.

That was the last thing they wanted; there was far too much else to do. Theo was organizing teams to scour the worst districts and find out who was starving. Nick was corraling his supporters. Even Miss Devine, as quiet and private as ever, had allowed them to fill her shop with bedrolls without a murmur, and was distributing a little of her own food and drink. Not that this surprised Mark—she was a woman who knew what was good for business. One or two of the louder supporters had already ventured back to her shop for a cheap sample of bottled calm.

So it wasn't until that evening, when the sun was only a reddish line over the edge of the buildings, that Mark had a chance to sit down. Pete, Verity, and Benedicta were still out, calming down those who had expected more fighting. So in the end, Mark, Theo, and Cherubina collapsed onto a beaten, chipped pew, with nothing between them but a desperately needed pitcher of water.

For a long moment, they didn't say anything, just relishing the chance to relax. But Cherubina never took her eyes away from Mark. He sloshed his water around in its little wooden cup, untasted. Theo threw his back in an instant, thirsty after his hours of work, and went to pour another, holding out the pitcher to Cherubina. Cherubina shook her head, tightly, without once taking her eyes away from Mark.

"Well?" Mark asked at last, too tired to play games.

"You ruined it," she said. Her voice was small, but still with a whiff of danger. "We could have kept on. One big victory, that's all we needed." She looked down at her hands. "We could have reached the Directory."

"You couldn't have," Mark replied, wearily. "You think that Snutworth would leave the Directory unguarded?"

"It would not have been worth the struggle," Theophilus added gently, filling his cup. "As it was, today you had a great moral victory. A lot of people's faith has been restored in the fight. There may yet be a chance for peace . . ."

"Peace!" Cherubina replied with scorn. "I was going after peace the only way it's ever going to happen. That's what Crede would have done—he'd have stormed on, overthrown the Director with his last man. That's all I wanted. To get something done."

"No," Mark said, interrupting her. "You wanted revenge." He stared into her eyes. She no longer looked like a child. "You wanted to punish Snutworth for all that time you were his wife," he continued. "I understand. It must have been worse than we could imagine. But you can't lead thousands of people to their deaths for that."

Cherubina scowled, but she did not reply. Mark didn't know what to say. Despite everything, he didn't want to be her enemy. She had been pushed into different roles her entire life—pampered daughter; obedient wife; Crede's symbolic crusader. He didn't want to stop her thinking for herself. But there were too many people's lives at stake. They had stopped one bloodbath today, but he didn't think that this could end without one.

Theo put down his cup and stood up, reaching over to take one of Cherubina's hands.

"Miss Cherubina," he said softly, his thin, tired face full of compassion, "we do understand. I'm quite certain that every person in that crowd had a real grievance that made them want to punish someone. But can't you see? For as long as anyone can remember, everyone in Agora has been alone—battling against friends and strangers alike to pull themselves to the top of the heap. But now, through division, we're united!" Theo wiped his forehead, getting into what he was saying. "People are helping each other, banding together. And through some accident of fate, they are looking to us to give them leadership." He paused, shaking his head, blearily. "We mustn't turn this opportunity into senseless violence, not when we can make a real difference. Not when . . ." he faltered, "not when we can finish what Lily started, and turn this revolution into something good . . . not when . . ." he blinked, harder, "not when the future could be . . ."

He fell to his knees. For a moment, Mark thought that he was overplaying the drama of his speech, and began to smile. Until he saw the sudden pallor that was creeping over Theo's face.

"Theo?" he asked, suddenly alarmed. "Theo, are you all right?"

Theo looked wildly from one to the other, grasping Cherubina's hand so tightly that his knuckles whitened. She looked down, scared, not sure what to do.

"Mark, what's happening?"

Mark looked up at her.

"Quick! Go get Benedicta; she's the best nurse we have."

Cherubina nodded, not offering a single objection, and forced her way through the suddenly interested and alarmed crowd.

"Theo? Theo!" Mark shouted. "What's happening? What should I do?"

But Mark could only watch, helpless, as Theo's eyes rolled up into his head, and he fell, convulsing, to the ground.

By the time Benedicta had been found, he was lying still, his breathing shallow.

"Is it one of the diseases?" Mark asked as Ben examined him. "Should I get some medicine?"

"It—it isn't like any disease I know," Ben said, her face pale. "Mark, there's this smell on his breath; I've only smelled it once before . . ." She turned to him, beckoning him close, so the crowd couldn't hear.

"Mark, I think he's been poisoned."

CHAPTER EIGHTEEN

Voyaging

LILY NEVER MISSED the sunset.

In her first weeks at the sanatorium, it had been her one sure way of counting the days. She usually missed sunrise. Her sleep had been troubled, full of terrible dreams, both natural and Nightmare-inspired, and Honorius had insisted that she needed her rest, even if she had to sleep until noon.

But sunsets were another matter. She found them soothing. Even in her half-addled state, she liked the way the sky slowly faded through comfortable pinks and reds, as though the day were breathing out, letting its troubles blow away, until the sun itself sank gratefully into the rippling depths of the sea.

The timbers creaked beneath her, and she shifted her weight. She remembered her first sight of the sanatorium—a great wooden edifice floating on the sea, behind the Cathedral. It was like a riverboat but far larger, with tall, wooden masts rising above it, and vast sails of red cloth bundled tightly around each one. Back then, as Laud half-carried her across the marshes, she had been so tired, and her mind so clouded, that she had not even questioned it. It was only later that Honorius had told her it was an ocean-going ship, the last ever to arrive from the lands across the sea, its cargo hold full of the coins that now decorated the Cathedral of the Lost. It had been left to rot, moored behind the headland at the edge of the marshes, but when Honorius had come to the Cathedral, banished from Agora like her, he had found a use for it. Officially, he was nothing more than the scarred porter of the Cathedral. But his true vocation lay here, attempting to heal the minds of those who escaped the clutches of the Nightmare.

He was a good healer. He had nearly been claimed by the Nightmare himself, once, and he had never forgotten that pain. There were only a few other patients, but he worked tirelessly with them, making sure each had a private cabin, where their nighttime screams and wails would not disturb the others. For the past three months, this long forgotten ship had been her home. Laud stayed in the Cathedral; he said that the roll of the water beneath the ship made him ill, but it had never bothered Lily. She had far too many other things to trouble her mind.

At first, Lily had resisted her treatment, not able to open up to a man she barely knew. Until, one day, Honorius had brought a visitor to see her. Wulfric—the Gisethi hunter who had guided her to the Cathedral the first time, the man who had been driven by the Nightmare to attack her. Lily had expected to be scared of him, but strangely, the reverse seemed to be true. The boiling anger that had driven his every movement was gone, and he seemed more uncomfortable when they met than she did. Honorius said that he had meditated long on his anger, and that Lily was a reminder of what the Nightmare had nearly made him do. Of how he had nearly killed her once in a paranoid rage. But now he faced his past with courage, and remembering that he could control his anger if he tried made him strong against the Nightmare's whispers. Of all of Honorius's other patients, he was the most recovered. Still bitter, of course, but humble, and quieter than ever.

After seeing that, she had begun to open up, and the healing had begun.

That was, she had to admit, the other reason she watched the sunset. It was part of her healing, part of facing up to her own troubles. As the sky darkened, it reminded her of Naru. Of that eternal half-light, and those buried, maddening secrets. As she recovered, she didn't need to think of that every day. But by then, watching the sunset had become a habit. And in any case, Laud usually joined her, and she didn't want to miss that.

"You really shouldn't spend so much time thinking, you know," a voice said behind her. She smiled.

"You'd rather I was talking to myself?" she quipped, as Laud leaned on the rail beside her. "I enjoy thinking, Laud. It's all I do at the moment."

"Just that?" Laud asked, with a smile. Lily looked back out to sea.

"Pretty much. It's relaxing." She kept looking. "No responsibilities, no prophecies, no one looking to me to lead them to a better tomorrow. Just me and the water."

"As I recall," Laud said, "you were the one who chose to start all of that."

Lily laughed. She liked it when he teased her. A month ago, he wouldn't have dared—too afraid that the horror would come back. But she had relived that a hundred times with Honorius, talking through it until it was almost like something that had happened to another person. She remembered how it had felt, the howling, overwhelming despair, but the feelings were sealed away. Honorius compared it to how he had made his own way through the

Nightmare all those years ago, searing his own flesh with a burning torch to focus his mind. Facing these memories was painful, yes, but now it was a pain she could control, and banish.

"Is Honorius going to join us?" Lily asked. "I know he's busy with his duties, but after everything he's done for us, the least we can do is spend our last evening here with him."

"Are you sure you still want to go tomorrow?" Laud asked, more seriously. "We could wait a few more days."

Lily wasn't completely sure if she was ready. Her sleep was better, and she hadn't felt so calm for months. But that was here, out by the sea. Returning to Agora would not be an easy journey. Laud said that many of the Naruvian tunnels had collapsed behind him, and in any case, with the Rail Nexus damaged, they would never be able to find the Hub again. The underground route was closed, for now. So the only possibility was the long overland journey, back through Giseth. But at least they wouldn't have to walk. Honorius had offered them another boat, a narrow paddle steamer that could take them all the way up the River Ora, to the gates of Agora itself.

She shook her head.

"No, it's time to go. Mark and Ben must be worried sick. It's only a few weeks until Agora Day; we've been gone for months . . ."

"They'll understand," Laud insisted. "You needed to fully recover. Remember, the whole world doesn't revolve around you."

Lily smiled.

"I know. And believe me, I'm so glad." She looked up at Laud, his hair glowing in the red of the sunset. "But you still chased me across half of Naru, didn't you?"

Laud didn't reply.

They stood there for a moment longer not speaking. Lily had been traveling for so long, it was good to have a moment of stillness. Just one more evening before the journey began again.

"I'm frightened," she said at last. She felt Laud squeeze her hand, but he didn't speak. He seemed to know when she had more to say. "Not of the journey, exactly," she continued. "Not even of going back to Agora, if we manage to get past the walls . . ."

"I'm sure that Honorius's trick will work," Laud said, reassuringly. "They would hardly have banished him for discovering it if it wasn't a way back in, even if he could never use it himself." Tentatively, he put an arm around her shoulders. "So what are you afraid of?"

"The Nightmare," Lily admitted. "I've never given in to it like that before. It'll be lying in wait." She dropped her eyes. "I don't ever want to let it rule me again."

Laud squeezed her shoulders.

"It won't," he said. "I don't really understand everything Honorius says, but he's sure that the Nightmare only feeds on fears you suppress, or your obsessions. And you're at peace with all of that now."

Lily smiled.

"Peace," she echoed. "Yes."

She remembered how desperate she had been to find her parents, how that had become the only thing that had mattered.

Well, she'd found them. One died in front of her; one didn't even remember her existence. Not what she had been hoping for. But now, when she thought of them, she tried to picture them as they had been, before all the prophecies and secrets had come to ruin their lives.

After Laud left, looking for Honorius, she spent a long time staring at the sea. She wondered if her father had ever stood here, watching the gentle swell of the waves. She imagined him bringing his new bride here to look out at the horizon, and wonder what the future held.

Perhaps, then, they had been happy. She hoped so.

* * *

The riverboat truly was a marvel of wood and brass. Long and narrow, with mechanical paddle wheels just beneath the surface and an always steaming funnel, Honorius had said that it would have been kept in the vault as a treasure if it had been small enough to fit. It came from the old world, one of the relics of the original Libran Society, designed for quick transportation up the river to Agora. Lily was rather pleased to think that it was finally fulfilling its function. At least the Libran relics hadn't all been as dangerous as Wulfric's flintlock pistols.

The morning had passed in a frenzy of activity. Honorius had spent it packing the steamer with food and fuel—anything to avoid listening to Lily's thanks. The scarred man had always refused to talk about himself, always turned the conversation back around to his patients. Even the reason he had been banished from Agora, the dangerous secret he had discovered, had been wrung from him only after many nights of questions. But after he'd told them what he knew—a secret way into Agora—Lily knew that it was time to return.

Just as Honorius finished stowing the last of the food, though, Lily had caught him. Managed to hug him, before he had a chance to pull away. Managed to ask him why he was really helping her. He rubbed the back of his hands before answering, and then set his jaw.

"Because no matter how much you hate it, you're a burning light of truth in all this darkness," he'd said, softly. "Not hard facts, like the Oracle. Real truth, real understanding. You'll break up these old ways forever. Agora needs that. I need that." He had turned away. "I'm sick of the shadows."

That image stuck in her mind, all through the farewells, as Laud untied the ropes and stoked the boiler. It was only as the engine thrummed into life that the reality of their journey sank in, and she waved brightly to Honorius as the sanatorium faded into the distance. He had given her a new life, and she wasn't going to waste it. And then she turned around, and took the wheel.

The marshes stretched before them. They were on their way home.

Over the next days, Lily generally steered while Laud kept the furnace stoked with wood. The funnel steamed, the paddle wheels turned, and the boat took them through the deepwater parts of the marshes at a reasonable speed. Not very much faster than they could have walked, but considerably drier.

But the most surprising part didn't come until nightfall, as they took turns either to stand watch or to curl up belowdecks. Maybe the Nightmare didn't know what to make of the steamer; maybe the sturdy boat just made them feel safe. But the Nightmare barely touched them. Once or twice as they navigated the marshy delta, Lily even had a dream that was not full of dark struggles and sudden, fitful starts.

Occasionally, it tried to reach her in the daytime, sowing doubt about wanting to return to Agora, and fears about the dangers she would face. But its call was weak, and Lily could understand why. The last two occasions, she had been here alone, or with Wulfric at his most distant and tense. But this time, she was here with Laud, under the summer sun. From up on deck, the marshes were striking, almost beautiful. And she was going home, to her friends, her real family. Not to peace—true—but free at last of the confusion that had dogged her for years. The Nightmare had no weapon against contentment like that.

After ten days, they left the marshes behind, and joined the River Ora. Now they traveled mostly at night, sleeping during the day. Lily knew that a few of the Gisethi villages were near the riverbank, and they didn't want to draw too much attention. In daylight hours, the plume of smoke that heralded their approach would be investigated, but at night the hiss and chug of the boat would be put down to another trick of the Nightmare, and determinedly ignored.

And this worked very well, until the sixteenth day.

Lily woke in the early evening to find Laud checking that the boat was firmly anchored, an ax and a pair of wicker baskets on the deck beside him.

"Anything wrong?" she asked.

"Nothing too bad," Laud replied. "But we're getting short on food and fuel."

Lily nodded.

"I think Honorius assumed we'd make faster progress," she mused, looking out at the gnarled forest a short distance from the riverbank.

"I'll deal with the fuel," Laud said, shouldering the ax. "Do you think you'll be able to find some more food?"

Lily grinned, picking up a basket.

"What, and miss watching you chop the wood?" she said, mischievously. Laud raised an eyebrow.

"I thought you objected to slave labor."

"I've made an exception, just for you," she said, teasingly, climbing down onto the bank. Then she looked up, more seriously. "Don't go too far in; the Nightmare gets pretty strong."

Laud landed on the bank beside her.

"Trust me, I'll remain focused," he said, holding up the ax. "What could be more thrilling than cutting down trees?"

Lily grinned, and was about to suggest a few alternatives, when they both began to laugh. By the time they parted, Lily's mood was so good that she barely even noticed the chill of the Nightmare as she stepped between the trees.

As she wandered through the dappled sunlight, searching for something edible, she couldn't help thinking back to the last time she had searched these forests for food. Back then, there had been frost on the ground, and she had come back with only a handful of mushrooms. But at this time of year, so close to the harvest, there were bound to be wild fruit trees she could plunder. She wished that she could approach the cultivated fields of one of the villages, but even if she found one, she didn't want to risk the questions that this would raise. Perhaps she would get away with being a simple traveler from a nearby village, but she knew that anyone who emerged from the forest was treated with suspicion.

As it happened, it was not as easy as she had expected, and it was well into the evening before she found an apple tree that still bore a good load of fruit. She picked all of the ones she could reach, but her confidence had been dented. The Nightmare around here was strange. She could feel it, snapping at her psyche, but it was different from before. In the forest, the Nightmare used to try to make her feel afraid. But now, every one of her feelings felt exaggerated. Each apple that fell into the mud made her want to curse aloud, each insect that she had to swat away caused her to fume with rage. Of course, she knew what to do—she concentrated, pushing it to the back of her mind. But still, it unsettled her. It was a little too like the unnatural anger she had felt down in Naru, as the Nightmare had targeted her frustration. As she walked back toward the river, she was glad that she didn't have to spend much more time in the forest. Whatever had gotten the local Nightmare so excited, she didn't want to meet it.

Something stopped her from calling out to Laud as she neared the edge of the woods. Perhaps she was still a little rattled. Or perhaps she didn't want to draw attention to her meager supplies. He would have had time to gather enough wood to sink the ship by now.

So it wasn't until she reached the boat that she realized something was wrong.

It drifted on the water, still and silent.

"Laud!" Lily called, softly.

No reply.

"Laud? Are you asleep?"

Still nothing. Lily clambered onboard, hastily dropping the basket, and began to look around.

The fire in the engine room was out. The cabins empty. Laud was nowhere to be seen.

Anxiously, Lily ran back to the side. Maybe he had found the woodcutting harder than he wanted to admit. Yes, she thought, as she raced back to the tree line, that would be just like him—to not want to admit defeat.

She stopped dead.

There was his basket, half filled with logs. There was one tree sapling on its side, and another, heavily scarred with deep notches.

But there was no Laud. No ax. Just a shape in the mud, where someone had fallen. And footprints, at least two sets, neither of them familiar.

She ran into the woods, trying to follow the footprints. But the ground was dry here, away from the riverbank, and she didn't know enough to spot the signs of their passing.

Whoever they were.

Lily leaned back against a tree, her thoughts in a whirl. Her breath was coming in gasps; her head swam. She felt sick and furious, all at once. And in the depths of her mind, the Nightmare's madness stirred. *Yes . . .* it said. *You left him alone. He'd never been in Giseth before, didn't know what to do, and you left him . . . and now he's gone . . . he's all alone . . . and the Nightmare will be back for you, with no one to stop it . . . Not unless you fight, and claw, and run wild to get him back . . .*

She pressed her knuckles to her forehead. The Nightmare wasn't going to have her again. Not when Laud was depending on her.

She closed her eyes, focusing on Laud. His face came into her mind, clear enough to send a shock through her system, and get her brain working again. How was she going to find him? She couldn't track him. She could wander through the woods at random, but that was a sure way to get herself eaten by wolves.

She cursed aloud. Why couldn't she think properly? How had she survived these woods before?

Mark. She'd survived because she wasn't alone. Because every time she was stuck, Mark had seen another way, had another idea. She thought harder, pressing her hands against the rough bark of the tree. What would Mark do? What strange idea would pop into his head?

She wished she could see into his mind now. Just like when the two of them had dreamed together, and plunged into her memories.

Dreamed . . .

And in an instant, Lily knew what she had to do.

She found a good clearing a short way into the forest—filled with moss and bracken, soft enough to sleep on. She lay on it, glad that it was a warm evening, willing her tension to go away and let her sleep. It took a while, but as she drifted off, she asked every star in the sky to let her not be disturbed until morning.

For once, fate was on her side. By the time the sun rose, the only problem she had was the layer of dew covering her, soaking her clothes. But as she pushed herself up, blinking, she knew that she had been successful. She had spent the whole night taking control of her dreams—a technique she had learned the last time she had been in Giseth, but had been too scared to use again until now. She had pictured herself beside a lighthouse, sending out a message through the shadowy half-world of the Nightmare, focusing on the one person she knew would be watching, unable to resist that summons.

Now all she had to do was wait.

A few hours later, she had her response.

Lily didn't notice anything, until the newcomer had almost

arrived. Then, a faint rustle in the bushes beyond the clearing gave Lily enough time to get to her feet, brush down her damp dress, and get ready.

The bushes parted, revealing a woman of middle years. She was beautiful, in an ethereal way, with long dark hair and green robes. In fact, the only thing marring this unearthly vision was her expression. She was staring at Lily with an expression of pop-eyed amazement.

Coolly, Lily looked the newcomer up and down, and raised an eyebrow.

"I'm glad you found me, Elespeth," she said. "I think you owe me a favor."

CHAPTER NINETEEN

The Addiction

THEO WASN'T DEAD. That was the best that could be said.

Sometimes he was well enough to speak. Whenever he did, he ignored any attempts by Mark and Ben to comfort him, insisting instead on giving instructions on medicines to prepare, and diagnosing any new illnesses that had come into the temple. He would sit up in bed, supported by an old, bundled blanket, and peer weakly at the latest line of patients. Then, all too soon, his health would fail him once again, and he would slip into unconsciousness. They had tried to find who might have poisoned Theo's water, but it was hopeless. There were too many people, and it wasn't as if they could report the crime to the receivers.

Verity cared for him most of the time, making sure that the curtains they had hung around his bed were secure—she didn't want anyone to know how ill the doctor was. But that left Mark and Ben in charge of an increasingly busy temple. Ever since Mark's

252

speech at the prison, the temple had become the center of the revolution, besieged by the hungry and the desperate. Even Nick seemed to look to them for ideas, when he wasn't trying to keep order in the streets. Mark barely had time to sleep, organizing rationing and watching the barricades. So it was left to Ben to keep their makeshift hospital going.

She never deserted her duties, but it was taking its toll. When she finished for the evening, she took off her smile with her shawl. Ben was starting to look almost like her brother, though she relaxed into worry, rather than sarcasm.

But Mark couldn't let himself think about Laud, or Lily. There wasn't time.

It wasn't until the hottest day of summer, though, that his composure cracked. And it all began with a cooking pot.

Mark had already spent the morning helping to haul buckets of river water from the banks of the Ora, so he wasn't in the best of moods. Mark knew that giving the patients river water without boiling it first would be a death sentence, but the big cauldron was still holding that day's soup, and the smaller one, the one they used for water, was nowhere to be seen.

Grumbling, Mark began to search around. Trying to control his irritation, he poked his head through the curtains surrounding Theo's bed. Verity, sitting beside the bed, nodding off after her night-long vigil, sprung awake.

"Have you seen the small cooking pot?" Mark asked. She shook her head.

"I think . . ." she began, "didn't Miss Cherubina take it yesterday evening?"

Mark frowned.

"What does she need it for? I haven't seen her cook a thing since she arrived."

That was certainly true. Cherubina worked when she had to,

but generally she sat, sulky and bristling. Now that she was no longer Crede's emblem of charity, the revolutionaries had little time for her. Mark had barely seen her for the last few days. She refused to talk to him, or to anyone. Even Ben, everyone's friend, got only a frosty look.

Verity shrugged.

"Perhaps she's finally joining us in the spirit of change?" she said doubtfully. Mark grimaced. He wished that it could be true, but the chances weren't good.

Thanking Verity, he began to ask around. It wasn't too long before he heard that Cherubina had last been seen going into Miss Devine's shop, next door. This was doubly puzzling. Miss Devine had opened her shop for their use, of course, but still very few took the glassmaker up on her offer. No one could easily forget her other trade, how she had drained their friends dry of emotion in exchange for food that her half-dead customers no longer truly wanted.

Still, he needed that pot. So, he steeled himself, pushed his way out of the temple, through the throngs of desperate and dying, and faced the thick curtain that served as Miss Devine's front door. In the blistering late summer light, the shards of glass set into the wall shone with painful brightness, making the curtain all the darker, like a slice of night.

Mark shook himself. He knew all about Miss Devine's kind of business. He'd bought from her, back in his old life. Her shop held no fear for him.

Even so, as he stepped into the gloomy little room beyond, he couldn't help feeling that the sudden chill wasn't entirely to do with coming in out of the sun.

Inside, the racks and shelves of tiny glass vials glittered back at him, lit from the sunlight streaming through the doorway. The liquids shimmered and squirmed as if alive. Perhaps they were. Who knew how emotions really behaved when siphoned out? As he got his bearings, the woman herself entered from the back room. She raised an eyebrow, and rested her long, thin fingers on the counter in front of her, but otherwise, she displayed little emotion.

"Can I do something for you, Mr. Mark?" she asked, in a tone that gave nothing away. "I wouldn't have thought that the leader of Downriver Agora would have time to visit." Mark didn't rise to the bait. He never thought of himself as a leader, though he supposed that people saw him as one.

"Is Cherubina here?" Mark asked. Miss Devine steepled her fingers, and looked at him sharply.

"Perhaps," she conceded. "But if she is, she doesn't want to see you."

"So, she is," Mark deduced. "I just need to see her for a moment." Miss Devine's mouth twitched.

"Is that an order?" she said. Mark glared at her.

"Are you going to let me see her or not?" he said, his temper flaring. Miss Devine leaned back, her arms folded. She didn't move. "Fine," Mark said, hotly. "I'll just have to find her myself." Without another word, he barged past Miss Devine, throwing aside the curtain that led to the back room.

"Very well, Mr. Mark," Miss Devine called out, not following him. "See for yourself what welcome you will receive."

The short corridor beyond was even darker than the main shop, and Mark had to squint as he entered a chamber lit only by one narrow window, high up in the wall.

The light fell slantwise across a tangle of glass tubes, snaking around the room, and gathering above a sturdy leather chair. It was Miss Devine's famous emotion distiller, and on any other occasion, Mark would have been impressed. But this time, he was far more concerned with the figure sitting on the ground at the foot of the chair.

Cherubina didn't look up as he entered. Her head was bowed, her ringlets falling over her face. She was stitching furiously, with long, dark thread, at something that lay crumpled at her feet. Surely that was too big to be a doll?

Mark came a little closer, and saw what it was.

"It's a good likeness," he said, aloud.

Cherubina didn't look up. Under her hands, the life-sized effigy of Snutworth was nearly complete. It was just as good as the dolls she used to make—she really did have a talent.

"You don't need to do this," Mark said, kneeling down beside her. "You think anyone needs to feel more anger toward the Directory? You've got your revolution; we'll go after the Director when the time is right . . ."

"No you won't," Cherubina interrupted, her voice small and tight. "You'll sit in the temple and do nothing, just like you always do. I'm going to show them who our real enemy is."

Mark reached out for Cherubina. With a flick of her wrist, she jabbed his hand with her needle, and he pulled back with a flash of pain. Mark massaged the wound, trying to staunch the little smear of blood that she had drawn.

"Don't interrupt," Cherubina growled. She pulled more rags from a pile beside her, and stuffed them into the lifeless body with surprising violence.

"I don't understand . . ." Mark said, trying to be gentle.

"We never truly understand each others' needs, Mr. Mark," said Miss Devine from behind him. She wandered into the room, and began to make adjustments to her emotional distiller. "We all have our addictions. Reason rarely plays a part."

Mark tried to ignore her. He brought his head down, trying to get a glimpse of Cherubina's eyes, but she turned her head away. He sighed. He clearly wasn't going to get anywhere here.

"Fine," he muttered. "But Verity said that you had the smaller cooking pot? We want to boil some more water for Theo."

"I need it."

Cherubina reached out, and touched the space under the doll's heart. It clanked.

"I built around it," she said. "Have to start with a core of something. And when it goes on the fire, the pot will melt and pour out." She looked up then. Her eyes were red-rimmed from weeping, but terrible in their intensity. "Pour out of his heart like so much metal slag. And then they'll see what kind of monster they're facing. Then they'll rally, and storm the Directory, and make everything better." She began to stitch again, furiously. "Don't you see, Mark, I need it!"

"No, you don't."

Mark wanted to be sympathetic. He wanted to reach out to this strange, damaged young woman. But he'd tried that before. And he didn't feel as sympathetic as he expected. The pinprick on his hand burned him.

"Didn't you hear me?" he asked, feeling his throat begin to choke. "I need that pot to boil some water. Our patients need it. Theo needs it," he kept his voice soft, but he could feel something hot building inside him. "You remember Dr. Theophilus, don't you? The man who hid us when we first escaped? The man who is still trying to save lives every day, even though he can barely move? The man who's doing more to help these people than your little crusade ever did?"

"How dare you!" Cherubina retorted, flinging down her needle. "You have no idea what I've suffered . . ."

"Really? Because as far as I can see, you've always managed to land on your feet!" Mark said, with biting sarcasm. "You were pretty quick to run off to Crede. Did you ever really believe? Or did you just want to cling to the most powerful person around, like you always do?"

"Stop it! Stop it!" Cherubina shrank back, but Mark wasn't finished. All the tension of the last weeks came pouring out.

"You petty, spiteful little girl!" he shouted. "Yes, all right, you had a terrible time when you were Snutworth's wife. No one's saying you didn't. But guess what? There are people here having an even worse time. Dying, suffering, bleeding because of the revolution you wanted just to get your own back! At least Crede believed! In his twisted way, he wanted what was best for others. And all this time, I thought there might be a little bit of you that thought of something other than yourself too. But no, you take one of our only metal pots, our only way of surviving in this plague-ridden city, and want to throw it on the fire, just because you can't get over your demons!"

Cherubina seized a pair of scissors. For one terrible moment, Mark thought she was going to attack him, but then she hacked at the front of the effigy—cloth and cotton flying. She stabbed, again and again in a frenzy, ripping open the doll's chest with a savage thrust, pulling out the pot and throwing it to the ground with a clang.

"There it is!" she said, hoarsely. "Take it and just . . . just . . . go away!" she shouted, tears coming to her eyes. Mark tried to speak, but Cherubina turned her back on him, so he snatched the pot up and stormed out of the room, past Miss Devine's mocking smile, fuming all the way. How could she think like that? Didn't she see the people all around her? Couldn't she imagine anything outside of her own life? She was as blind as . . . as . . .

He stopped in the middle of the shop, just a few feet from the exit.

As blind as he'd been, less than two years ago.

He had lived in the tallest tower of the city, deciding the fate of people he'd never met. He thought he'd been powerful then, when Snutworth had been playing him for a fool. But the cooking pot he held in his hands would change more lives than anything he'd managed back then. That was real power, and he'd taken years to learn it.

He looked down at his reflection in the battered brass pot. Cherubina might have been older than him, but she was just a child, inside. She'd been kept that way, always given orders, always told to change herself to fit those around her. And now he'd done the same thing, when he could have helped open her eyes. Just like Lily had done for him.

He couldn't abandon her now.

He put down the cooking pot and turned, pulling aside the curtain. He was about to hurry into the corridor, when he stopped. He could hear the sound of voices in the room beyond.

"Do not distress yourself, my dear," Miss Devine was saying. "He doesn't understand. No one would understand."

"He's so . . . so arrogant!" Cherubina was sniffing. "He thinks he knows best, all the time, even though he's made more mistakes than anyone I know. And he's lazy and never plans and . . . and . . ."

There was a sound of weeping. Mark shrank back.

"There, there," said Miss Devine, tenderly. "You know, I could make all those feelings go away . . ."

"No," Cherubina murmured. "I don't want that emotion taken away. I . . . I don't know what I'd be, without it. It keeps me going . . . in . . . this empty world." Through her sobs, Mark heard a scuffing sound, as though she had kicked the effigy. "Empty, like him. Like Snutworth . . . Like me . . ."

"Ah my dear," Miss Devine was saying, her voice dripping sympathy. "You misunderstand. I don't need to use my machine. I can make those feelings go away in quite a different way. All your worries . . . gone in a moment . . ."

259

Mark heard the shift in tone. It was only slight, but suddenly Miss Devine's voice sounded less friendly. Something was wrong, terribly wrong.

He jumped forward, racing into the dark chamber.

Miss Devine stood over Cherubina—a heavy glass jar raised over her head with both hands.

Mark leaped as Miss Devine brought the jar down. He plowed into her, and the two of them crashed back into the emotion distiller. Shards of glass tubes flew through the air. Mark felt one nick his cheek, and saw the jar shatter against the far wall. Cherubina sprang to her feet, pale and terrified, trampling on the effigy. Miss Devine clawed at Mark like a cat, struggling free from the pile of broken glass. Mark felt her knee in his stomach, and staggered back, winded. He spun around, but Miss Devine was already rushing at Cherubina, a long shard of glass in one hand. Mark seized the glassmaker around the waist, and brought her down. Miss Devine gasped as the shard cut deep into her palm, and blood welled up.

Mark sprang up, ready to defend Cherubina. But Miss Devine was no longer moving forward. She was lying on the floor, face-to-face with the broken effigy. Looking at it with strange intensity.

"You made him well," she said, quietly.

Cherubina stared down at her, pale and trembling.

"What does she mean?" she asked. "Mark, why is she . . . ?"

"You know Snutworth, don't you?" Mark said, interrupting. "Are you working for him? Spying on us?"

Miss Devine laughed. A low, painful laugh.

"Do you think he needs me to spy for him? He knows everything, boy. His control is absolute." She stroked the Snutworth doll's face, leaving a bloody smear. "He has been my master since we were children, since we were property. And I know my duties." She dragged herself forward, and Mark moved between her and Cherubina.

"What?" Cherubina was still confused. "Are you saying that you . . . love him?"

Miss Devine looked up at her from the floor, with an expression that was almost pity.

"Stupid little doll, always seeing the world like a picture book," she said, mockingly. "Who could love something like him? It isn't love; he's my addiction. We all have them, all have something in this crooked city that matters more than getting a good deal. And he is mine. His power—his certainty. This world is full of fools, and he is the only man I ever met who knew what he wanted." Her eyes grew harder. "He has a purpose. And in following him, so do I. That's more than anyone else has in this scrabbling city." She fixed her gaze on both of them. "You say rebellion brings you freedom, but it merely traps you in more choices, more decisions. You have no idea of the freedom of obeying, of giving up responsibility. I'd do anything for him, without a murmur. Have done, will do. I pushed him up to the top. I sold my wares to Ruthven, and made him fall. So many tasks . . . but only one failure. So far." Her look turned to poison. "Tell me, little poppet, did you really think that he would let you go? His trophy, his conquest?"

She pointed with one of her long, spidery fingers at Cherubina while still cradling the shredded face of the effigy with her other hand. It was grotesque. Mark wanted to stop it, but it had a terrible fascination.

"You know, I would have killed you when you came in," Miss Devine said, in a chillingly matter-of-fact tone. "After all these months of trying. But you had the image of *him* with you," her attention shifted to the effigy, but she continued without a pause. "For the first time, I felt a kindred tie. He was an obsession for both of us. But you were trying to break free, and that could not be allowed. You were *his*, little doll. You will always be his, and now you are broken."

In the midst of her dark words, something caught Mark's attention.

"Months of trying?" he asked. "You've tried before?"

Miss Devine tidied the doll's stringy hair.

"Such a lucky little girl," she muttered. "Always so close. Not drinking the water I brought, until that fool doctor had taken his fill. Not poisoned with emotions, of course, that would be too obvious. Something a little more traditional."

Cherubina gripped Mark's arm with a little gasp, and Mark felt a cold chill slide down his back. He had wondered who could possibly want to poison Theo. How could he have been so stupid?

"But that wasn't the first time. No, no," Miss Devine continued. "Standing next to Crede, the day I was given my instructions. I only threw one cobblestone. Just one. Pity my aim wasn't good; pity it smashed down your precious Crede. But, then again, it certainly stirred things up . . ." She smiled, wolfishly. "Perhaps that was his plan. He certainly wouldn't have told me. I served him with that stone. My great Director. You'll see. You think you're winning the revolution? He'll have prepared; he'll be using it to win . . . he always wins . . ."

Mark didn't see Cherubina move. All he felt was a rush of skirts, and then Cherubina was on Miss Devine. It wasn't in the least dainty—no scratching was involved. It was one solid punch to the nose. Mark found himself pausing, deliberately, before pulling Cherubina away. Miss Devine had plunged the whole city into war. She certainly deserved it.

The glassmaker got up, still maintaining her dignity, despite the trickle of blood running down her face.

"Well," she said. "I'm going to leave now, and you're not going to stop me."

"No," Mark growled. "You will pay for your crimes."

"Pay?" Miss Devine replied, with cold exactness. "Who will I

262

pay? The receivers? The Directory? You?" She raised her hand. Another long shard of glass was in it, wickedly sharp. Mark's eyes flicked around the room. He could charge her, but he couldn't be sure that Cherubina would be safe. Neither woman was thinking clearly at the moment. Nor, for that matter, was he. He had no idea what would happen if they fought again, and he didn't want to take that risk.

"You'll pay the People," Mark said, slowly. "We'll tell everyone what you did to Crede and Theo. They'll hunt you down."

"No you won't, Mark," Miss Devine replied. "Because you had the chance to do that to Ruthven, at the prison. That isn't your way." A tiny smile played on her face. "That's why he'll win, you see," she said, looking down at Snutworth's effigy. "That's why he always wins. Your strength lies in chaos, in raw pain, a hundred different voices clamoring to be heard. But he isn't confused. He's the shadow, the nemesis, the one who's always there. He's the one who has no limits, nothing he won't do. He's brilliance, and ice, and the crystal edge of a diamond." She lifted the glass shard, her own blood dripping on the floor. "His is the order of the new world. Soon, he'll be everything, and everyone. And then you'll all see him as I do."

And she flung the shard at them.

It was only a few seconds, as they ducked, covering their eyes, protecting themselves from the fragments of glass that rained down. By the time they looked up again, Miss Devine was gone.

Later, much later, Mark was sitting in the temple with Ben and Verity. They had listened to him without much surprise when he told them about Miss Devine. Benedicta, particularly, had said that she would put very little past the emotion peddler.

She had vanished, of course. Nick's men were combing the streets, but, as Verity said, they weren't likely to see her again.

Mark thought she was probably right. There hadn't been much reason left in Miss Devine's head.

He heard a cough from across the room. It wasn't a diseased cough, not one of the patients. It was small, apologetic—a sound to attract attention.

Mark turned his head. Ben smiled.

In the doorway, Cherubina stood. Mark hadn't seen her since earlier, after she had wept out her tears of fear and frustration. He had cried a couple of his own.

But now, her jaw was set, her eyes were dry, and her ringlets were tied back in a businesslike fashion. In her arms, she clasped a small pile of leather-bound books.

"I found these," she said, softly, "in Miss Devine's back room. I think they're medical textbooks." She brought them forward, putting them on the pew in front of Ben and Verity. "If we find the poison she used, could we make an antidote?"

Verity opened them, carefully, and showed a page to Ben. The redheaded girl nodded.

"My medical knowledge isn't as good as Theo's," Ben admitted, "but we might be able to do something with this."

"If not, I can go up to the Aries District tomorrow," Cherubina continued, "to the orphanage. Mother has some healer's skills, and it's time she helped . . ."

"We'll try this first," Verity said, pointing to something on the page. "But this will need two of us to make it, Ben. Three would be better, but someone has to stay with Theo."

"I'll stay," Cherubina said, in a tone that would brook no argument. Verity brushed back her hair, and smiled.

"Right. Ben, could you fetch the herbs? Mark, I think the mortar and pestle are over there."

Hastily, Mark got up, and picked his way through the makeshift beds to the altar, where the mortar and pestle were waiting.

As he picked them up, he saw Ben and Verity, hurrying down the stairs, having whispered their thanks to Cherubina. The blond girl hadn't moved. She stood by the pew, staring into space.

Mark returned, and put a hand on her shoulder.

"Thanks, Cherubina," he said. "You didn't need to go back into Miss Devine's shop, not after—"

"I did," she said, quietly. "It's my fault he's like that. I have to help. No . . ." she turned to Mark, and put her hand on his. "That's not it. I *want* to help."

Mark smiled. He understood.

And Cherubina leaned forward, and hugged him, whispering something in his ear.

"Thank you, Mark."

Mark shrugged.

"What are friends for?" he said.

Cherubina smiled. Then she turned, parted the sheets hanging around Theo's bed, and went to sit with the stricken doctor.

And Mark picked up the mortar and pestle, and went down to the cellar, happier than he had been in a long, long time.

CHAPTER TWENTY

L AUD WOKE UP, and wished he hadn't. He screwed his
eyes shut against the light.

He had been prepared for the Nightmare when he'd entered
the forest. Prepared for those little thoughts of doubt or fear that
would attack him, sapping his will.

He hadn't prepared for a stout branch to the back of the head.
Which, in the event, was quite an oversight.

It hadn't quite knocked him out. He remembered being seized,
and tied up, before someone had forced something down his throat
that smelled of sweet herbs and had brought instant sleep.

His thoughts were interrupted as he heard someone approach. He felt cool hands touch his face, and a bowl pressed to
his lips. He tried to push it away, but his head was aching fearfully,
and his throat was parched, so he let the water flow down his
throat. After a few seconds, the unseen hands pulled away, and

Laud found his voice again, in a stream of half-intelligible abuse at his captor.

To his amazement, he heard a very familiar laugh.

"Well, it sounds like you're fine after all!"

Laud's eyes sprung open.

"Lily . . . ?" he began, before his tired mind gave up, and he resigned himself to gaping. Lily frowned, and leaned forward to touch the back of his head.

"Does it still hurt?" she asked.

Laud stared at her. She looked freshly washed and well rested, and now that he was really looking, he could see that he was lying in a bed—wood-carved and comfortable, in a snugly constructed hut. Soup bubbled on the hearth, and little wooden toys were strewn across the floor. It was positively idyllic, and made no sense at all.

"Just checking . . ." Laud ventured. "I'm not still dreaming, am I? This isn't about to turn into some dreadful nightmare? It's just . . . either you were the one who hit me, or . . ." Laud trailed off; he didn't want to think about what that would mean.

Lily raised an eyebrow.

"Laud, do I really look like I'm being possessed by the Nightmare?" she asked, deadpan.

Laud squinted.

"No. You look happy, actually, which considering I'm recovering from a vicious attack isn't entirely welcome."

Lily scratched the back of her head.

"Ah yes . . . but you'll be fine; he didn't hit you very hard, and he really is sorry. The Order have sent several strangers to try to track them down recently, you see. They didn't know you were my friend; you're completely safe now . . ."

"Who are *they*?" Laud asked, wearily. "I've got a terrible headache, Lily, please don't be so mysterious."

He attempted a smile, and Lily laughed. Then she raised her head, and called.

"Owain! Freya! He's awake."

Laud wanted to be angry. He felt he had every right to be. This young man, Owain, had struck him with a wooden staff, and considering that he had the size and build of an oak tree, it was a wonder that he hadn't caused more damage. The young woman, Freya, had force-fed him something that had sent him to sleep, and both of them had kept him as a prisoner in their hut. He was very much the injured party, no matter how many times they apologized.

But tied around Freya's shoulders was a cloth sling, in which lay a sleeping baby. And no matter how much Laud felt like shouting at the young couple, he couldn't bring himself to wake their son.

Lily reached out, and gingerly stroked the little boy's head.

"Have I really been away so long?" Lily asked, amazed. "What's his name?"

"He's called Owain," Freya said, smiling. "After his father."

"Isn't that rather confusing?" Lily asked, beaming. Laud couldn't suppress his own smile. Not so much at the child, though he had to admit it was rather sweet, but at seeing Lily looking so joyous. Every day they had known each other had been besieged by worry and strain. He didn't think he had ever seen her look so happy.

The only shadow on all this bliss stood off to one side, leaning against a tree at the edge of the clearing. She was older than Freya and Owain, around forty summers, and wore green robes that made her look a little like one of the monks from the Cathedral. She had said that her name was Elespeth, and that she had guided Lily to Owain and Freya's hut, but otherwise kept her lips firmly shut.

She looked uncomfortable. Every time she caught Lily looking at her, her eyes flicked away. More than once, Laud turned to ask her something, and felt the pressure of Lily's hand on his. She didn't want to talk to her yet, either.

Instead, they sat down on the grass, damp with early morning dew, to eat a breakfast of mashed lentil potage, while Lily made proper introductions. It was a long story. She told him how Owain and Freya had been her and Mark's only true friends in Giseth, and how they had fled their home village to avoid punishment for loving each other. Now they lived in the forest, beneath the watchful eye of Elespeth and the rest of her people—the Brethren of the Shadows, a religious order that had learned how to live with the Nightmare. It was a fascinating tale, but it made Laud oddly uncomfortable, and not just because Mark had told him this tale once before, and he had mocked it as implausible. This was the part of Lily's life that was closed off to him—the year and a half she had been traveling in Giseth, while he had remained in Agora, not knowing if she was alive or dead.

It was not until Lily had finished her story that she turned to the silent woman.

"Now, Elespeth, do you want to talk about how you betrayed me?" she said, quite casually.

There was absolute silence. Strangely, the one person who did not seem shocked was Elespeth herself. She almost sounded relieved as she spoke.

"So, you know about it?"

Lily nodded. For once, Laud couldn't tell what she was really thinking. She seemed oddly calm, considering what they were discussing.

"Mark overheard you, just before you had him captured and sent back to Agora," Lily said, quietly. "I'd expected more of you, Elespeth. I knew you didn't like me, but I didn't think you'd betray us to the Order. Especially not to Father Wolfram."

Laud had expected a speech, some kind of moral rebuke. The old Lily, before her recovery, would have been fuming by now. But this was something different, something altogether quieter. Elespeth, for her part, held her gaze.

"In which case, why did you call to me through the Nightmare?" she asked. "Were you not worried that I would betray you again?"

Lily shrugged.

"You taught me to use the Nightmare—I used it. As far as I knew, it could be days to the nearest village, and I had no one else to ask. I hoped that you'd be feeling guilty."

Elespeth nodded, some of the tension leaving her shoulders.

"More than you can possibly know," she admitted. "When I agreed to Wolfram's demand, I thought he was doing the work of the Librans. But since then, Wolfram's obsession with finding you has grown . . . even his own people seem to be opposing him. His letters have become strange, full of talk of the Director of Agora seizing control of the Libran's plans, and 'the vessel being chosen on the Day of Judgment.'" Elespeth shook her head. "He has already corrupted some members of the Order of the Lost to his cause, and summoned them to Agora. Even a few of my own Brethren have joined him. He has continued to send me letters, but I have not replied. The Day of Judgment approaches, and I will not act against the Judges."

Laud shifted, irritably.

"Don't try any of that mystical nonsense. I'll bet that this 'Day of Judgment' never comes."

Elespeth smiled.

"The Day of Judgment is in nine days' time, Mr. Laudate," she said. "And even if you don't believe in it, there are enough people who do to make sure it will be a memorable day."

There was an uncomfortable pause. Laud and Lily exchanged

glances. They both knew what was happening in nine days' time. Agora Day. The Grand Festival.

And if everything went according to plan, they should get back to Agora in seven days. Just in time.

"What do you know about the Day of Judgment, Sister Elespeth?" Lily asked. Elespeth shook her head.

"Only that it will bring everything to an end. It is not the way of the Brethren to question the grand design."

"The Brethren have helped us, you know," Owain added, clearly trying to move the conversation away from this uncomfortable turn. "After Wulfric left, Elespeth looked after us. She even delivered our son. They've kept us safe from people from our old village, who were trying to find us. We owe her so much . . ."

"It's all right, Owain," Elespeth said, raising a hand. "Once, I helped capture one of her friends, but now I have reunited her with another, by bringing her here. In Agora, I believe that would be a fair trade."

Lily raised an eyebrow.

"No," she said. "I think you owe a little more than that."

Elespeth merely turned away.

The conversation continued, but Laud wasn't really listening. Occasionally, he nodded in confirmation, as Lily told parts of their story, but mostly, he thought about Elespeth. Yes, she had betrayed Lily, and he couldn't forgive her for that. But if she hadn't sent Mark back to Agora, would he have ever found Lily again?

"Laud," Lily said, softly, "I know that you thought we shouldn't involve anyone else in our plans, but we might need some local knowledge . . ."

Laud frowned, looking at the young couple. He wanted to be suspicious, especially as his head still ached from the blow.

But these were the only friendly faces he had seen for days.

And Lily was right. They did need help. He nodded, cautiously. Lily turned to her old friends.

"Owain, Freya, we need to ask your advice. It's about how we're planning to get home . . ."

And so, Lily told them what Honorius had revealed, back at the sanatorium. She told them the reason why he had been banished from Agora. About what he had discovered—and how they were going to use this secret to return to Agora.

After she finished, there was a long pause.

"That's . . . amazing." Freya breathed at last. "Completely crazy, but amazing. I don't know how you'll manage it on your own."

"We'll find a way," Laud insisted, although privately, he was wondering the same thing. "If we split up, the receivers probably won't recognize me . . ."

"I think they will," Owain said, thoughtfully. "If all you've told us of Agora is true, you won't be able to do this. Not on your own." A smile spread across his face. "So it's a good thing that you paid us a visit."

Lily's eyes widened in alarm.

"Don't think of it, Owain," she insisted. "It isn't your city; we can't let you risk it."

"One thing that you taught me, Lily, is never to take orders from anyone," he said, with a grin. But Lily was not so easily dissuaded.

"What about Freya, and your son? It could be weeks before you could return, even if everything goes according to plan. You can't just leave them."

"Lily," Freya interrupted, steel in her voice, "if it wasn't for you and Mark, we would never have escaped Aecer. Our son would never have been born. If Owain can help you in any way, then I'll cheer him on." She looked down at her baby, and held him close. "If I didn't need to nurse our son, I'd go myself. But I agree with one thing—Owain shouldn't go alone. You need someone more experienced in lying."

All eyes turned to Elespeth. The older woman bowed her head.

"This will not succeed," she said, softly.

"But you'll do it," Lily said, firmly. "Not for our sake, of course. But you wouldn't let Owain walk into danger alone, would you? Not when protecting this family is the only way you've redeemed yourself."

Freya and Owain fixed Elespeth with looks of absolute assurance, as did Lily. Laud watched Elespeth's expression. It looked from one to the other, searching for a way out. And then, defeated, her eyes sunk to the ground.

"If it is the will of you all," she muttered.

"Yes, it is," Freya said, triumphantly. "And this time, it really is. Except . . ." a flicker of doubt showed in her eyes. "Are you sure this is the best way to return to Agora? You'll be letting your enemies know where you are, taking the fight right to them."

"This isn't just about going home," Lily said, a trace of the old fire in her eyes. "This is about showing people the truth. I've been wrapped up in ancient conspiracies since before I was born. I've caused terrible harm, because I didn't really know what was going on. Well, I'm not going to force anyone to change, but I'm going to show them that they have a choice. That the world's bigger than anything they've ever imagined."

Up until that moment, Laud had worried that her time in the marshes and the sanatorium had dulled Lily's spark, made her cautious and fearful. But now, he saw her blaze to life again, discussing a plan that was dangerous, and foolish, and quite possibly brilliant. And he felt more confident than ever.

Lily was back. And he'd follow that guiding light anywhere.

CHAPTER TWENTY-ONE

The Return

ELESPETH TOOK A DEEP, shuddering breath. She made sure Owain was looking the other way, of course. It wouldn't do to let him know that she was nervous.

After parting from Laud and Lily, she and Owain had journeyed through the mountains for days, meeting up with other hooded pilgrims as they went. Wolfram's letters had spread far and wide through Giseth, reaching all of the Order and much of the Brethren. Most considered Wolfram mad for claiming that a new grand design was coming, and that all who wished to serve it should join him in Agora. But there were some who had taken him at his word, and made the journey toward the walled city.

At first, Elespeth had worried that the other pilgrims would suspect them, but fortunately, their fellow travelers were not particularly friendly. In all this time, they had barely spoken, and most had not lifted their cowls. Supposedly, they were allies, but most could not ignore that while some in the party wore the russet habits of the Order of the Lost—Wolfram's people—others were swathed in the green cloth of Elespeth's own Brethren of Shadows. That had been convenient for her and Owain; they had needed to borrow only one set of green robes that fit Owain to complete their disguise, but still, it disturbed Elespeth to think that her own people were responding to Wolfram's ravings. He was not only their enemy, but he was also the worst of the Order—vicious and unyielding in following their teachings, stamping out all dissent. To see him act like this, and follow the orders of the Director, a mortal man, was chilling. The Day of Judgment really was upon them—this was the end of everything she had known.

Their party was seven in all by the time they reached Agora and stepped through the tiny wooden door in the vast wall. Owain walked beside her, keeping his head down and his hood up. He had been silent ever since they had passed into the city, but she could tell that he hated these tunnels as much as she did. To be so far from the natural world, surrounded by dead, dry stone made her skin prickle. It was unclean, somehow. And everywhere, there were eyes. Guards in midnight-blue coats guided her and the other Gisethi visitors, watching their every step. It made her feel less than human—like some cog in an infernal machine.

But that was not the worst part. For the first time in her life, she could not feel the presence of the Nightmare. For most people that would be a relief. Owain, despite his nervousness, had said that he looked forward to a world without its influence. But Elespeth had lived with it all her life. It had guided her and tested her. It shaped what little power she had. Now she was alone, just one woman against the forces of this Director, wondering how she had been convinced to help.

The Nightmare had warned her that Lily would be trouble; every feeling she had upon looking at the girl was tainted by its fear. But she hadn't listened, because when she looked into Lily's eyes, she had seen her own face reflected in their dark depths, and seen guilt etched into every new line and wrinkle.

"Sister Elespeth?" Owain hissed. She put up a hand to stop him from talking.

"Hush," she whispered. "Wait for the moment."

They were passing one of the many branches of this dank tunnel—an old path, long disused, but standing unguarded. All they needed was the right distraction.

And then, they had it. One of the receivers, the guards of Agora, resplendent in blue and silver, turned, as though something had just occurred to him. He looked hard at Elespeth.

"Did someone just call you Sister Elespeth?" he asked. The witch nodded, pushing herself forward, pretending an arrogance she did not have.

"Yes," she said, thrusting her face forward until it was inches from the guard's. "Who wants to know?"

Heavy hands descended on her shoulders.

"Father Wolfram wants to see you," another of the receivers said. She struggled, of course. Just a little. Just enough for them to look the other way.

"You got anyone with you?" the receiver asked, peering into the gloom.

"No, I am alone," Elespeth replied.

Which now, of course, was perfectly true.

Lily stood in the bow of the steamer, waiting.

Around her, the calm lake lapped at the walls of the canyon. It was beautiful, but Lily wasn't here to look at the scenery. All of her attention was focused on the sheer cliff ahead, and the huge, dark wooden doors, set into its base, mirrored on the water.

Beyond the top of the cliff, Lily could just make out the distant towers of Agora. The River Ora could take them no farther—over the last days they had steamed upriver along the valley floor, but beyond this lake it was impassable by boat. Far to Lily's left, she saw the spectacular waterfall that filled this lake, plunging down from the top of the canyon, where the Ora flowed down from Agora.

But Lily's attention remained fixed on those vast wooden doors. Those doors were central to their plan. Because those doors were the reason that Honorius had been banished from Agora.

It had all been a terrible mistake. Back in Agora, Honorius had been a praise giver, like Laud. One of his clients had been a secret member of the Libran Society—a museum keeper who wanted to publicize a new exhibition on Agora's golden age. And when Honorius had come to collect some information, she had given him the wrong book. It had been only by chance that he had read the relevant passage before the receivers came to drag him away. But what he had learned was truly sensational.

He had found out how to open these doors. Not the tiny secret locks that allowed one small riverboat at a time to slip out of the city and down to Giseth to collect food. These doors led to a huge, old lock that would let even a ship the size of the sanatorium float up the Ora, split wide the walls of Agora, and sail into port.

Now all they had to do was wait for Owain to follow their instructions. Lily shivered in anticipation. There really was no going back now.

Owain shuffled through the city, his senses besieged by this new and unpleasant experience. It had been easy enough to slip down the tunnel, while Elespeth distracted the receivers. There, he had quickly found a door that led to the Agoran sewers, discarding his green robes as he went. He had trudged through the mud and worse, longing to find a way out, to escape this place of darkness and noise, worse than anything the Nightmare had ever shown him.

But when he finally found a grill and kicked it out, emerging on the riverbank, up to his knees in mud, it did not get better.

He could not believe that Lily and Mark came from such a place. They seemed so full of life, and goodness. But here the people pushed along in sluggish crowds, their faces wasted and blotchy, their clothes in rags. Lily had said that the building he was looking for was in the worst part of the city, and he hoped with all his heart that this *was* the worst place in Agora. Because if this was the best the city had to offer, he wasn't sure if he wanted to help Lily return.

No one here looked like the blue-coated receivers, so he began to ask the way to Lock Street. Most only stared at him as if he were mad. A few of the kinder ones offered warnings, that it was in the heart of the Pisces District, and that since the troubles had begun, it had become a place unfit for anyone but cutthroats.

In the end, Owain was forced to resort to intimidation. Despite his size, it was not something he was used to, and he hated himself for doing it. But as he collared one shifty-eyed man, he reminded himself that he was doing it for Lily and Laud. That they were depending on him.

"Lock Street," he growled, trying not to let a hint of apology show in his eyes. The man gave surprisingly good directions when suspended off the ground.

Owain slipped through the winding streets as quietly as he could, trying to avoid the eyes of the scraggly men and women who stared at him from crumbling doorways. They weren't attacking, yet, and Owain didn't want to find out how many he could fight off.

And then, he saw it. Lily had drawn the instructions on a piece of parchment. He couldn't read, but he could recognize symbols. And that sign, faded and broken, looked like the symbols that spelled out "Lock Street." The Clockwork House would be nearby.

He found the building with ease, the only one not filled with the sounds of arguments and crying. The door opened with a little encouragement, and he hurried in, stepping over the fire-blackened hole in the floor. Lily had told him that the Libran Society had once held their secret meetings here.

But that wasn't important to Owain right now, because ahead of him was the machine that gave the Clockwork House its name.

For a few seconds, Owain stood there, marveling. He had never seen such technology before. And this was just part of the mechanism—Lily had told him that it connected to steel rods that plunged deep into the earth, to open the lower doors, pump in water, and then winch up the great gates, splitting open the walls of Agora.

After all, there was a reason that this Clockwork House was on Lock Street, and it was nothing to do with keys.

But fortunately, he didn't need to know how it worked. All he needed to do was follow the instructions.

Wolfram hurried down the stairs to the depths of the Directory, his bad foot shooting pain up his leg with every step. He was used to it after many long years, but still, it did nothing to improve his mood. By the time he reached the cell, and laid eyes on Elespeth, he did not even pretend to welcome her.

"Why did you come here, witch?" he muttered, dismissing the receivers. He knew that they would wait just outside the doors, in case there was any trouble, but Elespeth did not look violent. In fact, she was maddeningly calm.

"Once, you invited me to join in your plans," Elespeth said, her voice betraying nothing. "But it seems you have found new allies. Even corrupting some of your fellow monks. I wonder what the Order would say about that."

Wolfram's hand clenched. He had always found it easy to keep his cool in Giseth, with the familiar presence of the Nightmare to keep him from letting his emotions reign. But Agora unsettled him—he and the Director were so close to their goal, but this revolution could ruin everything, and it made him jumpy. His reply came though gritted teeth.

"The time of the Order is over, Elespeth. The Day of Judgment is here."

Elespeth's mouth twitched. That was definitely a smile. Wolfram adjusted the hood of his monk's habit, unwilling to let this witch have the satisfaction of seeing how much she worried him.

"Yes, Wolfram. I believe it is."

Something was wrong. This wasn't the tone of a defeated woman. Wolfram got closer.

"Then why do you smile, witch?"

She met his gaze. Somewhere, out in the city, there was a strange rumbling sound, like ancient gears grinding into life. Even down here, they could feel it.

"Because I'm just the herald," she said, softly. "You never understood that, Wolfram. We—the Order, the Brethren—have always been there to represent forces greater than ourselves." She looked up, as the sound grew louder. "And now, it looks like it's time for one of those forces to arrive."

Wolfram felt an icy chill slip down his spine.

"What have you done?" he said, hoarsely.

And Elespeth replied, meeting his gaze.

"I've brought them the truth," she said.

Laud heaved at the rudder. Ahead, the doors ground open, moving outward, sending waves across the lake, rocking the boat. They saw the dark stretch of water within, the first of a series of locks that would bring them to their goal. The steam from the main funnel filled the air as they straightened their course, and headed for the darkness.

Lily stood on the prow, whooping with delight. Owain had done it. He'd opened the lock, the way up to Agora. They were so close now . . .

Lady Astrea looked out with amazement through a window in one of the Directory's towers. A tray lay at her feet, dropped, the teacups shattered, the tea soaking into the rug.

The wall was splitting open. The city wall!

Beyond the barricade, where the river sank from view, the great gray walls were starting to move. Houses pressed up to the walls creaked and groaned at the sudden vibrations. She could hear the sounds of shouts and screams. And then gasps. A whole city, gasping.

No, it wasn't part of the wall. It was gray, and ancient, and it was fronted with stone, but it was a door. An impossibly large door of iron and wood was sliding aside, churning up the river, and smoke and steam were billowing out. Something had come here, something from the barren, empty, impossible world beyond . . .

Ben ran down the stairs from the roof of the temple. Theo looked up from treating a patient—his first since his recovery from the poison. Cherubina's mouth dropped open. Mark ran forward.

"Ben, what's happening?" Mark shouted, above the sound of voices clamoring outside, and the deep, slow rumble that grew louder with each moment.

"The wall . . ." Ben gabbled, trying to get it into words. "The city wall . . . it's opening . . . and something's coming through it. It looks like a boat. I couldn't see properly, but there was someone standing in the prow, and it looked like . . . like . . ."

But she didn't need to say it. Everyone in that room knew that there really could be only one person making an entrance like this.

"It's Lily," Mark breathed, amazed. "It has to be. She's back."

Snutworth strode through the Directory. All around him, functionaries were panicking, receivers were being deployed, chaos reigned. But he was entirely calm. He always was.

"Flashy, Miss Lilith," he said, softly, to no one in particular. "But effective. You have just eliminated the need for several rather dull steps." And then, he smiled. "Well, now we can jump directly to the last stage. How pleasant."

After that, he was silent, watching the terror of his clerks. It was quite a show.

Mark forced his way through the crowds that thronged the Aquarius docks. He knew that Ben and Cherubina were in the crowd behind him, somewhere, but they had been lost in all of the jostling.

Normally, they would never have dared separate in this part of town, where the gangs had practically taken over since the receivers withdrew. But today, he knew they would all be fine—no one in this crowd had murder on their mind.

Normally, everyone would have noticed him—the boy who made a speech at the prison, one of the leaders of the temple. But now the people of Aquarius barely gave him a look. The air was full of shouts and chatter, amazement at what they had just seen. Everyone was asking everyone else if they had seen it too, if the walls had really opened.

As he got closer to the dock, the mood of the crowd changed. The nearer he got, the quieter it was. The faces of people around him were blank and uncomprehending, as though they were in a state of shock. At first, he was worried. Had something gone wrong?

And then he saw it.

There, at the water's edge, was a boat out of a legend. Steaming with living mist, it floated toward the dock. As it passed, people called out, throwing little gifts with joyous cries. Mark saw Laud, struggling with the rudder. But they weren't crying out for him.

There she was, standing in the prow. Lily, looking back at the adoring crowd with an expression of complete bewilderment. Mark struggled forward, shoving his way through. She wouldn't know how much Crede and Nick had used her as a symbol of their revolution. Woodcuts of her circulated through every street this side of the barricade. He had heard the sick call upon her name. And now, she was here, emerging through the walls—the eternal, unbreakable walls—like a goddess.

He reached the dock, and waved.

"Quite an entrance!" he shouted.

Lily didn't reply. Not until the boat docked, and Laud hopped out to tie it up. Only then, when Mark had thrown over a gangplank, and she had disembarked, did he hear her speak.

She looked out over the crowd. It leaned forward, ready to catch her first words, and send out her new wisdom to the whole city.

"By all the stars, Mark," she said, "what has *happened* here?"

CHAPTER TWENTY-TWO

The Reunion

LILY HAD LISTENED to three explanations of the last few months. First from Mark, on the dock, shouting over the cheers of her admirers. Then in a rush by Ben and Cherubina on the way back to the temple, taking her by back streets to avoid the crowds. And finally, when she was back at the temple, by an overjoyed Theo, who had the time to tell her in detail.

This didn't help. If anything, it made her more confused.

She'd expected a bloodbath. The way the Nightmare had made it sound, she had sometimes wondered if there would be any people left in Agora. Eventually, the only way she had been able to cope with the worry was to imagine that nothing would have really changed. She had almost been looking forward to coming home to a place she could rely on. Somewhere she could plan her next move.

Instead, she'd returned to find that Agora, the city where

children could be bought and sold, had become a revolutionary commune.

It was strangely comforting. Yes, this shattered Agora was very far from the charitable paradise she had once dreamed of creating—food supplies were nearly extinguished, rival gangs fought over scraps, and everyone knew that the receivers would soon cross the barricades and try to take back the streets. But still, her alms-house was the center of the downriver city, the place that gave everyone hope. People were volunteering to help, banding together against the oppressive forces of the Directory. Even Cherubina was willingly tending to the sick, which had almost been a bigger shock than anything else. Mark, Theo, and Ben had kept her dreams alive, and brought their own.

So, unfortunately, had people like Crede. And she remained the symbol, the one the crowds cheered even as they launched their vicious assaults against the receivers. If she had known that back in Naru, she would have been horrified. Even now, as she stood on the open roof of the temple, among the bedrolls of the sleeping patients, she felt a shudder run up her spine. It was a clear night, and distant fires were burning, consuming the buildings that stood near the barricades. She couldn't help but think of the founders, predicting that she would bring fire and destruction wherever she went.

Well, she thought, drawing her shawl a little tighter around her shoulders, maybe she did. Yes, everything she had inspired hadn't been good. Even if they won this battle, Agora would need years to rebuild itself, and she had been responsible for scars in her homeland that would never heal. But she also remembered the faces of the crowd that had come to greet her today. There had been grown men crying, children laughing, a whole city burning with hope, and faith in the future.

She'd been stupid to expect perfection; she knew that now. That was what the Librans had wanted. But they were bound to the past. They never believed these lands would grow beyond the bounds of their experiment. But the people of Agora had torn themselves free. They had a real chance to make a difference for the better, and whether they succeeded or failed, at least they were making that choice. That was worth any number of dreams.

She leaned her elbows on the parapet, and for the first time in nearly two years, she looked out over Agora. The others had gone to bed hours before, but she hadn't been able to sleep, and had wandered up to the temple's roof terrace for some fresh air. It wasn't a quiet night. Somewhere, around the flickering bonfires that dotted the city, someone was singing a marching hymn, just like the songs the crowd had sung as she returned. If it hadn't been for Mark and Ben hurrying her away through the back streets, the mob would probably have dragged her to the barricades and made her deliver a speech. Already Lily had reluctantly had to ask a large and intimidating man named Nick to set a few of his people to guard the steamer. Mark was afraid that some of the more desperate revolutionaries would hijack it, and sail it straight into the upriver half of the city.

Perhaps that was a plan to consider, when her mind began to focus again. Even now, at peace, she found the day hard to remember. She had been scared, of course, and worried. But those feelings had been pushed to the back of her mind by her joy at seeing Mark and Ben, and her amazement at Cherubina. And Theo, of course, dear Theo—who looked far more haggard and ill than she remembered, but still found time to welcome her with smiles and tears. She had begged him to get some rest, and after many protestations that he would happily talk all night, that Cherubina and Verity had worked wonders in nursing him back to health, he had left her to snatch a couple of hours of sleep.

And now, at last, she was alone. Now she had time to think, and to wonder what would happen next. Because whatever it was, the people of Agora wouldn't give her time to rest.

"What do you want me to do?" she whispered to herself.

"Just turn and look at me. That would be nice."

The voice was soft, barely audible over the noise from the streets. Lily shouldn't have been able to recognize it. But as she turned, her heart beating faster, she knew who it had to be. Laud had told her that she was living at the temple now.

"Hello, Aunt Verity," she said.

Verity hadn't changed at all. The veneer of brusque efficiency was gone, true. But that nervous, confused woman who had first welcomed her to the Directory, the one who had reached out to touch her face for a second or two—that was the woman who stood behind her.

"You don't need to call me that," she mumbled, looking down. "After everything I did to you, I don't deserve to be part of your family."

Lily thought for a moment. She was trying to feel something—hurt, anger, even forgiveness. But she was too tired, too relieved to be back among friends to have anything left to feel.

"My mother forgot that I ever existed," Lily said, softly. "My father sent me across the world to keep me away from some kind of ancient conspiracy. I don't think I've ever had a proper family."

"Really?"

Lily smiled, thinking of Laud, Mark, Ben, and Theo, sleeping downstairs.

"Well, not blood relations, anyway," she said, thoughtfully. Verity stepped forward.

"I wanted to tell you," she said, tripping over her words. "I wanted to find you again, after I realized that the orphanages in Agora wouldn't care for you properly, like a Gisethi village would

287

have. I wanted to raise you as mine, even though I was just a girl myself. The Director wouldn't let me, but that shouldn't have stopped me. I . . ."

"No," Lily interrupted, reaching out to the older woman. "You couldn't have done that. The Director wouldn't have let you. You'd have been thrown in prison, or worse, just to keep the Libran secrets safe, and I'd have had no one on my side in the Director's office, making sure I was protected."

Verity looked back at her, her eyes full of hope.

"Then you forgive me?"

Lily frowned.

"I don't know," she said. "You still took a baby and left her on a doorstep just because your big brother told you to."

Verity shrank back. Now she was no longer a woman of thirty summers. She was the frightened girl that Lily had seen in her dreaming vision. The girl who idolized her brother, and thought he could do no wrong. The girl desperate to believe in ideals, because the world was too big and complex for her to ever feel safe.

Lily didn't want to live in the past anymore.

"Yes," she said, softly, "I forgive you."

Lily let Verity rest her head on her shoulder. The older woman didn't cry, or speak. She didn't even embrace her, not really. For a second, Lily was almost disappointed, as though there should have been one last huge revelation—some great moment where aunt and niece affirmed that they would be family forever.

Except . . . her whole life had been like that. That was what the Librans had wanted. That was the part of her that was the Antagonist, whose every word and action changed the world.

But tonight, she was just Lily. Here, with her Aunt Verity, the only person in her family who was not lost to her.

And that had a kind of splendor all of its own.

* * *

Lily awoke to the sound of shouting.

She jumped up. The streets below were a frenzy of running footsteps, but the shouting itself was distant. Peering over the parapet, she could make out a cloud of dust and smoke hovering around the towers of the Gemini District, on the other side of the city. Now and again, she heard a low rumble, like venerable stonework crumbling into the streets.

She pulled her dress on over her nightgown and stumbled down the stairs, rubbing sleep from her eyes. Below, the temple was almost deserted. Only Mark and Theo remained, poring over a map of Agora they had spread out on the altar.

"What's happening?" Lily asked, as they looked up. Mark and Theo exchanged worried glances.

"The receivers have broken through the barricades in the Gemini District," Mark explained, pointing to the map. "We only heard the news about an hour ago. The people are fighting back. They've already set more of the buildings on fire—one of the museums went up before dawn."

Lily's tiredness evaporated in an instant.

"Are the receivers advancing?" she asked, hurrying over.

"Not yet," Theo said, worry clear in his voice. "The inhabitants of Gemini are keeping them at bay for now. But they have no leaders, no weapons, and certainly no plan. It could get very much worse."

"I should go there—see what I can do," Lily said, pulling on her apron. "You say they need leaders; maybe they'll listen to me—enough to pull back to somewhere we can defend . . ."

"No," Theo interrupted, firmly. "Laud and Ben have just set off to see if they can assess the situation. Cherubina and Verity have gone to find Nick and persuade him to bring reinforcements. The situation is under control." His face softened, though it couldn't lose the lines of worry. "At least for the moment. Rest, Lily. I doubt

289

you could step onto the streets right now without causing even more disruption." Theo turned to Mark. "And that applies to you too, Mark. After your prison speech, you're almost as famous as her."

"But we have to do something," Mark protested. "What if this is the final battle? We can't let Snutworth *win* . . ."

Theo looked troubled, but attempted a smile.

"I think the receivers will find it hard to take over this half of the city in just a few hours. And besides, you two can sway whole armies—we don't need to risk you on something that might only be a minor skirmish." He sighed. "And now, I'd better go and alert our volunteers. I suspect we'll have to prepare for some more wounds, at the very least . . ."

Theo hurried out of the door, and Mark turned back to Lily.

"Are you all right?" he asked. "You're looking a bit . . . surprised."

Lily nodded, a smile touching her lips.

"So . . . we don't have to do anything? Cherubina's helping the workers; Theo's taking charge . . ." she sighed. "This place really has changed."

Mark nodded. In the distance, they heard a splintering sound, as though another building was crashing down.

"Yes, it has," Mark replied, uneasily. "We're so glad to have you back, Lily. It's still pretty grim out there. Though I think your entrance yesterday made a pretty big impression. Half the city's still in shock!" He shook his head, marveling. "You know, we should probably sort out some more guards for your boat. I think we're going to need all of Nick's men to keep the receivers back . . ."

"The boat!" Lily gasped, suddenly remembering something. "I can't believe I forgot . . . it was just so overwhelming, seeing you all again . . ."

"What is it?" Mark asked.

"You remember I told you that Owain and Elespeth snuck into

the city, to open up the walls?" Lily explained, hastily, grabbing her apron from a hook on the wall.

"I'd hardly forget that—I still can't believe you trusted Elespeth after she betrayed us . . ."

"It worked, didn't it?" Lily interrupted. "Anyway, I suggested a couple of places they could find shelter after I'd arrived. I thought that they'd head here, but I did say that if they couldn't make it as far as the temple, we could meet at the riverboat this morning." Lily tied her apron and smoothed it down. "I really should go and see if they're there. They must be finding Agora pretty confusing, and I doubt Nick's guards will be friendly . . ."

"You're not going alone," Mark said, firmly.

"I think I can make it to the docks," Lily replied, lightly. "I doubt they've moved since yesterday."

"Things have been getting pretty desperate around here," Mark said, seriously, picking up his jacket. "There are some streets you'd better not walk down, fame or no. I'll guide you. Besides," he added, with a grin. "I'm not taking my eyes off you this time; you've got a nasty habit of vanishing."

Lily smiled. It was good to be home.

They ran all the way to the Aquarius docks, occasionally ducking into side alleys to avoid gangs of looters. The mood of jubilation from the day before had rapidly faded, and as the boat came into view, it looked like everyone was too busy with the Gemini skirmish to worry about investigating the steamer, although there were still a few gawkers clustered nearby.

The deck was deserted, but as Lily drew closer, she noticed a scrap of green cloth, tied to the side rail, and redoubled her pace—that was Owain's sign that he had taken refuge there.

There were a couple of large, surly men on guard, but they waved Lily and Mark onboard without a word. Lily bounded up the gangplank, and opened the door to the hold, while Mark investigated the boiler room.

"Owain? Elespeth?" she called out. Someone moved in the darkness beyond. She recognized the rough Gisethi clothing.

She stepped in a little farther.

"You in here?" she asked.

As her eyes adjusted, she made out a man sitting in the corner of the hold—head down, his knees up to his chin. Something was wrong. She had never seen Owain looking like this, not even when his whole village had tried to kill him. He looked crushed, defeated.

"Owain?" she said, more quietly, her good mood evaporating. "Owain, what is it? What's wrong?"

He looked up.

He wasn't Owain. He looked just like him, but his face was different—hollow, vacant. He stared at Lily with no interest at all. Lily took a step back.

"Who are—?"

A woman's hand clamped over her face and mouth. It was holding a cloth soaked in something that smelled thick and sweet. Her head began to spin

"You, Miss Lilith, have an appointment with the Director," said a tough female voice, far away.

And she fell into darkness.

CHAPTER TWENTY-THREE

The Appointment

MARK'S FIRST MISTAKE was to open his eyes.

It wasn't that his eyes still stung from whatever he'd been made to inhale. It wasn't that the light that shone toward him was uncomfortably bright.

It was that when he opened them, the first thing he saw was the face of Father Wolfram.

He jumped before he could stop himself, and felt leather straps bite into his arms. Wolfram moved the lantern closer. Mark could see nothing but his hard, uncaring face, the lines exaggerated by the harsh light. Mark tried to turn his head away, but something held it in place. His legs were bound too, uncomfortably. He was trapped in a sitting position, head back, vulnerable.

Wolfram shook his head.

"Always struggling against the greater good," he rumbled, in a tone of disgust. "No matter how many times I try to curb your nature, Mark, you are a twisted sapling, and would have made a crooked tree."

Mark didn't like the sound of 'would have.' He tried to speak, but his tongue lolled uselessly, and all he could do was groan.

"Do not attempt speech," Wolfram reproached him. "Not yet. The tincture will clear from your mind, soon. But for now, you must learn the virtue of silence."

Wolfram withdrew, taking the lantern with him. If Mark could have spoken, he would have remarked that Wolfram's own vow of silence seemed long dead, but perhaps it was best that he could not. The more he saw of this room, the more his heart sank.

It was not a big room, but the stones in the wall were built to a massive scale, as though this were part of a much larger structure. Without being able to move his head, all he could see was this rough-hewn wall, and to his far left, the edge of some contraption, covered in dials and tubing. It looked strangely familiar, but he couldn't place it.

Wolfram walked out of sight behind him, taking the light with him. Mark looked down, still unable to move anything but his eyes. With his head tilted back, he could barely see his arms, but the straps on them felt thick and tight.

There was a soft sound to his right. Mark tensed. Now the light was no longer blinding him, he could see a shape out of the corner of his eye. It looked like another chair, with another bound figure just coming to their senses.

"Wha . . . whu . . . what?" The voice came, so familiar. Mark groaned.

"L . . . Lily?" he asked, forcing his slack tongue to make words.

"Mark! What . . ."

That was as far as she got, before Wolfram struck her. Mark felt the force of it, even from where he was sitting, a ringing slap across the face. Wolfram stalked back over to Mark, and pushed the lantern so close that Mark felt his eyebrows singe.

"You will not speak," he growled. "If you do, Lily will receive your punishment. Be glad that I will not strike you. I might damage the apparatus."

Apparatus? Mark thought. There did seem to be an odd sound in the air, a humming hiss. And he had the sense that something large was hanging over his head.

Behind him, a door opened. Footsteps on the stone floor. And something else—the confident tapping of a cane.

"Well now, Father Wolfram, are the Judges awake?"

Mark knew that voice. Still reasonable, and calm, and deceptive.

Wolfram nodded. There were more footsteps, and the newcomer came into view. He propped his silver-handled cane against the wall, and smiled, warmly.

"Mr. Mark, Miss Lilith, welcome to the Directory," said Snutworth.

What struck Mark most forcefully was how unchanged he was. True, his coat was now trimmed with gold, but it was still the same formal black. He wore the same gloves, the same simple cravat, and the same expression of polite interest. He could have surrounded himself with finery, but he hadn't. In a way, that was all the more disturbing. This didn't look like a man who had reached his goal.

"Why have you brought us here?" Mark heard Lily say, her speech returning. "What have you done with Owain?" Wolfram glared at her, but Snutworth—Mark still couldn't think of him as the Director—raised his hand.

"No, Father Wolfram, I think that the Antagonist is entitled to an answer. Besides," he added, lightly, "we will scarcely make any progress if our guests remain silent, will we?" Wolfram bowed his head, and withdrew from sight, walking behind them.

"Now, to answer the simpler question first," Snutworth continued. "Mr. Owain is imprisoned elsewhere in the Directory, along with Sister Elespeth. I cannot pretend that they are particularly comfortable, but they are alive."

"And who was that, in the boat?" Lily continued. This time, Snutworth's expression hardened. Just for a second.

"That was Mr. Owain, naturally. I thought that you were famed for the clarity of your perception . . ."

"That wasn't Owain," Lily interrupted fiercely. "He looked like him, but it wasn't the same man. When he looked at me . . . it was like he'd never met me before . . ."

Lily trailed off. Snutworth's expression was hard to place. Was there a spark of triumph in those sharp green eyes?

"Nevertheless, it was him. Mostly. How else do you imagine Inspector Poleyn would have known where to find you? Really, I do wonder why you thought it would be a good idea to use the tunnels, or why it had not occurred to you that if one person may travel through them to reach the docks, so may a whole platoon of undercover receivers. Barricades are irritating, Miss Lilith, but hardly real barriers."

"Then why haven't you . . . ?" Lily began.

"Don't." Mark said, suddenly, surprising himself. "Don't ask him. He enjoys it."

He had realized what he had seen in Snutworth's eyes. No matter how hard he tried to disguise it, Snutworth loved to see one of his schemes to fruition. He remembered that look, back when Snutworth had been his assistant, and one of the deals had come in, increasing Mark's fortune and position. Of course, at the time he had thought that Snutworth had been pleased on his behalf, not that he was planning to take it all.

Snutworth nodded, sagely.

"I must admit to a little satisfaction," he said. "Ideally, I would have waited a few more weeks before launching my attack, to ensure that starvation would have rendered your defenders helpless. However, time moves on, and we must be prepared for tomorrow."

Mark tried to resist the urge to ask, he really did. But he and Lily were helpless, and whatever happened next, this was clearly important.

"What happens tomorrow?" he asked, guardedly. But it was not Snutworth who answered.

"The first day of Libra," Lily replied, with growing alarm. "My birthday. Agora Day, the end of the twelfth cycle of twelve years since Agora's foundation." She paused, Mark could almost picture her expression—the frown deepening on her face as the pieces slotted into place. "The Day of Judgment."

Snutworth clapped his hands, slowly, three times.

"There. I knew that you two were appointed the Judges for a reason." He moved to the device, just at the edge of Mark's vision. "Now, to business. There will be some important ceremonial duties tomorrow, naturally, but first I require a rather important piece of information." He touched some dials. Above Mark's head, something thrummed into life. He turned back, looking Mark directly in the eyes. "Where is the Descent into Naru?"

Mark tried to look far more confident that he felt.

"You don't know?" he said, quietly pleased to find that they still had an advantage. Snutworth nodded, almost amiably.

"Alas, my predecessor and I did not part company under the best circumstances," he said, smoothly. "Indeed, until Miss Verity left my service, I really did believe that the old man was dead. Which was rather frustrating, because since then I have learned that he had kept the location of the Agoran Descent to himself." Thoughtfully, he picked up his cane again and polished the handle with the edge of his sleeve. "Although the Directory records have much to say on the subject of Naru, the only entrance mentioned lies in the Cathedral of the Lost, which would be most inconvenient, and would probably require violence against the remaining members of the Order. So you can imagine my satisfaction when Verity, despite the threat of my displeasure, risked everything to steal a meaningless recipe from the Directory's vaults. It was obvious to me that this was a code of some kind, and one that could have only been planted by one with an intimate knowledge of our library, like the old Director. After that, well . . ." he caught Mark's eye. "It was simply a matter of waiting for the right moment to take charge of your schemes. And it seems that I was correct in my assumptions. Mr. Owain mentioned to me that you, Mr. Mark, managed to descend to the Land Below from somewhere here in Agora, doubtless with the aid of the former Director." He leaned back against the wall, entirely at his ease. "I think I would like you to share that knowledge."

"Owain would never have told you that," Lily hissed. "You're just trying to trick us!"

"Miss Lilith, you may believe whatever you like. Nevertheless, I know that there is a path down to Naru somewhere in Agora, and one of you is going to tell me."

There was a long silence. Snutworth moved his eyes from one to the other. Mark didn't know what Lily was thinking, but his own brain was racing, trying to think of any way to turn this one chance to their advantage. Lily spoke again.

"First, tell us why you want to know," she demanded. Snutworth shook his head.

"That is my concern," he said, simply. A desperate idea came into Mark's head

"We'll tell you," he suggested, "but only if you call off the receivers and start working out peace with the revolutionaries."

This time, Snutworth considered for a moment.

"No, I think not," he replied, still calm. "I must say, I do find your confidence admirable, but I fear that making demands is a waste of time. Consider—you are both my prisoners. No one except myself, Father Wolfram, and the loyal Inspector Poleyn know that you are here. There are no sympathetic guards who will take pity because of your youth, and no revolutionary supporters who can sneak in. Even if you were to escape, we are far from helpless, and I can assure you that after you caused the chaos in his village, Father Wolfram sees you as unholy creatures, fit for the harshest punishment." He came closer to Mark, his expression unwavering. "So I think it is fair to say that you have very little to bargain with. You have one piece of information I require. Give it to me."

Mark opened his mouth, and then firmly, defiantly, clamped it shut. Whatever Snutworth needed, it could only make everything worse.

Snutworth nodded, thoughtfully.

"Well, in that case, Miss Lilith, I have some good news for you," he said. "I shall answer one of your questions, and with a practical demonstration. Wolfram, would you adjust the mask?"

Snutworth moved over to the device in the corner, and began to turn the dials. The weird hum increased, along with the hiss of rushing air. At the edge of his vision, Mark could see Wolfram's hands reach up above his head, the long red sleeves of his habit blocking his view. Again, he got the sense of something above him. Something that shone like glass.

"What's going on?" Lily said, a note of panic in her voice. "Is that . . . ?"

Wolfram lowered a mask of smoked glass toward Mark's head. He felt his heart begin to race, and tried to struggle, but Wolfram gripped his head and fitted the mask tightly over his face, securing it with more straps. Snutworth turned back, although Mark could barely see him through the thick, translucent mask. He looked even more like a shadow to him now. Only his eyes, sparkling in the light, were still in focus.

"Yes, Miss Lilith," he said, his voice still maddeningly calm. "It is an emotion extractor."

Above him, Mark felt the sound of the rushing air intensify, as though the wind were pouring into his mind and soul.

"What are you doing?" Lily was shouting, but it sounded so distant. When Snutworth spoke, though, his voice cut through the confusion like a knife.

"Miss Devine and I were apprentices together. Our master was an alchemist by trade, and a true genius. He invented the first emotional extractor, an extraordinary achievement. And most of his imitators, from the worst glitter dive in the slums to the highest parlors of the elite, followed his original designs—relatively crude affairs. But Devine, now she was the best. She made several improvements to increase the purity of the extracted emotions, and yet she never realized what else she had managed to achieve. When I commissioned a copy of her device, some months ago, I did not quite appreciate it either." Snutworth paused, and Mark heard him turn another dial. The rushing wind in his head spread throughout his entire body. He tingled and shook, and in one horrible moment, he realized what Snutworth was about to say.

"Most emotion extractors require their subjects to be willing."

Mark's whole body felt light, as though something cold was seeping into him.

And then his every feeling blazed into life. He wanted to laugh, to cry, to howl, but his body lay rigid. Somewhere, far off, he could hear Lily shouting.

"I don't know!" she was screaming. "I don't know where the path is."

"Tell me, and I will stop." That was Snutworth, calm as ever. But to Mark, that voice no longer sounded rational. It was colored with a thousand different insinuations and implications. For a moment, all of the confidence Mark had ever felt took command. He believed he could break free of these straps with a single heave. He could see instantly what Snutworth's plan was—all the power that he could gain if he had access to Naru, and everyone's secrets. No, there was more to it than that, he was going to . . .

But then that feeling was gone, replaced by fear. Horrible, petrifying fear. He longed to curl up, to bury his head, to not think of what Snutworth was doing to him, what he could do to everyone. He felt tears running down his face and smearing on the inside of the mask. He could hear Lily more clearly now; she was afraid too, deathly afraid.

"But I can't say," she was shouting. "They never told me. You have to believe me!"

Why didn't she know? Why hadn't he told her?! Mark wanted to hit himself, his hands tensed as anger flooded him. He wanted to roar, to berate his so-called friend for never asking him how he'd reached her. He let out a sound somewhere between a scream and a curse, but the mask was tight, and it echoed around his own head.

"You misunderstand, Miss Lilith," Snutworth said, his very voice making Mark's innards clench. "It would be useful for you to tell me now, but not necessary."

He didn't need it! Maybe he was going to release them after all . . . maybe . . . he felt light and giddy. Suddenly, he loved everything, and everyone. Surely Snutworth could be redeemed; surely Lily could be rescued. Surely they could all go home, to the temple, where Theo waited, and Ben and Cherubina . . . all his dear, wonderful friends. Now every other emotion was out of the way, now he was free of worry, and fear, and anger. Now it was just love, and delight, in everyone and everything . . .

And it was gone. For a few more seconds, he felt an acute sense of loss. Then that was gone too. And there was nothing.

"You see, Miss Lilith," Snutworth said, as he carefully prized the mask away from Mark's face. "It doesn't honestly matter if you tell me, because Mr. Mark knows." He looked Mark in the eyes. Mark looked back, blinking.

"Yes?" he said, his tongue dull and slow.

"Tell me how to get down to Naru."

Mark looked back at Snutworth.

"Why?" he said.

"Do you find these straps uncomfortable?"

Mark looked down. They were causing his arms some pain.

"Yes," he said, truthfully.

"If you tell me, I will undo them."

Mark nodded.

"All right. The Descent is in the Last's old house in the Virgo District."

Mark heard Lily gasp, but he wasn't quite sure why. As the Director released his head, he saw a tangle of glass tubes in the ceiling, filled with fizzing gases of all colors. As he watched, they condensed down into fluids, running into several racks of tiny glass vials, each one holding a different color.

"You wondered what had happened to Mr. Owain?" the Director asked. "This. It is quite simple to obtain information from people, when they do not care about who has it."

Mark scratched an itch on his arm. All of the straps had been taken away, but he didn't see any reason to get up. There was nowhere else to sit, and his limbs were heavy and tired. Idly, he glanced around the room. He saw Father Wolfram begin to collect the little vials, which he supposed contained his emotions. Over to his right, Lily was crying. Her tears were dropping down to the stone floor. He watched one for a moment, running through a crack in the flagstones, before losing interest.

"Now, Miss Lilith," the Director continued. "I'm going to release you. As you know, if emotions are to be returned, they must be reabsorbed by their owner before a full day has passed, or they are lost forever. If you attempt to escape, or cause trouble, Father Wolfram will begin to smash the vials. I trust I make myself clear."

Lily nodded, biting her lips. Mark watched as Snutworth untied her. They looked like very sturdy knots. He wondered whether the Director had the rope made specially.

Now that Lily had gotten up, Mark realized that she had run over and started clinging to him. She was saying something, but it was hard to make out through all the snuffling.

"You should speak clearer," he said, flatly. "I can't hear you."

"I'm sorry . . ." Lily said. Mark shrugged.

"If you say so," he said.

Mark heard a clinking sound, and looked up. The Director was placing the little glass vials in a leather bag.

"Father Wolfram, would you go and inform Lady Astrea that she is in command of the receivers in our absence? Should the expected attack come, she knows what to do."

Wolfram left the room. As he opened the door, Mark glimpsed an ancient corridor, paneled in dark oak.

"Get up, Mark," Snutworth said. Mark did so. As he did, he felt Lily, who was still holding on to him, slump to the ground. He looked down. Somewhere in the back of his mind, he wondered if he should be doing something.

"Help her up, Mark," Snutworth said, gently rattling the pouch that contained everything Mark had ever felt. Seeing no reason not to, Mark held out his hand, and Lily took hold of it, pulling herself to her feet. She glared at Snutworth.

"What now?" she asked, her voice catching.

Snutworth smiled.

"Once Father Wolfram gets back, the four of us are going on a short journey, down to the land of secrets. And you two will fulfill the duty that was assigned to you a hundred years before you were born." He leaned forward on his cane, his eyes sparkling. "You will fulfill the last prophecy of the Midnight Charter."

For some reason, Mark felt Lily's hand tense in his.

He couldn't imagine why.

CHAPTER TWENTY-FOUR

The Leader

LADY ASTREA SAT in the Director's office, staring down at her hands. All of her life, she had dreamed of this moment—sitting behind the mahogany desk, the whole of the city at her command. Of course, she had imagined that she would have been appointed Director, not holding the fort against a city full of revolutionaries while the real Director disappeared.

Life had a way of being so disappointing.

"My lady?"

She looked up. Two receivers stood before her, both bedecked in midnight-blue uniforms trimmed with silver and gold braid. The young woman was scuffed and bruised, but bore the weary stance of a woman ready for more battle. The man was older, more cautious. His uniform was pristine, but of course, for the last few months he had been confined to his desk in the Directory. She sighed; this was not going to be an easy meeting.

She had read their reports. The battle in the Gemini District had been brutal, weaving in and out of houses, shops, and taverns. The receivers had the numbers, but they fought only with truncheons, while the defenders had broken bottles and knives. Neither side had come out of it very well, and the revolutionaries had managed to build a new barricade, deep into the Taurus District. By the time the receivers had regrouped, the sun had long since set, but no one was in the mood to sleep.

"How many receivers do we have left, Inspector Poleyn?" she asked the young woman, who saluted, smartly.

"Exact numbers are hard to say, Ma'am, but we sustained few losses at the Gemini skirmish."

"Losses?" said Chief Inspector Greaves, the older man and technically Poleyn's superior. "Please, Inspector, let us have no nice language here. Call them deaths. The deaths of our men and women."

"With respect, Sir," Poleyn replied, managing to make the word "sir" sound like an insult, "the losses were lower than we expected. We could easily make more progress, perhaps advance as far as the Piscean slums by tomorrow." She turned back to Lady Astrea. "If you would give the order, as Acting Director, we could send reinforcements from the barracks."

"Have you been to the barracks lately, Poleyn?" Greaves said—his tone still reasonable, but firm. "Our receivers are run ragged maintaining the barricades and protecting the citizens in our half of the city. They remember when their duty was to protect. Their contracts say that they will deal only with criminals and thieves, not take up arms against their own families and friends."

"They *are* criminals," Poleyn snapped. "Every one of them. They chose to reject our rule of law, to steal half the city. And come the end of this battle, they will all face trial."

"All of them?" Greaves said, his eyebrows raising, his craggy face unreadable in the candlelight. "How will you have enough judges, or prisons? There were thousands behind the barricades who didn't want a revolution, who were trapped in the wrong place at the wrong time. But we starved them into desperation. We have given them a reason to fight."

Astrea didn't speak for a moment. She was staring up at the portraits lining the walls. All of those ancient Directors. What would they think of her? What would they think of Snutworth, deserting his post in Agora's time of need?

But now was not time for history; now was time to act.

"You gave them a chance for peace, Greaves, and they responded with violence," she replied. "We shall continue the attack until they surrender. Their leaders will stand trial, and only them. The rest of the city will be pardoned."

Neither of the receivers looked happy, but they both bowed. Astrea relaxed a little. The rule of law still persisted within the Directory.

Poleyn saluted.

"Ma'am, you wished to see the prisoner now?"

Astrea nodded, and Poleyn blew on her whistle, the harsh sound grating on Astrea's already damaged nerves. The thick, ebony doors at the end of the office opened, and four burly receivers frog-marched in the prisoner. He was a large, brutish man, and despite the chains binding his hands and feet, Astrea was still glad that the guards remained in attendance.

The prisoner was flung to the floor.

"Look upon the Acting Director, prisoner," Inspector Poleyn barked. The big man looked up, pushing himself onto his knees.

"Can't stop chasing me, can you Inspector?" he said, leering at her with a smile that was missing a few teeth since that morning. "People will talk."

Poleyn turned away from him in disgust.

"He calls himself Nick, ma'am. Crede's closest lieutenant, and the leader of these revolutionaries."

Nick snorted.

"Better start checking your spies, girlie. That's old news."

Poleyn spun around, her truncheon in her hand, cracking Nick on the side of the head. Greaves frowned, and Astrea winced. She didn't object to this brutish man being taken down a peg, but she was not used to violence in her presence.

"You will be *silent* unless questioned!" Poleyn said, fiercely.

Nick pulled himself upright again, head weaving a little, but otherwise focused.

"Yes," Lady Astrea said, trying to take control of the situation. "We know that you are not the only leader; more's the pity. But Mr. Mark and Miss Lilith are both in our hands, and you will be able to avoid much bloodshed if you encourage your people to stop . . ."

"You think I can get them to stop?"

Poleyn went for her truncheon again, but Greaves put a hand on her arm, restraining her.

"We do want to talk to Mr. Nick, Inspector" he said, patiently. "Perhaps we should allow him to continue?"

Poleyn shrugged off her superior's hand, but did not strike the prisoner. The big man nodded to Greaves, and then turned to Lady Astrea.

"You don't get it, do you? I'm not really a leader. Sure, some'll follow me, if they're angry. If you want a fight, everyone knows that Nick's your man." He began to scratch at a recently stitched wound on his chest, through the holes in his ragged shirt. "But that's just because of Crede. He was a real leader. He always had a plan. Me and my friends . . . we were so angry, all the time. And Crede showed us how we could use that anger. Now half the city has that same rage, thanks to you."

Lady Astrea fixed him with a cold stare.

"I have read reports on you, Mr. Nick," she said, quietly. "A bully and a thug, half-drunk most days. You picked fights with my receivers and stirred up trouble wherever you went. And you would lecture us on leadership?"

Nick didn't reply; he just continued to scratch at his chest. Poleyn's lip curled.

"Nothing to say, Nick?"

The big man paused. And then, deliberately, he pulled his shirt open a little further. Poleyn recoiled from the smell.

"You see this wound?" he said, pointing to a mass of stitches. "I was on a barricade when it collapsed, a month back. I should've died."

"Are you boasting now?" Astrea asked, darkly amused. "I assure you, your just punishment will not be so easy to avoid."

"Thing is, I didn't die," Nick continued, slowly. "Because someone was there to stitch me up. Someone knelt down in the middle of a battle, with people grappling all around and rocks flying overhead, to sew up my wounds, and send me back for treatment. And everyone there saw it."

Nick met Astrea's gaze.

"His name was Dr. Theophilus," he said. "Before that day, I thought he was a fool. I thought everyone at the temple was a fool. But that's who we have to lead us now. Not fighters, like me. Healers. People who don't need to get ahead to win. And after seeing that, we're never going to let you turn it back the way it was," he rose suddenly to his feet. "Never."

He lunged forward. Poleyn blew another harsh blast on her whistle. The receiver guards descended upon Nick, beating him again and again, until he groaned in pain. Soon, he could no longer stand, and the receivers dragged him from the office. Poleyn followed, hastily bowing to Lady Astrea, and promising to have the man restrained.

Astrea sat back down behind her desk, listening to the commotion as Nick's curses faded farther and farther into the distance.

Only once silence had been restored did she look up at her one remaining companion.

"Set a new guard around the office, Chief Inspector," she said, trying to hide the slight tremor in her voice. The Chief Inspector nodded, but he still looked troubled.

"I worry about Poleyn, my lady," Greaves said, softly. "It seems to me that she can be as brutal as her prisoner."

"We are the representatives of order, Chief Inspector," Astrea snapped. "And order must be enforced."

Greaves considered for a moment.

"I have been a receiver my whole life, my lady. Under your husband, Lord Ruthven, under you, under many different leaders. I have dedicated all my days to the preservation of the law. But law is there to preserve the peace, and allow our people to lead lives without fear. Without that, it is no better than the mob."

Lady Astrea raised her head, imperiously.

"Your comments are noted, Greaves. You may go."

He bowed, turning to leave. And then paused.

"This will not end today, my lady," he said, quietly. "Tomorrow, the battles will be ten times worse. Our people are going to die. So many of them, on both sides. We are armed, but the revolutionaries have the numbers."

"But we will win, Greaves," Astrea said, firmly. "We have to. For the sake of all of Agora."

"Perhaps we will, my lady," Greaves said, looking back, his expression unreadable in the candlelight. "If there are enough of us left when the fighting finally stops."

Lady Astrea barely noticed as he left. She sat in the Director's office for a long time after that. As the hours went on, the receiver guards she had requested arrived—experienced men and women, warily poised. There were no truncheons here; the Director had trained them to use swords. She didn't think she had ever seen anyone use a sword before—these were not the elegant rapiers of stories. These were thick, heavy, brutally sharp weapons. They would take many lives before their wielders fell.

The guards nodded to her as she sat behind the mahogany desk, but made no other sound. They had their orders, and they were the same as hers—to protect the Directory, and its secrets. For the fifth time that evening, she slipped open a drawer in the mahogany desk, and glanced at the contents. Two little boxes, filled with glass bottles, each one labeled with the names of the two Gisethi prisoners. She slid the drawer shut with a shudder. She wondered if she would ever truly understand the Director. Not that it really mattered. She was his now; she could never break the link. Never stop herself from being compromised by the man who owned her life, who could crush her a thousand ways.

She wished her children were here, but they were cowering with the rest of the elite in the Leo District, wondering if they could ever return to their old, familiar world, or if they would emerge into a new one that would take their livelihoods, or even their lives.

But that would be down to her. When the rebels found out that Mark and Lily were missing, she knew there would be only one course of action. And she had to be prepared. Tomorrow, everything would be decided. Tomorrow, Agora would rise from the ashes. One way or another.

So even though she barely knew them, she got up from behind the desk, and walked to each of her receivers, thanking them, and they replied with a salute. Then she walked away, down the corridors—the last defender of Agora.

"Let them come," she said to the empty air.

But still, before she could sleep, there was something she had to do. Ghostlike, she slipped down the corridors, deeper into the building. She passed the scribes, still working feverishly, ignoring everything but their endless records. She passed a few cowled Gisethi monks—guests of Father Wolfram, who did nothing but stare at her as she passed. They had their secrets; she had hers. They were not inclined to share.

And then, at last, she came to an oak door, with a mother-of-pearl handle. This was a part of the Directory that very few frequented. Even the clerks didn't know about this room. The Director probably knew, but if he did, he hadn't left a sign of his passing. These were the guest quarters. Most people thought them unused. But it was here that she kept her greatest secret, and weakness.

Softly, so softly, she opened the door.

"I'm back, my dear," she said.

CHAPTER TWENTY-FIVE

Orders

LILY PRETENDED TO SLEEP. It was the only way she could find an excuse to keep her eyes shut.

Mark had said that the journey was nearly over, that after four long hours of descending into the well beneath the Last's house, and a further couple riding the newly repaired mine carts through a long, black tunnel, they were almost back at the center of Naru. Normally, Lily would have been full of curiosity—even with her eyes closed, she could tell that they were shooting down the tunnels at phenomenal speed. And she would have been checking to see if Wolfram and Snutworth were distracted, so she could work out if there was any chance of escape when they reached their destination.

But she couldn't, because if she opened her eyes, she knew what she would see. She would see Wolfram standing in the front of the cart—silent, but full of suppressed energy. She would see

Snutworth, his eyes fixed on nothing, his thoughts impossible to fathom.

And she would see Mark's blank stare. It was bad enough every time she heard his voice. It had the same pitch as before, but not his cadences, his phrases; all of the music of it was gone. Looking at him was even worse—he was little more than a walking corpse that had forgotten to stop breathing.

Occasionally she wondered why Snutworth hadn't done the same to her. Not that he needed to. He hadn't even bothered to tie her hands. Because Mark's emotions lay in a bag in Snutworth's pocket, and she knew that if she did anything wrong, he wouldn't hesitate to crush them. And if he did that—Mark would be no better than dead.

Without warning, the rattling cart screeched to a halt, pitching Lily over. She scrambled to stay upright. If Snutworth had fallen, maybe she could . . .

But no. Wolfram was picking himself up, cursing. Mark lay on the floor of the cart, like a marionette with cut strings. But Snutworth had kept his balance, leaning nonchalantly on his silver-topped cane. He gently tapped the pocket of his coat. Lily heard the delicate chink of the glass bottles.

"Do not fear, Miss Lily. I would not be so clumsy," he cast a look over at Wolfram, "unlike some. Get up, man; we're nearly there."

Wolfram rose to his feet with bruised dignity, and dragged Mark up by the wrist.

"You're hurting me," Mark said, in a matter-of-fact tone. "Stop."

"Be quiet, or I'll hurt you some more," Wolfram said, with equal straightforwardness. Mark closed his mouth.

They began to walk down the last stretch of the black tunnel. Lily tried not to be disturbed at the way their footsteps made no sound. She wondered if Laud had felt the same way when he had first stepped into Naru.

Lily felt a stab of pain in her chest. The image of Laud had ambushed her in her weakness. Was he all right? What would Laud do when he found that she was missing? Of course, she worried about all of them—Ben, Theo, even Cherubina. But Laud had seen her at her weakest. Laud was prepared to stagger for weeks through tunnels and marsh to find her. He'd do something stupid, and it would be her fault.

And the worst part was, she was rather hoping he would. She couldn't bear the thought that he might have more important things on his mind.

Distractedly, she slipped her hand into Mark's, and held it tight. He didn't react—didn't even curl his fingers. But it was something. She needed to feel that she wasn't alone.

"Incidentally, Miss Lilith," Snutworth said, as they approached the end of the tunnel and the light from the communal dining cave became visible. "I should mention that you are to not speak while we are in Naru. Not a single word. I am well aware that you have spent time with these people, and may wish to convey a coded message." He turned back to meet her gaze, as polite as ever. "The instant you speak a word that I have not requested, the vials containing Mr. Mark's emotions will be smashed. May I remind you also that in his current state, he will hardly leap to your defense, and that Father Wolfram and I, though not in the first flush of youth, are not above the use of physical violence." To illustrate his point, he twisted the handle of his cane, and pulled, revealing an inch or two of the long blade concealed within. "Crude, yes, but I have never been one to underestimate my enemies. Do I make myself clear?"

Lily wished that she had a snappy comeback. Instead, she tried her best to look dignified, bit her tongue, and nodded. Snutworth smiled.

"Excellent. It is always pleasant to keep things civilized.

Speaking of which," he turned on his heel to face the mouth of the tunnel, and strode forward. "Good afternoon, I wonder if any of you fine people could direct me to the Conductor."

Lily dragged Mark to the mouth of the tunnel; Wolfram following behind. Beyond, the tunnel opened up into a room that Lily had sat in several times—the Hub dining room—where she had eaten with the strange inhabitants of Naru, before exploring the Canticle of Whispers had taken over her life. She barely had time to take in the crowds of amazed faces looking up from the trestle tables, or the smells of the meat boiling in the cooking pots, before a familiar rotund figure got up from the head of the largest table, brushing crumbs from his multicolored robes.

"Lily, is that you?" the Conductor exclaimed, rushing forward, the cluster of Naruvians parting like water around him. "Several of us said that we heard an echo of your voice in the lands above, but the Oracle wouldn't tell us what had happened. And we've been so busy repairing the Rail Nexus and the carts that . . ." The Conductor trailed off, noticing the others for the first time. "You have brought friends with you? Today of all days? Then that must mean . . ."

"Indeed it does," Snutworth said, cutting him off. "I am afraid we do not have time for pleasantries. I invoke the rights of the Midnight Charter," he intoned, his voice carrying across the whole cavern. "The Day of Judgment has dawned, and I speak for the will of the Judges."

The Conductor took a step back, as a buzz of excitement filled the room.

"Is this true?" asked the Conductor, looking from Mark to Lily in astonishment. "Is this man your chosen vessel?"

Wolfram whispered something in Mark's ear.

"Yes, he is," Mark said, automatically. The Conductor blinked, but before he could interrupt, Snutworth had turned to Lily.

"I believe this gentleman requires an answer before we proceed, Miss Lilith," he said, and tapped his pocket. Lily heard the chink of the glass vials.

"Yes," she muttered. It was barely a whisper; the mood of the room changed. The buzz grew, but now it was tinged with fear.

"You all heard them," Snutworth proclaimed, while still managing to keep his voice sounding reasonable. "I am their chosen representative, their vessel. I shall begin the judgment on their behalf."

This time, Lily couldn't contain herself. She started forward, desperate to warn the Conductor that this was wrong, that this man was a liar, a monster . . .

She felt Wolfram's iron grip on her shoulder. It stopped her. Mark's emotions were still at stake. But Snutworth could make as many speeches as he liked; nothing had changed, yet.

"Very well, sir," the Conductor said, his voice resigned. "Then . . . you wish to be taken to the Oracle?"

"Yes," Snutworth said. "But first," he looked back at Mark and Lily, "you have guards here?"

The Conductor shifted, uneasily.

"We do not appreciate physical contact, sir, but we have some who act as guardians. They might be suitable for such duties . . ."

"That will do," he said. "Summon them."

Lily bided her time. She remained silent as the guardians arrived, their faces swathed in cloth and their hands gloved to minimize the sense of contact as they marched them through the tunnels, deeper and deeper toward the Oracle's throne room. As guards, they didn't look particularly skilled. But there were at least ten of them, and Lily couldn't count on any help.

With every step, she lengthened her stride, just a little. With every movement, she crept closer to the Conductor. It was a slow process, trying not to draw Snutworth's attention, but as they passed the Hub, scintillating with a million distracting colors, Lily seized her chance.

"Conductor," she hissed, "what are you doing?"

"Please, Miss Lilith, don't question me," he said, without lowering his voice. "This is an ancient duty, from long before either of us was born. Every Naruvian must serve the Judges, or their chosen vessel. Why do you think I helped you when you arrived? I'm sorry to say that it was not all charity, much as I grew fond of you." His voice dropped to a whisper. "If I fail to carry out my purpose, I forfeit my right to be Conductor. And most of my people would follow this man just to see what would happen."

Lily pulled back, stung by the defeat in his voice.

"Of course," she said, bitterness welling up inside her. "I'll feel so much better being betrayed by someone who feels guilty about it."

The Conductor didn't reply, but his shoulders slumped.

"Miss Lilith," Snutworth said, without turning back. "If you would kindly recall our conversation about speech? Another lapse of concentration would be unwise."

Lily clenched her fists, but bit back her response. He had her. There was no way to wriggle away from that fact. No matter what Snutworth was planning, she couldn't risk leaving Mark in that state.

So she went back to waiting, to putting one foot in front of the other as they descended the steps to the Oracle's cavern, hoping that something, anything, would show her what to do.

But by the time Snutworth drew aside the curtain that led to the throne room, her mind was still blank.

Lily felt a shudder as she entered the chamber. It wasn't that there was anything surprising—quite the reverse, the Resonant Throne was exactly as it had been when she was last here.

There was the same odd light, glowing from every corner, and the same stone bridge, cracked but sturdy, leading up to the throne. And there was the same sound—that half-whisper, half-vibration that seeped into her head and settled there, like a bad memory she couldn't quite forget: the Canticle of Whispers, the source of all of the Oracle's knowledge.

Lily kept her eyes averted as they crossed the bridge. She didn't want to see the Oracle, not ever again. But as Snutworth stepped forward, and made a sweeping bow, she couldn't help stealing a glimpse.

The Oracle had not put her mask back on. Lily wished that she had. There it was, her mother's face, so like hers and yet so different, gazing down with perfect detachment.

"You are Snutworth, Director of Agora," the Oracle said. It was a statement of fact, not a question. Lily searched in vain for some flicker of surprise or alarm in that too-calm voice. She shivered; at least Mark had an excuse for sounding so cold. Her mother had made herself like this.

"I am," Snutworth said, standing tall, but with a hint of tension in the hands that grasped his cane. "And you know why I am here."

"You would present yourself as the vessel of the Judges—the chosen representative of our lands?" Was it just Lily's imagination, or did she detect a note of distaste there?

"I present nothing," Snutworth said, quietly. "But as it says in the Midnight Charter itself—*Once the Judges have found their harmony, they shall choose either to rule the lands themselves, or to select one to be their representative, their Vessel. They shall then present this decision to the Oracle on the Day of Judgment, and the Vessel shall complete our task of perfection with the assistance of all of the knowledge of Naru.*" He swept his hand through the air to point at Mark and Lily.

"The Judges have affirmed me their vessel, within the bounds of Naru. Surely you do not need them to repeat it."

"They did not intend to select you," the Oracle replied, the Canticle flaring up a little as she did so, letting the whispery echo of her voice fill the cavern.

"Nevertheless, they did," Snutworth said, coolly. "An undeniable fact. The Charter makes no mention of intention."

"No," the Oracle replied. Lily felt a shudder pass through her, a vibration thrum through the throne room. Was the Oracle angry? It was hard to tell. The base of the Hub, suspended above her mother's crown, pulsed with a harsher light as she continued. "You are not presented yet. The Protagonist is incomplete. You must be presented by both."

Snutworth nodded.

"Yes, of course. I suspected as much. Mark, come here."

Mark came forward, as Snutworth reached into his inside pocket, withdrew a leather bag, and tipped out a handful of tiny vials. Mark's emotions lay in his palm, concentrated into thick, viscous liquids. He looked down at them for a moment.

"Conductor, the Judges should be restrained," he said.

"I . . . that is . . ." the Conductor hesitated. Father Wolfram glared at him.

"Would you deny your purpose now, Conductor?" Wolfram growled. "The Charter gave you your power, your reason for living. Obey it."

The Conductor let his head drop.

"Hold them," he sighed.

Lily struggled, of course, as gloved hands closed around her wrists, but it was almost out of habit. Snutworth was about to return Mark's emotions—she couldn't interfere with that.

Mark offered no resistance at all. Not even when the guardians made him lie on his back, arms spread-eagled. Snutworth came and stood over him.

"Now then, Mr. Mark, please try not to move."

Delicately, Snutworth pulled out the glass stopper to each bottle, dropping them onto the ground where they rolled off the walkway, and dropped down to the crystal-shard floor far below with the tiniest of pings.

"Hold his arms tightly," he instructed, kneeling. And then, without warning, he grasped Mark's jaw, opened his mouth, and poured in every vial in quick succession.

Lily tried to leap forward, as Snutworth emptied the last one and jammed Mark's mouth closed. She knew what happened if emotions were taken too quickly. They were supposed to be inhaled gently, not poured in all at once. But the guardians held her well.

Mark's eyes began to widen. His limbs thrashed, veins standing out on his forehead. For a second, the beginning of a scream escaped his lips, but Snutworth pulled a handkerchief from his pocket, and rammed it into Mark's mouth. As Snutworth got up and walked away, Mark's convulsions grew wilder, and tears streamed from his eyes. Lily couldn't bear to spectate any longer. She tore herself free from the guardians, and ran over to Mark. She knelt down, grabbing his shoulders, trying to stop him from beating his head against the stone walkway.

Slowly, so slowly, Mark began to calm down. His face was almost purple, distorted from pain. He was sobbing in deep, painful heaves. Gently, she plucked the handkerchief from his mouth. The sound that escaped was something between a moan and a cry.

"Lily . . ." he said, woozily, "what . . . what . . . ?"

"There, Oracle," Snutworth said, cutting through everything. "Two Judges, complete and whole. Now, do you accept me?"

The Oracle looked down at Mark. Above her, the crystal pulsed again, and the Canticle rose up in strength. Lily felt it in her gut, like the whole room breathed out. And then, the Oracle nodded.

"Yes," she said.

"Good," Snutworth replied. "Now, would you vacate my throne, please?"

And in one, horrible moment, everything made sense. All this time, Lily had wanted to know why Snutworth needed Naru, when he ruled Agora, and even commanded some of the monks who controlled Giseth. Surely that was enough?

But it wasn't. Snutworth didn't want the power of law, or armies. That kind of ruler could fall, like Directors before him. Snutworth ruled through knowledge, through manipulating those around him—their secrets were his tools.

And now, Snutworth would know everything. Everyone's little weaknesses would be revealed, everyone's strings would be visible to him. Powerless, she saw the Oracle rise, and step down. She saw Snutworth hand his cane to Wolfram, pass her mother on the steps up to the throne, and sit down. For a second or two, he shut his eyes, a look of pain creasing his features. And then, he smiled. It was perhaps the first genuine smile she had ever seen on his face.

"Wolfram," he said, quietly, the Canticle ebbing and flowing with his voice. "Stay for a while; I must instruct you. Everyone else is to leave, for now." He looked at the Conductor, and pointed. "But tell your people to prepare. There are so many places you must travel to—so many people you must meet, and tell them . . ." he nodded, listening to something too faint for anyone else to hear. "Tell them what they need to hear."

The Conductor bowed his head.

"As you command, Oracle."

Lily felt her feelings drain away, even as Mark's returned. She felt numb. Snutworth was the Oracle. He had all the knowledge of the Canticle, every thought in every land since the Librans had first arrived from over the sea. He had a cult of his own to spread his whispers. It didn't matter what she did. It didn't matter what any of them did. He could control the world without ever having to leave his throne.

"Lily . . . what's happening . . . ?" Mark said, finding his voice at last. Lily looked down, lost for words.

"He's won, Mark," she said, her voice small. "He's won."

Chapter Twenty-six

The Storm

BEN SANK HER HEAD into the collar of her receiver uniform as she sprinted through the streets, the rest of her "squad" around her.

She was still running from that battle in the Central Plaza. Short, sharp, and brutal, the revolutionaries had burst over the barricades at the seventh hour of the morning, just as the chimes from the clock in the Central Plaza were fading. Laud had wanted to attack at dawn, but as Theo had pointed out, the receivers changed shifts at dawn, so there would be twice as many defenders there.

It had worked. The receivers were so obsessed with pressing forward in Gemini and Taurus, that the Central Plaza had only a token resistance. Already, behind her, Ben could hear the bulk of the revolutionary forces, hurling pieces of the barricade, tearing through to this side of the city. The streets were deserted—the remaining elite and artisans were hiding behind bolted doors, and in the confusion, this retreating receiver squad hadn't cared that two of their number were unfamiliar. Or that their uniforms, made only the night before by Cherubina, were suspiciously fresh and unmarked by battle.

Ben raced to keep up with Laud, trying to signal to him, to warn him not to draw attention to himself when they were supposed to be keeping a low profile, but he was already barking out orders to the other receivers, instructing them to split up. Fortunately, his plan seemed to be working. They were nearly at their target, and the squad was scattering down different streets, until it was just the two of them, emerging onto the square before the Directory.

For a second, they stood in awe. Despite everything, the Directory of Receipts had lost none of its grandeur—its solid gray mass, fronted with ancient wooden doors, exuded a power that momentarily stopped them in their tracks. But then they saw the doors creak open, some "fellow receivers" beckoning to them, and their focus returned.

Ben's heart sank as they slipped through the main doors. There were at least twelve receivers on guard here—far too many for them to overpower—and the doors themselves were bound with iron. Even if the mob managed to reach the Directory, they would never be able to open the doors for them, as planned. Ben and Laud exchanged glances. So much for backup.

"Keep those doors open!" a voice called out behind them. Alarmed, they turned, and the door guards around them scrambled as a small group of receivers appeared on the far side of the square. They both recognized Inspector Poleyn hurrying toward them, blowing her whistle. Ben felt Laud touch her shoulder. She would see through their disguises in an instant.

"Excuse me, Captain?" Ben piped up to one of the harassed

guards. "We need to get a message to the Director. He said it was urgent . . ."

"Director's gone, didn't you hear that?" the captain barked back, not bothering to turn around. "Took his new prisoners and left, along with that creepy monk."

Ben grabbed Laud's arm, stopping her brother from lunging forward to grab the captain. If they asked any more about that, they would draw too much attention. Her mind raced as Inspector Poleyn got closer to the doors.

"Where should we take it then, Sir? Only, it's urgent . . ."

"Take it to Lady Astrea!" the captain growled, gesturing further into the Directory. "And then get back here. We need everyone we can get."

"Yes, Sir," Ben muttered, dragging Laud down the corridor. As soon as they were out of sight of the doors, she turned and looked him in the eyes. "Tell me you weren't going to demand to know where they've taken Lily and Mark," she said. Laud scowled in response.

"They're not even here," he muttered. "Our people are going to arrive to find the Directory sealed up, and we won't even rescue our friends . . ." he kicked the wall, furiously. "How did Poleyn get back so quickly?"

"So we'll change the plan," Ben said, hurriedly trying to soothe her brother, before anyone else noticed them. "We managed to get into the Directory, didn't we? There has to be something we can do."

Laud shut his eyes, his breathing fast and shallow, as Ben put a concerned hand on his arm. It wasn't just that he was angry. They were all angry. After Mark and Lily had disappeared, even Theo had agreed that their assault on the Directory couldn't wait. They knew that as soon as the capture of Mark, Lily, and Nick became common knowledge, there would be no way to stop the mobs from forming. At least this way, they could take charge, perhaps even attempt some tactics.

But no one had reacted like Laud. He'd never been easy to get along with, but for as long as Ben could remember, he'd been the controlled one—the big brother who kept his cool and sneered at the world. But back at the Central Plaza, she'd watched him fighting his way through the receivers, before he slipped into his disguise. He'd pushed one receiver up against a stall, beating him again and again with his own truncheon, until Ben had torn him away, still spitting with fury. This new rage scared her. He seemed so desperate.

Carefully, she reached out toward him, conscious of the growing commotion down the corridor. They needed to get moving. *Now.*

"They've got her, Ben," Laud said, suddenly, his eyes still tightly shut, his whole body trembling. "They took her away from me again . . . Every time I think I've found her, she's gone . . . she's gone and I couldn't save her . . ."

And in that moment, Ben understood. She took her brother's hands, putting her head close to his.

"She's not gone," she said, tenderly. "Not forever. Maybe the captain's wrong. And even if she isn't here, we've gone too far to stop now. There're hundreds of people depending on us to open the Directory doors for them. Maybe there's a back door? Or a tunnel they didn't think to guard? Come on—there has to be something." She squeezed his hands. "Lily wouldn't give up."

Laud took a deep breath. When he opened his eyes again, his face was full of the old determination.

"All right," he said, glancing around. "You try that corridor; I'll try this. Remember, try to give the impression that you know what you're doing."

Ben attempted a smile, but there was no more time for words. Already, they could hear the commotion farther down the corridor.

327

They had promised that they wouldn't split up. But all their plans were useless now—if Poleyn caught them, Ben doubted they would even get a trial.

She hurried down the candlelit corridors, her passage making the flames flicker, casting crazed shadows on the walls. She knocked on a hundred doors, and opened them to dusty libraries and offices. Occasionally, she found a clerk or secretary, but she quickly waved aside their panicky questions, trying to ask for Lady Astrea with an air of authority. But no one knew where she was, until a frightened old man, who proclaimed himself the Director's secretary, mentioned that he had seen her heading for the guest rooms, and pointed the way.

Even here, in the depths of the building, she could hear the muffled sound of commotion growing louder. And was that a thumping noise, like someone battering on the grand doors? She kept running until she found herself in a corridor lined with elegant tapestries. This looked like the guest quarters to her. She moved along the corridor, pressing her ear to another door, trying to see if she could hear Lady Astrea's refined tones. But all was silence.

Eventually, she reached the end of the corridor. There was only one door here, but it caught Ben's eye. The last few doors she had passed had been simple affairs, probably storerooms. But this one was made of beautifully carved oak, and had a striking mother-of-pearl handle.

She put her head up against it. There was definitely something in there. She could hear a low rumble. Tentatively, she tried the handle, easing the door open a crack. Just enough to look in.

Beyond lay a richly furnished chamber, dominated by a large four-poster bed. The room was dark, but a crack of light from the door fell into the room, illuminating a sleeping man on the bed.

He looked small, and shrunken. Even his snores—the rumbling sound Ben had heard—were weak. But there was something familiar about him. She knew that she should carry on—that anyone who was being kept in such luxury clearly wasn't a prisoner. But curiosity got the better of her. She opened the door a little farther, trying to get a look at his face, without waking him.

But . . . surely that was . . .

"My lady, are you there?"

The voice was deep and strong, and Ben recognized it at once. A few months ago, she would have been glad to hear Chief Inspector Greaves. Not anymore. It was coming from behind her, farther down the corridor.

"Lady Astrea, ma'am! You are needed!"

That was Inspector Poleyn. The figure on the bed stirred uneasily. Ben knew she'd never be able to hide in there, and shut the door as swiftly as she could. Then she cast around, urgently, as the sound of footsteps grew closer. The corridor was narrow, and the only way out was back toward them. Ben braced herself to run, to try to slip past them so fast they wouldn't be able to give chase. She didn't have much chance, but she wasn't going to let them take her without a fight.

And then, to her relief, she caught sight of another door, half-hidden in the wood paneling. She scurried forward, trying the handle. It swung open.

Offering silent thanks to all the stars, she dived through into the darkened room beyond, pushing the door shut behind her.

She leaned back against the door, her heart pounding in her ears.

In the room, something moved.

It was only now that she considered that hiding in a completely dark room was not the wisest action. The light creeping around the door illuminated only the first few feet of the bare chamber. She could just make out a candle and tinderbox on the edge of a table.

There was another sound, louder this time, like someone

throwing themselves against a metal door. Her hands uncertain, Ben grabbed for the box and tried to spark a flame.

The first flash illuminated something on the other side of the room. Something in a chair. She tried again; this time she got the candle burning. She held it high.

A pair of dull, dead eyes stared back at her.

Ben jumped back, but didn't make a sound. She couldn't. Those eyes were still staring at her. And she was wrong; they weren't dead at all.

A young man sat in a wooden chair on the other side of the room. He was large, tanned, and strongly built, and dressed in rough fabric. And he was looking right at her.

The man didn't move. Neither did Ben, but her mind raced. There was something wrong here. Why hadn't he spoken? Why hadn't he raised the alarm?

Why had he been sitting in the dark?

"Who are you?" she whispered. Outside, she could hear the sound of Greaves and Poleyn. Their voices were raised, as if they were arguing.

The young man looked back at her, without interest.

"Owain," he said.

Ben started. This couldn't be Owain. Laud had described him as one of the friendliest people he had ever met. This person was looking at her as if she were no more interesting than the wall.

She was about to speak again, when there was another banging noise to her right. She moved the candle. This room was surprisingly bare, but there was a second door set into the wall—a heavy-looking metal door. There was a key still in the lock, and the metal door shook as something was hurled against it from the other side.

"What's that?" Ben whispered. The man who called himself Owain shrugged.

"That's Elespeth. She's been in there for hours now."

Horrified at his callousness, Ben put down the candle, turned the key, and pulled open the metal door. A woman of middle years, her long black hair straggling over her face, nearly fell through the door, and out of the tiny cell beyond. Her hands were tied behind her back, and her mouth was firmly gagged. Seeing her wild expression, Ben reached up, and pulled loose the gag.

Elespeth screamed.

Ben tried everything she could to stop her—even attempting to pull the gag back over the woman's mouth, but it was too late. The door to the corridor was flung open.

Greaves, at least, looked sorry to see her. Poleyn gave the impression that she would like to start the execution immediately.

"Spies!" she snarled, striding into the room. Elespeth tried to hurl herself at her, but her hands were still tied, and Poleyn felled her with a single professional blow. Elespeth hit the floor hard, writhing in pain. Ben shrank back. Poleyn normally looked oddly delicate and refined for someone in her position, but the barricade assault had stripped that away. She bore a black eye, her uniform was tattered and smeared with dirt, and she looked every inch as capable as any street receiver.

"Was that necessary, Poleyn?" Greaves asked, coming into the room. "The woman was clearly bound."

"Appearances cannot always be trusted," Poleyn said, seizing Ben's arm. "Some people dress as receivers to try and spread their revolution. Don't they, Benedicta? Did you think I wouldn't recognize you from my captain's description? Do you think all of my receivers are idiots?"

In desperation, Ben looked over at Owain. Why was he just sitting there, looking down at Elespeth, collapsed at his feet? Why wouldn't he help her?

331

"A moment, Poleyn," Greaves said, stepping in. "That scream which alerted us to her presence—that wasn't Miss Benedicta, I'm sure; that was an older woman's scream."

"Probably the Gisethi witch," Poleyn muttered. "And with respect, we can investigate later, Sir. Right now we have a revolutionary rabble coming for us . . ."

But Greaves wasn't listening. He had knelt down and raised Elespeth's head. The older woman was weeping, silently.

"What's this?" Greaves said, examining the strip of cloth that now hung loosely around her neck. "Why would this prisoner have been gagged? That isn't normal procedure. And come to that, why is she so tightly bound? The young man isn't even shackled . . ."

Ben tried to speak, but Poleyn clamped one gloved hand over her mouth.

"Sir!" Poleyn insisted, dragging Ben half out of the room. "There is no time for this. We are needed to defend the Directory . . ."

"What is going on here, Poleyn? Why is this woman such a threat?" Greaves insisted.

"She underwent the process," Owain said.

Slowly, Greaves looked up. The whole room seemed still.

"Process?" Greaves asked.

"Nothing but the words of a madman . . ." Poleyn began, but Greaves ignored her.

"To remove emotions," Owain continued, as disinterested as ever. "The Director said that her process was incomplete, that it would be more appropriate to leave her with rage and sorrow. Unlike me. I have nothing left."

Ben realized her mouth was hanging open. It wasn't the revelation itself; it made a horrible kind of sense. No, it was the proof of it, the way that Owain talked about the Director hollowing out his mind without once changing the tone of his voice. He almost sounded bored.

Chief Inspector Greaves got to his feet.

"Did you know of this, Poleyn?" he said, quietly. Poleyn was still dragging Ben toward the door, her head down. Ben dug in her heels. Poleyn wasn't going to get away that easily.

"With respect, Sir," she said, "we need to warn our people at the main doors. If we send out a runner, we can summon our forces back from the barricades, crush these rebels between us . . ."

She trailed off. The Chief Inspector's face hadn't moved. He was still looking at Owain.

"Forgive me, but I feel that this is an important question," he said, his voice catching. "Did you know about this?"

Ben felt Poleyn's grip on her arm loosen, just a little. The Inspector was uneasy.

"The Director ordered a few of us to retrieve the Gisethi spies, and to bring them here after they were subjected to the process," she admitted, her voice becoming stiff and formal. "I did not enjoy it, Sir. I do not often enjoy following my orders. But I serve the Director. No, I serve Agora, and right now all of that is threatened. And frankly, Greaves, it's time you began to show where your loyalties lie."

Greaves looked at Poleyn then, a look that was almost pitying.

"I see. Thank you, Inspector. That makes everything so much clearer."

Then, moving faster than Ben had ever seen from a man of his age, he slammed Poleyn into the wall. Poleyn raised her arms to fight back, letting Benedicta go, but Greaves grasped her wrists, trying to fling her to the ground.

"Traitor!" Poleyn shouted, jabbing him in the stomach, winding him. Ben saw Poleyn reaching for her truncheon, and looked around, wildly. Her eyes fell upon the candle.

Ben lunged for it, grabbing it half a second before Poleyn realized what she was going to do, and jabbed the burning candle into the inspector's wrist. Poleyn yelped as the hot wax seared into her, and her truncheon clattered to the ground. She rounded on Ben, spitting with fury.

And Greaves took his opportunity. He barreled into her, knocking her back into the cell that had once held Elespeth. He slammed the iron door, reached for the key, and turned it with a click.

For a minute, both he and Ben leaned against the wall, panting, listening to Poleyn hammer on the inside of the door. Then, as if nothing had happened, the Chief Inspector straightened up, looking almost serene.

"Now," he said, all business, turning to Owain and Elespeth. "How long ago were you subjected to this appalling practice?"

"Twenty-two hours, forty-three minutes ago," Owain replied, blankly. Elespeth merely moaned. Greaves nodded.

"Time enough then. Let's hope the Director kept the bottled emotions in his desk. He wouldn't have thrown them away. Not him. We may yet have time to return our guests' emotions; I believe after a full day the effect is permanent . . ."

Greaves was halfway through the door before Ben was able to speak again.

"But . . . I . . ." she stammered.

"No time, Miss Benedicta," he said, hurriedly. "Poleyn was right in one respect. We must act fast to prevent bloodshed."

In the distance, there was a great, grinding crash, and a howl like a maddened beast. The mob had broken down the doors.

Greaves pinched the bridge of his nose.

"Well now, that could complicate matters . . ."

The mob was merciless. It poured through the corridors, a thousand trampling feet bringing bedlam to these sacred halls. As Ben caught up with it, she could see the flaming torches up ahead.

Already, one of the ancient tapestries in this corridor was smoldering, smoke beginning to fill the air. Ben pushed forward, her small shape darting between the packed bodies, thanking the stars that she had changed back into her own clothes and that Greaves had chosen a different route through the Directory. This mob would have torn apart anyone wearing a receiver uniform.

Even this wasn't quite as bad as she'd feared. Not everyone was shouting and cursing. Some cheered as they ran, while others wept. This wasn't just a mob of hardened thugs; there were children, and old women, even a few dressed in the rich fabrics of the elite. All of Agora was here, demanding to have a voice, at last.

But as she struggled toward the front of the crowd, into the antechamber before the Director's office, it got worse. Here were the real troublemakers—Crede's old crowd. Some were battering on the old, oak doors that sealed off the way to the inner sanctum, while others were piling up scrolls and books, a hundred years of Directory records. As Ben watched, powerless, one lowered his torch into the pile of paper, and it went up in flames, the smoke in the corridors growing worse. Then, to her horror, she saw the prisoners. Dazed-looking clerks, a few lowly receivers, even the Director's secretary. Bound and terrified, being jostled toward the flames of their own books. Ben could hear them choking, could see the sweat on their faces as the crowd took up a chant. *Burn them,* it said, *burn them with their words. Agora is free . . . free . . . free . . .*

She opened her mouth to shout, to tell them this wasn't their way. But it was. It was Crede's way. A way that many of them hadn't abandoned, no matter who they said they were fighting for. And as she drew in a breath, the smoke filled her lungs and she coughed, eyes streaming, as the old clerks were pushed closer to the flames.

"Enough!"

Theo stepped out of the shadows. One by one, as the mob saw him, their chanting began to fade. He wasn't Mark or Lily, but they all recognized him—the doctor from the temple who had never given up, even on the verge of death.

"Look at yourselves!" Theo said, his voice ringing in the sudden silence. "Is that what you've fought for? The right to take revenge? Is that why you joined us breaking down the barricades?"

All eyes were on Theo now, but not all of them were friendly. Two of the ringleaders, a married couple of ex-thieves with cruel smirks, walked up to the doctor.

"Yeah, it is," the woman said, folding her arms.

"We'll follow your attack plans, Doctor," the man continued, waving his torch under Theo's nose, "but who says we have to listen to everything you say? There are no leaders anymore. Especially not the sons of nobility."

There were a few rumbles of agreement from the crowd. But most had fallen silent. Theo looked down at the couple with cold disdain. And then, he spoke.

"You're listening to me now, aren't you?"

The woman scowled.

"Not for long, Mate. Not for long."

To everyone's surprise, Theo smiled.

"I didn't need you to listen for long. Just for a minute. Just long enough for my friends to prevent you from becoming savages."

The ringleaders looked around, suddenly, but it was too late. Their prisoners had been released. Ben, whose eyes were sharp, was just able to pick out Pete and Cherubina, disappearing back into the smoky half-light, guiding the fleeing clerks to safety. The air filled with cries of alarm, but Theo didn't give the couple and their supporters a time to react. He carried on, his voice cutting through the hubbub.

"Turn on me if you must," Theo said, commanding their attention again. "Yes, I tricked you. And I would again. A doctor knows when drastic measures must be taken, to stop the poison." The couple stepped nearer to Theo, snarling. But no one else joined them. The crowd seemed unsure. These two didn't look like leaders anymore. They looked like fools. The husband turned to the wife, floundering, and she grabbed the torch from his hand.

"And what about now, Dr. Theophilus?" she said, putting as much contempt into his long, noble name as she could. "What does a doctor do when he's leading a gang of rebels?"

Theo looked over her shoulder, and smiled.

"Sometimes," he said, "all you need to do is wait."

There was a loud creak.

The crowd turned.

The door to the Director's office was opening.

For a brief instant, Ben was delighted. She saw Inspector Greaves, a bunch of keys in hand, pulling back one door. And Laud, wrenching open the other, flashing her a look of triumph. That was how Greaves had escaped the mob. Laud had helped him—receiver and revolutionary, working together.

And then she saw what waited behind the door, and her happiness died away. The light from the burning ledgers glinted off the swords in the hands of Lady Astrea's guards.

It was a hopeless fight. There were hundreds of rebels, while the guards numbered only twenty. But they had a look in their eyes that made one thing clear—the first to attack would be the first to die. They would take no prisoners. And no revolutionary seemed ready to step forward.

Inside the circle of steel, behind a grand, mahogany desk, Lady Astrea sat. The Lord Chief Justice was signing a document, her fingers stiff and tense on the quill, but clearly determined not to give the rebels the satisfaction of showing her fear. The moment stretched on forever. No one moved, except to cough as the smoke from the burning books floated upward toward the high, wooden ceiling.

Eventually, Lady Astrea spoke.

"I do not believe that you have an appointment, citizens," she said.

"My lady," Greaves began. "This is not necessary . . ."

"You are a traitor, Chief Inspector," she interrupted, with dignity. "Consider yourself relieved of your post." Greaves bowed.

"With respect, my lady," he said, "I did not swear my allegiance to you, or to the Director. I swore it to Agora, and her citizens. I regret only that the Director's actions did not alert me to this sooner."

"You may choose any excuse you wish, Greaves, for allying with these savages, but you will share the blame for bringing down Agora. That will be on your conscience forever."

Ben thought back to the little room she had found, just before discovering Owain and Elespeth. The little door with the mother-of-pearl handle, and the sight she had seen when she had opened it.

"We're not savages," Laud shouted, finding his voice. "*We* don't twist the truth, and rob people of their emotions. We didn't want power; we just wanted to get on with our lives . . ."

Lady Astrea laughed.

"Power is *all* you want," she said, rising to her feet. "If you were happy with having no power, you would accept any injustice. You would make the best of what you had, instead of fighting. I know about power, boy. Power is everything."

"I don't believe that, my lady."

For a second, Ben looked around with everyone else to see who had spoken. And then she realized it was her own voice. She had spoken without realizing. And she knew why.

"I don't believe it," Ben continued, "because I've seen into your secret room."

Lady Astrea raised an eyebrow, but didn't respond. The whole crowd was silent.

"I've seen him, my lady," Ben continued, attempting a smile. "I've seen Lord Ruthven. Your husband."

And there it was, the flash of concern, the break in her haughty mask.

"What does that matter?" Lady Astrea said, drawing herself up. "I am not defined by my husband. If I chose to keep him safe after his disgrace, after he was nearly executed at the hands of your rabble, it changes nothing."

"It changes everything," Ben said. "It shows you care about something other than power."

Lady Astrea laughed, bitterly.

"Personally, I have a weakness, yes. But I *am* Agora now. I am the keeper of the city's past and future. Personal concerns do not matter. My husband would expect no less. *I* would expect no less."

Beside her, Ben heard Theo step forward.

"My lady," the doctor said, "you must admit, you cannot win. We could force you to step down, if we wanted. We would risk injury and pain, true, but no worse than everyone behind me has experienced every day of their lives. We've known suffering, and starvation, and violence, and we've gone too far to stop." Theo's expression hardened. "Can you smell the smoke, my lady? At the moment, some of us keep a restraining hand on our anger—we fight it back with reasonable words and trickery. But if you defy us again, we will fight with true desperation. Without honor, without conscience. You will fall; your husband will fall; your people will fall. But your people are *our* people." He sighed. "There has been so much destroyed, my lady. So much harmed. All we want is a chance to heal."

Lady Astrea looked at him then. Her gaze was penetrating.

"We would have nothing," she said, her voice trembling. "No certainties, no order. You are asking me to unmake a perfect city, Doctor."

"We don't need a perfect city," he said, with quiet passion. "We don't want ancient pacts or grand designs. We just want to make it possible to live here without being a symbol, or a pawn." He smiled. "We just want to be human."

Lady Astrea didn't answer. She was looking beyond Theo, her gaze sweeping across the portraits of the former Directors, staring down from the walls of the grand, ancient office.

The room held its breath. The receivers readied their swords.

Lady Astrea made her decision.

CHAPTER TWENTY-SEVEN

Words

MARK KICKED the small wooden chair across the cave again. It crashed as it hit the wall, finally splintering into pieces.

Lily looked up from where she sat on the floor.

"That isn't helping," she muttered, listlessly.

"It's not helping *you*," Mark corrected. "It's definitely making me feel better."

Savagely, he stamped on the one remaining chair leg, and couldn't help feeling a tiny spark of satisfaction as it cracked under the blow. His mind still felt as though it was burning, and it was taking every ounce of his self-control not to hurl himself against the wall and beat it until his fists bled.

It wasn't just the theft of his emotions, or their traumatic return. Yes, they had been overwhelming at first, enough to make him scream like a madman as the guardians dragged him to this cave. But this anger felt more real, though he wasn't sure whether he was angrier at Snutworth, or at himself.

He tried to believe what Lily had said—that he had no choice, that without his emotions he literally hadn't been able to care about anything. But that didn't comfort him at all. He'd led Snutworth here. He'd given him this power. It was all his fault.

He felt violated. He'd already tried to take out his frustration on their guards, but the guardians were strong, and they were quick to swat him back into the cave, with looks of disgust at having to touch him to do so. He already had a nasty swelling on his forehead from when they had sent him sprawling.

He seized the leg of the chair, weighing it for balance. There was no other furniture in the cave, but this seemed sturdy.

"Maybe if I crept up on them . . ." he began.

"You might be able to knock them out," Lily completed. "Then what? Snutworth controls this entire land!"

"Great! Just great . . ." Mark growled, flinging the leg to the floor. "Then what do you suggest we do?"

"Maybe take a moment to think?" Lily suggested, sourly.

"You think there's something we overlooked?" Mark asked, sarcastically. "Have you *noticed* who we're sharing a cell with?"

He pointed over to the other side of the cave.

The former Oracle sat on the floor, her knees drawn up under her chin. Down from her throne, away from the mysterious light of her chamber, her dress no longer sparkled. It looked heavy and awkward, like her limbs. Her eyes were focused on something far away.

"We're in prison with the fount of all knowledge," he said, a little more calmly. "And somehow, I still feel as though this chair leg is going to be more use."

"She won't help," Lily said, her voice cracking. "She doesn't know how."

Mark felt a stab of guilt. Because of the power of the newly returned emotions washing around inside him, he hadn't had a chance to stop and think what all of this was doing to Lily. That was her mother, sitting there. They were alone at last, and neither of them was talking. What was the matter with him? The least he could do was comfort Lily.

But instead, he felt another burst of anger exploding through him, and clenched his fist. He wondered if Snutworth had given him back all of his emotions. He still felt a little odd. He stuffed his hands into the pockets of his jacket, and pulled out the glass vials that he had picked up off the floor. Most of them were empty, but there was one that still contained a drop or two of deep blue liquid. Midnight blue. Well, that was appropriate.

"I'm sorry, Mark," Lily continued, half to herself. "I didn't want to help him, but I couldn't see you like that." She looked over at the Oracle, her eyes narrowing. "I couldn't see you empty, like her." Lily rose to her feet, angrily, still looking at her mother. "Why won't you just give us something?" she said. "You sat on that throne for years. Is there nothing you heard, nothing that can turn the Naruvians against him?"

"Nothing," the Oracle replied, at last. Without the echoes, her voice was feeble. "He has invoked the rights of the Charter. We live and die by its laws."

Mark turned the last vial over in his hand, thinking.

"But what happens now?" Lily insisted, kneeling down to look her mother in the eye. "What happens after the Day of Judgment?"

The Oracle's face didn't move at all.

"Nothing," she said. "The last commands are to obey the Judges' vessel. The experiment is ended. We have served our purpose."

Lily's lip trembled, but her eyes were full of cold disdain.

"Then what was all your knowledge *for*?" she asked. "What good will it do in his hands? Is this really what the Librans pictured? A man who's only desire is to play with the lives of others? Is that the final result of their great project?" She pulled her face into a sarcastic grimace. "I think something might have gone wrong."

The Oracle stared at her. For a second, Mark thought he saw something. A tiny twitch in her face—of anger, or regret. But then it was gone, and all she did was to nod.

"So be it," she said.

Lily turned away, her arms wrapped tight around her. Mark approached the older woman, but Lily caught his arm.

"Don't bother, Mark," Lily said, tightly, on the verge of tears. "She's never going to help us."

Mark looked at the Oracle. The vial in his hand sparkled.

"Perhaps she just needs a little motivation," he said, an idea occurring to him.

Mark kneeled down in front of the Oracle. She focused her gaze on him.

"What are you going to . . . ?" she asked. She didn't reach the end of the question.

In one sudden movement, Mark grasped her chin, readied the vial, and tipped the last drop of his emotion onto her tongue. It evaporated with a hiss, the thick blue steam rising, and flowing down into her mouth.

Lily stared.

"Mark?" she gasped. "What did you do? You needed that!"

"I've taken most of it back," Mark said, trying to sound more certain than he was. "I don't feel any different. A drop or two of regret isn't going to matter to me—I've got plenty." He watched. Very slowly, the Oracle's shoulders were beginning to shake, and her eyes were filling with tears. He nodded with satisfaction. "The question is, Oracle, can you say the same?"

The Oracle opened her mouth, but she seemed to be struggling to find her voice. She grasped at him, her hands clenching uncontrollably.

"What . . . did you . . . you . . . I . . . ?"

Her voice dissolved into a moan, and then a wail. Tears streamed down her cheeks. Her body convulsed. Horrified, Mark grabbed hold of her, trying to stop her from bashing her head, and Lily dropped back to the ground to help.

"I didn't mean to do it!" Mark shouted, over the sound of her wails. "I just thought . . . a tiny bit of regret might help her see things our way. That was barely a quarter of a normal dose, it shouldn't be doing this to her . . ."

"Do you have any idea how long she's been keeping those emotions suppressed?" Lily shot back. Mark swallowed.

"No," he admitted.

"Neither do I," Lily replied. "But she didn't remember me, so that must be sixteen years at least . . ."

"I wanted to remember you."

Lily and Mark stared down. The Oracle struggled to speak, her voice choking with sobs.

"I didn't want to give you up," she stammered. "But I had to. I was to be Oracle, the greatest honor a Gisethi can be given. It must always be a Gisethi, you see—Naruvians don't have the understanding, and Agorans would try to use secrets for their own advantage, but an Oracle must be clear-sighted, impartial, . . . cold." She clung to Lily. "To be Oracle, you must leave behind everything that is you, lest the Nightmare use it to turn the echoes deadly. Even the Canticle itself hides any echo of ourselves from us. You cannot sit and record a million broken dreams and spoiled lives if any of them matter to you. You can't remain on your throne forever if you've known what it is to live." She clutched at Lily's hair, a faint smile breaking through the tears. "Such beautiful hair, even when you were born. I remember that now. But I'd already been chosen. Thomas wanted me to stay after you were born, at least for a few days, but I had a duty . . . my duty . . . oh stars and heavens forgive me . . ."

The Oracle clung to Lily, her sobs growing louder. Mark stepped back, scuffing at the floor. He wished he was elsewhere. This was private; he didn't belong here. Instead, he stood by, awkwardly, as the sobs died down.

"Thank you, Mark," the Oracle said, her voice still shuddering. Mark turned back. The Oracle was looking at him with real warmth for the first time. "I thought I should say it, while I still could." Her voice began to change in tone. She grasped at Lily's face, turning it toward her. "I feel this false emotion leaving me. If there is anything you want to ask the woman I was, anything you need from Helen d'Annain, you must be quick."

Lily stared back; she opened her mouth, but no sound came out. And then, swallowing hard, she asked her question.

"Did you ever love me?"

The Oracle bowed her head.

"Not enough, Lily. Not enough to forego my great duty." She looked up at her daughter, letting fresh tears trace shining lines down her face. "Not until now."

Lily held her mother then, not speaking. Held her as the last of the warmth drained from her face. By the time Lily got up again, brushing down her dress, her mother was once again vacant—a cold and perfect shell.

She walked over to Mark, and he squeezed her hand.

"Look, Lily . . ." he began, but she shook her head.

"It isn't the time to talk about this," she said, softly. "Right now, we need to stop Snutworth, and the Oracle's just told us how to do that."

Mark frowned.

"Really?" he asked. Lily nodded, her eyes flashing.

"Snutworth is on the Resonant Throne now, but he hasn't forgotten his past life. Oracles are supposed to forget."

"But that just makes him all the more dangerous," Mark began, but Lily cut him off.

"Exactly! You remember what happened when I found out who she really was," Lily said, gesturing to the crumpled form of the Oracle. "How the whole cavern shook because she *felt* something in those memories? Well, just imagine how Snutworth is feeling. He's been wanting this his whole life."

Mark began to see what she was getting at, and felt a prickle of excitement down the back of his neck.

"You mean, if he gets carried away, the Canticle will go wild?"

"I barely touched the surface of the Canticle, and I nearly lost myself," Lily continued. Mark could almost see the cogs in her mind turning. "Just think about it, all those millions of thoughts, even he can't keep track of everything. Not if he's trying to keep hold of his own mind."

"Snutworth's never really cared about anything in his life. Do you really think he'll start now?"

"Maybe not," Lily pondered. "But perhaps we can spread a little confusion, see if we can get all those thoughts to overwhelm him, to break his control. And if not, well . . ." she picked up the chair leg. "Two against one, right?"

Mark frowned.

"But won't he already know what we're planning? I mean, if he can hear every word spoken . . ."

"What if he does?" Lily said, firmly. "Even if he's bothering to listen to us, do you think he'll really care? He doesn't think we can do anything to hurt him now."

"But how are we even going to get to him?" Mark pointed to the thick curtain covering the cave entrance. "The guardians are out there, remember?"

Lily pondered for a moment. Her eyes drifted down to the figure who sat on the floor, staring into space. A strange look passed over her features. It was almost mischievous.

"Maybe I can call in a little family assistance after all . . ."

Mark and Lily ran down the tunnel. Behind them, they could still hear the shrieks of the guardians.

Mark still couldn't quite believe that Lily had pushed her own mother into the guards' arms. The Oracle hadn't resisted; she barely seemed to have the will to move under her own power anymore, but she stumbled just far enough to startle the guardians. And the second the guards were distracted, Lily tore the protective covering from their faces, and Mark spat on them.

He felt like an animal, but it had done the trick. The guardians were more accustomed to contact than ordinary Naruvians, but they had still scrabbled at their faces as though they were being burned by acid. Now, the guardians were chasing after them, but the network of tunnels in this area was complex, and their shouts soon disappeared into the distance.

"If we live to tell people about this, maybe we'll leave out the escape," Mark gasped as they ran. "It wasn't particularly heroic, was it?"

"This isn't the time for heroics," Lily replied, breathing hard. "I think the Oracle's throne room is this way . . ."

They plunged down another tunnel, this one only sparsely lit. The light from the crystals set into the wall seemed weak and sickly, and the farther they went, the darker it got. They passed Naruvians, huddling along the edges of the tunnels, staring at the fading crystals with horror, but they didn't have time to stop and ask questions. They didn't need to slow down to know that something was wrong.

And then, without any warning, they were in the right tunnel. Mark recognized the steps cut into the floor—they were nearly at the Oracle's chamber. He also noticed that there were no guards posted. That was odd. Surely Snutworth wouldn't leave himself defenseless? But he pushed that thought away. They had to keep going, keep racing on, because if they stopped to think, they would have time to realize that they had no plan, no real way of knowing what awaited them.

Ahead, the tunnel opened up into the antechamber. The curtain was partly drawn aside, the odd, flickering light from beyond illuminating the room. Lily came to a sudden halt, and Mark nearly fell over her. They exchanged glances. All they could hear were their own ragged breaths. Mark swallowed. This was it.

He tried to think of something encouraging to say as he met Lily's eye. She shrugged. She knew there was nothing that could be said.

"Well now." The voice of Snutworth penetrated the curtain, and echoed around the antechamber. "What a pleasure. Please, do, come in."

Almost unconsciously, Mark and Lily linked hands. And then, together, they pushed aside the curtain, and walked into the chamber of the Resonant Throne.

The cavern was different, somehow. It was still impressive, the long walkway of rock, extending out over the jagged forest of crystal shards far below, each one glinting and sparkling in the half-light. But when the Oracle had been here, the atmosphere had been thick and mystical—the Canticle of Whispers had filled the room, and the air itself had swirled with possibility. Now, the air was still, cold, and clear. And the Canticle no longer floated everywhere at once, but seemed to beckon, to draw them forward to the center of the chamber, and the figure on the throne.

Snutworth sat back, watching them. He was alone, but entirely at ease. His dark coat, traced with gold, flowed over the stone chair, making him look like some rare and precious ore. Above him the vast, tapering crystal, the base of the Hub, was almost drained of light. Only intermittent pulses flickered across its surface, making the shadows in the room shift. But somehow, Snutworth's eyes were still visible—bright green sparks in the darkness.

As Mark's eyes began to adjust to the dim light, he noticed that the walkway had changed too. Up until it nearly reached the throne, it was the same as ever, a spar of rock, extending over the jagged crystals at the base of the cave, the one safe path forward. But then, abruptly, the rock crumbled away, leaving a chasm twenty feet wide, and much deeper down. And on the other side of the drop, Snutworth looked back. Even now, trapped on an island of rock, he sat with calm assurance, one hand resting lightly on the arm of the throne, the other extended in welcome.

"Now, this is an interesting situation," he said, quietly, his voice echoing through the chamber. "I had wondered whether you would simply run back to Agora. I think you would have been much happier if you had. The whispers have brought me all sorts of news. Even as I speak, the Directory is falling, your friends Mr. Owain and Sister Elespeth have been restored to their former selves, and . . . yes, Lady Astrea is handing over her power—my reign as Director is over." He smiled. "Which is terribly convenient, I must say. It saves me the bother of resigning and installing my own puppet ruler for the city. People are so much easier to control if they believe they are free."

"Control?" Lily shouted back, scornfully. Mark could tell that she was frightened, but trying to mask it, and he too tried to show no fear.

"Please, Miss Lilith, do not trouble to shout," Snutworth said, gently. "I assure you, I can hear every word."

"How are you going to rule from here?" Lily continued, walking forward until she reached the edge of the broken causeway. "You're trapped."

Snutworth nodded.

"A small precaution. Everyone here is loyal, to a point, but the echoes brought me news of your escape plan, and I could not take the risk that you two would find your way here while I was alone. I always enjoy a little conversation, but you are young, and might have been able to physically overpower me. So, therefore, a few large mining hammers were called into use." He gestured to the broken causeway. "A somewhat crude solution, I grant, but serviceable. I have some rope to assist my exit, when necessary, but for the moment I am quite prepared to wait. At least until the guardians think to disobey my orders and come looking for you here." He tilted his head to one side, slightly, listening to the whispers as they washed around him. "Yes, already they've discovered that you haven't taken the mine carts back to the Last's Descent. It won't be long before they work out where you would go. And this time, I think I will instruct them to execute you. Wolfram will see to the actual blow, of course—I think spilling blood might render a Naruvian entirely useless. Don't you agree?"

Mark frowned. Why was he no longer looking at them?

Mark moved instinctively. He didn't even see Wolfram coming, though he felt a rush in the air. The old monk lunged, but Mark fell to the ground, rolling away. He shouted a warning to Lily, but she moved just a little too slowly. By the time Mark found his feet, she was struggling in Wolfram's grasp. Now Mark could see the dark corner by the entrance where Wolfram had waited, cowled and hidden. They must have passed right by him.

"Wolfram," Snutworth said, casually, "would you kindly put Miss Lilith in some danger?"

Wolfram spun, knocking Lily's feet from under her with a

sweep of his leg, and produced Snutworth's cane—or rather, the blade that had been hidden inside. He held it to her throat.

"Thank you," Snutworth said, amiably. "Now please, Mr. Mark, do not approach Father Wolfram, or Miss Lilith will be dispatched."

Mark stopped in his tracks. Something was strange here. The blade was still steady enough, but beneath the cowled hood, Mark could see that the monk's lips were tight and bloodless.

"Please don't stare, Mr. Mark," Snutworth chided. "I believe Father Wolfram is feeling a little delicate at the moment. Though I assure you that this will make little difference to his effectiveness."

Mark tried to blot Snutworth out. He was just a voice—he couldn't reach them. But Wolfram was right there. He caught Lily's eye. Despite everything, he could still see the spark of curiosity there.

"What happened, Wolfram?" she asked. Wolfram's jaw remained tightly clenched, the rest of his features hidden beneath the hood of his robe.

"Father Wolfram is about to perform a rather useful task for me," Snutworth said, thoughtfully. "He is going to begin a project I have long been preparing, and convey some choice information to my agents in Agora. They are unassuming people—trained to be unnoticeable. Some are native Agorans, but most are former members of the Gisethi orders. Wolfram has been recruiting from Giseth for quite some time, and I must say, I am very pleased with them. They are used to following commands without question—their faith is remarkable. Under my guidance, they will become my voice in the lands above. They will whisper the right secrets in the right ears—have a few people shamed, and a few others inspired. Reputations will be ruined, my own chosen elevated, and my control assured, all without needing to leave this throne." He settled back. "I must confess, some of the things I have learned from only a few hours on this throne have made me unwilling to return to the lands above. Dear me—the things people think when they are alone, such nasty little secrets, such dark desires. And yet so useful, if revealed at exactly the right moment . . ."

Mark's eyes widened.

"What did he tell you, Wolfram?" Mark asked. Wolfram twitched, but didn't respond. The tip of the blade hovered a hair's breadth from Lily's throat.

"Whatever it was, it was lie," Lily said, her voice tight. "He lies to everyone . . ."

"No, Miss Lilith," Snutworth said, firmly. "I do not lie—quite the reverse. Lies are never as powerful a weapon as the truth." He smiled. "You have searched for 'the Truth' your entire life, and has it ever brought anything other than misery and pain?"

"What? Are you going to claim that you'll usher in some perfect world?" Lily snarled, and then gasped as the blade moved a little closer. Snutworth waved his hand, airily.

"Not in the least. But I don't suppose mine would be worse than they could manage on their own. And at least my world will follow a plan. Our lands were not designed to run themselves. They are not natural. They need a guiding intelligence, or they will descend into chaos."

"And you think you should be the one to guide us?" Lily said, her voice dripping with defiant scorn. "I'll try the chaos."

"Well now, you would say that." Snutworth leaned forward in his chair. "The sad thing is, you truly believe that you do all this for the greater good. But I have listened to the Canticle, Miss Lily. I know all of your thoughts, even the ones you don't realize that you have. And let me tell you something, I know exactly why you want chaos. Because that is where you shine. You, the symbol of charity, the savior— all those people look to you, and it makes you feel wonderful."

Lily grew pale. Mark wanted her to deny it, to throw Snutworth's words back at him. But he knew that she couldn't.

"And why would *you* stand against me?" Snutworth asked, his

353

green eyes moving to take in Mark. "Don't you hate all of this chaos, Mark? All this fighting, and running, and changing the world? All you wanted was a quiet, stable family. That was the only time you were truly happy, wasn't it? When you used to play on the riverbank, before you knew any of this. Don't deny it. I have heard your thoughts."

Mark tried to muster a response, but suddenly he felt tired. The air around him thrummed with whispers, and so many of them were familiar. The voices of his dead mother, brother, and sister.

"You poor children," Snutworth said, sounding almost heart-felt. "But of course, you were never truly children, were you? Poor Lily, abandoned by a father who sent her to live in a cruel and heartless city, and a mother who knew everything in the world except her own name. Poor Mark, watched over by a mother who could offer nothing but stories, and a father who sold him. Such sad lives. But I can change that." He smiled. "All you have to do is leave this chamber. I will let you live. And from now on, nothing will be your fault. No responsibility, no pain. People around you will still believe that they control their own lives, sadly, but you will know the blissful truth. That I know their every thought, their every desire. And when it suits my whim to change the world above, I will summon one of my followers and issue my instructions. A single word in the right place can change the course of lives, or end them altogether." Snutworth smiled, benevolently, and all around him the Canticle surged with power. "The ancient Librans were extraordinary people, but they never truly understood what they had created. They only meant for the Oracle to observe. They never saw the potential to manipulate, to control, and all under the illusion of freedom." His voice rose, the whispers echoing his every word. "Until today, I was merely the ruler of the lands above. Now, I will *be* the lands above. Agora, Giseth, as much part of my will as my own body. Others will struggle, others will rise and fall, if I so choose. But you two will live in peace. You can be children again, knowing that I am watching over you, that you will never have to make a decision again."

Mark and Lily met each other's gaze. Through all the fear, Mark realized that he did want that. He wanted it so desperately it hurt. He'd been running and fighting for so long. He just wanted to go home, to see his friends again, to not have to worry anymore.

Which was why he could never let Snutworth win.

Lily elbowed Wolfram in the ribs, just as Mark charged. The monk fell to his knees, the sword dropping from his grasp. Lily squirmed free, diving for the weapon. Wolfram shoved her to one side, scrabbling for the blade, but Mark stamped on his hands, and Lily snatched up the sword, jumping up and backing away.

Wolfram rose to his feet, and Lily held out the sword, pointing it at Wolfram's heart. Neither moved.

Cautiously, Mark crept behind Lily. From here, he could feel her trembling, a little, but the monk didn't get any closer.

"Dear, dear," Snutworth said, placidly, "not your finest moment, Wolfram. Still, it is of no matter. These two are little but a distraction. Go. Begin your task."

To Mark's surprise, Wolfram didn't move. He simply stood, head bowed. It was impossible to see his face in the shadows of the cowl, but Mark was sure he was staring at the tip of the sword.

"Do you hear me, Father Wolfram?" Snutworth said, with a trace of irritation. "It is time to begin the great work—to use the secrets I gave you. Forget the children. What harm can they do us?"

Again, Wolfram didn't move. Didn't even raise his head. Mark risked a glance at Lily. He could see a bead of sweat running down the back of her neck. Wolfram's stillness was unnerving, and he was standing between them and the exit.

"I gave you an order, Wolfram," Snutworth said, his tone still measured. "I understand the need for revenge, but you have duties to perform."

"No," Wolfram said. His voice was quiet, but it had a rasp to it that Mark hadn't heard before.

And then, he pulled back his hood.

Mark stiffened, and he saw Lily take a step back. In the shifting light of the cavern, much of Wolfram's hard-lined face was in darkness. But what he could see was enough. He had never seen an expression like that on the face of a living man. There was no emotion there at all. No anger, no fear, not even his old look of hard determination. And when he spoke, his voice was hollow, and dead.

"These things you have told me," he said, his gaze never moving from the sword, "these secrets you have shared, they will not work. They cannot, because they cannot be true . . ."

"They are, Wolfram," Snutworth said. "Every word."

Deep inside him, Mark felt a familiar, unwelcome presence. The Nightmare was lurking close by, inside every whisper of the Canticle. But it was different than any time before. This time, it wasn't interested in him, or Lily.

"They *cannot* be true," Wolfram said, his voice growing louder. "Because, if they are, these people you seek to control are not worthy of our attention. They are not worthy of life," he began to breathe heavily, his voice changing, filling with hatred. "I thought that I knew darkness; I had made darkness my tool. I knew why you wanted control, to bring order to this bestial world, and I supported you. But I didn't truly understand." He stepped forward, his whole body tense. "Not until you made me understand, Director. Not until you showed me what mankind has done. What secrets they hold in their heads." Mark could feel the Nightmare, thick in the air, and through it all, Wolfram's voice continued, deep, and loud, and broken. "You showed me there is no truth. There is no true virtue; no love, or faith, or duty in their minds. Everything is corrupted, mixed in with lies, and deeds that are worse . . . far, far worse. The things that they think, and do, when the world cannot see them . . ." Wolfram's voice rose in anger. "I wanted a better place for mankind. I defied my church for you, so you could be their master, and save them from their own base desires. But now I know—mankind isn't worth controlling." His lip curled in disgust. "We are filthy, and vile, and we must be purged. One by one."

Wolfram sprang.

Lily had no time to react. The monk ran at her, snatching back the sword. He made a grab for her, but she twisted, slipping under his arm, just as he slashed the air. He spun around, lunging at her again, and his eyes fell on Mark, still frozen to the spot.

Mark turned to run, but too late. Wolfram grabbed his shoulder, wrenching him back. Mark struggled, desperately, kicking and punching, but the monk barely seemed to feel his blows. He tightened his grip, and Mark gasped in pain, his arm going numb.

Wolfram lifted the sword to Mark's throat, letting out an almost animalistic growl. Mark's heart skipped.

And then Lily was there. She sank her teeth into Wolfram's wrist, and he let go of Mark, staggering back toward the edge of the abyss. Mark sprang free, but Wolfram seized Lily's hair. He threw her to the ground, her chin striking the stone. For a second, Mark watched, powerless, as the monk stood over her, the sword in his hands, his eyes full of the mad light of the Nightmare.

He swung up the blade, and brought it down toward her face.

Before he knew what he was doing, Mark slammed his whole body into the monk, sending him sprawling back, toward the edge of the stone walkway. At the same time, Lily kicked out, striking at Wolfram's bad foot. He yelled in pain, arms spiraling, trying to regain his balance.

And he fell, plunging off the walkway.

The Canticle took up his scream, magnifying it a thousand times over. For a few seconds, as Mark and Lily stared in horror, the Nightmare surged in their minds, triumphing, making them feel Wolfram's rage, and fear, as the huge jagged shards of crystal grew closer.

His scream stopped.

There was a terrible silence. Mark stared at Lily, his whole body shaking. Lily, looking dazed, crawled forward, to look over the edge, but Mark sprang up and pulled her back. Neither of them needed to see that. He was gone, and they had done it.

Up on his crystal throne, Snutworth sniffed.

"Regrettable," he said, "But it matters little. I have many more servants. The Naruvians will send my messages, for now. And the Canticle will reveal to me who will make an appropriate chief agent in the days to come. My message will be spread, my dominion assured."

Mark felt sick. He had hated Wolfram; he couldn't mourn or regret what he'd done. But at least he felt something. Not like Snutworth.

"He's dead!" Mark shouted fiercely, turning to face the Resonant Throne. "Can't you feel anything? He was your friend!"

"He was my servant," Snutworth said, placidly. "Soon, I will have so many more."

"And what, you'll play with the world until you get bored?" Lily asked, equally angry. Snutworth smiled.

"Perhaps. Or I may improve it, or make it worse. There are so many fascinating possibilities. These lands were built for experimentation, but now that the old Librans are dead, their plans will live on."

Mark felt Lily squeeze his hand, and they looked at each other. He could see the strain he felt etched on her face, too. He wanted to run, to curl up, to have a chance to feel something over what had just happened. But they couldn't give up now. Not when they had Snutworth talking.

Mark swallowed hard, burying his morbid thoughts in case

Snutworth could hear them. Lily let go of his hand, and both of them turned again to face Snutworth, refusing to show fear.

"What about new ideas?" she shouted. "Or new lives? What about freedom?"

"Freedom," Snutworth replied, contemptuously. "Who deserves this freedom? You? Your friends, perhaps? Like my little wife, who runs to anyone with a modicum of power because she can't face the world? I can hear her thoughts Mark. She's thinking of you right now. Listen . . ."

The Canticle around Snutworth seemed to reach out, and the voices grew louder, more distinct. Mark stepped back, alarmed. But then, one voice—a voice so clear and familiar to him—rose above all the others.

Mark can't come back now. Not right now, I couldn't bear it . . .

She sounded so lost, so uncertain, and Mark felt a stab of pain. "Maybe she's in danger and doesn't want me to get mixed up in it," Mark said, defiantly.

Snutworth raised an eyebrow and turned to Lily.

"Or perhaps you would like to hear Mr. Laudate?" he said, leaning forward. "Do you want to hear how he thinks of you? All the thoughts he barely acknowledges, all his doubts, and fears? Do you know what he thought when he first met you?"

On command, the Canticle rose up, and with it came Laud's voice—speaking in that harsh, sneering tone that he had used when he had first come to the almshouse.

Silly little girl. Someone should teach her how the real world works . . .

"He still sees you like that," Snutworth said. "He doesn't think of you as your own person, just a bundle of ideas that need to be protected. Proud little Lily, what will you think of that . . . ?"

"I don't care!" Lily blurted out, obviously shaken. "They're his private thoughts. Everyone has stupid thoughts they don't really mean."

"And even if he does, maybe it's a good thing," Mark added. Lily looked at him incredulously, and Mark shrugged. "He thinks you're something unique that needs to be protected. I'd say from Laud, that's a pretty big compliment."

"But how many can you excuse?" Snutworth said, his tone darker. "How many nasty little thoughts can you stand?"

And suddenly, the air was full of them. Cajoling, cringing voices, all around—mocking and sneering, and all of them full of doubt and pain.

We'll never do this, never cure this sickness. I should never have tried to help. They don't deserve my help.

That was Dr. Theophilus, his voice weary and resigned.

"Such a pity that your reliable healer breaks so easily . . ." Snutworth laughed.

It's Lily's fault. Her fault my sister is dead. Her fault my brother abandoned us. Her fault we're all about to die in a stupid revolution.

Benedicta spoke, full of bitterness. Mark saw Lily screw shut her eyes, as though she had been physically struck.

"What a shame Miss Benedicta didn't hold the faith when you were away," Snutworth proclaimed with undisguised glee.

Mark should have stayed in prison. Then he couldn't have caused any more trouble.

That was Pete. Mark tried to block it out, only to hear Verity's voice ring loud and clear.

My brother died waiting for her. And now she's gone. What was the point? Why should she live and he die . . . ?

"How many do you have to hear?" Snutworth shouted. His voice seemed to buzz with the Canticle now, as a thousand known and unknown voices blended with his own. Mark could feel the vibrations beneath his feet—the room shook with the force of Snutworth's passion.

Why are we allied with Mark? He was one of the elite once, and he'd still be if he hadn't been stopped . . . he's just like the rest of them . . .

What's the point of fighting when my children are starving? Who cares about others? I need to look after my own . . .

I won't follow . . . they're just children . . .

What's the use?

What's the point?

"Stop it! Stop it now!" Lily yelled, clamping her hands over her ears. Mark felt cold and empty inside. He wished he could deny what they had heard, but somehow, he knew that the Canticle could never lie.

"I thought so," Snutworth said. "The great Judges are just as willfully blind as any other. Truth stings you. But *this* is the Truth. When you strip away the self-deception, all of the little tricks that you all use to make yourselves respectable, this is all that remains—banal, selfish little creatures that don't deserve control over their own lives."

"I didn't mean stop *them*," Lily said.

Mark looked over at her. She was looking up again now, and her eyes had a kind of fire to them that Mark had seen before. She wasn't defeated.

For the first time, Mark saw Snutworth hesitate, and Lily leapt in.

"Stop your foul commentary on it all!" she shouted. "What are you trying to prove? That our friends had a moment of weakness? Haven't we all? But that doesn't mean they really believe it."

"Only in their worst moments will you find the truth," Snutworth said, with a flourish.

Suddenly, the air was filled with a voice that was all too familiar. Mark listened, dumbfounded, as Lily's echoes resonated through the throne room.

She's wrong! Can't they see the Speaker's wrong and I'm right! No, what are you doing . . . I don't have time now, Gloria. I'll see you tomorrow . . . Mark might never see his father again, but mine are out there, somewhere, and he has to come with me . . . I don't care . . . I have to know everything! . . . have to do anything to know . . .

Every time she had caused suffering, every time she had been too weak, or too stupid, to stop another's pain—the Canticle summoned them all. Lily stood absolutely still, an expression of horror fixed on her face as the darkest moments of her life returned in mocking, rushing echoes. The air was split again by the memory of Wolfram's dying scream.

"See yourself, children," Snutworth said, his voice resonating around the cavern. "See yourself as you are. Liars, murderers, destroyers . . ."

Mark knew what was coming, but even so, as Lily's voice was replaced by his own, he couldn't help gritting his teeth.

You know your way out, Gloria . . . It's not my fault . . . I'm not going to ruin my reputation to make you feel better . . . Stupid old man, what does he know . . . ?

"That isn't the truth!" Mark shouted, trying to drown out his own voice. "That's me at my worst. I've been better than that, we all have. You say you understand people, but all you can see is their failings."

Lily opened her eyes wide, a new confidence spreading across her face.

"That's it! Don't you see, Mark, that's how *he* sees the world." She looked straight at Snutworth. "That's why the Canticle sounds so angry. You can't hear it properly, can you? All you can hear is what you believe in. You think you're showing us the Truth about ourselves, but all you're revealing is the truth about *you*. You're empty, Snutworth. You don't see people—all you see are their weaknesses, their strings that you can use to manipulate them. But the rest of us are so much more than that."

Snutworth straightened on his throne.

"I don't need to listen to this," he said, his calm starting to fray. "You know nothing of the world, nothing of my design . . ."

"We know more than you," Mark said, defiantly, moving to the edge of the causeway, so Snutworth couldn't avoid his gaze. "We see people as they are, not as a set of weaknesses to exploit."

"Try it, Snutworth," Lily continued, pointedly. "Try listening to everything."

Snutworth hesitated.

"Do you think to surprise me with love, or kindness, or friendship? I know of these things—how else would I have known how you would react when I took Mr. Mark's emotions." He leaned forward, intensely. "Can you never admit when you've lost?"

"Maybe there's something you don't know," Lily whispered, her voice nearly blending with the Canticle. "Maybe you need to listen."

Mark barely dared to breathe. As long as Snutworth saw the Canticle as a tool, as something he could use to his own ends, he could control it. But if he really opened up to it, if he really tried to listen to everything, then maybe their plan could work.

For a moment, Mark thought Snutworth wouldn't take the bait, that he would laugh and banish them from his presence, that this last, tiny chance would vanish forever.

But once, Snutworth had been Mark's servant—Mark had known him better than anyone else in the world. And if there was one thing he had learned, it was that Snutworth never wanted anyone else to know more than him.

Snutworth closed his eyes.

The volume and power of the Canticle began to increase. Snutworth clenched his jaw, concentrating, as it thrummed through the air. The whole chamber was beginning to shake, the ground rolling beneath them.

"There is nothing here I do not know," Snutworth said, triumphantly, his voice splitting into a hundred, buzzing echoes. "Just the same old banalities, the same petty concerns, a million times over."

"Exactly," Mark shouted over the noise, staggering to maintain his balance. "The same. A million people, all as complex as the next, each with good points and bad, and so much in between . . ."

"Or are they all different?" Lily picked up the argument, dropping to her hands and knees as the chamber rocked, and dust fell from new cracks in the ceiling. "All filled with a thousand thoughts that pull them every way, until you can't tell which one will carry the day?"

"You want to know why the Librans wanted two Judges?" Mark called out, everything falling into place in his mind. "Because there're always two sides to everything. Always a hundred different ways to see. And that's why you'll never control the Canticle. Because you think too *small*. You hear all these people?" He shouted. "Listen—every one of them is wonderful."

"Every one of them is terrible," Lily added.

"We're devils," Mark said.

"We're angels," Lily said.

"We're simply human . . ." Mark screamed as the Canticle rose into a wail.

". . . and that's the most complex thing of all," Lily concluded. Snutworth's breathing became ragged. Mark could feel the vibrations in the air; the throne began to hum with a deep tone.

"No . . ." Snutworth exclaimed, his calm tone trying to reassert itself. "I am apart from this. I am pure. I see . . . everything . . . I understand . . . all . . ."

"You could have had a life, Snutworth," Mark said, almost pitying him. "You could have made your own way, but instead, you're just everyone's shadow. An empty man whose whole life is based on controlling others. It doesn't matter how many times you pull the strings, you're not part of our world. And you never will be, now."

"Our world!" Snutworth spat. Mark saw that Snutworth had thrown off any semblance of his old calm—dredging up these thoughts was taking its toll on him. "A falsehood—a tissue of lies to prove an old argument. Agora, Giseth, Naru—none of it is real, no one can have a real life here. We are nothing but dreams."

"We might have been like that once . . ." Lily said, powerfully, the echoes beginning to cluster around her. "But not anymore. No one told us we were supposed to be an experiment; no one said that we were supposed to think a certain way. And now, we don't. We've changed; we're human. We have lives of our own that don't depend upon prophecies or ancient plans. We're our own people, and we always will be."

"But what are you, Snutworth?" Mark said as the Canticle began to rise again, stronger than ever. "Have you found your place?"

"Is it here, with all these old secrets?" Lily continued, driving her point home as firmly as any knife. "Why do you want all this knowledge? What will you do with it?"

"I . . . I . . . control . . ." Snutworth gasped out, his voice barely seeming his own anymore, it carried so many half-heard echoes.

"Control what?" Lily continued. "What do you get out of it? If everyone is so stupid, out for whatever they can grab, why do you want secret power? Why don't you want the glory? Why hide here?"

"You're nothing," Mark said, and meant it.

"No . . ." Snutworth said, his voice barely human.

"At least the Oracle did what she did out of a sense of duty," Lily shouted. "But you, you're empty. Just a little boy who never knew when playtime was over."

"All you have left are dead thoughts, Snutworth," Mark said, his voice filling the chamber. "We're not your playthings anymore. The world's outgrown you."

The Canticle screamed.

A million echoes filled the air, their whispers frantic and meaningless. The whole cavern was vibrating now. And in the midst of it all, Snutworth stood up from his throne with a jerk, as though it had burned him.

"Help . . . me . . ." he said, so softly that Mark could barely hear him. But it was too late.

Great shards of the ceiling crashed down, shearing off more of the walkway. Snutworth looked around him, suddenly clear-eyed, and terrified. Above him, there was a dreadful cracking sound.

"The Hub!" Lily yelled. Mark looked up. The Hub itself was vibrating, faster and faster, until the chamber rang. Any second now, it would fall. Lily and Mark scrambled backward as the walkway crumbled beneath their feet, and Snutworth stared around, looking for any way out.

But there was nothing. The gap that he had made was too wide. Too wide for him to escape, even if he used his rope. Too wide to jump. Mark, standing in the entrance, saw the moment that Snutworth realized this. Saw the understanding in his eyes.

And then, Snutworth turned, and sat back down.

Softly, he rested his hands on the arms of the Resonant Throne.

And he smiled. A smile that would live in Mark's memory for the rest of his life. It looked, at last, as though he were at peace with himself.

The Hub shattered.

The Cavern of the Oracle collapsed.

Darkness fell.

CHAPTER TWENTY-EIGHT

The Judgment

LILY COUGHED DUST into the air.

She tried to sit up, but there was a crushing weight on her chest, and she hadn't the strength. Still winded, she wriggled her arm, trying to loosen the rubble, and touched something that felt like a hand. She turned her head, blinking to get the grit out of her eyes. She made out Mark, lying on his front, half buried beneath loose pieces of stone. He didn't look too bad, though he was covered in rock dust. They had been lucky; they were standing in the entrance when the Chamber collapsed so they had escaped the worst. But Snutworth . . .

She had seen the Hub splinter as it fell. Seen the largest shard as it plunged down toward him.

He was gone. And the Canticle had gone with him. For the first time ever in Naru, she heard nothing but the beating of her own heart.

367

Beside her, Mark stirred. He raised his head, and mustered a smile.

"Well . . . that worked," he said, weakly. He heaved himself up onto his elbows, and looked back at the former entrance to the throne room. A small piece of tattered curtain was still visible under the rubble. He frowned. "That's it, then?"

Lily nodded, slowly. She had to admit, it didn't feel much like a victory.

"Do you think we should have . . . I mean . . ." Mark hesitated. "Wolfram . . . Snutworth . . . Did we just kill them?"

"Wolfram was mad," Lily said, shakily. "If we'd hesitated, he'd have killed us both. And Snutworth trapped himself over there; he has only himself to blame."

"Yeah . . ." Mark said, "but . . ."

"We needed to break his connection to the Canticle," Lily said, ignoring the pang of guilt. "We didn't know it would bring down the whole chamber."

Mark met her eyes.

"No?" he asked. Lily looked away. The truth was, they'd both known it was a possibility. They both remembered what had happened when the Oracle had become upset; the whole of Naru had shaken. Lily sighed. She didn't think she would be losing much sleep over either of them. She just hoped that none of the Naruvians had been hurt.

"I . . . I don't care about Snutworth," Mark admitted. "But Wolfram . . . he had his beliefs, Lily. We all have those."

Lily frowned.

"We live for our beliefs. He tried to kill us for his," she sighed. "I know, it's not perfect, but I'm willing to live with it if you are," she said.

Mark nodded, uncertainly.

"All right," he agreed. There was a silence.

"So . . ." Mark ventured, "home now?"

Despite herself, Lily laughed, coughing again.

"That's it?" she asked. "All those plans and prophecies, leading up to this?" She thought about it for moment. It did have a certain appeal—it was definitely the last thing the old Librans would have imagined.

She heaved at the stones. Miraculously, she didn't think she'd broken anything, but the lower half of her body was pinned under the rubble, and she couldn't move. Every time she tried, she felt the rocks shift ominously.

"You too?" Mark groaned, struggling. "You think anyone will come if we call for help?"

Lily listened. In the distance, she heard shouts, and a storm of approaching footsteps clattering on the stone.

"Actually, I don't think we need to."

Mark twisted around to look, just as Septima and Tertius came into view. Their normally bright robes were streaked with grime, and they looked wild-eyed. As soon as they saw the rubble, though, they stopped dead. They stared, speechless as other Naruvians caught up with them, until, eventually, the Conductor arrived, red-faced and panting.

"Why have you stopped?" he wheezed. "We must make the vessel tell us why our land is wracked with torment . . ." he trailed off. For a long minute, he stared stupidly at the rubble, until Lily couldn't stand it any longer.

"Conductor, aren't you going to dig us out?" she asked, as politely as she could manage, coughing up another gout of dust. The Conductor didn't respond. All he could do was look at the pile of stone that had once been the entrance to the Oracle's chamber. Lily looked at Tertius and Septima, but they seemed equally dazed.

"The harmony is gone," Septima whispered. "The Hub is cracked, and the crystals are silent . . ."

"Where will our knowledge go?" Tertius added, panic beginning to set in. "What will we do? How will we live?"

"We'll help you," Mark said, hurriedly, "we promise. But please, you've got to get us out of here . . ."

A few guardians at the back, still swathed in gloves and masks, looked to the Conductor. He gave them no instructions. There was no color left in his face.

"You have destroyed everything," he said, numbly. "We have nothing. Nothing but empty, silent caves . . . for ever and ever . . ."

Lily shut her eyes. She did feel sorry for him, of course she did. But every second that passed, it was getting harder to breathe. She didn't have time to be gentle.

"Conductor," she said, firmly. "Our so-called vessel is gone. That means we're in charge again, right?"

This stern tone got a reaction; the Conductor frowned.

"I'm not sure. There was no guidance on this, and the former Oracle is refusing to talk to me . . ."

"Then you're going to have to make this decision yourself," said Mark. "The plans are over, the prophecies are gone. This is just you, Conductor. What do *you* think should happen?"

The Conductor passed a hand over his brow. He looked lost, as though he were waking up from a long, peaceful dream.

He looked down at Lily. She stretched out her hand to him. He jerked back, but she kept her arm extended.

"It's a new world, Conductor," she said. "New life. New ways. Don't be ruled by the past."

The Conductor glanced back at his people. They were silent, their large, dark eyes fixed on him, and Lily.

He steeled himself.

And he took her hand.

Amazed whispers rippled through the crowd. One or two of the

Naruvians sank to the floor, looking ill. But the Conductor held on, shaking only a little.

"Guardians!" he said, suddenly. "Clear this passage. The Judges need our help."

The guardians worked quickly. By the time the Conductor had pulled Lily out of the rubble, Mark was already standing. Lily's knee twinged alarmingly; Mark had a nasty cut across his back, and both were bruised all over, but for now, they could move.

As soon as Lily could stand on her own, the Conductor withdrew to a safe distance, wiping his hand on his robe. He looked a little queasy, but oddly proud.

"Thank you," Lily said, not quite sure what else to say. She could feel the stares of the Naruvians all around her. She wondered if she should apologize, but what could she say? She and Mark had changed their world forever; it would hardly matter to them that they did it for the best of reasons.

"What are your commands now, Judges?" the Conductor said, with dignity. Lily met Mark's eyes. He looked as tired as she felt.

"I think . . ." he said. "I think we need to go home. Is the way clear back to the Last's Descent?"

The Conductor nodded, silently. But Septima was not so dignified.

"You can't go!" she cried. "You're the Judges!"

There was a clamor of agreement from the other Naruvians, but Mark shook his head.

"You don't need us anymore," he said, raising his voice over the hubbub. "You need someone who can send you supplies, or help you contact the other lands. And when we get back home, we'll try to do that. But we can't do anything more from down here."

This seemed to only add to the Naruvians' confusion. But it was Tertius who stepped forward, looking directly at Mark and Lily.

"But . . . who will tell us what to do?" he said, hesitantly.

Lily and Mark looked at each other. For a few seconds, Lily was tempted. This was an extraordinary opportunity. Every person in Naru was looking to them. They could change anything they wanted. They could remake this place with everything they'd learned. They could turn it into a paradise.

But that had been Snutworth's plan, not theirs.

"That's up to you," Mark said, gently. "This isn't our land; it's yours. You have to decide what you want to be."

"But," Lily added, "if you're looking for somewhere to start, I wouldn't look to the world above." She looked around at the confused Naruvian crowd, and to her own amazement, managed to smile. "There are more than enough wonders right here."

And without another word, Mark and Lily set off to climb the stairs away from the cavern of the Resonant Throne. There was still a long way to go to the Last's Descent.

As they turned the corner, they noticed the Naruvians had begun to talk to each other, earnestly. They noticed the Conductor was gathering others around him, a new sense of purpose in his bearing.

And they noticed Tertius take Septima's hand. She didn't pull away.

They didn't speak as the mine cart whisked them back to the Last's Descent, nor as the metal platform slowly winched them back up toward the surface. Lily knew that once they started, there would be too much to say. And right at the moment, all they needed was rest.

So it wasn't until they were nearly at the top that they started to wonder aloud if what Snutworth had said about the rebels taking over had been true. Were they about to emerge in the Virgo District as they had left it, full of locked doors, scared merchants, and wandering receiver patrols? Or would it be a violent storm of revolution? Either way, it was with some trepidation that they emerged from the secret room in the Last's house, padded through the corridors, and pushed open the iron-bound front door.

What they hadn't been expecting was utter stillness.

Mark stared around, puzzled. The early evening sunlight outlined the faded buildings around them, a welcome return to normality after the last couple of days. Most of the houses were still shuttered and barred, but here and there a door had been thrown open, and left creaking in the breeze. At this time of day, even in the quietest parts of the city, there would normally be a steady stream of people making their way home. This emptiness was eerie.

They began to walk down the cobbled streets. Lily half expected to run into a receiver patrol, lying in wait. But the only noise was a far-off rumble, like the sea crashing against the cliffs by the Cathedral of the Lost.

She stopped.

"Mark," she whispered, "do you hear that? What is it?"

Mark cocked his head to one side.

"I think . . ." he said, "isn't that . . . shouting?"

Lily dropped her head. She couldn't cope with another mob. They were probably coming for them already, tearing through once-proud Agora—the final result of her attempt to make the city a better place.

"No . . ." Mark continued, cautiously. "It's . . . cheering . . ." a smile began to grow on his face. "I think it's coming from the Central Plaza! Come on!"

And despite their aches and bruises, the two of them ran through the streets of Agora.

The closer they came to the Central Plaza, the louder the noise became. Now it was easier to pick out individual voices from the wash of sound—yelling slogans, calling to friends, even singing. Lily was sure that she recognized the Sozinhos, singing that same song of Glory that she had heard three years before—on the day of the Grand Festival, the day she and Mark had truly begun the paths that had led them here.

Three years exactly. Today was Agora Day too—her day of birth. The thought stopped her in her tracks. Mark skidded to a halt in front of her.

"What are you waiting for?" he asked, exasperated. "Don't you want to know what's happening?"

Lily paused.

"Do you think there's any way we could find out without going there? This might be a celebration of the Directory crushing the rebels, you know."

Mark's face lost a little color. He clearly hadn't thought of that. And then, just as suddenly, he smiled.

"Well, there might just be one place where we could get a better look . . ."

It was an extraordinary sight. The plaza was filled to bursting. The crowds spilled out onto the bridges, through the archways, and into the streets beyond. The remains of the barricades floated in the river, or had been trampled underfoot. Lily had never seen so many people gathered together. Even here, in the Observatory at the top of the Astrologer's Tower, she could still hear them singing.

The Astrologer's Tower was deserted; they were sure of that. No one had been living there for weeks. Mark had thought that would be the case—if Snutworth had left Lady Astrea in charge, she would have had to move into the Directory, away from the front lines. Behind Lily, Mark adjusted the great brass telescope that had once belonged to Count Stelli, angling it down to focus on the plaza itself, and get a closer look. But Lily was enjoying just staring through the windows, gazing down on the rooftops of Agora as they turned red and purple in the sunset.

"Lily!" Mark called, pulling his head back from the eyepiece of the telescope. "Come and look at this!"

Lily tore herself away from the vista and put her eye to the telescope. For a few seconds, the image was blurred, as Mark adjusted a few dials, and then . . .

"By all the stars!" Lily exclaimed in delight. "Is that Theo?"

But she didn't have to ask. Now she could make out their friend clearly. He was standing on the remains of the barricade, making some kind of speech. She didn't even need to hear it—she knew what it would be. It was written all over the faces of the crowd, and reflected in the cautious smiles of Laud, Ben, and Cherubina, standing beside him on his improvised podium. He would be reassuring the people gathered below, telling them that the worst was over, that there was hope. Mark shifted the telescope, and Lily saw others in the crowd nearby. She saw Inspector Greaves, solemn, but glad. She saw Pete, with tears of relief in his eyes. She saw Elespeth, looking wary, and Owain, cheering louder than any other. She saw Lady Astrea—her head bowed, but her carriage erect. And she saw receivers mixing with civilians, elite next to debtors, all cheering together at Theo's words. Tomorrow, Lily was sure that most of them would be back to normal, ready to drive their fellow revelers into the dirt to get the best deal. But for today, the revolution was over; peace was restored. And that sounded like a victory to her.

"Do you see that, Count Stelli?" Mark said, softly, into the air. "Look at Theo now—making predictions about the future in the Central Plaza, on Agora Day." He dropped his eyes. "He's your grandson after all."

Lily pulled away from the telescope, exhilarated by what she had seen. She wanted to laugh, to dance, but there would be time for all of that, and more, when they reached the plaza.

"All right," she said, "we've been cautious enough. Time for some fun!"

She was halfway through the trapdoor out of the Observatory when she realized that Mark wasn't following her.

"I don't think we should go," he said.

Slowly, Lily came back up the iron stairs. She didn't even bother to hide her disbelief.

"We just escaped from Naru," she said, incredulously. "We just stopped Agora and Giseth from falling under Snutworth's control. And as far as our friends know, we could be dead. Don't you think they'd want to see us?"

Lily trailed off. Mark was shaking his head. Lily realized that he didn't look particularly sad, or nervous. More than anything, he looked thoughtful.

"Would they? Right now?" he said, quietly. "Just . . . just look through that telescope."

Puzzled, Lily walked back over to the vast brass machine and put her eye to it. Everything was the same as before. Theo had clearly come to a particularly rousing part of his speech, because all those around him were cheering. She saw Laud, applauding vigorously, and her heart skipped a beat. Suddenly, more than anything, she wanted to get to him—to fling her arms around him, and show him that she was back, and she wasn't leaving again.

And then she noticed Cherubina. She was smiling, of course. But still, she looked around, nervously, as though expecting something to go wrong at any moment.

"Look at them," Mark said, coming close to Lily. "Look at our friends. They've done it—they've led the revolution to victory. But if we appear now, while the crowd is still looking for leaders, they'll make *us* take over." Mark stared out of the windows. "We're the big symbols of this revolution, remember? Without your almshouse, none of this would ever have happened."

Lily smiled, beginning to understand.

"Without your speech at the prison, the revolution would have become a massacre," she replied. Mark nodded.

"Exactly. The Librans wanted us to run the show, and I don't know how it happened, but we did. We set it going. But . . . I don't want to rule." Mark stuffed his hands into the pockets of his threadbare jacket. "I don't think we'd do that good a job."

Lily met his gaze. He was right, of course. They knew how to cause trouble, how to topple power and discover new ideas. They knew how to spread chaos. But Agora had been through their fire. It needed something else now.

Lily walked over to the glass walls of the Observatory, and let her gaze trace a path through the streets, past the wreckage and crumbling buildings, marked with violence and struggles, until she reached the Central Plaza.

"You know, Agora is almost broken," Lily mused, looking straight at Theo, his tall, awkward frame just visible from this distance in the midst of the crowds. "I think what it really needs the most is a healer."

Mark smiled.

"So . . . what do you think?" he asked. "How do we get back to the temple without them spotting us?"

To her amazement, Lily felt herself grinning.

"We'll take the upriver route. There are more bridges over the Ora that way, and I don't imagine there will be too many receivers wandering around."

"That's a long way," Mark said as he began to clatter down the iron stairs to the antechamber, Lily following close behind.

"True," she said, as they walked through the bronze door, and out onto the stone spiral staircase where, four years ago, they had first met. "But I don't fancy a trip through the slums. Getting stabbed in a back alley by the one desperate debtor who didn't hear the good news is *not* my idea of a perfect end to the day."

Mark laughed, sauntering down the steps.

"Fine, but it'll be longer before we can sleep. You realize that this is probably the only time that the temple is going to be empty for a long while? You remember what peace and quiet were like, right?"

Lily passed an open door. She stopped. There was something familiar about the room beyond, its furniture swathed in white dustsheets. Beneath her, farther down the steps, Mark stopped. He turned back, looking up at her from the gloom, his face suddenly serious.

"Lily . . . are you sure we're doing the right thing?"

"I'm sure they'll understand," Lily said, still distracted by this little room that niggled at her memory. "They'll be back at the temple soon . . ."

"I didn't mean that," Mark said, scratching the back of his head. "Can we just walk away? I mean—over a hundred years of planning, the Librans founding three civilizations, all leading up to us, the Protagonist and Antagonist, the fabled Judges . . . and we're just walking away? Shouldn't we have fulfilled our role? Chosen a leader? Shouldn't we have made some kind of judgment?"

Lily looked into the old room. For a second, the sun shone through the slit window, and illuminated her face. And she remembered. She remembered the day she had met Mark, the moment their lives had become intertwined, and all Agora had begun to change. For a second, as she stared through the window, all of the city was laid out before her, in all its crooked splendor. So similar to how she had first seen it, but thanks to her, and Mark, and all their friends, so completely different. It looked brand new, as though she were seeing it for the first time.

She smiled, looking down at Mark, and heard another far off cheer as Theo finished his speech.

"I think we did," she said.

And she closed the door.

Chapter Twenty-nine

𝕭eginning

MARK FOUND LILY on the edge of the cliff, staring out to sea.

"I'd have thought you'd be helping to pack the ship," Mark said, coming to stand beside her. She flashed him a smile.

"No chance," she said. "Laud and Honorius are still arguing about how the last few provisions should be stowed. We were supposed to leave at dawn, but I don't think that's going to happen now. I could wait onboard, but I think I'll just leave them to it. It might be a long trip, better that they sort out their differences now."

Mark nodded, understanding. They had reached the Cathedral only a week ago, and there had been so much to prepare for the voyage. None of them really knew how much time it would take to cross the sea. Honorius had taught himself navigation from the notes of the long-dead captain, but it was still a risky venture. Mark suspected, for Lily, that was half the appeal.

As for the other half, Mark could just hear the sound of him shouting at their captain, over at the dock behind the Cathedral.

"So, I can understand why you'd want to go on a sea voyage with Laud . . ." Mark said, slyly. "But really . . . taking Ben along as well? Isn't that going to make things awkward?"

Lily swatted at him, playfully.

"We'd be in more trouble if we tried to go without her. It's not as if there aren't a lot of other Agoran diplomats going with us—and I'd say Ben is one of the best. Anyway," she added, growing a little embarrassed, "I think she knew about Laud and me before we did."

Mark nodded. He'd seen less of Laud and Lily over the past months than he would have liked, but it took only a couple of minutes in their company to feel it. It wasn't an obvious passion; they didn't spend all their time holding hands, or giving each other long, lingering looks. But whenever they were together, they looked relaxed in a way that Mark had never seen before. As though for the first time in their lives, the world around them, with all its faults, didn't really matter.

"Besides," Lily continued, hastily changing the subject. "She gets on well with Honorius, and we need to keep him happy. It was hard enough getting him to agree to leave his patients, even though it'll only be for a few months. I told him that Owain and Freya would look after them well, but . . ." Lily's lightheartedness faded a little. "Honorius saw his patients as his children."

Mark knew better than to say anything else about family. Lily's father was now buried beneath the Cathedral. Verity was not going on the voyage—although she and Lily had talked about it, she had decided to stay behind. She was the new Director's secretary, and Mark suspected that she might be something more, soon. And as for Lily's mother . . .

On the Conductor's last diplomatic visit to Agora, he had brought the former Oracle. Lily had tried to talk to her, but her

380

mind seemed to have shut down completely. Elespeth had suggested that living for a while in the care of the Brethren of the Shadows might help her reconnect to her damaged emotions. They could only hope.

Mark put a hand on Lily's shoulder, and she reached up to touch it. For a while, neither spoke, watching the waves ripple in the pre-dawn light. They were both well wrapped-up in thick, Gisethi jackets, but they didn't really need them. The spring morning was still and mild. In fact, this winter had been so gentle that it was hard to believe that six months had passed since the Day of Judgment.

Lily broke out of her thoughts first.

"Anyway," she said, briskly, "enough about that. Did you bring it?"

"Cherubina found it for me, in the vaults of the Directory," Mark said, swinging the worn leather bag off his back. "I still don't know how I'm going to explain this to Lady Astrea when we get back to Agora," he said, as he pulled a thick roll of paper from its depths. "I know that there's a copy in the new Libran Museum in the Astrologer's Tower, but this is the last original version they had. It's a priceless antique."

Lily laughed.

"Lady Astrea has to remember that she's not the Director. Anyway, she was a Libran, wasn't she? I thought they appreciate symbolism."

Mark grinned.

"I think that's the problem. She doesn't like what this symbolizes, not one bit. And she particularly doesn't like it coming from me—she still won't call me by my title, you know."

Lily raised an eyebrow.

"Well, 'Official Adviser to the Director of Receipts' is a bit of a mouthful. If Theo ever gets his election ideas working, you've got to work out something snappier."

Mark laughed.

"I'd just be happy if Astrea didn't call me 'the boy' when she thinks I can't hear."

Lily sighed, taking the roll of paper from Mark and beginning to unwrap it.

"You keep an eye on Astrea," she said. "I know that Theo needed advice from someone with experience of government, but give her a chance and I think she'd try to take over the city again."

Mark shrugged.

"Chief Inspector Greaves is looking after her while we're out of the city, and the receivers are loyal to him. Even Poleyn is coming around now that she's out of prison. Besides, Astrea knows that Theo could have her husband locked up again, and she won't risk his safety. We'll be fine."

The last of the paper fell away, abandoned on the ground. Mark couldn't stop himself from feeling a little nervous as he looked at the contents. It really was beautiful, a roll of creamy parchment, with hand-painted illuminations. One of a kind.

But they had agreed to do this together.

Mark took one end of the heavy scroll. Lily took the other. They walked to the edge of the cliff.

And then, with one throw, they flung the last original copy of the Midnight Charter over the edge. For a moment, it turned, gracefully, end on end. And then it fell, and disappeared beneath the waves.

Lily breathed a sigh of relief.

"No more prophecies," she said. "No more experiments, no grand plans."

"We're free," Mark said.

They stood in silence, for a moment. Mark felt as though they were standing up straight for the first time ever.

Lily looked over to the dock. In the distance, under the

lightening sky, Mark could make out a redhaired figure, waving. Lily smiled.

"Looks like we're all set," she said, softly. "There'll be a lot of goodbyes to say."

Mark stuffed his hands into his pockets.

"No need to make them too long," he said, tightly. "I mean, you won't be gone forever. This ship isn't huge, so it can't be so very far to the old lands."

"You know," Lily said, her voice full of sincerity, "there's plenty of room onboard the ship. If you wanted to come, I'm sure we could wait . . ."

Mark smiled. He'd considered it—he really had. The chance to discover why the old world had abandoned them, to really know what had happened out there. A voyage to discover all of their history, their *real* history, before the Librans came in with their blanket of secrets. It sounded like quite an adventure.

But he'd had enough adventure for a while. And there was so much to do back in Agora. The city was still being rebuilt. There was a new, open government to set up, and new, fairer laws to pass. Diplomatic envoys had to be met from Giseth and Naru, which was tricky when most Agorans were still not used to the idea that there were other lands out there at all. And there were always those days when the Director just needed someone to talk to. And with Lily, Laud, and Ben leaving, even if it was only temporary, Mark was going to be the one the Director turned to more and more over the coming months.

And of course, he'd promised his father he'd join him on one of his fishing trips. He wouldn't miss that for the world.

"I think," Mark said, meeting Lily's gaze, "that there'll be enough adventure to keep me happy here until you get back. Besides," he added, "I've been struggling for sixteen summers. I think I'd like a quieter year."

Lily nodded, understanding.

"Well, I suppose it's time to go . . ." she said, looking over his shoulder. "Laud looks as if he's going to explode if I don't hurry up."

Mark couldn't suppress a grin.

"You know why that is, don't you?" he said. Lily raised an eyebrow. Mark pointed to where the reds and pinks of dawn were visible on the horizon. "Come on, this is Laud. He knows how to sell an image. He wants you to sail away into the rising sun."

Lily looked out over the waves. And she laughed.

"Well, he'll be lucky," she said, turning her back on the sea. "Honorius said it might take hours to get all those sail ropes working . . ."

"You watch, Laud will have them all ready," Mark laughed, as they began walking back toward the Cathedral.

"Anyone would think you were calling my Laud all style and no substance . . ."

"Well, you'd know . . ."

"You see, this is why we're not taking you with us . . ."

And laughing, chattering, and for all the world feeling as though nothing important was happening at all, Mark and Lily walked down from the cliff, the light of the dawn shining behind them.

And, as far as Mark was concerned, that was exactly how he wanted it to be.

Epilogue

THE RED SAIL disappeared out of sight over the horizon. Theo let out the breath that he hadn't realized he had been holding.

He squinted against the high morning sun and saw Mark, still standing and waving at the edge of the dock. Theo thought about going over, but decided against it. There would be plenty of time later for reminiscing, for admitting how much they would miss their friends. He didn't want to interrupt Mark's moment.

Theo drew his dark, silver-laced jacket around his shoulders. The sun was bright today, but it was still only a few days from the Gisethi Spring Festival—and the breeze was cool. Perhaps he should return to the Cathedral. His days in Agora were so busy now, and the Cathedral was a place of blissful quiet, now that Wolfram and his supporters were gone. Even Wulfric, their rather wild-looking new porter, knew when to leave him to his thoughts.

"Director . . ."

Theo looked down. Verity was standing beside him. Her eyes were wet, but she was bearing up well. Lily had talked to her for a long time before she left. Perhaps, one day, Theo would ask what she had said.

"You know, Verity," he said, gently, "you don't need to call me Director, especially here. I still can't get used to that title."

Verity looked up at him, shaking her head, fondly.

"And believe me, that's why you're the best Director Agora has ever had," she said. Theo shrugged.

"Well, I don't think Snutworth was a hard act to follow," he admitted, hoping to make her laugh.

To his delight, there was a slight trace of a smile. That was enough, for now.

He looked back at the dock. Mark had stopped waving, and was staring out to sea.

"Would you like some time alone?" Theo asked Verity, gently. "I could wait up at the Cathedral."

She shook her head, firmly, but with a sad smile.

"No. Keeping busy always helps." She reached into the pocket of her jacket. "That reminds me—the monks wanted you to have these, as a symbol of the new friendship between Giseth and Agora."

Verity pulled out a small drawstring bag, and dropped it into Theo's hand. It made a slight clinking noise. Curious, Theo undid the knot, and poured the contents into his other palm.

"What are they?" he asked, prodding at the gold and silver metal disks. "They look like those decorations that cover the Cathedral."

Verity nodded.

"They are," she said. "Apparently, when the ship originally arrived, all those years ago, the sailors who survived thought they were the most valuable thing aboard the ship—more than food or water. The new Bishop pried a few loose for us. He thought we might want to take them back to Agora."

Theo held up one of the disks, engraved with the head of a long-forgotten man. It was only a little piece of gold, but something about it seemed dangerous.

"You know," he said, "I'm not entirely sure that would be a good idea."